Rebellion

Rebellion

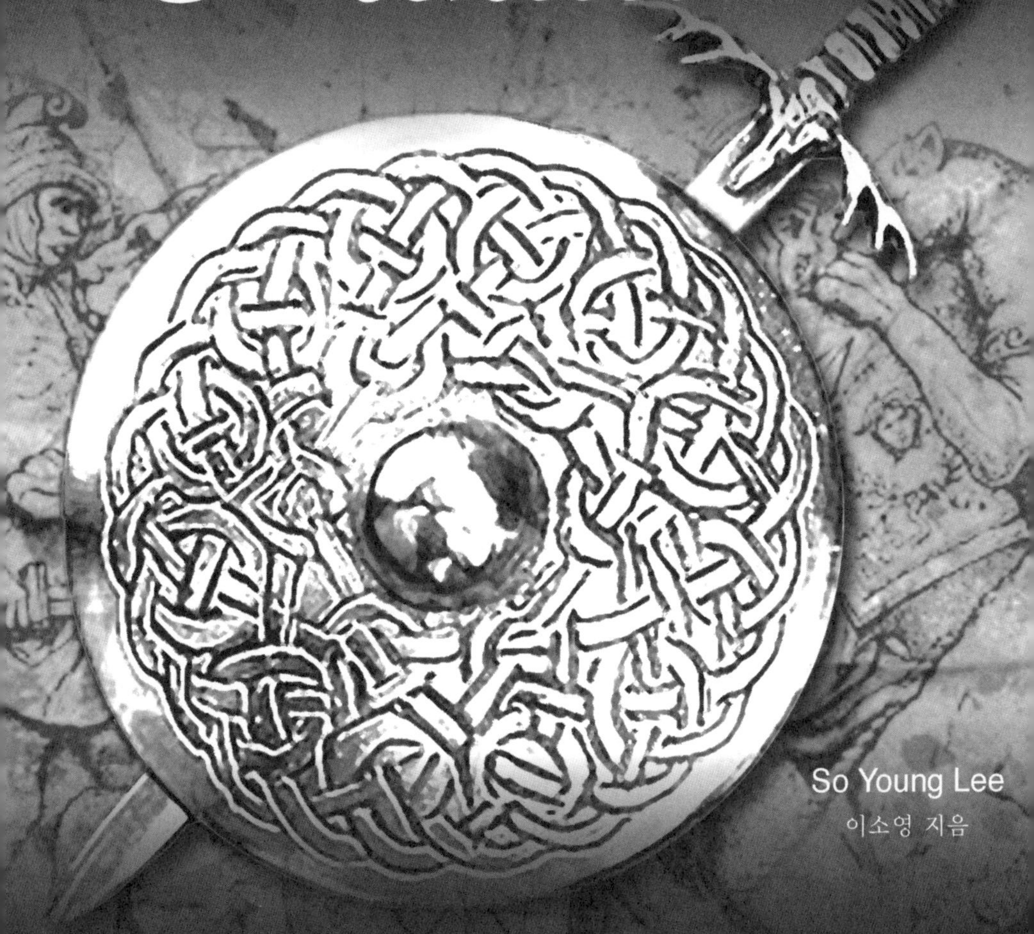

So Young Lee
이소영 지음

일등북

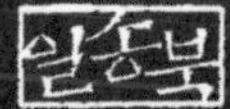

추천의 글

소설 『리벨리언』에 대한 나의 느낌이랄까 소감은 3번 바뀌었다. 일송북 출판사의 부탁으로 처음 이 원고를 받아들었을 때 나는 다소 멍해지는 느낌이었다. 우리나라 중학생이 A4용지로 무려 302쪽에 달하는 영어 장편소설을 썼다니. 그것도 1학년 때 초고를 쓰고 2학년 여름방학 때 완성했다니. 그러나 다음 순간, 영특하긴 하지만 그래도 중학생인데 쓰면 얼마나 잘 썼으랴 싶었다. 그런 가벼운 마음으로 책장을 넘겨갔는데……. 내 안에서는 차츰 경악에 가까운 놀라움이 일었다. 우선 중학생이 썼으리라고 도저히 믿어지지 않는 고급 영어 구사에 놀라고, 아마도 초등학생 때의 독서 체험을 근간으로 삼았을 터인데 그 해박한 역사 지식 수준에 감탄했고, 이렇듯 영어로 장편 소설을 쓰겠다고 덤벼든 용기와 완성해낸 끈기가 기특했다. 어린 작가의 그 모든 특장점을 한 단어로 뭉뚱그려 부른다면 아마도 '천재성'이란 말이 되지 않을까 싶다. 그래서 나는 흔쾌히 영어 교정과 번역을 맡아주었다. 오래 교직에 있어선지 될성부른 떡잎을 키우고 돌보는 일보다 더 큰 보람을 나는 알지 못하기 때문이다.

소설 『리벨리언』은 고대 로마의 검투 노예 스파르타커스의 반란을 그 역사적 배경으로 한다. 폭정과 일상의 억압에 맞서 저항하며 자유를 갈급하는 사람들의 모습이 생생한 감동을 전해준다. 우리는 이 소설을 읽으며 로마의 전쟁사를 일별할 수 있고 그 여러 전쟁들에서 목숨을 바친 병사들의 충정을 느낄 수 있다. 또한 이 소설에는 우리의 감성을 자극하는 미묘한 로맨스가 녹아있다. 한 마디로 이 소설은 모든 연령층의 누구나 즐길 수 있는 최고의 소설이다.

오 영 숙

전 세종대 총장
현재 한국외국어대 통번역대학 영어과 외래교수

For Mom, who encouraged me whenever I was feeling depressed
For Dad, who listened to my tedious stories on Roman history
For Gaius Julius Caesar, my parrot, who has sparked my interest in Rome

Then there are my friends, who also encouraged me. To some of them I have revealed the plot, and I thank them for telling me that it was "readable". Whether or not they said it in earnest, those words still cheered me up, and I would like to thank them for that. In no particular order, my friends who have helped me are Jeong Yoon Son, Hannah Hyun Jeong Nam, Da Hae Jung, Seung Joo Yoo, and Ye Eun Lim. I would also like to express my gratitude to all friends and teachers who have taken an interest in my novel, though due to space restrictions, I cannot specify all their names.

Lastly but not the least, there is the publishing company, Ilsongbook, which has made it possible for me to publish my book, and Young Suk Oh for her valuable comments.

Thank you.

Historical Note

The War of Spartacus, or the Third Servile War, is one of the most ambiguous wars. Not only is it because the slave army did not keep a record of what happened, but also because the Romans were ashamed at the fact that it took them so long and so many lives to conquer "just" a revolt by "mere" slaves—and thus, they were reluctant to write down facts about the revolt. Later on in history, some classical Roman writers, such as Appian and Plutarch, have recorded facts about the Third Servile War; however, their accounts of what happened differ greatly from each other. The motivation of the slave army is also not known—Appian claims that it was to march on Rome itself, while Plutarch argues that Spartacus merely wished to escape Italy and move into Gaul.

However, both Appian and Plutarch do somewhat agree upon the earlier events of the rebellion. According to them, in 73BC around seventy gladiators escaped Lentulus Batiatus's

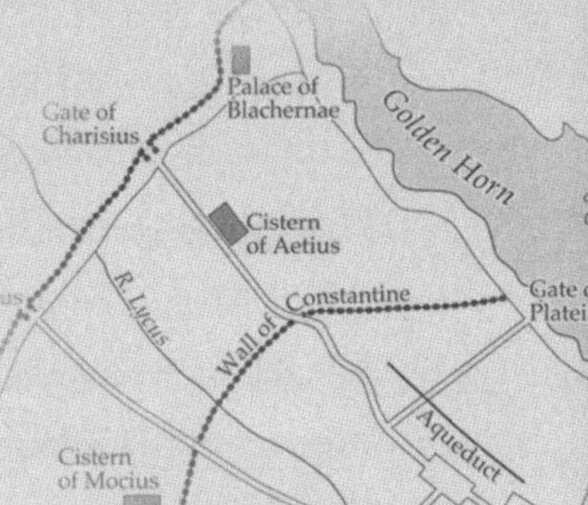

gladiator school, and using their gladiatorial weapons, defeated the legionaries in Capua. They also say that Spartacus and his followers plundered the rich region around Capua, Campania, having set up a base in Mt. Vesuvius. Even at this point, the Romans considered the slaves a very insignificant matter, something more like a crime wave than a real threat.

Later that year, the Roman senate sent Gaius Claudius Glaber as praetor to put down the rebellion. However, it is evident that the Romans did not think of the gladiators as threat, for they did not give Glaber regular legions to command, but a militia comprising of three thousand men. Glaber blocked the only known route to the mountain, hoping to starve the slaves. Spartacus, though, had a plan of his own. He made ropes and ladders out of vines and using them, climbed down a cliff opposite of Glaber's troops. The slaves then moved around the base of the mountain and were able to flank an unsuspecting Glaber, annihilating the Romans.

Unlike the occurrences in the novel, the slaughter of Glaber's army and Varinius's army did not happen in one day. After hearing the loss of Glaber, the senate gave Praetor Publius Varinius command of regular legions and ordered him to defeat the gladiators. He, however, was not able to succeed either. The part where Varinius is forced to escape half—naked is true?he had been bathing in his friend's house when the rebels attacked. After defeating Varinius, Spartacus and his followers were able to conquer other cities such as Nola, Nuceria, Thurii and Metapontum to spend the winter of 73BC. The leaders of the slave rebellion were, apart from Spartacus, Crixus, Oenomaus, Gannicus and Castus, though Oenomaus was lost sometime in the winter.

In the spring of 72BC, the senate, who had finally taken the rebels as a threat, dispatched the consular legions under Lucius Gellius Publicola and Gnaeus Cornelius Lentulus. For plot purposes, I put Gellius, Lentulus, and Varinius under Crassus's command, but the fact is not so.

Meanwhile, the rebels split into two groups, one under the leadership of Spartacus and the other under the control of Crixus. The exact motivation of this happening is unknown.

Gellius defeated Crixus's army, killing Crixus in the process. What happens after is not clear, due to contradicting sources (sources that may not be contradicting but at least mentioning different events) by Appian and Plutarch.

Their records reach a consensus though, when in early 71BC Marcus Licinius Crassus took charge as praetor with eight regular legions at his command. The first big confrontation between Crassus and Spartacus happened near Picenum, according to Plutarch. Here, he gave two legions to Mummius to maneuver behind the rebels, warning Mummius not to engage the slaves. However, Mummius disobeyed, and it led to a complete rout of the two legions. Crassus managed to win the battle despite this, though Roman casualties were heavy. Crassus is reported to have used decimation after this battle, though the number of the Romans decimated varies according to historians. It is also after this battle, Appian records, that three hundred legionaries taken as prisoners by the rebels were forced to fight and die like gladiators.

According to Plutarch, Spartacus, after his loss in Picenum, negotiated with pirates to transport him and his men to Sicily. However, he was betrayed by them in the process. Modern historians such a M.J. Trow suspect that Crassus might have had a part in the betrayal, offering a greater sum than Spartacus had offered.

Spartacus's troops were then forced to retreat to Rhegium, where they were besieged and starved by a Roman "human— wall" that ran from top to bottom of the toe of the Italian peninsula. Later, some of the rebels under Castus and Gannicus were able to break through the human wall and escape, but were eventually killed or caught by the Roman legions. Rebels under Spartacus also broke through the siege—Spartacus met the Roman legions about eighty kilometers northeast of Rhegium, bringing down his entire strength on the legions for a last stand. Spartacus's forces were routed completely in this battle.

Meanwhile Pompey had also participated in the war, coming back from Hispania after conquering the revolt there by Quintus Sertorius. While on the topic, I would like to say that Pompey and Caesar would never have had a chance to meet in Hispania for Caesar's quaestorship was in fact attained three years later. Pompey made the destruction of the rebel army complete by either slaughtering or capturing the remnants of Spartacus's rebels.

For the aftermath, both Pompey and Crassus were elected consul in the following year, 70BC. Around six thousand prisoners were crucified on the Appian Way from Capua to Rome, and according to stories, the rebels' bodies remained on the crosses long after they had died as a warning to other slaves. Whether or not it was because of this, it is true that there was never another slave rebellion in Rome.

And it is also true that, no matter how much the Romans tried, they could not find the body of Spartacus.

Allegiances

Romans

- **Gnaeus Octavius Lupus**
  Rank : Tribunus Laticlavius (Normally called Tribune. The second in command of a legion.)
  Relations : Nephew of Crassus, friend to Lucius, Titus, Lucia, Julius Caesar, gladiator Spartacus
  Senior Officers : Crassus, Suetonius

- **Quintus Lucius Maximus**
  Rank : Centurion (A middle ranking officer who normally leads a century (60~80 men))
  Relations : Brother to Lucia, friend to Octavius, Titus, Spartacus
  Senior Officers : Crassus, Suetonius, Octavius

- **Titus Aemilius Flavius**
  Rank : Centurion,
  Relations : Adopted older brother to Octavius. Friends with Lucius, Julius Caesar
  Senior Officers : Crassus, Suetonius, Octavius

- **Marcus Licinius Crassus**
  Rank : Praetor (An annually elected magistrate of the ancient Roman Republic, ranking below but having approximately the same functions as a consul. Mostly related to military.)
  Relations : The wealthiest senator of Rome, uncle to Octavius. Friends with Julius Caesar, Suetonius

• **Servius Hortius Suetonius**

    Rank : Legate (The commander of a legion. (4800 men))

    Relations : Senior officer to Octavius, friends with Crassus

    Senior Officers : Crassus

• **Gaius Julius Caesar**

    Rank : Quaestor (Any of various public officials in ancient Rome responsible for finance and administration in various areas of government and the military.) of Hispania

    Relations : Friends with Marcus Lupus-father of Octavius, Octavius,

                  Crassus, Titus

• **Caecilius**

    Rank : Veteran Centurion

    Relations : Friends with Octavius

    Senior Officers : Crassus, Suetonius, Octavius

• **Lucia Maximus**

    Relations : Friends with Octavius

• **Quintus Arrius**

    Rank : highly respected senator

• **Gnaeus Pompeius Magnus**

    Rank : Commander of his own legions

Slave Army

- Spartacus

  Thracian gladiator, the commander of the slave army

- Crixus

  Second in command of the army, a ruthless gladiator

- Oenomaus

  Second in command of the army with Crixus. A patient, Gallic gladiator

- David

  Jewish gladiator, an officer in the slave army

- Castus

  An officer in the slave army

- Sempronius

  A Roman pirate merchant who agrees to help Spartacus

—75 B.C.—

Part 1

Acquaintance

"…eyes that did not portray the joy of victory but the agony of having to kill a friend, hatred of the Romans for making him do so… A part of his mind tugged at him, his innocence, his morality, telling him to shout for the loser to live?"

— Text

~ *1* ~

He felt his stomach lurch. He closed his eyes, not wanting to see anymore. He shouldn't have come. He should not have.

"Octavius," his friend, Lucius, called, his voice portraying excitement. "Look at Spartacus! He's twirling his sword, getting ready..." For a long time there was silence, Lucius being completely mesmerized by the scene.

Lucius grasped Octavius's tightly clutched hands, leaning forward to see better. "Are you seeing this, Octavius?" he asked, swiveling his head to look at his friend. Octavius felt the movement and opened his eyes, not wanting to show his weakness, his weakness of not being able to stand a death of a person. He hated it. Other people could stand, and even enjoy a death scene, yet he could not.

"I'm seeing it," he responded tensely.

"Are you enjoying it?"

"No."

Lucius smiled at his response. "Oh, come on. Don't be so childlike," he said, and smiled a crooked smile, knowing it was a comment that would get Octavius going.

Octavius shot a sharp look at Lucius, otherwise ignoring his comment. Spartacus had already managed to topple the opponent onto the ground, and some of the more belligerent members of the crowd began to shout for the death of the loser.

"I don't get why you hate the killing part so much," Lucius started.

"You asked me to come, I did. Quit it now," Octavius said.

"Or maybe it's because you're two years younger than me," Lucius said, ignoring Octavius's comment. There was a certain unspoken rivalry between them, and Lucius knew Octavius hated to be behind others—even when it came to unchangeable things such as age.

Octavius chose not to respond, and instead decided to focus his attention to the crowd. He watched the crowd debate with a sickening feeling. How come he was the only one who hated the killing? Was he weaker than others?

The questions rang in his mind, discomforting him.

Lucius smiled an innocuous smile at Octavius when the crowd began to go for the side of killing the loser. Octavius sullenly glared back at him, and averted his eyes to the ground of the coliseum where Spartacus was standing.

Spartacus. Octavius, in a way, envied the man when it came to sword skills. There was no one, at least people who he knew, who could beat Spartacus. Spartacus's fights always had a pattern. Spartacus would toy with the other gladiator until the other gladiator would lose his strength and nerve, and then would start inflicting severe blows in a consecutive motion. Before one strike had been delivered, another part of his body was preparing to deliver the next blow.

The man literally flew across the ground, agile in his feet as he was with other parts of his body. Strike, dodge, strike again. Lucius would always talk about him, how absolutely beautiful his sword tactics were, persuading Octavius to go watch a gladiatorial game with him. He had finally acquiesced, agreeing to go watch a game, and from the first moment, he had become captivated in Spartacus's fighting skills.

Watching Spartacus, watching a game was interesting. What Octavius was not interested in was the killing part. The gruesome images swirled in his head, as he hope that today, he would not see someone die.

"Boo," the crowd bantered. "Kill him!" they cried, their voice a unified one suddenly. Octavius groaned. He looked toward Spartacus, curious of what the gladiator thought of the verdict. Then he stared, shocked at what he saw in the man's eyes. His eyes were full of agony, but his eyes also burned with fury, dangerous hatred that reflected the enthralled faces of the crowd. Spartacus's eyes looked around the crowd, a little desperateness showing... and their eyes met.

Octavius held the gaze, still shocked, at the eyes that did not portray the joy of victory but the agony of having to kill a friend, hatred of the Romans for making him do so, as he continued to stare down at the gladiator. A part of his mind tugged at him, his innocence, his morality, telling him to shout for the loser to live.

Spartacus seemed to sense the younger man's wavering feelings as he continued to stare up at Octavius, his eyes pleading. Octavius tried to tell him that it would be no use shouting out 'Live!' alone, but the beady black eyes would not leave his face.

"Lucius," Octavius said, his gaze still on the gladiator.

"Yes?" Lucius replied casually.

"Today was not a death match. I mean, there's no need for anyone to die. Isn't it against the rules to kill a gladiator when it's not a death match?"

Lucius rolled his eyes. "The crowd makes the rules here. And don't say that to me, say it to the crowd."

"Me? To the crowd?"

"Yeah. You," Lucius said, a smile forming on his lips. Octavius, although ambitious and outgoing, always seemed to become an introvert when he entered the coliseum. Octavius would not, could not, do it, he decided.

Octavius sensed his friend's feelings, scowling. He then stood up with a flourish, doing it on purpose to let his friend see what he was doing.

Lucius looked at him with wide eyes, sputtering out unintelligible words.

"Citizens, I plead your attention for just a few seconds. Today was not a death match. There is no need for anyone to die today. Let him live, and he will return to the arena again, later, and provide us with better entertainment. With one more gladiator around the area, we will be able to experience even more various types of games. Let him live," Octavius shouted, as loudly as possible. People near Octavius paused their chant to stare at him, first in scorn, and then in respect. It helped that his father was a renowned advocate, also his status as a patrician (the highest ruling class of the Roman society), and perhaps most importantly of all, that he was the nephew of the richest man in Rome, Senator Crassus.

Their chants slowly died down, and those who were afraid to voice their thoughts, it being contrary to the popular opinion, began to shout in accordance with Octavius. Soon the arena was chaos; with people all yelling different opinions. He spotted some small brawls that were happening in the midst of the crowd, arguing over whose opinion was righter.

The announcer began to shout for order, and Octavius sat down in his seat again, giving the baffled Lucius a crooked smile.

"You didn't think I would do it, did you?" he said smugly.

"No," Lucius responded sourly. He had wanted to see some real blood. He pouted slightly as he saw Octavius gloat over the commotion he had created.

Octavius glanced around the coliseum, which was still noisy despite the announcer's efforts. He managed to meet Spartacus's eyes, which flashed him a genuine thank you before averting them to somewhere else.

When Octavius looked up from his seat, surprised by the sudden quietness, he could see the announcer preparing to make a speech. His face was full of childish delight as he called for silence.

"Excuse me, but I shall announce a special guest who has just come to Capua. Uh…it is quite a surprise for us. If we had known sooner, we would have staged a special gladiatorial fight for him… We formally greet a famous advocate of Rome, a famous pirate slayer—" the announcer yelled, drawling, dramatizing the condition.

The announcer held the suspicion long enough for the crowd to fidget uncomfortably. "Let us all welcome Gaius Julius Caesar!" Octavius broke into a grin, thrilled to see the man after a long time. The people cheered madly, making Octavius wonder if they did anything else but cheer.

The figure at the entrance of the arena bowed to the crowd. Julius was very well known due to his recent victory involving the pirates. Not only that, but he was the nephew of the late—consul Marius, one of the best known and best loved figures in Rome. He and Octavius's uncle, Crassus, had a special relation. Octavius smiled a little to himself as he thought of the relation. Julius had enormous amounts of money in debt, and that made the two impossible to separate.

Julius felt delighted to see Octavius in the arena. He had come looking for Octavius, who was almost like a brother to him. When Sulla the Dictator had hunted him after Marius's death, he had taken refuge in Octavius's house for a few months. Sulla had literally wiped out almost every supporter of Marius, his political enemy. Julius, the nephew of Marius, had also been hunted—if Marcus Lupus had refused to shelter him, during his daring escapade from the clutches of Sulla's soldiers, he would have died a long time ago. It helped that Octavius's family was a subtle supporter of Marius, though Julius later found out that Marcus was only pretending to be subtle.

"We were just deciding the fate of the loser here, sir. I believe your opinion counts as well," said the announcer, interrupting his thoughts. Julius noticed how the announcer was staring at him in awe, and hid a grin. Only six years ago, he had been a refugee, and now, he was greeted as a hero.

Julius looked at Octavius who had a wide smile on his face. The bond they had made during Julius's flight was still there. Julius cast an inquiring look at Octavius, and when Octavius shook his head slightly, he nodded, smiling at his innocence. He had certainly never been in battles, Julius mused.

Julius turned to address the announcer. "I have a very

urgent appointment in Rome, with Gnaeus Octavius Lupus. A senator, Senator Crassus, is calling. By the laws of Rome, we should leave immediately," Julius claimed. "We have no time for this, though I love the honor of being able to decide a gladiator's life. Keep him alive until I come back, and I will decide then."

Octavius hid a smile. Julius could be gone for years; the gladiator would have his judgment some years from now. He felt Julius dragging him out of the arena, and he followed, with a baffled Lucius behind. "Come on, before the crowd realizes what I've just said," Julius whispered into Octavius's ears. This time, he grinned freely.

It turned out that Crassus had called for Octavius, though it was not an urgent business as Julius had said. Octavius thanked Julius for siding with him and vowed to himself that he would never be goaded into watching a gladiator death match again. Bidding Lucius a good bye, Octavius headed for his house with Julius walking beside him, listening to his heroic stories of capturing the pirates.

"Julius! It's been years," Marcus exclaimed as he hugged Julius.

"No legionaries, huh?" Marcus asked jokingly and Julius laughed whole—heartedly.

"Yes, actually," Julius answered with a mischievous grin. He gave a low whistle, and three legionaries marched into the house. "I'm an officer now," he announced proudly. Marcus clapped Julius on the shoulder chuckling slightly. Marcus offered Julius some wine as he asked about the pirates.

"I've heard of you. I've heard that you have been taken by the pirates as a prisoner on your way to Greece, and how you had threatened them with the stories of crucifixion. Something that you didn't forget to carry out after you were freed," Marcus said, his eyes glittering with interest.

Julius nodded. "Actually, I hanged them before I put them on a cross. It was my way of thanking them for their hospitality for the forty days I was on their ship. It had been quite entertaining in fact, in its own sense. Anyway, I did carry out my promise, hanging the most legendary pirates in the Mediterranean, and I guess the exaggerated story about that made me something of a hero in Rome. The mob regards me as a ruthless, intelligent patrician youth, expecting much of me. I'll have to try hard to satisfy their expectations," Julius said, his expression thoughtful.

Marcus nodded his head. "It'll be a tough job. You can't even imagine the stories they tell about you."

Julius smiled, and Octavius got the feeling that Julius did not dislike the exaggerated rumors about him. Marcus and Julius continued with their conversation, catching up on each other's news. Octavius stood by them, immersed in his own imagining. He saw the battle scenes flashing vividly in his mind. Boarding a ship, chasing the pirates, the battle... he heard the distant sounds of clashing swords, saw the Romans gaining lead, and finally, the winning legion returning to land with the civilians calling them heroes. Adrenaline pursed through him as he saw himself standing in the same position, receiving the congratulations from others.

He had not known the world outside of Capua until Julius had intruded in his life on one day when he was still nine. Since then, he had learned the powerful force that was moving the world—the city of Rome. It was then when he had noticed the world of power, domination and ambition. His dreams had continued to improve from then on.

He broke from his daydream at a boisterous laugh from Julius. "That was a good one, Marcus. When did you start to joke?" he said. Then, without giving Marcus any time to respond, he let out a startled sound. "Oh, Gods, look at the time," Julius said, suddenly gasping as he looked at the sun. "We need to get going," he said, shooting an apologetic look at Marcus as he clutched Octavius's arm gently. "I'll come back as soon as I can," he said, flashing a smile.

"So soon?" Marcus asked as he gave the younger man a hug. Julius nodded apologetically once more and headed to his horse.

Octavius smiled, also hugging Marcus good bye. He turned to his mother, and shyly turned his head at her kisses. Julius had already mounted his horse and was waiting. Octavius was about to follow him when he was jerked back by Marcus.

"I know this is not your first trip to Rome, Octavius, but I want to give you some warnings," Marcus said, his face grave.

"I know. Don't disturb Crassus, be on your manners, don't eat sloppily… The rules you always warned me of," Octavius said, smiling. His smile faded as he saw that his father's face remained serious.

Marcus took Octavius closer to him, embracing him in his chest. His voice was a mere whisper as he spoke. "I want you to give this to Julius. Don't open it and most of all, never tell anybody else," he said, handing Octavius a parchment scroll wrapped repetitively—almost so that the scroll became double the size.

"Your uncle too must not know of it," Marcus said, warning him.

Octavius stood still, perplexed. "Why me? Why not give it directly to Julius?"

Marcus looked pained for a moment, his face reflecting his doubts. Finally, he chose to tell his son what he was thinking. "Give it to Julius when you reach Rome. He wouldn't want me involved…I don't think he would accept it if I just gave it to him right now. Remember, never—never—tell anybody else. I trust you, Octavius. Or else I would not have given it to you," he said. With that, he embraced Octavius tightly and gently pushed him toward the horses.

Octavius stared back at his father, his face bemused.

"Just do it," Marcus said, a little impatiently.

"Will you tell me what it's about?" Octavius said, putting the scroll inside his tunic.

"Later, later," Marcus said, his face pained, gently pushing him toward the horses again. "Please. I swear to Jupiter I will tell you when you get older, or when I believe is the appropriate time."

Octavius thought about arguing that it was hardly a promise but thought better of it and stiffly nodded his head before heading toward the horses, where Julius was calling to him impatiently.

⁕

Octavius felt cool wind run through his tunic. Rome, he thought. Octavius loved going to Rome—a city that ruled the world. He glanced back at the three legionaries riding behind him.

He rode slowly and carefully, afraid that he might drop the scroll his father had trusted him with. It seemed conspicuous—every time Julius looked at him Octavius stared back uncomfortably, as if Julius could see through his tunic. He fidgeted a little, trying to keep his face straight. All he could think of was the scroll. What was so important about it that it should be a secret to everybody?

"You rode horses better when you were nine," Julius called, teasing. "Speed up a little. You're crawling."

Octavius frowned slightly. "I'll explain later why I'm going at this pace," Octavius said. He looked at Julius, and he saw Julius give a shrug.

"You don't need to explain why you are going so slowly, but please, hurry up. I have to report to your uncle by tomorrow noon."

"Why do you have to go by noon?" Octavius said, glancing suspiciously at Julius. Julius just laughed mischievously, winking, and Octavius didn't press. He knew Julius enough not to press.

❖

"Julius?" Octavius glanced around. He frowned, trying to remember where he was. He had been riding a horse... yes, Julius must have carried him here when he fell asleep last night, he thought. He still could not understand why Julius had ignored his complaints and argued that they should ride through the night. He made a note to ask Julius later. He relaxed as the familiarity of the room settled in. He had always slept in this room when he visited his uncle. As he dressed, he tried to collect his thoughts together. No doubt Julius was with his uncle in the lounge, talking about politics.

Octavius gasped suddenly, as he remembered the scroll. He patted his chest where he had put it and let out a sigh of relief as he checked that it was still there.

Octavius checked himself in the mirror one last time before he stepped out of his room. Outside, slaves were scuttling around preparing for a grand feast. He was invited to Crassus's house a few times a year, and he usually came alone, though it was good to have Julius with him. It was a pleasant surprise.

He opened the door, stepping out to the corridor cautiously. He felt the scroll unusually heavy inside his tunic. He tried to concentrate on walking down the corridor without seeing suspicious. A legionary automatically touched the hilt of his gladius as he approached the lounge. Octavius frowned at him and smiled inwardly as the young soldier gave him a perplexed look. "I have come to see Crassus. My name is Gnaeus Octavius Lupus, his sole nephew. Open up," he said. The legionary glared at him for a moment, sizing him up, and then took his hand off the hilt of his sword and retreated inside the room. Octavius could hear him announcing his arrival. It took a few seconds before the soldier came back out and waved him in.

Octavius stepped in, and was greeted warmly by his uncle who was sitting on a comfortable looking chair. "I expected you to come," Crassus said. He was a plump man, with sandy hair unlike Octavius's dark brown hair. Crassus looked at his nephew, and inwardly sighed at the little resemblance they had. Octavius was lean, and his eyes were brown with a light shade of blue. Octavius's hair was hazel, closer to dark brown, turning into a normal brown when he received sunlight.

His were a lighter brown, almost blonde. He tried to console himself as he thought of their similarities. He knew his nephew well enough to find them. Octavius seemed like an innocent boy from a small town, yet Crassus knew that he was not. He had ambition lurking inside him, the want to be recognized and famous. It was the same characteristic that had drove him on when he had been younger.

"It's nice to see you again, Uncle," Octavius commented, in which Crassus smiled. Julius, who sat facing Crassus, waved his hand to an empty chair. Octavius took his seat, and patiently waited for the men to continue with their talk.

Crassus, however, had no intention of doing so. "Octavius, have you seen my new collection of statues?" Octavius looked crushed as he realized that he was about to be excused.

It was Julius who came to his aid. "It's all right, Crassus. He knows."

Crassus looked horrified. "Who told him?"

"I did, actually. I think he has a right to know. What's more, I am not embarrassed that I owe a large amount of debt to you. The whole Rome knows it. He too would know it soon enough, and I thought it would be better if I was the one who told him. Oh, and remember that I gave some of my best legionaries to you. Should have equaled some of the debt," Julius noted as he poured himself some wine. "And those five thousand pieces of gold I got out of you today is not a debt. I earned it fair and square."

"Gold?" asked Octavius, and Julius nodded.

"Remember yesterday?" Julius winked. "Your uncle wanted you here quickly—he has no patience," he said. Julius glanced slyly at Crassus who shook his head as if in pain. "I was only paying a visit to your uncle when your uncle talked about you. I said I could bring you here by tomorrow noon, and he refused to believe me. He said that he'll give me five thousand pieces of gold if I kept my word, and I did. We arrived in the morning, when you were sleeping like a pig," he said, snickering.

Octavius just stared. He could have been amazed, or he could just have been stunned. "That's... something," he finally commented, leaving the two older men to laugh.

"Octavius, maybe I should take Julius to the slave markets to have him pay off the rest of the debt," Crassus said, looking for a chance to take revenge. "I'll buy him, and he can serve us until he dies. The so called hero Julius Caesar serving at my house. That'll really be something."

"Crassus, I think you know what I'll do if you really take me in." Julius commented wryly, his snickering expression gone.

"You'll strangle me." Crassus said curtly.

"That is a possibility." Julius replied. Then, he added "Remember, I gave some of my best legionaries to you."

"Including that unfriendly man out there," Octavius intervened. "He didn't recognize me, which means he's new—

from you, Julius."

"Right. The best," Crassus commented lightly.

Julius turned to shoot Octavius an irritated glance before continuing. "Most of them are really good. They'll make good guards, and if you want to create a new legion, do it with them. Veteran soldiers—well not actually veterans, but experienced and staunch nonetheless. Besides, Octavius, soldiers are not meant to be friendly. Overall though, they are great, on my honor," Julius responded, without paying heed to Crassus's taunts. Crassus rolled his eyes when Julius mentioned his honor.

"I have always wanted a legion, Julius. I am thinking about creating one. I just need a good reason for me to do that."

"Reasons are everywhere," Julius commented, his face thoughtful. "By the way, is every thing working out in the senate?" he asked, changing to a more serious topic.

Crassus frowned, and took a sip from his wine. He seemed to consider what to say. "Hmm... No, not really. The ones supporting Sulla—Senator Cato now—has taken over the senate," He looked guiltily at Julius, for he too had been a Sulla supporter once. Julius, to his relief, did not seem to mind much. Crassus gave a fake cough and continued. "And of course, there's Pompey, who's gone now, to crush a rebellion in Hispania. He's always crushing and slaughtering people, just like his nickname 'Boy slaughterer'"

Julius stared at the man sitting in front of him. Crassus was not on either side of the political parties now, but he had been a supporter of Sulla. He had been there when Sulla had ordered him to be chased and murdered. Crassus had not prevented the armies from chasing him. He was uncomfortable with this man when it came to politics, but he tried to keep a calm face. There was no better political ally, and there was also no one else who would lend him a bigger amount of money.

"Pompey is only 6 years older than me," Julius remarked with some remorse, and nobody knew what to say. Crassus looked at his wine cup, stirring it gently mainly because there was nothing else to do. Octavius pretended to check his gladius.

Octavius could understand Julius's sorrows. Pompey already had his first triumph, the dream of any Roman general. He had his triumph when he was mere twenty two, the youngest record for a Roman general. Plus, Pompey was well known for routing pirates and was told to have a great skill in commandeering. Not only that, but he was also a famous politician, feared by opponents.

The silence continued until Julius broke it with an unexpected comment. "Octavius, you care to have a sword fight with me?" Julius remarked suddenly, watching Octavius finger his sword. Octavius looked up, surprised by his question.

"With you, Julius? I…I don't have armor," Octavius stammered, partly in shame. He did have one, a very ancient one back at his home, which was mostly used for displays. He'd worn it only twice—he felt the rust in the armor. It was an artifact, thought Octavius bitterly.

"You should join the legions later on. They give out good armor," Julius said, with some of his good humor returning. "Actually, I'll buy you the armor. You would need a strong one. Legion armor isn't as strong as private one," Julius offered, and Crassus waved his hand.

"With whose money, Julius?" he asked, with a raised eyebrow. "I will buy Octavius the armor myself. My sister never had a taste for fighting men, and your father is preoccupied with dull laws, though they sometimes come in handy. No wonder they never bought you armor," Crassus rose, glad not to be discussing politics. There was something about Julius when it came to politics; it was as if he could see the man thinking, conspiring of some dangerous plan. And Crassus believed that Julius had the will and the power enough to carry it out, even if it may not be now. On the other hand, money was something he could always spend and he felt confident in talking about it.

Julius rose too, and Octavius automatically rose after Julius. Crassus noted how Octavius trusted the young man, and a kind of jealousy sprang up inside him. He was the uncle, not Julius Caesar. "I'll buy you the best armor from the best smith," he said, surprising himself. He had not planned to buy such an expensive armor, but looking at Julius had made him want to say that. Julius looked at Crassus and smiled, as if he could read Crassus's mind. Crassus sweated inside his toga. It was just this that he felt nervous about Julius. He seemed to be very genial on the outside, but ambition lurked underneath like a crocodile waiting for a good prey. His scrutinizing eyes didn't help either.

The surprised Octavius shook his hands. He did need armor, and he was grateful to his uncle for his suggestion. However, it made him guilty to think that his uncle would be buying the best armor in Rome. He was not a commander—he was not even in the army yet. He had no need for such an expensive armor. "No, Uncle. I have no need for armor, let alone an expensive one," he said, voicing his thoughts.

"Octavius. Armors are meant to be worn for years. You will go to the legions, and when you join, you'll need to have a nice armor to protect you from savage blows," Crassus said. Octavius knew that young Roman patricians went to serve in the legions at least for two years— it was an almost mandatory step in becoming a senator, the most privileged rank in Rome.

"Uncle, I am only fifteen years old. I've got time. The minimum age for joining the legions is seventeen," Octavius said.

Crassus shrugged. "It's a pity Marius changed the law. If not, you could be in the legions now," he said, and immediately regretted it. He knew how protective Julius felt of Marius. He glanced briefly at Julius, who just smiled. Cold sweat broke out. "You'll turn 16 soon," he said, glad to change the topic. He gestured at a slave and told him to prepare horses for a journey to the smith. The slave bowed, and scurried off to fulfill his orders.

Crassus left the lounge with Octavius and Julius behind him. The two would need some time to arrange their baggage and dress up. He told them to come out to the front gates an hour from then.

Octavius walked slowly to his room, sensing that his uncle was watching him. He turned, waved slightly, and opened the door to his room. When he entered, the room was completely different— his things were packed neatly in a corner and his bed made. No doubt a slave had done so, and Octavius was grateful for the bed. However, the slave had touched his belongings, and it showed that he or she could rummage through his belongings to simply organize the room as well for personal purposes— or... by an order from Crassus.

He had no idea why his uncle would do so. He trusted his uncle, or, he had trusted his uncle completely until yesterday, when his father had warned him not to speak anything about the scroll to his uncle. He had thought that his father and his uncle shared information and worked together—it had been quite a shock to know that there was some big secret between them.

He kept telling his mind to shut up. Maybe the scroll was just about some personal stories that his father was too ashamed to tell his uncle. He clutched the scroll inside his tunic. No matter what it contained, it would be better to dispose of it soon.

The sooner, the better, before someone else managed to get hold of the scroll. Besides, he was not even sure if he could hold on. He was dying to see what was written in the scroll. Octavius was afraid that if he had the scroll for a much longer time, he might not be able to resist the temptation and read the parchment paper.

Octavius opened the door again, stepping out to the corridor once more. No one was there. He walked briskly to the end of the corridor to a room, where he had seen Julius enter before.

"Julius?" he called, knocking. His voice cracked a little. Soon slaves were bound to come to this side of the building, and even though he was sure that they would have no suspicions for him to wander about because he had done so many times before, it was still good to be careful.

He heard noise from the room and a creak as the handle turned. He came face to face with a slightly irritated looking Julius.

"Octavius? What are you doing here?" he asked. Octavius did not answer and merely stepped into the room, closing the door behind him. He marveled at the room. The room smelt of ripening apples and delicate aromas and like the richest man in Rome, his uncle had a taste for fancy interior. At one corner a Greek statue, slightly too large for indoor display, was posing gracefully. It depicted a Greek lancer, the pose of a man in his young twenties, with powerful bulging muscles and intensely focused features. It was one of those statues that disgraced you whenever you stood next to it. The curtains were deep mahogany and laced around the edges. Outside the windows he could spot a full view of the inner courtyard, where a tall fountain stood, spouting water energetically.

He took a moment to admire the scene before taking a big breath to talk to Julius. "My father gave this to me just before I left. He said it was a secret. He told me to give it to you when we reached Rome," he said.

Julius frowned as he took the scroll from his hands. Octavius cursed inwardly when Julius turned around so that he could not see what was written in the scroll.

It took only a few seconds.

Julius turned around again to face him, his face serious.

Octavius looked carefully at Julius, detecting signs of distress and a little anger. Julius seemed a little distant as he began to speak.

"Octavius, thank you for bringing me the scroll. Please keep it a secret from everyone. Your uncle must not know. No one must. Don't look at me like that. Your uncle is not dangerous, nor is he in danger. It is just that... it is information your uncle cannot know," Julius explained slowly.

"What is it?" Octavius asked.

For a moment Julius looked almost pained. "Yes, you have a right to know. Maybe later. When you are a little older, I promise to tell you," Julius said. Octavius glared at him, disappointed. After all, it was hardly a promise. No clear dates. Just 'when you get older.'

"When? That's exactly what Father told me," he asked, persistently. He could be a zealot if he wanted to.

He almost regretted asking the question. Julius's face became crippled as he sought the right words. "It's not... that important, Octavius."

"Then it won't do any harm to tell me. I can keep my mouth shut."

"It's not that simple either," Julius said dryly.

"I can understand," Octavius said, putting on his most

innocent expression.

"I love you, Octavius, and so do your parents. They wouldn't want me to tell you this nor do I want to tell you because it has some serious risks," Julius said.

"Risks? You just said it wasn't important," Octavius said stubbornly. "I carried it all the way here. I could have peeked but I didn't. I kept my side of the bargain."

"We had no bargain, Octavius," Julius pointed out. Then he said, "I'm sorry, Octavius. I don't want to keep secrets from you. Look, what I mean by it is that it has more risks than it is important. This thing dates back to a long time. The fraction between Marius and Sulla. Both are dead. It does not matter much now. I would not want to risk you on such a long dead issue. I mean, this thing probably won't be an issue about two or three years from now. The fraction is already easing. Look at me, entering Rome like a hero. It would not have been possible if the fraction was still going on strong. The issue, as I have said before, is dead. It does not concern you. It has almost no importance to those who did not take part in the fraction. But it still can be danger-ous. Are you following?"

He gave a resigned shrug, knowing that Julius's mind was made.

"Octavius. You might get to know the meaning of this scroll a week later, if lucky," Julius said slyly.

Octavius shrugged again and glared at Julius one last time to tell him his disappointment and was about to leave the room when he saw several gold pieces shimmering near the scroll. It had not been there when he had first come in.

It was new, from the scroll.

Lucius sighed. He had been hoping to practice his sword skills with Octavius, but apparently, things were not working out as he planned. Octavius was gone, taken by the fat uncle of his. He had nothing to do after he finished his studies.

Lucius idly drew a big circle on the ground and practiced sword motions on his own. He danced in the circle, drifting along, yet being careful to not step outside the circle. Jab, duck, defend. Jab, duck, defend. Spar, jab, and slam.

Unlike Octavius, he never liked the soldier manuals. All he liked about it was looking at the exemplary sword tactics. He was more of a field type than Octavius, who had a talent for, and loved, planning."

His parents would always tell him that if he could not scheme, he could never become a commander. Lucius didn't care. He could always memorize the manuals later, but sword tactics came only through practice.

He wanted to challenge someone just to relieve his stress. Octavius was gone, and the other boys around here were too weak to match him. He thought about challenging one anyway, and suddenly remembered Spartacus. Spartacus had only been in Capua for a few months but was still regarded as one of the best swordsmen in the district.

Lucius prided himself that among the youth in Capua, he was the best swordsman. Every sword tournaments in the area he had won. People gazed at him in awe when he strutted by, the sword champion.

Lucius wondered why the thought to challenge a gladiator had never occurred to him before. Now that it did, it seemed a fascinating idea. Gladiators trained every day. Even the worst of them had bulging muscles.

He dressed in his best armor, one that he had received as a present a few years ago. The fancy iron chest plate alone was enough to intimidate anyone. Even Octavius was in awe of it. Spartacus would certainly be intimidated, Lucius thought with some happiness. Intimidating the enemy first is the most important; his sword tutor had once said to him. The tutor no longer taught him anymore, due to Lucius's rapid learning.

He jogged lightly to the arena, sweating hard in the heavy armor. Lucius cursed the weather under his breath. It was supposed to be fall, but the sun still glared down at him—and he felt like some clay being baked in a fire stove. He spotted a legionary wearing a centurion's armor guarding the entrance of the coliseum. "Quintus Lucius Maximus, son of Governor Gaius Maximus," he shouted as he came near the coliseum, and the legionary saluted smartly.

"Hello sir. The show's finished," he said.

Lucius smiled. "I know. I want to see Spartacus."

"Spartacus? May I have the reason? I'm sorry, but you were not expected."

"I want to have a sword match with him, centurion. Is it against the rules?" Lucius asked, his voice slightly daring.

The centurion frowned. "So that was why you were wearing the heavy armor," he said to almost to himself, ignoring the tone of the voice. "You should probably ask Lentulus Batiatus for permission. But see, maybe you'd want to rethink it. I don't want anybody getting hurt while I'm staying guard. Spartacus is really—"

"Let me in, centurion," Lucius intervened. The centurion shrugged, as if it was 'your own neck' he was risking. He told the legionaries next to him to guard the entrance well, and turned to Lucius.

"I'll show you to the gladiator school, sir."

"No need. I can go to the school myself. It's right behind the coliseum, and I promise I won't trip while crossing the arena," Lucius grinned, and the centurion showed a slight smile.

"I'm sorry sir, but you can't go into the gladiator school without a soldier to accompany you. There are a lot of rowdy men in there, and you might need someone to assert your authority, or else they'll be all over you. It's their domain in the school, especially since we will be entering through the back door. I'm actually surprised that Lentulus Batiatus had survived in there for all these years— and, this is a rule." Lucius stared at the centurion, weighing his words. Then he gave a nod, and the two walked into the arena.

The entrance of the school was blocked by three legionaries who let them in without a backward glance. It was illegal, the centurion had explained, to go through the backdoor, but nobody would object to the governor's son, and it wasn't a serious law anyway. The centurion unsheathed his sword as he opened the door, and Lucius gave an inquiring frown. He was affected by the soldier's nervousness and found himself rubbing the hilt of his own gladius. Lucius stepped in the dark interior and was momentarily blinded. Even before his eyes could see, he heard whispers as he was noticed. Lucius grimaced, and looked around as soon as his eyes adjusted to the dim light. There was a long aisle, and alongside it were the prison cells for the gladiators. He could see men peering at him between the bars of their prison cells, and felt a shudder go up his spine.

The whispers stopped. They just all stared at him, sizing him up, nobody saying anything. Their muscles bulged vigorously, recreating the image of Titans. Many had scars on their body, each a horrible gash on the skin. Some were just leaning on the wall of their cells, eyes hopeless, staring. Others were gazing at him from the bars like a hungry lion ready to pounce, a sneer on their face. Lucius rubbed his wet hands together, and started to walk down the aisle. He was grateful for the bars that protected him from these beasts. He now could understand the centurion's warnings of coming here. He felt glad to have listened to the warning and have agreed to have the officer escort him.

"Bastard!" one yelled. Lucius looked closely at the dirty man out of curiosity. He was anything but gutless, Lucius determined, a character Lucius admired.

"Who are you?" he asked.

The man glanced up at him with malice.

"That is not your business."

"You speak good Latin. You must be from Rome," Lucius remarked, and the man looked away. "Why did you call me a bastard?"

"Because you are one," the man replied, and Lucius unsheathed his gladius.

"I will ask one more time. Who are you, why are you here, and why did you call me a bastard?"

"Just as I said. I called you a bastard because all of you Romans are one. Living in a tight shell made of power and money. The rotten Roman Republic will collapse soon, and that day, I will rejoice. If I survive until then, I will personally go around and kill patricians, or better, make them fight against each other," the man said with a smirk. "My name is Crixus, by the way. Remember it because I'll personally kill you when Rome collapses."

Lucius resisted the urge to drive his sword into the bars before stalking off.

The governor's son walked with his lips tightly pressed and his eyes narrowed. His good mood had vanished into thin air. He wondered where Spartacus was, searching the faces.

Eventually, they reached the end of the long corridor, and Lucius saw a heavy gate guarded by two legionaries. They saluted to their superior officer and the governor's son, and opened the gate for them to pass through. They were shown into a large hall made of marble, which was so polished that it gleamed. Lucius watched in fascination as he recalled the prison cells. It was like two different worlds from each end, only separated by an iron door.

He entered the hall in awe. It was better polished than his house, the house of the vain Governor Maximus. He spotted a scribe sitting on a desk, and went towards him. "Lentulus Batiatus, the master of this school. Tell him that Quintus Lucius Maximus, son of Gaius Maximus is here," he said, and the scribe rushed off to fulfill his order. "Thank you, centurion. It was quite nerving— the prison cells," said Lucius, with a dry smile. The centurion bowed his head and saluted as he headed for the gate once more.

Lucius was pacing around in the marble hall, marveling at the quality of marble, when a polite cough came from behind. Lucius turned around, and hailed the man who was standing before him. The man returned it, and the two stood silently for a while, not knowing what to say.

"I came here to challenge Spartacus for a swordfight. I

thought I should get your permission first. After all, he's your gladiator," Lucius said bluntly. The man nodded, and smiled a little. Now that he could get a good glimpse of Batiatus, he knew that the rumors about him were true. Rumor, the only thing, that he cared for in the world was money. His calculating eyes told him so.

"Spartacus is… well, somewhat ruthless. Are you sure you want to challenge him? I don't want the death of the governor's son becoming my fault."

"Don't worry about that," Lucius said cheerfully. "We'll do it in the traditional way of a sword tournament—whoever draws first blood wins."

The elderly man gave a slight frown. "That's why I'm worried. Spartacus, though polite, he might… Let's just say that when he loses his composure, there's nothing that can stop him. He, along with other gladiators hates Romans, even though he doesn't show it, and it might go further than first blood. He can be very rash, you know," he paused, looking worriedly at Lucius, and then continued. "If you have a guard, a legionary with you, then the soldier might be able to prevent that situation from happening."

"So you're giving me permission?" Lucius asked.

"Yes, but I still recommend that you keep a guard—"

Lucius shook his head. "I'll manage. Where is Spartacus?"

The schoolmaster just shrugged, another of the 'your own neck'. "He will be in his own room."

"Cell," Lucius corrected with a knowing smile.

"You've seen it? The cells? No, that is for the losers, new men, and bad—tempered trouble makers. Our best gladiators have their own small rooms. You can't even imagine how much a gladiator needs to be taken cared of," the master of the house explained, a little wistfully. Lucius nodded, thinking of Crixus, and asked the older man to call Spartacus down for him.

The older man had just turned around when Lucius called him back. "Excuse me, sir, but I'd like to ask one question. Who is Crixus?"

Batiatus paused uncertainly. "You've seen him?"

Lucius smiled. "Oh, we had a very pleasant conversation just a few minutes back."

"Ah... I'll apologize instead. He is not new, but he is too bad tempered. I doubt he has a piece of morality left in his heart. He is a Gaul, captured in a fight a few years back. He's been with us since then. He had grown up as an anti—Roman; I believe he hates Romans as much as Hannibal hated us, if not more."

"He speaks good Latin," Lucius commented.

"Yes, he is ruthless, but I guess intelligent in his own way. He's been caught trying to escape, twice. He almost made it once, three men tailing behind him. Nobody else has ever managed to do that," Batiatus said, seeming a little disturbed by the memory. "He's a hero among them. The Germans and the Gauls especially honor him very much. He's got his own circle of admirers, and we can't dispose of him because... well, he's quite a spectacle. He's a good fighter, next to Spartacus. If it wasn't only for his temper...anyway, he knew Latin before he came here, so he was able to curse all of us from the very first day we met. Ha. His Latin has improved— I guess you can call him intelligent. Not a lot of slaves around here can do that."

Lucius nodded. The man he had seen in the jail was an image of another person, or a beast. His black curly hair was long, oily and shabby. His beard was also tangled up in a mess, his coal eyes bright like a lunatic's. His thick fingers clutched around the bars, his stout figure ready to pounce...

"I'll call Spartacus down now, if you please, Lucius," he said and Lucius thanked him gratefully.

Octavius drew in a sharp breath. The smith had called for an outrageous sum for his new armor. Crassus had asked the armor to be made in the finest and strongest iron. He also asked the smith to compact the iron so that not only will it be strong, but it would be lighter. Octavius couldn't quite make out how compacting the iron would lighten it, but the smith had reassured him and told him that it would make him more mobile. Crassus also had asked for a special design portraying Jupiter and Mars. The smith had nodded his head enthusiastically and said that he would put in more intricate designs than just that.

"Uncle, this is unnecessary," he repeated for exactly the twenty seventh time. Crassus ignored his nephew and continued on ordering the shield and the gladius "This fee alone would feed a thousand plebeians($\substack{\text{common people} \\ \text{of Ancient Rome}}$) for more than a week," he mumbled to himself.

"I want a gladius, though it needs to be a little bit longer than the standard one. With gold carvings, iron that would never break and elaborate design on the hilt. Make sure the grip is a tight one and the helmet, of course, needs to be light and comfortable," Crassus let out a string of commands. The smith nodded his head as he scribbled notes on a sheet of paper.

Julius, who had been standing next to Octavius, grinned. "Your uncle is going through a lot of pain. But Octavius, you shouldn't mention plebeians in front of the general public, unless you are required to do so."

"Why?"

"I'm just telling you to watch your mouth. It makes you sound like a member of the populares*, you know, like a supporter of Marius. I know your family supports him, but still, no," he whispered softly.

* a party composed of aristocratic leaders in the late Roman Republic who wanted to strengthen the power of the plebeians such as sharing riches of the nobility with the people. Its most notable leaders are the Gracchi brothers, Gaius Marius and Julius Caesar. (Single: popularis)

Octavius looked at Julius, confused. "But why don't you like it? You are the nephew of Marius and are no doubt a strong supporter yourself. Sulla died; what's the danger? I thought it was you who said that Marius and Sulla were dead issues?"

"Didn't you hear your uncle? Supporters of Sulla, the optimates (the pro-aristocratic faction of the late Roman Republic. It was opposed to the populares, and its most notable leaders are Sulla and Cato.), are still powerful, and they would not want to hear Rome's richest man's nephew becoming a solid popularis. Maybe not now, but later, they will hate you for it. You will become dangerous—you will have the money, possibly your own legions, and an advocate—your father—who would always support you. You will also have some powerful allies like Crassus, and...

maybe me also." He smiled wryly at the last part, and
Octavius smiled also. Julius's face became serious once more.
"Later maybe, but now is too dangerous. They might try to
cut you off before you become powerful, sensing the poten-
tial danger in you."

Octavius nodded, but doubt still showed on the teenag-
er's face. "You told me a few hours ago that it didn't matter
anymore," Octavius repeated cynically.

Julius decided to ignore him. "Octavius, you know Tiberius
Gracchus, from your history lessons, right? He was murdered,
and his main mistake was that he opposed the senate with
the plebeian thing before he had enough power," Julius continued. He paused for a moment, and renewed, "I'm sorry
Octavius. I never meant it to sound so serious. There is no
way that what you say to your uncle and the smithy here
will be reported to the senate. I'm talking about later, when
the senate starts to take an interest in you. I'm sure you will
take care of yourself well, but I just want you to be safe. You
have absolutely no idea how beastly those senators are. They
are addicted to power. They would do anything to gain
more, murders, robberies, wars. I doubt that there is one
who has never conspired. They are always wondering about
how to kill the opponent. And so, if you have many who

hate you, you will get killed in one way or the other, simple as that. I don't want you to become so. Talking about equality with the plebeians would put you on their black lists, and trust me; you won't live long after that."

"I understand what you mean, Julius," Octavius said softly. "But the Roman Republic is dying. Rome is rotting from the inside, not only in this city, but in other places, like Capua. The governor has three mansions while the plebeians live in cramped insulas," Octavius waved at the direction of Crassus as he continued, "and this is one of the examples," He glanced to Crassus to check whether his uncle had heard or not. He hadn't, to Octavius's immense relief. "Rome's crawling with slaves and beggars. One day, I'm afraid, it will all collapse."

Julius smiled. "I know Octavius. Capua's better off. You should see Rome. Sometimes it's a surprise that there are no plebeian or slave rebellions. I think that it is only a matter of time for a revolt to start," he said. Octavius nodded thoughtfully.

<hr>

Lucius grunted as he defended himself with his shield. At first, he was able to make a good headway on his light feet.

However, as time passed and as he tired, it was growing more and more difficult to dodge blows. He needed to use his shield, and lifting the heavy shield was too tiring for him to continue doing it for long. Spartacus was a head taller than him and was more heavily built. As Lucius fended off the blows, he thought himself lucky to fight a gladiator trained in the Roman legionary style. I know the Roman legionary patterns, he thought with some comfort.

He thrust his sword towards Spartacus, but Spartacus fended him off easily and counterattacked, making Lucius back off in surprise. He glanced at his left hand, and was relieved when there was no blood. Lucius blew at the sweat that was blinding his eyes, as he swiftly dodged a mortal blow. For a second his vision blacked out due to extreme tiredness. He was panting hard by then, and it was on that moment Spartacus let his sword go.

"I think I won," he said, not cockily, but quietly.

"No one drew first blood. It's not over," Lucius countered.

"You would die from exhaustion," Spartacus said in a very cool manner. Lucius hesitated, and then he resigned, sheathing his sword.

"You are really good. Better than my teacher," he complimented.

"Thank you," Spartacus replied, and they sat silently for a while.

"Where are you from and why are you here?" he asked. Spartacus seemed to consider the question for a moment and replied quietly.

"I'm from Thracia. And I was captured in my homelands by some slave merchants and was sent here," Lucius regarded the gladiator, and started to walk away. "Where are you going?" He heard Spartacus ask, and wheeled around.

"We fought a nice contest. I thought you would be honest with me—man to man. You have served in the legions, Spartacus," Lucius spat, betrayal surging over him. Spartacus looked surprised.

"No, I—"

"Your sword patterns are the traditional legionary style. Don't lie to me," Lucius said.

"I was just trained here."

"Of course you were. You are using tactics that normal gladiators would never know. It's straight from the manual," he said, glad to have remembered that part. He always did look closely at the fighting manuals, even though the planning part never suited him.

Spartacus looked at Lucius for a moment, and hung his head. "I guess it doesn't matter anymore," he paused, then continued. "Three years ago, when I was living in Thracia, I was forced into the Roman auxiliary. I didn't want to fight for the corrupt Republic. After a few months, I ran away, but they managed to find me. I killed a few soldiers while resisting, and the commander, the Legate, thought that I was a very good swordsman. Instead of stoning me, like the traditional legionary style, he bound me in chains and transported me here, to this gladiator school."

"Serves you right," Lucius replied, but Spartacus continued without heeding his barbed comment. He seemed distant.

"Then after my first few contests, I became a hero and was given my own room. I was their champion. When important people came to Capua, I was the one who fought in front of them. You know this already, don't you?" Lucius gave an unsympathetic nod. "I'm not treated as a slave or a deserter here, but I still am. They say that. Once I had been a farmer in Thracia, living happily with my wife. I would have still. If it hadn't been for Romans, that is," His face clouded as he said the last few sentences.

It was plain that Spartacus had been drafted in one of

those forced recruits. Still, he was from a Roman province, and he should have done his duty as by fighting for Rome. To run away was one of the most shameful acts that one could do, and to think that this fierce gladiator had been so cowardly was almost unbelievable.

"If you fight well, like now, you'll earn your freedom and you can go free," Lucius found himself saying, despite his promises to himself to be apathetic and silent.

"No. That will be a decade or two from now, when I'm old. Even though I do earn enough money to buy myself, they'll keep me until I'm too old to put up a good performance. Who knows what will happen in the meantime? Will my wife be alive? More, will I be alive?

"I never minded the fighting. It's about killing, killing friends, in front of people who enjoy it. One of my wishes is being able to force those arrogant Romans to fight among themselves, as we gladiators do," Spartacus said, almost to himself. Lucius looked at the big man with some shame. His face burned as he thought of the times he booed.

He just inclined his head slightly to show that he was sorry; it was all he could manage. He had actually planned to ask Spartacus if Spartacus could teach him sword techniques. He was already better than his sword masters, and the only one who had managed to beat him was Spartacus. It would be worth learning from him. Lucius stole a glance at the gladiator. He wasn't sure if it was the right time— the talk had become more serious than he had ever planned. Spartacus was looking at nothing particular, lost in his own thoughts.

Lucius frowned, trying to think of a good way to ask him. For the hundredth time that day, he wished that Octavius was here with him. Octavius would know the right words. He racked his brain, thinking of what Octavius would say. Octavius would negotiate. Yes, that was it. He would negotiate.

"Spartacus?" Lucius asked cautiously. "I have a nice idea... What do you say to teaching me how to fight?"

"I'm not sure—"

"Look, I can save you and your friend's life," he continued. Spartacus looked inquiringly at him. "You said that you hate the killing. I will vote for the loser, always, whenever you fight. That way, you won't kill your friends— at least; I'll try so that it would work out that way." Spartacus shook his head slightly and Lucius remained crestfallen before he suddenly remembered Octavius. "Octavius is the young man you saw today, who made that little speech about saving the loser. I guess you owe him," he said, suddenly glad that Octavius had spoken up after all.

Spartacus made a big 'O' with his mouth when he heard of Octavius, but that was practically it. "Octavius is my friend. I have a hunch that he will also love it if you teach him. Perhaps you can teach both of us and we'll always vote for the loser when you fight so you don't have to kill your friend." Lucius offered.

Spartacus seemed to think about it and then shook his head. "It's not allowed. Batiatus would never allow it."

"It's a common practice."

"Not here."

"Is it fine with you?" Lucius asked. Spartacus nodded tentatively.

"But Batiatus—"

Lucius smiled. "That man will do anything for money."

❦ 4 ❦

Julius stared at the scroll Octavius had given him as he gently massaged his temples. The time for carrying out Marcus's plea had come. He thought carefully, wondering how they would take in the piece of information he was about to give them. Wondering how Octavius would swallow it, he chuckled slightly to himself as he imagined their reactions.

He placed the scroll gently inside his cloak and headed out of his room, nodding to a few guarding legionaries. He smiled fondly at them, and they saluted back. Still loyal to him, Julius mused happily.

"May I ask you where you are going, sir? Senator Crassus would wonder," a sentry said.

"No, you may not," Julius said, grinning. "I have some business to tend to with some other advocates. I'm preparing for a court case, you know," Julius lied easily. The sentry opened his mouth to say something else, but Julius was gone before he could actually say anything.

⁕⟨⟩⁕

Octavius rocked with his horse, carefully observing the poorer districts of Rome. Each time he turned a corner, the plebeians would stop their work to stare, and continue as they realized that he was not an officer of the legions. The streets were a mess, full of litter, and smelling of urine. It was difficult to drive a horse in such narrow roads. Not only that, but there were also many obstacles— plebeians hurried back and forth pushing carts full of cement. Many worked in construction sites, laboring away in the hot sun. Their powerful arms glistened with sweat as they heaved and hauled, grunting and yelling playful curses at each other.

Octavius had escaped from his uncle's house for a few hours earlier. His uncle would never let him go to the plebeian districts, and Octavius was sick of looking at polished patrician houses and government buildings. He wanted to see something different— the real Rome. He was also tired of having two guards tagging behind him— it seemed as if they watched him, not guarded him. Today, he was alone, with no guards, in the very district his uncle had forbidden him to come. The guards would be all over Rome by now, searching for him frantically, dreading Crassus's reaction when they told him that they could not find him. The freedom was sweeter than he had imagined it to be.

His gaze strode towards the two men leaning on a wall of an insula. They were sitting down wearily, and it was pretty obvious that they shared a father and son relationship. The older man looked as if he was very ill, and the younger, vibrant man was tending to the older man. The father limped, coughing frequently. Octavius observed that some of the skin loosely hung from his face, giving him the suspicion that the man had once been fat.

He gazed at the two for a while and was about to move on when he saw a young boy entering the insula, carrying a water jug. He had not felt the thirst before, but as he heard the lucrative sound of water sloshing in the jug, he felt a sudden craving for a drink. He dismounted from his horse, tied the horse to a wooden pole and approached the boy. He knew that many people would flock to get a good look at the horse, but he doubted that they would ever dare to touch it. The horse would be safe for a while.

Octavius slowly approached him, being careful not to upset him. He was carrying a big jug that looked too heavy for one such age to carry.

"Excuse me," he said, clearing his throat. He could have settled with 'Come over here, boy' as many other patricians preferred, but he suspected that it would just cause more unnecessary tension.

The boy did not turn, and Octavius was forced to call once more before the boy turned to have a peek at who was calling him. The boy saw him, and it was Octavius who was more startled. The boy's face carried the feeling of complete panic and hatred, something that Octavius had not expected to find.

The boy, who seemed to be a little older than ten, glared at him hostilely with such a guarded face, that all Octavius could do was gape stupidly at the boy.

He recovered a few seconds later, putting on a calm and smooth expression. "May I have a drink?" he asked, pointing to the jar of water. He had exploited his options- thought of ordering the boy to give him a drink but soon put that out of his head as he realized that the order would only make the boy run away from him.

This time, it was the boy who looked surprised as he gaped back. Octavius took slow steps toward the boy, as if approaching a wild animal, satisfied that the boy did not run. When he was only a meter away from the boy, he extended a hand.

The boy hugged the jug tightly. "S'over there. The well," he said—a clear refusal. Octavius sighed. Maybe he should have tried the 'come over here, boy' thing after all.

He had left the main road and had entered one of its numerous branches, branches that got worse as it got further away from the main road. He could catch a glimpse of the father and son, still leaning on the insula.

"I'll have just one drink," he said, showing a small, sparkling coin. The boy's face lit up at it, and he suddenly beamed. "Just a small gulp," Octavius added, all the while wondering to him why he was bothering to go through all this process. If anybody else knew, they would have a good laugh about this.

He nodded his head. "'Kay. Small drink, no more. Ain't got enough for me and me family."

Octavius nodded. He took the jug and sipped the water carefully, enjoying every moment of it. From the corner of his eyes he saw the father and son, both standing straight now.

He held the jug back, wiping his lips. The boy held out his hand expectantly and Octavius gave him the silver coin, still savoring the cool taste.

He headed back to his horse when he stopped in mid

step. Standing straight?

He glanced back to the father and son, who were stand—ing straight, without a limp. The older man had stopped coughing. A third person had joined the party, and the three were conversing. The third man's face was partly covered by the wall, his face shielded from Octavius's view.

Out of plain curiosity, he approached the three men casually, though he knew his expensive clothes would attract attention like bees near a particularly good smelling flower.

The third wore a hood over his head and had stopped conversing as he approached them. He saw the hooded figure going rigid. Too rigid.

Octavius leaned closer to them, making his interest obvious now. The hooded figure turned slightly, covering his face. He wore a cloak over him.

He saw the figure, standing there, before him, resembling something…

"Do you have any business around here?" the son said, his voice not unfriendly but not welcoming either.

Octavius was taken aback. "Just taking a look," he answered casually.

The son smiled crookedly. "Nothing much to look at here. I advise you to get out of this place quickly, before the gangsters hear that a rich patrician boy is lost in this unwinding, never ending maze of streets. You are quite conspicuous, you know. Look at your horse. See the people gathering?" he said, pointing at Octavius's horse. His voice was cool and composed, without much slang. It was abnormal for a beggar.

"There's much to look at," Octavius said, smiling a knowing smile.

"Such as?"

"You. And your father. And the mysterious third party."

"Not much to look at either."

Octavius smiled. "Your father was sick a few minutes ago, but obviously, he has shaken off the illness in a matter of minutes. He does not have a limp anymore. Your mysterious third party refuses to show his face to me."

The son's face hardened and then came back to normal so quickly that Octavius doubted if he had actually seen the son tense. "You have made keen observations. Sometimes, it is not wise to disclose all you know," the son said, his voice threatening. He was still smiling. The son reached behind his back, disclosing a gleaming gladius.

Octavius gasped in response. The son seemed to be more stoutly built, resembling Lucius. He wished desperately for his friend. It seemed as if there would be a brawl, and the odds were not good. He hardened his face, ready for the assault. Whatever happened, he would not run.

The son slinked back and forth, unsheathing the gladius. Then he let out a great roar and lunged, a killing blow from the start. Octavius ducked the blow, aiming for the legs. The son jumped, at the same time retaliating. Their swords met in midair for the first time with a large clang. The father was keeping his silence, just watching.

It was the third party that stopped the fight.

"Stop! Titus! Put down your sword!" he said, grasping the son—Titus's—arm. Titus still leered at Octavius.

"Titus, I'll count to three. One, two..."

"I'll put my sword down when that bastard puts down his," the son replied.

The third party grunted. "Just do as I say, please, Titus."

Titus shook his head stubbornly as he lunged again. The third party grabbed him again, jerking him back with more force.

"Titus, you first. I'll make sure that he puts down his after that," the third party said.

"But he's dangerous! Look at his symbol of his cloak. Crassus's symbol," the son wailed.

"Crassus is not with Sulla or Cato these days, and this man is far from dangerous, so just do as I say, Titus."

Titus reluctantly sheathed his gladius, retreating into the corners. Octavius stood, panting. He had prepared himself mentally for the fight and almost wished the son had continued attacking him.

They leered at each other for a while before the third party interrupted. "It would be better if you went," he said to Octavius.

Octavius ignored him, his eyes narrowed. Crassus? Were they plotting against his uncle?

It seemed as if the third party had read his thoughts. "No we are not plotting against Crassus," he said. Octavius stayed silent, focusing on the pitch and rhythm of the voice.

"Julius?" Octavius finally said.

The third party tensed, too much.

"Julius?"

"Who's Julius?"

Octavius rolled his eyes. "Now that was a really lame question. Your voice. Your actions. Your features. They are too similar. What are you doing here?" Octavius asked, frowning.

The man gave a sigh and unveiled himself. "Hanging

around with old buddies," Julius said with a smirk. "I'll tell you later, when you are a bit older—"

"Don't give me that crap again, Julius. It works only once."

"It's only once because it is connected to the scroll you gave me."

"Gods, Julius. I'll never trust you again," he said, his face coloring. Julius seemed hurt by the remark. Then, Octavius saw Julius perk up smiling a crooked smile, and narrowed his eyes at Julius, sure that the man had some mischievous thoughts.

"All right," Julius said easily, and Octavius narrowed his eyes even further.

"I want the truth."

"Are you suspecting me?" Julius asked innocuously and dragged him into an alley where they would not be easily spotted. Titus followed with his father.

"Octavius, this is something that you can never confide in... to anyone." Julius took in a deep breath. "I mean, can't we have this discussion when you are a little older? The things that I am going to tell you date back to the times when you were not even born. To say it nicely, it is useless. You are just dragging yourself into old secrets that don't even matter."

"You are not telling him," Titus said stubbornly, still glaring at Octavius. The father also nodded.

"He's the one who brought me the scroll. He's the only son of Marcus Lupus," Julius whispered.

"Marcus?" the father asked in surprise.

"Yes. Him."

The father groaned and shrugged his shoulders, something Julius took as permission. Julius pulled Octavius closer to him.

"To start with, his name is Titus Aemilius Flavius, son of Publius Flavius," Julius said, jerking his head toward Titus. "Publius is of equestrian (the lower of the two aristocratic classes of Ancient Rome, ranking below the patricians and above the plebeians) rank, but it didn't stop him from gaining power. He had many powerful allies in the senate, corrupt like them too." Julius talked in a low voice making sure that the father and son could not hear.

"He was a senator for a few years before a big change happened. He was a staunch popularis, and when Marius died, he decided to withdraw from the senate. He thought it would be dangerous to remain in the senate because of the major political shifts that were taking place." He paused.

"It did not protect him, however. When Sulla gained power, he set his mind on eliminating every Marius supporter. Some subtle supporters who lived far away from Rome were left alone, like your father. Of course, he was only pretending to be subtle, but that is another story. Every staunch supporter was hunted down, even in places such as Africa or Far Hispania," Julius said.

Octavius interrupted. "How do you know all this?"

"I was in the middle of it when it happened. Plus, I knew Titus since I was young. We grew up together. He's a few years older than me. Don't interrupt. Anyway, Publius foresaw Sulla's move and told his son, who was a young centurion in the legions then, to resign. The son, Titus, did as his father said and tried escaping out of Italy— almost made it too. This is a year after my escape. He was almost killed in the process and came back to Rome, working as a dealer in the markets. It worked for some time until a senator saw through his identity and ordered him to be pursued. He roamed Italy for more than a year until he came back to Rome—again—to settle with his family in the back streets, where no one would be able to recognize him. Sulla died a short while after that, but Titus found it impossible to find a job again. So this has been going on for a while now.

"Nobody can live on these streets just by begging. You have to do illegal stuff, but old Publius just could not tolerate himself to do such 'lowly' acts. I mean, he did it very well when he was a senator… Anyways, they were half dead by the time I accidentally tripped on them. You know of my loans, right? Many of them go straight to them. I have some inner pleasure in using Crassus, who was the very general who pursued them. In fact, it is him who is keeping them alive by funding them. He'd crack up if he ever knew of it…" Julius said, smiling widely. Octavius felt obliged to smile along.

"Your father and Publius had once been very intimate. He had thought of Publius as dead when contacts stopped, but after I told him of them being alive, he wanted at once to fund them with some money. I told him not to get involved with this, because there is always the risk of someone finding out. I don't want him to get in trouble, and there's going to be serious trouble if Crassus finds out. That's why he told you to give me the scroll when we reached Rome, in fear that I might refuse the bundle of gold. And a letter," Julius said, pointing at the two.

Publius was holding the gold pieces, counting them and putting them into his bags. The old man's face was creased with a wide smile. Titus was reading the letter, his face hard. As soon as he finished reading the letter, he spat onto the ground, cursing. He half threw the letter to Publius who only glanced at it. He was more occupied with the gold.

Titus turned to glare viciously at Octavius, who smiled crookedly and turned back to Julius. "What's gotten into him?" he asked.

"The letter," Julius said, smiling slyly.

"What's it about?"

Julius's grin widened. "Octavius, do you seriously think I would have told you all this if I thought that you would never be able to find out these secrets on your own?"

Octavius just gaped at him. "I don't follow."

Julius laughed. "What I mean by it is that I would not have told you any of this unless you were going to learn of it sometime soon. The letter… it is an invitation from your father to adopt and raise Titus. A better environment for your son, the letter says," he said and smiled an angelic smile.

"What the… Oh," Octavius remarked. "Damn the gods," he cursed when his senses returned. He quickly veered to look at Titus who was staring as if he wanted to rip the Octavius's guts out.

"I'm not going, father," Titus said.

"Why not? You would never achieve your dreams living down in these ghettos," Publius remarked lightly. Titus was about to object when Publius's face turned serious. "Go,

Titus, go. I have no wish for you to be trapped here like a bird in a cage. Marcus Lupus is a trustable man, and I have no doubts about his son. He is a respectable man, Marcus."

"What about you?"

"I like it here. I'd be more of a burden if I followed you. Come and visit us when you can, Titus," the man said, his face jovial yet his tone serious.

"No, I'm not going alone."

"Don't be a fool."

"I can't leave you out here," Titus objected. The old man said nothing, but just opened his arms and moved to hug Titus.

"Dramatic," Julius drawled with a silly smile on his face. Octavius poked him to be silent and Julius rolled his eyes.

"Forget your life here. Go back to the highly respected centurion you once were. Give Marcus my thanks, Julius," he said, suddenly turning to Julius. Julius's face grew sharp and compassionate suddenly as he nodded solemnly. It was now Octavius's turn to roll his eyes.

"Go," the old man whispered, pushing Titus towards Octavius and Julius. Titus obeyed, shooting one last venomous look at the 'bastard'.

❧ 5 ❧

Octavius closed his eyes as he dived into the pool. He did feel guilty about Titus, who would be spending the day uncomfortably watching out for gardeners. Crassus had decided to throw a pool party and Titus, naturally avoiding Crassus, had decided to stay hidden in the gardens. Julius had told Titus that Crassus would not realize him, even if he might realize his father. Nevertheless, Titus had refused to take the chance. Octavius's trip to Rome had been rescheduled because of Titus, and so it had been decided for him to leave the very next day.

Octavius, however, decided to put it out of his mind for this moment, and enjoyed the cool water on his face. He was the only one in the pool. Everybody else was enjoying the hot bath in a large tub which was located next to the pool. Most of the famous senators of Rome were there, enjoying the party. The women were talking in the dining hall while the men talked in Crassus's private bathhouse.

Julius Caesar was sitting on the edge of the pool, dipping only his legs. When Octavius gestured at him to come in, Julius said something about the freezing water and rolled his eyes. Octavius smiled as he did another lap. When he swam, the silver necklace around him brushed his face—a necklace that brought sweet memories.

That necklace had been a present from Lucia, Lucius's younger sister. She was a year younger than him, and a year ago, she had thrown the necklace out of the window at Octavius. Octavius had understood immediately and had given her a golden pin in response. Nobody knew of the exchange yet. His body burned even in the cold water as he thought of her.

No one knew of their secret ridings in the forest together. They raced each other in the forest near Capua, just enjoying each other's company.

"Octavius! Aren't you cold?" Julius shouted at him, snapping Octavius back to the present. Octavius was about to respond when he thought better of it. He swam toward Julius, and pulled Julius's legs in a swift motion. Julius dropped into the pool, cursing. They splashed around for awhile, earning weird stares from men closest to them.

"I don't want barbarians in my house," Crassus said, frowning at their direction, and Octavius laughed heartily.

"You are bathing in olive oil, Uncle," he remarked, pointing at the slave who was busy rubbing the oil onto Crassus's body.

Crassus scowled again, but the expression soon disappeared. "Gentlemen," he cried, addressing the public. "This oil is not just any oil. It is imported from the East. It is one of the rarest oil you can find," he bragged.

One patrician dragged himself out of the hot water and commanded attention by clapping his hands. He looked uncomfortable, as if he was choked by the thick steam. "That is nothing. I have an animal, a gorilla, imported from Africa. That too is very rare, as you might well know. Would you like a trade, Crassus?" Soon the bath house was full of people shouting out their rare goods. Some had a book written by Alexander himself, some had a collection of ivory tusks and so on.

The talk was cut short when Crassus clapped loudly, causing the slaves to appear. The slaves held plates of fruits, meat and wine. All dishes and cups were plated with gold, and had at least one gem embedded onto it.

A slave approached the pool, offering Octavius and Julius

wine cups. Julius took one, and Octavius was about to refuse when Julius prodded him on the back. "Octavius. Surely you have drunk wine before?" Julius asked, and Octavius gulped. He was too ashamed to admit he hadn't, leaving him with only one choice. To take the cup.

Octavius carefully took a sip. The first part was all right, but the wine began to become bitter in his mouth as he held it. He quickly swallowed, but the bitterness still lingered in his mouth and he wanted to gag. He placed his cup gingerly on the edge of the pool and pretended to swim. What he was really doing was drinking the pool water. It wasn't hygienic, he knew, but there was no alternative. Octavius grimaced as he realized that he would have to go through this routine every time until the cup finally emptied.

He came back to the edge of the pool, joining Julius. Most of the bitterness was now gone, but he did not dare to go through that routine again. "Wine's good." Octavius heard Julius comment, oblivious to Octavius's feelings. The two stayed silent, each deep in his own thoughts, before Julius spoke again. "Mind if I have your wine?" he asked, pointing to Octavius's wine cup, which was practically full. Octavius nodded eagerly, and almost spelt the wine in his eagerness to give it to Julius.

Julius drained the cup, and looked at Octavius, "Well, what do you think of the plebeian districts?"

"Refreshing sights. All I've seen in the past few days are polished houses of wealthy senators. It's getting tired of comparing whose house is better polished," Octavius responded.

"Yes, I agree with you."

They sat in silence for a while before Octavius interrupted again. "Was it that bad? The fraction between Marius and Sulla?"

"Worse."

"How?"

"Like every day Marius supporters would be killed brutally in the Mars square. It honestly smelled of blood. No one dared to enter the square because it reeked with blood, perspiration, and conspiracy. I'd almost been killed there myself, but Sulla pardoned me at the last minute. He regretted it the day after that, ordering his soldiers to put on a chase. I was long gone by then," he whispered.

Octavius nodded thoughtfully before answering. "I feel guilty about Titus," he whispered back.

"Oh, he'll manage," Julius said with a sly smile.

"Won't he... escape? He's not quite fond of me."

"Are you?"

"Well… I'm not that fond of him either," Octavius answered truthfully.

"He's just a little too rigid. You'll love him later. He's a great friend. Very constant in his loyalties," Julius answered. "And as for the escaping, he won't escape. Trust me on this, Octavius."

<hr>

"Capua," Octavius called loudly. Both looked around expectantly and smiled in satisfaction as Titus came sluggishly toward them, answering their secret signal.

"You look as if dead," Octavius said, half jokingly. Titus did not smile back. Julius noticed the tension building up again and clapped them both on the back smiling at them patronizingly.

"Be good boys, all right? I've got some business to tend to. Got to run. Sorry," Julius said.

Titus growled at him. "Why did you tell me to sleep in the garden? I could have managed on the streets," he said.

Julius smiled again. "I was afraid you hated Octavius so much that you would run. Or maybe because you loved your family too much—you might have decided to go back during the night. Then I would not be able to fulfill Marcus's pleas to send you over to his house in Capua. And I know that if you are here, you would remain here because you are not stupid enough to try going over Crassus's manned walls by yourself in the night, trying to escape. You'll be dead in a matter of seconds, because Crassus keeps good guards—my legionaries," Julius explained matter—of—factly with a slight smirk.

Before Titus could say anymore, Julius waved them a farewell, and left hurriedly. Titus turned to glare at Octavius who just gave a neutral shrug. After a good night's sleep, he was feeling content, content enough to ignore Titus's silent rage.

"Let's go. I've bidden my goodbyes to my unhappy uncle already. He asked me why I was going so soon, and I had a hard time thinking of the excuses," Octavius said.

Titus still glowered. "I couldn't have a good night's sleep. Oh, by the way, your uncle probably will not be able to realize who I am unless I am with my father, or unless I disclose my full name."

"So? That's exactly what Julius said yesterday," Octavius retorted.

"Trying to be useful," Titus said, sarcasm thick in his tone.

"Thanks," Octavius answered. "I'm going to Capua right

now.”

“And me?”

“Wherever you want,” Octavius answered casually.

“I’m not going.”

“Great. By doing that, you are letting me, Julius and my father down, not to mention yourself,” Octavius said. He deliberately poked at the man’s self esteem, observing the man to be someone who regarded esteem as the top priority.

He was right. “I don’t give a damn about you and your reputation,” Titus said. Nevertheless, he settled a horse in the stables.

“That’s Crassus’s horse,” Octavius added helpfully.

“Let him mourn,” Titus answered as he galloped out of the stables first. Octavius was quick to follow, ready to provide excuses if they should be questioned by sentries.

<hr>

The two traveled in silence for a while. The journey normally took about eight hours, but the journey seemed even longer to Octavius who became gradually depressed by the silence. Thankfully, the silence was broken by Titus.

“You sure of the road?”

“Yeah.”

They rode in silence again, the sound of their horses trot ringing in the plains. They glanced at the wide plains that were spread out in front of them, admiring the tranquility of it.

"Tell me about yourself." This time, it was Octavius who broke the silence.

"You first," Titus answered. Octavius paused to glare at him but decided that no harm would come out of speaking first.

"There's nothing much to say. My name is Gnaeus Octavius Lupus, normally called as Octavius, nephew of Marcus Licinius Crassus, son of Marcus Lupus, who is an advocate."

"Do you want to be an advocate?" Titus asked, surprising Octavius. He shook his head slightly.

"Why not," Titus asked with genuine interest, surprising Octavius even more.

"He tried to make me an advocate once, making me memorize all the laws, making me speak in front of people."

"And you don't like it?"

"No, I like it fine. It's just that he keeps on trying to make me pursue that career and most of all, he is trying to prevent me from becoming a senator. He was not like that when I was young, but then, as I grew up, he sort of became like that. I don't know what changed him, but he wants me to stay away from power. It's something I'd rather not do," Octavius said hesitantly, wondering why on earth he was saying all this.

"He's just trying to protect you. He probably went through too much bloodshed during Marius's and Sulla's reign," Titus offered, without sarcasm.

"Marius too?"

Titus rolled his eyes. "Maybe you have all heard this from Julius, who can't be blamed for being biased. After all, Marius is his uncle, and Sulla was bent on killing him. Marius killed as many as Sulla, though maybe in subtler ways. Anyway, both were ambitious politicians who hated each other's guts and killed as many of the others as possible when they had power. It's not only Sulla, remember that, Octavius."

"Still, I'm not going to age in Capua. The city is boring, nothing compared to Rome. I want to live in Rome."

"Anyhow, nice dreams."

Octavius decided to ignore the first Titus's remarks about ambition. "I really do. I envy those who live in Rome."

"What about me? I lived in Rome until yesterday," Titus said with a straight face, his eyes gleaming to hide a crooked smile that was forming.

"Except for you," Octavius concluded simply.

"I bet Crassus would call you to Rome soon enough, so that he can polish you to become a nice, obedient general or senator or whatever," Titus said, almost wistfully. Titus had no idea how correct he was. He also had no ideas whatsoever on what was about to happen in Capua, nor did anyone else. They lived in complete blissful ignorance, until a fuse was ignited… by no one else than Octavius.

73B.C.~72B.C.

Part 2

Defiance

"The real death occurs inside you, where all the decent morality dies off with time… It's time for something that I had planned for years…
It's a pity you won't be alive to witness my great plan, Octavius"

– Spartacus

$$\sim 6 \sim$$

Octavius paced around in the room, thinking of a good escape plan. "He knows it, Octavius," Lucius said, disturbing him from his thoughts. "My father knows that we always vote for the loser when Spartacus is playing, and he also knows that it is influencing his popularity from bad to worse."

"Tell him about the deal. Both of our sword skills have improved a lot because of Spartacus."

"Are you nuts? He would kill me if he knew that I was taking lessons from a slave," he said. Batiatus had stuck to his word and gold, not mentioning anything of Spartacus tutoring the governor's precious son.

"Your tutor's also a Greek slave. Plus, it's a common enough practice. Training with gladiators."

"It would most likely be training with former gladiators, not gladiators. Besides, you know my father," Lucius said grimly, and Octavius admitted it with a faint smile. The governor was very conservative when it came to ranks. He despised plebeians and associated with only a few selected equestrians. He hated to associate with those below his rank, the patrician class, and he would never even hear of his son being taught by a slave.

Also, the governor always decorated himself and his estate so that it would stand out from other peoples' houses. No one knew how many expensive and rare treasures he had accumulated since being appointed to a governor post, both legally and illegally.

"Ask Lucia to get us out of this room. She can open it from the outside. Your father is a very great man, and very persistent. He locked us up. Seriously. Locked us up," Octavius said, shivering. When the governor had prohibited them from going to the coliseum, they had tried to go there secretly. The governor, finding out their plan beforehand, had locked them up in this storage room.

The room was full of exotic goods, and Octavius might have been tempted to take a look at it if not for his current mood. What right did the governor have to lock them up here?

Lucius rolled his eyes. "What should I do? Shout to her to rescue us out of here! So that everybody can hear that we are secretly going to escape!" he said, emphasizing the word secretly.

"I'm going to sue him for locking me up in here without permission," Octavius declared.

"A fine chance you'll have of suing a governor."

"Why not? But we need to do something. We stroke a deal, and today Spartacus is fighting with his best friend. He practically begged us to come," Octavius said, marveling at the room structure. Gaius Maximus had locked them up in a big vault where there were no windows— no possible means of escape but a heavy metal door. The metal door was locked tight.

Lucius stayed silent for some minutes before speaking. "There's nothing we can do."

"No, there is always something we can do. Keep thinking. I intend to keep my promise," Octavius said firmly, more firmly than he believed in himself—he was not sure if they could get out of the room soon enough.

Octavius had been skeptical. Learn lessons from a gladiator? One who had betrayed the Roman legions? Lucius had calmed him down, telling him that Spartacus was even a greater fighter than their sword masters. After exchanging a few blows with him, Octavius understood instantly that the man was no ordinary gladiator. Naturally, he had lost the contest. He still remembered how it felt. How the sky had circled around him, how he had almost waited for Spartacus to put a foot on his chest and kill him, like he had done to many other gladiators. So this is how it felt, he had thought.

"You're too slow," Spartacus had commented during their fight. "Oh. And your sword will not listen to you if you wave it around like that. Don't get frustrated." Octavius had given an enraged battle cry and tried to hit Spartacus, but Spartacus had jumped away easily. He was still advising Octavius. "Never attack first. Let them get at you and then attack back. Watch what the opponent's doing. Don't let your mind wander."

Octavius smiled a little at the thought of Spartacus. His skills had improved much because of Spartacus. And of course, there was another teacher... the Titus.

Titus, a stout patriot who had gotten closer to him with each passing day, helped him with the swords. Titus advised him in a strict, disciplined way as if he was a centurion again and Octavius one of his legionaries. He pitied them after three minutes of training. Unlike the lavish sword styles of Spartacus, Titus's was straight to the point, and

surprisingly efficient. It felt great to surprise Spartacus sometimes with a new technique of Titus's.

Once, Titus had even followed Octavius to challenge
Spartacus. They continued on for more than twenty minutes, each panting yet no one getting anywhere. The match
finally ended when Titus threw a handful of sand into the
gladiator's eyes and thrust him off balance. No rules against
sand, right, he had said smugly after beating Spartacus.

Over the two years, brotherhood had sprung up between
them, and now they treated each other as close friends.
Octavius understood Titus as a typical Roman soldier, hard
on discipline, while Titus understood Octavius as an ambitious young man yet a man who hated bloodshed. Ambitious
and peaceful don't go together, Titus advised, especially
when you are in Rome.

Titus was also the first to recognize the relationship
between Lucia and Octavius. He had first recognized it on a
grand party to celebrate the governor's birthday. The two
had talked, not intimately, just casually, but Titus could see
through their veils of casualty. Their heads were too close,
and they talked for more than a few minutes, which was the
record time Titus had counted when it came to girls with
Octavius. He normally shied off from others.

He, on the other hand, was a different issue. He enjoyed himself immensely when there were parties—he would go around, speaking to as many of the women as possible. After a round of speaking to them, he would slink off to the men and participate in their drinking and gambling— something he had not been able to correct after his few years as a centurion in the legions.

❧ *7* ❧

Spartacus looked at the seats. Where were they? They had always kept their promise despite their declining popularity. People were slowly noticing what they were doing, and showed their displeasure outwardly. But they wouldn't betray him now, of all days. He would be fighting Jacob, a Jewish slave who had been his companion for years. Even though Jacob fought well, there was no gladiator who had yet managed to beat him. Jacob would not be the first, and Spartacus was pretty confident about that. Still there was no sign of Lucius and Octavius. The cornicerns sounded the note to start, and he desperately searched them one last time. He could not see any friendly faces.

Assuming and hoping that they were just late, Spartacus saluted to the audience, a signal that the match would officially start. Jacob did the same, and the two aimed their swords at each other.

Jacob attacked first, swinging his long sword towards Spartacus's legs. Spartacus knocked the blow off easily, and retaliated by throwing his sword towards Jacob's thigh. Jacob managed to avoid the blow by jumping to the side. Spartacus quickly swung his sword for a mortal blow at Jacob's undefended right arm. Jacob dodged to one side, but the blade still had scratched him. Blood trickled down from his arms, soon turning into a stream of blood.

Spartacus saw Jacob grit his teeth, and his mind filled with remorse. He had hurt his best friend. Jacob lunged at him, but his footsteps were awkward, as blood began to flow out more and more. Spartacus side stepped, and swung his gladius—a blow that was blocked by Jacob's shield. The Jewish gladiator, however, looked stunned by the blow. Spartacus whirled his sword around expertly, eyeing the audience for his friends. He could not see them.

Jacob saw his friend whirl the sword from left to right with ease. There was no hope that he could win the Thracian slave. Panic clenched at him as he realized that today would be the end of him. Today's sunrise was the last that he would ever see. Spartacus was closing in at him, and he could detect the pain in his friend's eyes. There was no stopping however. It was my life or your life.

Spartacus rammed his shield against him, and Jacob just received the blow. Panic had frozen him. He felt another blow cut through his cheeks, and distantly heard the crowd booing. He had had enough.

The favored gladiator saw his friend sprint towards the end of the arena, dropping his shield and sword while running there. Don't, you fool, he wanted to scream at Jacob. This was not a death match they were fighting. No one needed to die. The audience seemed to be in good humor. If Jacob fought bravely, Spartacus was almost sure that they would not vote against him. It had always been that way. Brave gladiators did not get killed, or else, there would be more than a dozen dead in each month. Gladiator school owners could simply not allow that—they had financial situations to think of. They liked it when the audience voted for the loser to live, and the audience knew it too. They liked to please the gladiator school owners because if he was pleased, he would provide even better entertainments. The Roman audience was not a brutal killer. They were Romans, Romans who valued courage. If only a losing gladiator would show courage, they would vote for him.

His experience told him that Jacob's actions were of a crazed man who knew that his death was coming. The

Jewish slave was clutching frantically at his hair, moaning words that nobody could understand, while the crowd booed at his cowardly actions. There was no hope that the crowd would vote for Jacob and allow him to live now. The crowd yelled at him to kill Jacob and he cast a fleeting look toward Batiatus, who looked hesitant but still nodded his head in agreement with the crowd. With that, his last hope vanished. Spartacus felt grief overwhelm him as he clenched his fists in anger. They never understood what it was like to kill a friend. Lucius and Octavius. They were no different. He had thought that they were, but they had betrayed him today. That was all it mattered. Spartacus walked over to the moaning figure. The figure looked up at him, but there was no recognition in the eyes—just complete panic. "I'm sorry," Spartacus whispered, as he, with a swift motion, drove his sword into Jacob's torso. It would at least be a fast death.

They saw with glee as Jacob fell to the ground, life seeping away rapidly. Spartacus saw them, gloating over a death. He felt uncontrollable fury as he leered at the audience. It should be them who he should kill, not his fellow gladiators. It was them who deserved to die. And it was then when he knew what he should do. For Jacob. For other gladiators. For himself.

Octavius sprinted to his feet when he heard the door creaking open. Behind the door, there stood three muscular guards with Gaius Maximus at their head. The vain governor walked lightly over to Octavius and patted him patronizingly.

"The gladiatorial games are over. Your friend has won a decisive victory."

"And the loser?" Octavius asked.

For a moment a look of contempt crossed the governor's face. He shook his head slightly and then shrugged, as if Octavius was being too naïve. "Jacob the Jewish gladiator met his death in a crazed state," he said, eyeing the reaction of the two young men. Octavius clenched his fists until the knuckles became white, but said nothing. "I am sorry for locking you up, Octavius. Though I believe you would have seen much better things," he said, indicating the antiques in the room.

"Yes. It is not every day you get to spend a few hours in a prison filled with exotic goods," Octavius replied, and stalked off without a backward glance. He did not care about respect to his elders. That was something that should be paid to people who deserved it. He did not care that he had offended the governor of the city, one who could decide someone's life. All he cared was that he could not, he did not, keep his promise to Spartacus. Spartacus had to kill his friend in the end. The result, as always, was the most important in gladiatorial games.

Octavius pushed the three baffled guards out of his way, and continued his way toward the gladiatorial school. He needed to apologize. What will Spartacus think? Will he believe his innocence? His breath grew shorter and faster as he approached the arena entrance. The guarding centurion tried to deter him, but with no avail. Octavius ignored the soldier's shout and went on, his eyes fixed onto the back door. His pace grew faster along with his breath. He finally reached the back door of the gladiatorial school and ignoring the cursing and jeering gladiators, he ran on, opening the door to the main hall of the school. There he roughly called to the scribe, and ordered him to bring Spartacus down for him. He waited, pacing around in the hall, rubbing his sweaty hands together. How should he apologize?

"He will not see anyone today, sir. I would not recommend it either—he's very unstable at the moment. After the battle, he threw his sword at the audience, though thankfully, no one was hit. Batiatus tried to calm him down but failed. He is...well, mad." The scribe called from behind, and Octavius turned towards him, his anxiety turning to irritation.

"Tell him that Octavius is here. He'll come then," he said, and the scribe bowed. The little man scurried up the stairs and soon returned with a disappointing answer.

Octavius cursed under his breath and strode to the base of the stairs. He could hear the scribe calling to him that he was not allowed to go up, but he did not care. Explaining himself to Spartacus was the only thought that Octavius had now, and the thought dominated every part of him. Octavius climbed two steps at a time, reaching the top of the stairs in a matter of seconds. The stairway was connected to a gloomy dark lit corridor with rooms aligned on the left side.

Two legionaries were standing guard, or rather, sitting guard, because they hastily stood to attention when Octavius appeared, their faces still foolishly grinning.

"Gnaeus Octavius Lupus. I'm here to see Spartacus," he said, trying to hide his disappointment in their lax attitudes. No matter what they were doing, they were Roman legionaries, and he believed that they should live up to that name.

"You are not allowed up here. It does not matter who you

are. Only guards and authorized men are allowed," the soldier said with a slight slang, and Octavius glared at him.

"Get out of my way," he said. "Please," he added for a good measure.

"Do you have permission?" the man asked.

"I'll get it after," Octavius said, trying to conceal his impatience and irritation.

The man shook his head stubbornly. "Under the laws of the school—"

"Under the laws of the school, shouldn't you be punished for staying guard like that? I have some thoughts about going to Lentulus Batiatus and report on your lax attitude," Octavius said, smiling a dangerous smile.

The soldier froze slightly. He threw a quick glance at his companion, who looked thoroughly unhappy. Octavius could see them wavering.

"Look, let me in, and I'll keep my mouth shut," he said, seizing the chance. "Give me the key too. I'll be quick."

"Well—" the legionary started, but was cut short by his companion.

"Aw, let him in. What's that gotta do with us?" the man said as he withdrew himself to let Octavius pass. As the youth passed, the man handed over the keys, and pointed to a room. "Spartacus, you say? The second room, right over there. I won't recommend it though. That guy's sorta crazy."

Octavius nodded and went to the room where the man had pointed. Behind the youth's back, the two men giggled as the legionary who had given Octavius the key pulled out an amphora from his back. "Let's give this our best shot," the man said, opening the bottle head and pouring the wine into his large mouth. His companion eagerly waited for his turn. They would fall asleep soon, from too much wine. Not that it mattered. Nobody checked. They knew that their attitudes were lax, but why not? There was no war in Capua right now—they didn't need stand attention that sharp, did they? No, they decided. Carpe Diem, they said to themselves as they giggled.

Little did they know how much they were helping Spartacus.

<hr>

Lucius stared after his friend in shock. Octavius was always calm, never rash. The behavior today was something that Lucius had never imagined even in his wildest dreams. To talk like that to a governor! Octavius must have been furious, he thought. His father too had been shocked, and after the initial shock followed a string of curses directed at Octavius.

Lucius however, could understand his friends' feelings. He also knew where Octavius would be headed, and decided to follow Octavius to the gladiator school.

⚍

The key was turned, and Octavius stepped into the second door. It was a small room, with a cot placed on the far end. There even was a small table, and a chair, which surprised Octavius. He had heard that famous gladiators were very well treated, but he had never imagined that they were treated this well. The dim light ominously reflected shadows.

"Spartacus?" he called quietly from the door way. Nobody answered him, and Octavius sighed. He walked over to the cot, where he thought a figure was lying. On his way, he unwittingly placed the key on the table, by habit.
His guess was true—there was someone lying on the bed, and he gently shook the figure. Octavius was about to start the apologetic speech he had prepared when a dagger was suddenly hurled at him. Thanks to all his practice that he had done, he managed to avoid the blow, though awkwardly.

Spartacus was now standing before him, resembling Hercules. There was a dagger in his hand, and the dagger glinted dangerously in the dim light.

"Spartacus? I'm Octavius. I'm really sorry about—" he started but was cut off by a dagger blow. Octavius drew his gladius from his belt, comprehending the situation. He had not been mistaken for somebody else. The blow was for him from the very beginning. The dagger slashed through air again, and it was countered by Octavius's gladius. Even though the gladiator was great, the gladiator could not possibly defeat him with a dagger, or so Octavius hoped.

The big gladiator stalked to the opposite side of the room, blocking Octavius's only exit. And while he did so, Spartacus managed to get a glimpse of the key. Spartacus paused slightly to make sure that the key was the key he had hoped it was, but the move was so subtle that Octavius did not recognize it. He then snuffed out the only torch in the room. There was only infinite darkness.

<hr>

Octavius clamped a hand over his mouth. His breath seemed too large in the small room. He could hear a slashing noise now and then, and each noise brought him fear that he never had known. He also knew that someone was out there, in the same room, holding a dagger so that he could plunge the dagger into him.

Spartacus was blocking his only exit, and the gladiator knew this room way better than he did. He had no choice but to remain standing in the corner, waiting for Spartacus to come to him. He shivered, and he understood what the governor had told him. He understood the gladiator Jacob, about running around in a crazed state. He was not sure if he could say the negative for himself, now that he was face to face with a powerful gladiator who craved for his blood.

Minutes ticked away, adding to Octavius's nervousness. He felt like a trapped deer, waiting to be stabbed to death. Once or twice, he heard Spartacus lunge randomly. One lunge had come so close to the young man that he felt the wind swish in front of him. Spartacus knew where he was, and he would be killed anyway, he thought. No, he told himself, pressing down his fear. He would survive. How? The question rang in his mind, driving Octavius crazy.

"You did not come. You betrayed me. Betrayers die. Talk!" the gladiator rumbled, and Octavius kept his silence. He knew better than to respond. The darkness still had not cleared up, and it seemed as if every space of the dark was trying to reveal him to the gladiator. This could not go on forever. Spartacus would start moving soon, and in the end, he would meet his death. If he was to meet his death anyway, then he would show contempt for it, and for the gladiator.

"You betrayed the Roman legions," he croaked, and he felt a light breeze ruffle his hair. Spartacus now had a clear aim. "Plus, it was the governor who locked us up in a vault so that we could not get out," Octavius continued nonetheless.

The gladiator did not answer, but only swung his dagger again. The breeze grew stronger. Octavius closed his eyes, and tried to maintain a peaceful face. His face would not be writhed in pain when he died.

"You are powerless, Octavius. Admit it! I'll accept your excuses, though it does not mean that I am going to pardon you. I had begged you to come. Please, I had said, he is my best friend, a companion who had been with me from the start. How would you feel if you fought Lucius and was forced to kill him? You cannot help me anymore. You are powerless against the governor. Admit it. In other words, my friends' life, and my life also, are still endangered. I had been a fool to believe that you could protect me from practically everything. It's time for something that I had planned years before. But when I met you, I discarded the idea on the term that it was too risky. I thought there was no need for my plan because you and Lucius would protect me and me from killing my friends. Now it's time to reactivate the plan, and you have helped me very much, though unwittingly. It's a pity you won't be alive to witness my great plan, Octavius.

"The deaths you see in the arena aren't all. They are actually quick, less painful death, and even those deaths don't occur so often. Death matches are rare. The real death occurs inside you, where all the decent morality dies off with time. No friends, no loyalty. You have to fight your opponent, whoever it may be, in order to save your own life. Slowly, the power to love deteriorates, and so does your innocence. My hands are very dirty, Octavius. They've killed more than you realize, not only in body, but also in spirit."

The words just glanced off Octavius's ears—he was too busy thinking about a way to save himself. If it had been in some other situation, Octavius would have analyzed the man's words... and would have known what he meant.

However, in this situation, all he could do was just to ask "What did you plan?" in hopes of delaying his death. The more Spartacus talked, the more chance there was for somebody to come to his rescue. Spartacus did not respond, instead waving his dagger toward the voice. Octavius drew back sharply.

He could feel the hostile darkness even though he had closed his eyes, his teacher, and his friend, turned into a sudden assassin, and fueled by revenge.

Then he could see light. Light of Pluto, the god of death, he thought. Was it over? Was he now truly dead? He had heard from his some elders in the town that when you died, you saw a bright light that flashed for a moment. It would guide you to the Underworld.

The light did not recede however, and a piercing scream penetrated his ears. His eyes shot open, and they saw Hercules clenching his left thigh. Behind the Hercules, he saw a man. The man came towards him, and Octavius's eyes flooded with tears of relief as he recognized the man. Lucius.

Lucius smiled to himself. He had rescued his friend from death, from the rash gladiator. He had escorted the dazed Octavius to his home, where he bragged about himself. It was worth bragging, though he had stabbed Spartacus mostly by accident. He was not going to tell anyone about that. Octavius's parents could not find a way to thank him enough, and Titus looked as if he might kill himself. Titus had somehow taken over the roll of an older brother, and he felt a sort of an obligation to protect Octavius from any harm that might come to him. And now his younger brother had almost died, while he had been lying around idly in Octavius's home.

Marcus Lupus knew Publius Flavius very well—their relations dated back to the dictatorship of Marius, and he had welcomed Titus like a son, going through the legal adopting process on the spot. Titus too had felt pleased about it, especially since the man had known his father and was still a popularis.

He would now be considered a hero among the village folks, Lucius mused. He was deliberating on what he would say when people congratulated him when he heard a shout come up from the first floor of his home. Startled, he grabbed his gladius and hurried out of his room.

Being on the second floor, he could see what was happening on the base floor and in the courtyard of the mansion. Slaves ran in all directions, screaming. Even the men were running frantically, and Lucius had to shake a slave a few times before the slave could answer him.

"Invasion," the slave gasped. "Not soldiers," he stammered, and the slave, in his hurry, pushed his master away to escape. By now, screams were exploding from everywhere. A fire started in the corner of the courtyard. What were the legions doing? He did not have time to think of an answer. Somebody swung a sword at him, and Lucius countered it. His attacker lay on the floor, helpless. Lucius veered towards the attacker, and the attacker lay still, with his eyes closed. Lucius lifted his gladius, but he could not bring it down, maybe on a practice target made of straw, but not on real human flesh.

"Who are you?" he asked, instead of killing him. The man opened his eyes, and looked around him, as if he was surprised that he was not dead. Then, he jumped up, and aimed his sword at Lucius.

"Weakling. You can't kill anyone, can you?" he sneered, and ran away swiftly. Lucius thought about following him, but decided against it. Knowing about the invaders was much more important than chasing one man down. He hurried down the stairs, calling to the centurion who was supposed to guard the house. The centurion appeared a few seconds later, with twenty men behind.

"Sir, we need to evacuate for the moment. Your parents are safely away, and I was told to bring you back."

"Who are the invaders?" he asked, and was answered by an informal shrug.

"That is of no importance at the moment. I have sent two men to warn the rest of the village as your father have instructed. I have horses ready at the stables. The attackers have not reached there yet. The family is to rendezvous at the summer mansion nearest to here. Hurry!" the centurion said, gently pushing him towards the stables. Lucius broke into a fast run, and the soldiers followed him as best as they could, panting.

Screams followed Lucius as he ran into the stables. It was quiet in there, and Lucius felt comfortable in this small sanctuary. He mounted his own horse, and motioned for the other soldiers to ride. The centurion mounted, followed by other officers and veterans. Other men had to walk because of the lack of horses. The veterans were not veterans at all, but just men who were a bit older than the others, Lucius thought bitterly. This attack was probably the largest attack that this village had experienced in a century.

He had jogged his horse at least a mile before he thought of his younger sister. "Centurion! Where is my sister?" he called desperately.

"With your parents, sir," the centurion replied casually and kept on jogging his horse. The men who were told to walk were panting vigorously by now. Lucius nodded, apparently relieved, and continued on.

<hr>

"Village under attack! Village under attack!" the young soldier cried as he raced his horse up and down the streets of the small village. Children ventured out to see the cause of this commotion and were quickly pulled back. Young men filled out onto the streets, each holding a crude weapon of some kind. The soldier could also see the women preparing hot water to pour down on the invaders. They were better than the inexperienced legionaries who practically ran away, he thought. When he believed that he had warned the village quite enough, he galloped to Marcus Lupus's house as instructed, and shouted his presence loudly.

Marcus Lupus cautiously opened the front gate himself, and gazed calmly at the soldier. He told the soldier to come in, and the soldier obeyed. He was quickly led across the courtyard and into the main house, eventually into a big dining room.

"Who is it? Is it a gang of thieves?" Octavius's mother asked. She was sitting nervously on a chair, rubbing her hands together unconsciously, and Marcus also looked anxious. The soldier replied that he did not know, and told them that the legions were having a hard time putting them down. All of them had superb sword skills, and the invaders had managed to kill half a century in only a matter of minutes. The rest had run off or had gone to away to 'escort' the governor.

Marcus sighed. None were guarding the civilians. "Are they dangerous enough to evacuate?" he inquired, pacing continuously in the room.

"The governor's family has. They have attacked the

governor's mansion first, meaning that they are looking for valuable things. This house may be attacked too, if that is the case. The town militia might hold them up, but it's only a matter of time," The soldier replied with some sadness in his voice.

"Our family has had enough for today. Octavius will lose his mind if he hears about this. He is upstairs, resting peacefully with Titus, trying to recover— and this is what happens!" he cried, enraged at nobody in particular. The soldier dropped his eyes, partly feeling guilty at the fact that he had been the one to bring the bad news.

Marcus called to a few slaves. He beckoned to one to prepare the house guards and chose another one to inform Titus about the invasion without Octavius knowing. While he was doing so, Licinia, Octavius's mother, turned her gaze to the soldier.

"What is your rank, soldier?" she asked, with kind eyes that made him think of his own mother. She would be worried when she heard the news about the revolt.

"I'm just a normal infantry soldier, ma'am," he said, blushing. He wished that he could have mentioned a higher rank.

"Have you gone through any wars before?" she inquired

again, and he nodded.

"Not a real war, but I did go through some skirmishes like this one. At least I'm more experienced than the others around here." he said, blushing again. She smiled, and nodded encouragement.

She was on the verge of saying something when Marcus interfered. "This is getting serious. Maybe we should evacuate after all."

"No, we might not be able to defend our own wheat fields, but I'm not going to lose the house to some barbarians," Licinia said, showing passion that surprised Marcus.

"I thought you hated violence," he mumbled, partly to himself, and finally nodded assent. "Our house guards are of top rate. They should be able to defend the house, at least I hope so," Marcus concluded though he looked unsure of himself. Marcus was continuously rubbing his ring, a sign that he was very anxious.

"You help out the militia, soldier," she whispered quietly to the infantry soldier. He blushed, saluted smartly, and ran off.

⋯⊰❈⊱⋯

"And, as I was saying, Titus, Spartacus snuffed the lights

out. I moved into a corner—"

"Sir!" A man rushed in desperately through the door. Octavius looked up at the man, annoyed that he had interrupted the climax of his story.

"What is it, Galvix?" he asked frowning, not concealing his irritation. The slave looked up; looking worried as if Octavius might go crazy at any moment. Octavius frowned even more. The shock had worn off hours ago, and he was now back to his normal self. He couldn't bear to see others looking at him like a fragile cup that was might shatter at the slightest disruption.

"Actually, it is for Titus, sir," he said, and Titus looked at the slave in surprise. He was lying on a bed that was situated on the opposite side of Octavius's armchair. He stood up, and asked him what was going on.

The slave said that it was important news for him, and gestured impatiently for him to come out. The slave even tried to drag Titus out, and Titus shook him off. He had been an equestrian, and he did not like the way that these slaves treated him. They eventually learned about his past as a beggar, and seemed to think him as one of their own. That frustrated him more than anybody could imagine.

"Enough! I am going out," he partly yelled, and Octavius

tried to hide his grin. Titus valued his honor as much as his father did, he thought, thinking of the events a few years ago.

"What is it?" Titus grumbled, closing the door behind him.

"There has been an invasion in the village. Nobody knows who they are, at least yet. The governor has evacuated, but the master has decided that we will keep our house instead of evacuating. You are not to tell Octavius anything about the raid," he said, almost as if ordering, and Titus grabbed the man's tunic.

"Stop being so insolent!" he growled, and freed the frightened man after almost chocking him to death.

Titus thought that Octavius was recovered well enough to know about this raid, but the slave shook his head furiously. He repeated that it was Marcus Lupus's orders, and that he should never disobey it in any circumstances.

"Then what are the legionaries doing?" he inquired, and was answered that they had been either killed or that they had gone to escort the governor.

Titus looked at him, and waved the man off in irritation. Those cowardly men did not even have the right to bear the legion flag. If he had been their centurion, he would not have let them retreat in such a cowardly way. In fact, he would have killed the deserters himself. Pathetic bunch of vagabonds, he thought. Before he entered the door, he checked if his gladius was well sharpened. In his nervousness, he wanted to fasten his armor on, but he could never hope to do that without the keen Octavius getting suspicious about it. He had no choice but to enter casually, and he did.

Octavius was nibbling at some grapes. "What is it, Titus?" he asked, and Titus hesitated. He tried to mumble a lie, but Octavius waved it off.

"You were never good at lying. Now, what is it?"

Titus glanced around him, thinking of a good excuse. While doing so, he recognized a plume of smoke coming up from the direction of the village outside the window. He moved swiftly towards it and pulled the curtains.

"Is there anything that I shouldn't know about outside the window?" Octavius asked, looking suspiciously at him.

"Octavius. I— Look. I promise that I will tell you everything tomorrow."

"Why is it tomorrow, of all days? Can you not tell me now?" Titus shook his head apologetically. Octavius let out a sigh of resignation and slumped even further into the comfortable armchair. He popped some more grapes into his mouth, and closed his eyes. Why was everyone keeping secrets from him? He frowned, trying to think of a good answer to his own question, but soon gave it up. It seemed as if his head was in a dead lock and would not function. He would wait to hear the 'secret' until tomorrow— it wouldn't kill him. And he needed a bath. Yes, a warm bath would refresh him.

Titus studied Octavius carefully. Maybe Octavius was not fully back to his normal state, he thought. If he had, then Octavius would have been all over him, prodding him on. But nobody could blame him for being tired and impassive. After all, he had almost died today.

"So, your story," Titus said, mainly to keep his mind from wandering.

"I told you the ending before," Octavius said curtly, more than he had intended to do.

"I'm sorry, Octavius. I really am."

"Yeah," Octavius responded without any cynicism. "I'm just tired suddenly." Titus shrugged his shoulders at this sudden change of behavior. If he knew Octavius, the young man would come back to himself soon.

Octavius rubbed his eyes roughly and yawned. "I feel

dizzy," he said, as he lied down on his own bed— next to Titus's. Titus moved to snuff out the lights for him, and Octavius shook his hands furiously. "No. There's no need for that."

"Scared of the dark, Octavius?" Titus laughed jokingly, trying to cheer his younger brother up.

"Yes. Had enough of it already," Octavius snapped, looking into his eyes. The younger man did not laugh; there was only seriousness in it. Titus felt the grin on his face fade away, and he just shook his head at Octavius's behavior.

"Well, I'm sorry about forgetting… that. Good night— or good evening. It's not completely night yet," Titus said, and rose to leave. If Octavius went to sleep, it would be better for him. He would guard the house with the other guards, resume his post as a centurion, even if temporarily.

"Don't leave me, Titus. And don't tell anyone about… about what I said about darkness. Just my nerve, it's gotten a bit sharp. I'm okay. But don't leave me alone, please." Titus sighed. If only he could tell Octavius what was happening outside. Octavius would understand then. But he could not tell Octavius, and that was the end of the story.

Titus sighed, and picked up a book from the corner of a desk. He held it up to Octavius to reassure him that he would stay, and took his seat in his chair. He moved it closer to Octavius, and squeezed Octavius's hands warmly before opening his book to read. Of course, no word made sense. He could not understand them— the letters were impeded by images of shouting, pillaging, and fighting.

❧ 9 ❧

The soldier urged his horse to go faster. He was almost there. He could hear shouting and screaming.

When he arrived, he was momentarily blinded by a streak of fire. He instinctively crouched himself, pressing flat against the horse. Something that looked suspiciously like a torch flew past him. Panic flared inside him as he realized that he had been discovered. Before, he had always been with officers who knew how to handle things. At least he had been with fellow legionaries who guarded each other when they were at peril. However, he was alone now— the rest probably dead or in the governor's summer mansion. He gritted his teeth as he thought of them. None of them had as much experience as he had, and he had been only in three minor skirmishes before. They had just run away when a bigger force attacked.

Why did he ever listen to that woman? If he died, it

would be because of her. He spotted one of the townsmen standing in the middle of the battlefield, and ran his horse towards him.

"What happened? Who are they?" he asked frantically.

The man tried to answer him. The soldier looked at the man in horror as the man let out a sputter of blood and slumped to the ground. His eyes were glazed, leaving only emptiness behind. A sword had penetrated his body, and the legionary traced up the sword to an arm, an arm to a head, a head to a face— one that he had seen before.

The soldier froze, as the man showed a grin on his face. His horse wasn't much better off. It kept neighing nervously and pawing the ground. The man pulled his sword out of the already dead man and aimed it towards him. The legionary felt pain. Pain, as he had never felt before. Time had slowed. He screamed as he saw the man withdraw his sword from a body he recognized as his own. As he fell off his horse, he recognized the man. His gasp widened, and he tried to grab onto something. He needed to tell someone who the attackers were. He opened his mouth to shout, then there was only darkness. Only one thought prevailed until the last minute:

Spartacus.

~ *10* ~

When Octavius awoke, light streamed into his room through the window, warming and lighting every object in the room. He gave a big yawn as he pulled off his bed sheets and stepped onto the carpet. Where had he put his home shoes again? He lazily looked around for it, and found them lying untidily on a corner of the room. Octavius stepped into them, and walked out of his room, treading softly on the carpet. Titus was nowhere to be seen, as usual. He didn't have much sleep.

Octavius did not meet anybody on his way down to the dining room, something that struck him as unusual. He didn't mind though. No servants were better than bothersome ones who always decided to interrupt the tranquility of the morning, or noon, as he judged from how high the sun was up.

Then he came across something that he did mind. No

food was set for him on the table. Where was his breakfast? And more, where were the people?

"Aula? I'm starving," he called, only to be met by silence. Panic suddenly clutched him. Nobody was here. Where were they? Did this sudden disappearance have any relation to the secret that was kept away from him yesterday?

"Aula? Mother? Father? Titus?" Nobody answered him. Octavius's breath grew faster, and he rushed up the stairs toward his parents' room. Nobody was there. He looked carefully around for a note, and found none. He repeated the same process in his room and Aula's, but was met with the same result. The only thing that he had noticed was the fact that Titus's book was almost unread.

In his panic, he ran around the house, opening every door—even the servants' quarters. He knew they would hate him for it, but it didn't matter. After completing the journey, he slumped down, dejected. The house had become a ghost house in only one day.

He tried to calm his mind and tried to think reasonably. Had he missed any rooms? No. Wait. He did not check the sick room, a room that he had been warned not to enter. The room was an infirmary, and his parents of course did not want him to frequently visit the 'sick' room. Octavius also knew that fewer people walked out of the room then those that had gone in. Instead, they came out covered in linen. The room had a long history— it was used as a sick-room since his ancestor who had built this house had died in there. The room had seen the death of the houses' ancestors, servants and slaves. Rumor had it that there was a ghost living in the room. There were always servants, freedmen, slaves, who are willing to testify, and Octavius shivered slightly at the idea.

Octavius never even had an abstract idea on how the room looked like. After hearing the rumor about the ghost, he had not even ventured close to the room, nor had there been any reason for him to consciously go there. It seemed that the time to venture had come.

As he ventured nearer, he thought he heard whispers, grunts, and sometimes yelps. A shiver ran up his spine. Damn the ghosts. He continued on, holding his breath. The corridor was sunlit; no ghosts came out when there was daylight.

He took a deep breath and turned the knob of the door. All he needed to do was to jerk it open. He shut his eyes tight, and pulled. He opened them, and came face to face with his father.

"The militia lost, and the army ran away."

"They escorted me to this house!"

"That is your own business. Your days as a governor are numbered. The consuls have advised you to keep a trained century, and you said that you had one. Now your trained century— half dies and half escorts the governor to his summer mansion." The man had a sleek nose, and eyes that darted nervously around. He was tall and imposing, compared to the relatively short but stout governor. He grinned faintly, showing his teeth— in a way that reminded the governor of his higher authority.

"As a representative of Rome, I deliver this warning. No amount of money shall be given to you. You take money out of your own funds, and recover Capua to its original fertile state. If it is not done, the senate will be obliged to… well, I'll leave that to your own imagination, governor," the man said in a cool voice. He was impassive towards the governor's distressed looks and his grunts of surprises.

"This was completely unexpected. The walls are tight, as you have ordered. Who would have imagined a gladiatorial rebellion?" the governor cried, and the man shrugged.

Lucius felt guilty as he just sat there, on the table. He could not bear to see his father so helpless. But there was nothing he could do to help but to stay silent and not provoke this man any further.

"That, as I have said before, is your own business, as well as your own duty as a governor. Now, I'm a busy and tired man. I have ridden all dawn and morning to come here—there would have been no need to do so if this rebellion was put down quickly. Thankfully, a nearby villager saw the commotion and sent a warning to Rome very quickly. Anyway, I need to visit the house of Lupus before I go back, so if you'll excuse me, governor. Oh, remember, the deadline to restore Capua is one year. The senate is very upset about this rebellion. The fact that it ever took place, the fact that the gladiators had successively escaped out of Capua, the fact that the legionaries—your legionaries—could not put a stop to the rebellion." A smile lurked beneath the man's face as he said so, a smile that showed contempt for everything in the house, including the governor.

<hr>

"What are you doing here?"

"What are you doing here, father?" Octavius asked

suspiciously.

His father stared at him, and Octavius held the gaze. He would not be intimidated— he had a right to know what was going on in his house. His father finally looked away, sighing. Octavius tried to hide his grin. Everyone in Capua knew about his stubbornness, his unwillingness to give up once he set his mind on something. It could be good or bad, depending on the situation. He concluded that this time, it was good.

His father led him deeper into the infirmary, where he roughly glanced at many beds lying in a neat row. A few chairs were also there, and on them, he noticed his mother, Titus, and Aula sitting there.

Aula broke into a smile when she noticed him. "Octavius! I'm so sorry. I should have left a note or something. In my haste, I completely forgot about leaving a note. I just noticed the time and was about to go down."

Octavius smiled, and nodded to reassure her that he was all right. All he wanted to know now was what had happened while he was sleeping. He looked toward Titus in a questioning way, and Titus just waved his hands towards the beds. On the beds were sheets, some neat, some crumpled. On a closer examination, something seemed to be beneath the sheets. Titus stood up, and stalked towards the nearest bed.

"Octavius. I promised that I would tell you everything today. Now, ready yourself." Frowning, Octavius focused his complete attention onto Titus's hands. The hands grabbed the corner of a sheet and was about to jerk the sheets back when Aula screamed.

"No. Don't show that to Octavius." She was joined in by Licinia, who also nodded her head in approval of Aula's words. Octavius glanced at his father. Marcus also didn't seem to be comfortable in what Titus was doing, and seemed to be wavering between a yes and no.

"What is it? I believe that enough secrets have been kept from me," he announced, but no one seemed to be heeding him. They, now joined by Marcus, were shaking their heads, no.

"Octavius, as a patrician youth from a renowned family, will have to go to the army sooner or later," Titus said and Marcus just glared at him. "Sir," Titus added for a good measure, and Marcus gave a resigned nod. Titus took a big breath, and without waiting for a nod of assent from the adults, continued. "Yesterday, Spartacus escaped by leading a gladiatorial rebellion." Octavius just gaped his mouth, his brain not processing the information just yet.

"He led about eighty men, or so we think, and pillaged the village. The legionaries were either massacred or scared away by the rebellion, and it was the militia that helped to reduce the size of the rebellion. The reduced number of gladiators came to our house, and we managed to scare them off with our twenty infantry house guards and ten archers plus the surviving militia. Of course, we have suffered many casualties also," Titus whispered to him, his mouth set tight grimly. "They are the losses," he said, jerking the bed sheets away.

Octavius stood, frozen to the spot. He just stared, and stared at a man whose face was covered in dried, reddish brown blood. Octavius's gaze drifted to the man's torso, which was otherwise clean except for a patch of red on the middle of the man's chest.

Octavius's hands, which were clasping each other, were trembling furiously. The knuckles were white, and his face was drained of color.

He trembled with a sudden coldness, and faintly felt Titus's hands steady him gently. He had never seen a corpse so close, only from the far away back seats in the coliseum. This was certainly different.

"He had a clean death Octavius, compared to others. Should I show them too?" he asked with a bit of humor at the youth's reaction. Octavius shook his head, still frozen to the very spot. Would he also have looked the same way if Lucius had not come to rescue him? The image of him lying there had overlapped with the man's bloody face. No. Never. He shook his head to clear the images, but they came back, each time more frightening than before, as if taunting him.

"Who is he? I don't recognize him," he said, his voice faltering. He did not want to know— most of all, he did not care. He had just asked the question to focus his mind on something else.

"A brave young man from the town militia," Titus answered.

"Where are the rest of the servants? Are they dead too?" Octavius kept pouring out the questions, afraid that if he let his mind rest for even a second, he would see horrible images of him lying on the bed.

"No. They are surveying the wheat fields for the losses. The rebels took whatever wheat they could find and burnt the rest that they could not carry off with them." This time, his father spoke aloud. Then, in a more quiet voice, he asked, "Are you all right?"

"No," Octavius answered, being truthful. He would not pretend that he was not shaken by the dead man who stared back at him.

"It's natural. It's your first time" Marcus said quietly. Octavius stayed still, futilely trying to erase the picture of him lying on the bed, covered in dried blood.

Aula quietly rose, and brushed Octavius's shoulders, as if trying to comfort him. "Time for your breakfast, Octavius," she said, tip toeing her way out of the room. Octavius had always felt amused when he saw her walk like that— it was just funny to see her obese body on tip toes. However, now, he just stood there, staring after her, feeling nothing.

"I don't want to eat anything," he whispered, mainly to himself. Aula closed the door after her, without hearing him.

His parents stood up. "We understand. Actually, it was also my first time experiencing real combat... and dead men. I was like you at first, but it got better overnight. Trust me, you'll feel better too." Licinia announced as she tenderly hugged him from behind. Octavius just stared after her in disbelief. She hated violence. And if she was so nonchalant about the corpses, then there was definitely something wrong with him. He was just staggered by the fact that no one seemed to be as shocked as he was. His father was calm, his mother was too, and so was Aula, at least it seemed so. Titus, he could understand, but the rest... it made him blush suddenly. Why was he the only one who was terrified of a dead body that could not move? Was his cowardice showing?

His parents stood to leave, discussing the recovery job in low voices. Octavius stared at Titus who seemed to be more at ease than he was yesterday evening.

"So this was your big secret?" Octavius asked.

"Yeah. I had strict orders to not tell you because of your mental shock that you received from Spartacus trying to kill you."

Octavius smiled half heartedly. He was suddenly burdened with the idea that maybe he might have been the cause of the revolt. Since he did—or could—not go to the arena to save Spartacus's best companion Jacob, Spartacus had tried to kill him in his irate state, saying the words that had hurt him. That had hurt him because it was true: *You cannot help me anymore. You are powerless against the governor. Admit it.*

Yes, he admitted it. He was powerless against the governor, and more, he was also powerless against the mob. Octavius had thought that Spartacus would know. Their agreement was that they would try their hardest to try to increase the survival of both himself and his friends, not guarantee it. The lives of the gladiators could never be guaranteed, and that was a stark fact. Spartacus, he believed, had interpreted the meaning as 'always guarantee the survival of.' Spartacus had interpreted the meaning correctly only yesterday and it gave him such a sense of anguish, disappointment, despair, and most of all, the understanding that his life and his friends' lives could never be guaranteed, that he had decided to revolt. Such was the theory Octavius had formed.

If only he had gone. If he had, then Spartacus would have been content to live in his own shell of comfort, or more likely, blissful ignorance. The revolt that had taken the lives of many innocent civilians would not have occurred.

He voiced his thoughts to Titus, who shook his head. "Even though the rebellion might have happened earlier because of you, they would have rebelled anyways. It was too organized for it to have been a sudden spurt of anger." The words calmed him down a little, as he thought of what Spartacus had told him the day before. Yesterday, he had not heeded to Spartacus's little speech much, too occupied with other thoughts. But now, as he rethought the entire conversation, he could catch the line— *'It's time for some —thing that I had planned years before. But when I met you, I discarded the idea on the term that it was too risky. I thought there was no need for my plan because you and Lucius would protect me and me from killing my friends. Now it's time to reactivate the plan.'*

He gasped in agony as he thought of the warning. If he had only given it a thought—the rebellion had been pre-dictable. It could not have occurred. The feeling of guilt did not die down.

Then his thoughts moved onto the next sentence, 'and you have helped me, though unwittingly' How? He had never helped Spartacus escape. He mused about the fact for a moment before he finally comprehended the meaning.

The key!

He had left it on the table.

"Gods, Titus, I helped him," Octavius said, stunned.

"What?"

"I left the key on the table… he must have used it to get out," Octavius said morosely. Titus opened his mouth to blame him, but then closed it again on a better thought. It would only burden the youth more, who clearly was antago-nizing himself with that.

Titus sat down on a chair next to the dead man and gazed calmly at Octavius, thinking of what to say.

"You seem more comfortable with them than you are with me," Octavius commented dryly and Titus laughed.

"A few months in the legions and you will become like me, trust me."

"I don't think I'm ready for that yet," Octavius said, his voice crestfallen. He hated his cowardice—or so he thought—of killing.

"You won't go even if a job is offered?"

"In Capua? You should have seen the legionaries yesterday, how they were staying guard. I think that they were even drinking. It's no surprise that Spartacus was able to escape so easily. I'm not joining them," Octavius said.

"No, not here. This is just a town force. I mean in the regular legions."

"I don't know. I might not… as I said, it doesn't seem like I'm ready for it," he answered. They lapsed into silence again before Titus began to narrate him the story of what had happened yesterday.

"The militia was great. But the problem was that they did not have any proper tools—"

Octavius was still disturbed by both his cowardice and

guilt. If only he had been there when Spartacus had fought Jacob… these people might still be living.

"However, we had good weapons that could block them off, or else, all might have been lost. There was a guy from the militia—"

What was Spartacus thinking when he revolted? The legions would all be on him like flies on food soon. Rome was not forgiving to rebellions. Even though Spartacus had tried to kill him, he hated to think of what the Roman generals would do to Spartacus after they caught him. He knew how much Spartacus had craved for his freedom. A part of his brain actually congratulated Spartacus on having the guts to revolt. A much larger part of his brain told him that Spartacus's rebellion would and needed to be conquered soon, for the sake of innocent Roman civilians and for the republic itself.

"A smart aleck. But he could fight real well. The legions—Octavius, are you even listening to me?"

"Hmm? Yeah," Octavius responded, looking down. He hadn't meant to ignore Titus.

Titus rolled his eyes. "Fine. Here's some information that might interest you," he said, emphasizing the word interest with some spite. "Spartacus is currently on his way to Mt.

Vesuvius. When they fled from our house with all the wheat they could gather, they picked up rural slaves. I know because a scout reported more than two hundred men."

"A scout already?" Octavius asked, jerking up his head.

Titus nodded. "Rome's got good roads, good legions and good scouts. The legions would probably depart soon to crush the rebellion."

They were just about to leave the room when Aula jumped into the room.

"Come quickly! A representative of the senate has just arrived!" she panted, heaving her large body. Octavius looked questioningly at Titus, and Titus lifted his eyebrows.

"Told you. There's nothing that can beat the Roman scouts."

Octavius fidgeted uncomfortably in his clothes. Not that he hated them, but he liked casual clothes, unlike these that were too elaborately designed. Aula had dragged him into a room and fastened these clothes on him with other garments. He had the uncomfortable feeling that all these additional garments made him look like a circus fool.

The tunic, which was made of pure silk, felt cool compared to his sweating body. A representative of the senate, of Rome, of the people! Even though he had met many Senators during Crassus's typical pool parties, he had never met a representative on an official duty. Cold sweat poured off from his body as he thought of the powerful man who he would meet today.

He glanced at Titus, who also looked unnatural in his clothes. Titus, who usually wore only a light tunic, was wearing a sincere looking toga. He thought that the toga didn't fit Titus very well—it was far too big and heavy looking.

"You look like an old man," Octavius said, giggling nervously. Titus wrinkled his face in distaste at the words before retorting.

"You, look like an overgrown child in his father's toga."

"My coming of age ceremony had been conducted a long time ago. I am quite legitimate to wear a toga," Octavius snapped matter—of—factly.

"Yeah, if a long time means a couple months," Titus said, not bothering to hide his smirk.

"And yours had been conducted decades ago, judging by the wrinkles on your face," Octavius said grinning and was about to tease Titus further when the door opened, and a tall man with nervous brown eyes entered. Marcus followed respectively behind the man, Licinia right next to him.

Octavius and Titus rose to greet the representative, and he just nodded. The man took his seat at the head of the table, and gestured them to sit down. He stole quick glances around the room, frowned, and then glanced at each one of them carelessly. After sighing enormously, he said, "Wine." Aula scurried off to fulfill his order, and the man closed his eyes, content that he was being well obeyed.

"Gentlemen…and lady," he said, glimpsing at Licinia.

"You probably suffered a lot from the revolt. I saw the burnt fields while coming here." Marcus bowed his head in assent. Aula returned with wine, and he sipped the wine carefully and slowly, as if it might spoil his exotic looking toga. "I am not here as a representative from the senate, but as a friendly messenger from Senator Marcus Licinius Crassus," he said and paused slightly. Octavius sighed inwardly. He had been hoping to see a senator on duty. Arrius seemed to be unaware of the young man's feelings as he continued. "He demanded to know whether you were safe or not. When the news reached us at dawn, important senators were contacted and it took us less than an hour to decide what to do and who to send as a representative. That's why I was able to arrive here so fast—if we had a meeting with the other useless blabbering senators, we would still be debating over what to do," he said, smiling faintly and waving his hands elegantly. Octavius could feel at once the arrogance that radiated from the man.

"I am also here to search for more evidence on this revolt and to persecute anyone responsible—but I believe that is another story. I am not here to discuss that now," he said, staring at each one of the face to see if there was agreement or not. Octavius smiled, showing assent, as he guiltily thought of the key he had so stupidly left in the room.

"Good. Well, for Crassus's question, you are undoubtedly fine except for some financial losses. Yes? Right. He also wanted to know if that young boy over there could come to Rome," he said, gesturing carelessly at Octavius while looking in Marcus's direction. Before Marcus could respond, he turned to Octavius. "I believe we've met before," he said, smiling greasily. Octavius tried to recall him, but he could not remember where he had seen the man, let alone recognize him.

"We were both at the pool party of Crassus two years ago. You've grown a lot," he commented, smiling the oily smile again. Octavius shook his head blushing. He didn't recall seeing the man. "No?" he asked, playing with one of the gold rings on his fingers. He smiled patronizingly, as if he was pardoning the younger man's stupidity.

"Ah. That is too misfortunate. Anyway, Crassus wants you at Rome because he wants to enroll you in a military post," he said and stopped to look around, enjoying the gaping mouths of people at present. "He believes that this rebellion would last for a long time. The legions in the Italian peninsula are not experienced unlike the ones at the borders, and the legions on the frontiers are too preoccupied with dealing other enemies—so, he and I have decided that the best way would be to train the nearby legions better, and to recruit new ones. He will need new officers, if you know what I mean," he smiled. Only this time, the smile did not look greasy at all. "What do you say?"

Octavius didn't even glance at his parents for their opinions. "This is one of my best opportunities, and I'm not going to let it go, sir." Titus gave him an inquiring look as he rolled his eyes. Octavius had clearly forgotten the rows of dead bodies in his ambition.

"Are you sure Octavius?" Marcus asked, alarmed.

"Yes, father," he responded more confidently that he felt.

Licinia shook her head defiantly and Marcus said, a little wistfully, "He needs to serve anyways if he wants to become one of the highly respected senators."

"I thought you didn't want him to become a senator?" Licinia asked, aghast.

"No, I don't, but it's up to him, not me to choose his future. If becoming a senator and general is what Octavius wishes, I have no thoughts whatsoever to take away that wish from him."

"But Marcus—" Licinia protested weakly. Then she turned to Octavius. "Are you sure? Is this what you want? You'll see more of those corpses, and you'll be in constant danger and you—oh gods," she said and broke up due to lack of breath.

"I'll be fine," Octavius answered, somewhat meekly.

"Everyone says they'll be fine," Licinia retorted sharply and Marcus put a hand on her shoulder.

"It's up to him, Licinia. Up to him," Marcus whispered and Licinia finally acquiesced, though she shot deadly looks at Marcus, Arrius and Octavius. If looks could really kill, the three would have died in a matter of seconds.

Arrius clapped his hands delicately as the family reached a consensus. "Any questions?" he asked Octavius as if this was just a normal orientation practice.

"What if the rebels are easily conquered?" Octavius inquired.

"Just pray that they won't be," the man said, with the everlasting smile still on his face.

———◆◆———

Octavius felt his pulse quicken. He would serve two years in the legions, and then start to climb up the political ladder to becoming a senator, a consul perhaps.

He touched his helmet. The helmet did not have a plume attached because he was not an officer— yet. He would become one, one of the greatest that Rome had ever seen.

He would become one who his parents, Crassus, Julius, Titus…and Lucia would be proud of. As his Greek philosopher teacher had once said 'A war brings a start to many heroes.'

Octavius admired himself wearing full armor in the mirror. He had usually refrained from wearing it, unlike Lucius, because it was too heavy. He had no clue on how to fight nimbly in this heavy iron prison, especially in the hot weather. Octavius then gently put on his helmet and immediately winced at the weight. He quickly decided that he could live without the helmet—he took it off and decided to carry it.

Octavius mounted his horse after the man, who had introduced himself as Senator Arrius. The Senator seemed to be very impatient about the delay— even though he was the one who invited himself to rest at the Lupus's house and depart the next day. Titus mounted after him. Yesterday, Titus had begged to Marcus to send him along with Octavius, to write a letter of recommendation so that he could get a post in the legions. Please, it's been the very thing I had been waiting for, he had asked. He had also told him that he would always stand by Octavius's side and guard him. Marcus fell for that. Octavius stayed silent yet he looked on the scene with his face showing contempt— he knew one thing Titus hated the most, baby sitting him. Although Titus had fallen into the role of being his older brother, he hated guarding Octavius. That boy is old enough to protect himself, he would always say to others.

He turned around to face his parents and saluted to them as best as he could, grinning. They smiled back, and watched until their son could not be seen anymore.

The three men rode in silence when Octavius suddenly reined his horse. Arrius looked at him in a both irritated and questioning way. "I need to visit someone before I go," he said and Arrius shook his head. "Please. It will take only ten minutes."

Arrius contemplated on it and decided that if they were late already, an extra ten minutes would not matter. He waved his hand carelessly, indicting that he would remain here. Titus wanted to follow but Octavius shook his head. He then raced his horse off toward the opposite direction of Rome—Capua, the governor's summer mansion.

He reached the governor's mansion in a matter of few minutes, driving his horse wildly. He was stopped at the entrance of the mansion by the soldiers who were in a grim mood. Octavius saluted them slightly and they let him pass after recognizing him. He initially asked the centurion to call down the siblings but as the man was going off to obey his order, Octavius stopped him. Lucius would ask him too much questions and his subtle jealousy would probably ruin his currently good mood. It would only delay them and Arrius would no doubt be furious. He changed his amends for just Lucia, swallowing his guilt.

A moment later Lucia came out, looking sleepy and annoyed. Octavius jumped off his horse and gave a mock bow to her, causing her to frown and yet smile.

Lucia saw the boy she had once known in full armor—more likely a man now. She looked up and down at him and Octavius grinned.

"You look all right," he said and she just nodded.

He twitched his fingers nervously. "Lucia. I'm going away," he said and Lucia suddenly felt panic. They had never made their feelings clear in the public, just remaining as childhood friends. She had known Octavius all her life. He was the closest man she knew besides her brother. He listened to her—he never thought her as inferior to men as others did.

"Going away?" she asked, incredulous.

"Yes. To Rome. I am receiving a military post. No, I don't

know what it will be though I'll mail you soon enough."

"Are you going to fight?" Lucia asked, her voice suddenly high pitched because of the tension.

"I might. Though I think this slave revolt will be over before I even get my post," he said, a little dubiously.

Octavius inhaled slightly at her aroma, noting the black, silky hair falling behind her back. He blushed as he thought of it, and looked away, trying to focus on the conversation. He could not help noticing her concerned hazel eyes— the eyelashes just the right length... her slender figure...her strong personality...He pushed himself away from her consciously, breaking the charm.

"You are not fighting, Octavius," she said with her lips pursed. For a moment Octavius longed to stay and talk with her, not follow the snaky Arrius. But he could not. This was the first step to what he had dreamed all his life—being in Rome, being in power—and he could not just let it drop. After all, it was not as if he was not coming back.

"I'll be back," he said and she shook her head. Sometimes she wished that she had been born a man, joining Octavius on the adventures. She was sure that she was smarter and more able than most foolish men who had become senators just because of their gender and birth status.

"I have to go now," he said, slowly and reluctantly. "But I promise I won't get myself killed. I'll live out the war—if it really happens... and maybe after...we can," he halted.

"I'm not a child, you know, so don't try to put me off by all your 'don't worries'" she said in a more icy voice than she had intended.

Octavius blushed immediately. "No, of course not. That was not what I meant. I'm sorry" he labored out and Lucia suddenly felt sorry about her response. She was making it harder for him.

"I know, Octavius," she said and Octavius's face brightened conspicuously. "Just don't get yourself killed all right?"

Octavius smiled at that, returning to his normal self. "I can take care of myself. You stay out of danger."

"There's no danger in Capua. It's a boring city."

"Maybe outside the walls."

"There's only the dull forest. I will certainly never get killed in that boring forest. Wish you luck Octavius." Octavius fought the urge to hug her as he gave a polite bow and mounted his horse. As he was riding toward the gates he put in one last word.

"I'll send Lucius a letter when I reach Rome. Just don't tell him anything about this meeting, or else he'll be all over me…" he said and Lucia nodded, immediately understanding.

"And…" he said, taking a big breath. Just do it, he told himself. "I'll miss you." With that, he galloped toward where Arrius would be without once looking back, his face burning.

<hr>

"I'm back, uncle," he greeted Crassus, who was sitting with his back towards him. The plump man veered around, his mouth forming a big smile.

"Octavius! I didn't even hear the door creak open!" he cried, indicating the heavy door with his pudgy hand. "I must be getting old, huh?" he asked playfully, and stood up to hug his nephew. Then his face turned more serious, "So it is true, the rebellion. They are…"

Octavius gave a grin. "All okay, though most of the crop is gone. Stolen or burnt." Crassus waved his hand and instantly telling him not to worry. Then, he waved to a slave, and told him to transport a thousand denarii to the house of Lupus.

"Tell Justinus to carry out the job well. A thousand denarii—I'll check to it that it was safely delivered. Now, go!" The slave rushed out, bobbing his head in a series of bows. "I can trust that guy," he said, partly to himself and partly answering Octavius's questioning and doubtful looks, "and don't object to my offerings, Octavius. It is my thanks for letting you come to me."

Octavius shook his hands. "Actually, it should be me thanking you. I've... always wanted a post in the legions."

"Ha. Well your career, as a general and as a politician, starts today. Just to say, you look fabulous in that armor. The best I've ordered in a few decades," he answered, smiling proudly all the while. He could feel some kind of destiny as he gazed at the young man's handsome features, someone who any general would like to have on a battlefield.

Octavius blushed, and Crassus motioned for him to sit down. He poured his nephew a cup of wine, and noticed how much his nephew was blushing.

"Wine's good. Try. Or did that moral Marcus Lupus never teach you how to drink?" That caused Octavius's already pink cheeks to become even redder. He saw Crassus having a fun time, enjoying himself and took a big breath. He smiled gently, as if he appreciated the joke and drained the cup. He felt a sudden giddiness come over him and had to blink a few times. He instantly regretted his decision but now there was nothing left to do except to pretend that nothing was wrong. Crassus looked back at him in appraisal, looking a little surprised.

"Uncle, my father wrote to a letter to you," Octavius said, trying to hide his giddiness.

"Did he now?" Crassus heaved himself up from the armchair and took the letter from Octavius's outstretched hands. He rolled the scroll of parchment paper flat and was about to begin reading when his nephew's voice interrupted him.

"There is a man who came with me from Capua, apart from Senator Arrius. He is legally my adopted brother, older brother, and he is outside the door, waiting for your approval."

"My approval? Over what?" Crassus inquired, and was met with a gesture towards the parchment.

Dear Senator Marcus Licinius Crassus,

It has certainly been a while, Senator. The revolt took everybody, including me, by surprise, and so there are many severe losses to the town. This event, however, might have been predicted because Spartacus had tried to kill my son Octavius on the very day. From the way I hear, Octavius and his friend Lucius- the stout, strong boy you saw on your visit last time- had made a deal with Spartacus that they would protect his friends in the coliseum if he taught them sword lessons. The man fights very well, and I privately believed that he was pretty well composed to teach my son. That was my mistake.

Spartacus, angered at the fact that they did not keep their promise (as I have it, the governor prohibited them from going by locking them up in a storage room) tried to murder my son when my son went to him to apologize for breaking the promise. No one knows how he escaped, but he did, leading a revolt of about eighty men. The revolt, though, may well have been planned rather than been an instantaneous thought because they were very well armed, as far as their gladiator arms would get them.

Senator, before I continue, I thank you. Thank you for your consideration- of recommending Octavius. I know that Octavius has craved for a military post, or for a political seat to achieve his dream. I cannot thank you enough for providing this opportunity for Octavius.

I can also guarantee that you will not regret in making your decisions. I believe that my son would be very useful to you, mainly because he has known the gladiator more than anyone in this town. He will know the man's strengths and weaknesses, possibly his ways of action and battle style. I also know that innocent as he might seem to be, he will be firm and constant in battles, and I have my complete faith in him that he will carry out his tasks well enough.

Furthermore, I recommend Titus Aemilius Lupus, aged twenty three. He is my adopted son, senior to Octavius. He is the only son of a friend of mine — who had some financial problems. He thought it would be better for me to adopt his son, which I gladly did. Titus Lupus, my son, has been with us for nearly two years, and is a very trustworthy, energetic and intelligent young man. He is deeply trusted by our family, Octavius especially. He has served as a centurion once when he had been younger. Titus also is famous for being one of the best swordsmen of the town- I deeply believe that you will not regret in appointing him a post, if you will excuse my saying so.

Thank you, with all my heart,
Marcus Octavius Cornelius Lupus
Licinia Crassus

Crassus looked blankly at the parchment paper, and gave it to Octavius to read. Octavius blushed when he read about his father recommending him. His face lightened up at the recommendation of Titus, his friends whom he always needed and looked to for advice.

"Well?" Crassus intervened.

"Sir?"

"What do you make of the recommendations? Do you think you are fit enough?" Crassus asked, and Octavius just stared down at his sandals, not knowing what to say. He did want that post, but he also didn't want to sound too rude, bragging about himself. Crassus clapped his nephew play-fully, a blow that caused Octavius to wince.

"I say that you are," he said, his face cracking up in a

bigger smile. Octavius smiled back, apparently relieved. "But I'm not sure about the guy named Titus Lupus."

"Meet him for yourself," Octavius said, gesturing at the door.

Crassus bellowed loudly to the legionary to let a man named Titus Lupus in. Soon, a legionary opened the door, followed by Titus. Crassus stood up, and examined the new man from head to toe, sizing him up. The young man seemed a bit unsettled at first, but when he realized that the Senator won't stop, he did the same to Crassus. Crassus admired his daringness to do so— most men would just drop their glance and shuffle about uncomfortably. He at once noticed the broad shoulders, the short cropped light brown hair that made him look powerful. The man was a head taller than him, intimidating the medium sized Senator a little.

"Your name?" Crassus asked him as shortly and unfriendly as he could. He always had the urge to make a bigger man subordinate to him.

"Titus Aemilius Lupus. Called Titus," he answered back in the same unfriendly style, and Crassus felt both admiration and irritation at the same time. Admiration that the man had guts enough, and irritation that his plan to make him more subordinate had just failed.

"Tell me about yourself."

Titus glared at him. "I am under no obligation to reveal my past to you, Senator. But, I'll tell you that I am twenty three years old, has experience in the legions, is an adopted son of Marcus Octavius Cornelius Lupus, and is completely willing to assist Octavius during this war," he said, in a very cool manner.

Crassus irritatingly looked at the strange man standing in front of him. He would certainly be fit for a legionary. And if Titus would only obey his command, he would have a powerful sword at his side. The man's turquoise eyes bore down at him, and the Senator turned his gaze away. Brave, daring, energetic and intelligent—according to Marcus. If he would only come to him.

"You're in," Crassus said dryly, and instantly regretted what he had said. He didn't want the man to realize that this had been some sort of sizing up test. Octavius stepped in between them, sensing the awkwardness between them, both valuing their pride more than anything, both head-strong, both stubborn. He should have expected this.

"Uncle, this is Titus Aemilius Lupus. He's my best friend and my older brother. Uh...He always cares for me very much, and he taught me sword skills along with Spartacus. He also told me of legions—their style, their ranks and more—very resourceful and intelligent," he paused. He abused himself for not saying things more smartly and more clearly. Crassus looked at him venomously, and Octavius blushed again. Why did his uncle want to undermine Titus? "Titus. This is my uncle, Marcus Licinius Crassus. He has helped our family very much, from finances, political businesses, military businesses and more. This time, he called me for a post in the legions— my life now would have been very different and very boring without my uncle." It was getting a bit easier now.

Titus winked at Octavius out of Crassus's eyeshot. He smiled, rolled his eyes and made a round gesture at the side of his head. Crazy old fool, he mouthed, and Octavius put a hand to his mouth to hide his grin.

"Nice to meet you, Senator," he announced, putting back his serious face.

"We've already met," Crassus snapped. Then, he waved his hands as if he was bored with dealing with the younger man.

"Octavius. You know where your room is, right?" he said, and Octavius nodded. "Titus. You—"

"He will share my room, if that is okay with you, Uncle. My room is too big." Octavius cut in before Crassus could say something provoking. Crassus glared at him for a few seconds, and then nodded his head in assent.

Crassus turned his back to them, and picked up a scroll of paper that was marked with the symbol of the senate. He stayed still, and he spoke only when Octavius was going out the door.

"There's a feast today. 7 o'clock. Come to the dining hall. Oh, and as soon as you get settled in your room, come down to me, alone." he said curtly, stressing the word alone.

Octavius announced that he understood and carefully closed the door after him. The legionary stepped back to his post in front of the door and continued to look forward, his hand on the sword hilt ready to lash out at any invaders. Octavius had the feeling that he was staring at some rock statue instead of a human being. One of the best, he remembered Julius saying. It certainly did look like it.

"Poor you, to have an uncle like that," Titus broke into his thoughts. He seemed rather amused than frustrated or inferior.

"He's usually not like that. Actually, he was fine before you came in," Octavius paused, unsure if he should say this or not. He decided to say it, "I think he wants to intimidate you," Octavius said carefully.

Titus nodded, laughing. "Well, he failed entirely. That's probably the reason why he was so irritated. By the gods, you have a difficult uncle."

Octavius smiled at his contagious good mood. He shrugged, and continued to lead the way to their room. He noticed that Titus stopped several times to gaze at marble statues, curtains, rugs, and antique furniture.

Titus couldn't believe that a man had so much money as to own all this. Under one finely made statue, there was a name card that read— Scipio Africanus. The statue was black and shiny— even Titus who didn't have much interest in rocks could see that the statue was made from one of the finest rocks. Very well polished too.

There was also a pure white lion statue that glinted sunlight back to him. It depicted a lion rising to claw at some unknown foe. This one looked newer than others, by the way it shined so much. It also had a cleaner surface than others, with less dents and scratches.

"Your uncle must be really rich. He— whoa, look at that. That one's red. I've never seen a red statue before," Titus said, gaping at a red orange statue of an eagle, Jupiter's bird, which had a golden head.

"Rumor has it that he could buy more than half of Rome," Octavius said, rubbing the gold head fondly. Titus kept on gasping at the statues, the silk curtains without any embarrassment, as they climbed up to their room.

12

The soldier who stood in front of the meeting room stepped away automatically as Octavius appeared. Octavius smiled at him, and went inside, fidgeting uncomfortably when the guard did not smile back.

He saw Crassus reading a handful of parchment papers marked with the senate emblem. Crassus gazed up at him, and smiled. "I loved the guy. Is there anyone else you would like to recommend?" he said, and Octavius checked his uncle for some irony, but found none. "I really did, but don't tell him that."

"Why?"

"Oh, just, because I did like his manner. Too many men are weak in Rome these days, and it's been a while since I saw such a proud, strong, upright man." The senator smiled, and Octavius gave an uneasy laugh. What a strange guy.

"Right," Octavius said. "There's a young man called

Quintus Lucius Maximus. You probably saw him before on your last visit to Capua. He's a stout guy who loves fighting, and is also good at it. His loyalty to the republic is beyond doubt. I know it because he is my best friend, someone who I can trust and rely on. You will not regret it if you take him in," Octavius said. He knew Lucius would love a post in the legions and he also knew that this action would help ease Lucius's jealousy a little.

"Good. I hope the Lucius would be as good as Titus," Crassus said. He was willing to recruit men who would be loyal to the legions, to the Roman republic, and to him. He needed a legion to gain military influence. He had the money—he only needed a couple of legions. There was no better chance than now, when a slave rebellion had just started.

Octavius took a seat as the senator talked. "Yesterday we got the news that there was a gladiator rebellion in Capua. Important senators talked over the matter... I guess Arrius would already have told you this part. The man, Octavius, you need to be careful of him. He is the most dangerous senator here, with all his information, ready to blackmail anyone of us and also ready to fling derogatory remarks to any who do not suit his purpose. Anyway, to get to the point, you know why I called you, right?" he asked, and Octavius nodded enthusiastically. "What post are you expecting?" he asked again and Octavius blushed. His uncle was capable of making him a legate— the commander of an entire legion, but then he was too young and inexperienced. He was now barely seventeen, the minimum age of entering the army. He shook his head to tell his uncle that he did not know, and his uncle smiled.

"Have you ever heard of the tribunus laticlavius?"

"The head of the military tribunes, second only to the legate?" Octavius asked, trying to control his voice that quavered with anticipation. This was more than he had ever expected. A centurion had been the highest thing he had expected, but a tribune? Tribunes were the staff officers and would lead detatchments from the legion. There were six of them, tribunus laticlavius included, and they were of higher rank than a pilus prior, a centurion who led a cohort, or a primus pilus, the most senior centurion of the entire legion.

"Am I allowed?" Octavius added.

Crassus smiled. "Of course, the post is usually taken by young patricians in their twenties, though I believe we can make an exception. I also have the confidence that, even though you lack experience compared to them, you would not lack any skills," he said warmly. Octavius smiled, blushing. His initial blush had widened to his neck, and Crassus smiled, sensing it. Octavius blushed even more.

"I… This is better than expected…"

Crassus laughed, and his face suddenly turned serious. "I need to confirm your post in the senate. But don't worry about that. Trust me. Tribunus laticlviuses are men who are friends of the commander or the sons of the richest men in Rome. You fit very well into both of the categories." He winked as he said it.

Crassus felt himself blush as he looked at his young nephew. All he had done was to offer a military post, and his nephew was cheerful as if he had become Jupiter himself. He felt a prick in his conscience when he thought of the real reason he was offering his nephew a post. Even though he was the richest man in Rome, he only had only a group of soldiers—used mostly as guards— under his command, and he knew from his experience that a general with soldiers could be more powerful than any others, regardless of his status, or wealth. He thought again of the need to make new legions, and how the revolt in Capua was a good reason to do so, especially since the revolt had not been put down yet.

New legions could prove to be difficult without officers

that were completely loyal to him. He had seen a legion mutiny against their overall commander, and he shivered at the thought of his legions revolting against him. The last time a legion had done that, it had been on a battlefield, and the commander had met his death brutally, alone. He needed talented and loyal officers, and he knew that nobody would be more loyal to him than his kin, Octavius especially. Octavius would never mutiny his legion against him. He would seed his new legions with loyal officers.

The only thing that stood between him and new legions were the senators. He would need the senators' approval for a new legion, and they were very difficult to handle. He thanked the gods for the Capuan revolt, and Arrius for promising to ally him when it came to legions. Arrius was a very influential and dangerous man, and he would need the man's full support for new legions.

Octavius refrained himself from yelling with joy. He would need to live up to his new status. His helmet would now be decorated with a red plume that would assert his rank, and the thought made him overflow with joy. Unable to contain it, he went and hugged his uncle as strong as he could, making his uncle give a pained grunt.

"Enough, unless you want me to die before I even enter

the senate building," Crassus said painfully, and took in a deep breath as Octavius let him go.

"That man, Titus. He has served as a centurion before?" Crassus asked.

"Yes, uncle."

"Then he will regain his post as a centurion," he said. He was not sure how much he should believe Marcus's letter, especially when it came to the Titus's upbringing. The man was no doubt a son of some Marius supporter, but that didn't matter now. He seemed to be constant in his loyalties, and as long as Octavius stayed with him, the man would be loyal to him also. He laughed as he saw Octavius's grin widen.

"Are you going to appoint him in the senate too?" Octavius asked, and was met with a shake of head.

"No. If I am granted a new legion, or legions, then it is completely up to me to appoint my centurions. Only the legate and the tribunes need to be approved by the senate." Octavius nodded at his uncle's words.

"What about Lucius?"

"Yes, I was just about to mention him. What was his full name again?" Crassus inquired, frowning. His memory was beginning to get shorter these days.

"Quintus Lucius Maximus, uncle," Octavius responded, looking eagerly at him. Crassus gave a slight jolt in his chair. "Is he the son of Governor Gaius Maximus?" He saw Octavius's face light up.

"Yes. You know the governor?"

"The governor is well known to the senate for a certain revolt." Crassus said, rolling his eyes.

"Uncle," he paused, an idea suddenly striking him. He looked uncertain as he continued. "I just thought of this— he might refuse to accept the post if he is appointed to a lower post than mine. He has such a strong pride that he would never agree to serving me as his senior officer."

Crassus weighed Octavius's words before speaking. His eyes were cold as he spoke. "Well, no senator would agree to him being appointed as a tribune, in the situation his father is in right now. Also, if you want to be in the same legion as him, he can not be of the same rank as you because there is only one tribunus laticlavius per legion. I promise that I would promote him to a tribune as soon as there is an empty spot, but he would have to settle for a centurion for now. And if he is not pleased with that, I cannot give him a post."

Octavius opened his mouth to object and closed it on a better thought. He nodded, and said that he would inform his friend by sending a messenger. Crassus agreed, and clapped his nephew on the shoulders. "Be ready for the feast, Octavius. There will be many important men, including Senator Arrius and your future legate, Senator Suetonius. The dinner meeting shall be convened in the dining hall. You know where it is, right? Good." He watched as Octavius's eyes flickered with interest.

"What about Julius?" his nephew asked, and Crassus felt a prickle of jealousy as the name was mentioned. Why did his nephew like the man so much, especially when it had been him who had offered him a position? He shook his head, and Octavius nodded, still seeming content. There was nothing that would ruin his current mood. He rose, excusing himself. There was only a few hours left before the feast, and Octavius wanted a hot bath to clean of himself all the dust that had enveloped him during the ride.

⁂

Octavius sat down nervously on the right side of his uncle. He was followed by Titus, who took a seat next to him. Titus looked grim in his toga, and Octavius stifled a laugh. He quite couldn't get used to Titus in a toga, though he too was wearing one also. The fabric felt heavy and useless, but Crassus had insisted. "Formality is important to them," he had said. At least, his toga was not so oversized.

Octavius knew that Crassus was charming these people so that he could get more votes for his appeal tomorrow. No doubt everyone here knew it too. His thinking was interrupted when a man took a seat facing him. The man had dark hair, and calm, dark brown eyes that seemed to take everything in with some warmness. His eyes rested on Octavius, and Octavius held the gaze, looking into the man's deep eyes. The man gave a light smile of acknowledgement and looked away.

"Gentlemen," Crassus began, and Octavius realized for the first time that there were no ladies present. "You all know why I have called you—for the construction of my new legions," he announced, and everybody nodded their heads. Some were wearing senatorial togas that marked their status as a senator, but some were also wearing their full armor, though they had taken off their helmets out of courtesy. "I have always craved for new legions, because those who have legions have power," he said, thinking of Marius and Sulla before him. These people here were his clients, those who were almost completely loyal to him— maybe except for Senator Arrius.

"I will have my chance tomorrow. There has been a large gladiatorial revolt in Capua, and we will need new legions to put it out. The size of the rebellion has been reported to have grown in numbers," he said, silently thanking Arrius for this bit of information. He could always rely on that man to be informative. "And the men who will lead the new legions will be you, my honorable friends," he announced, and was met with a loud clapping. Crassus and they knew that their posts were not yet certain, for they did not have the approval of the senate yet. However, they were pretty sure of Crassus's power in the senate, and they clapped as if they had already been appointed to the post. "To the legions, and to my new officers," Crassus said, as he lifted his wine cup.

As food was brought out, the solemn mood soon turned into a cheerful mood of men joking and laughing with each other. Octavius heard men talk of their military experiences good humouredly, and with pride. He began to understand that this gathering was aimed at solid military supporters of his uncle who would make up the core of the legions.

He noticed some senators, in their purple lined senatorial togas, and Senator Arrius among them. Arrius gave him a nod as their eyes met, and quickly shifted his nervous eyes to a pair sitting in front of him. The pair seemed to be bragging about some experiences they had in battles.

Most senators conferred among themselves after deciding that they had heard enough war stories for one day. They joked and laughed, and from what Octavius could hear, they were making fun of Cato, Crassus's political enemy.

A dark—brown—haired man sitting in front of him talked with his uncle. The man seemed to be very dignified, and calm. He also chose his words very carefully and he bore an aura of command.

Crassus noticed his nephew looking at him, and spoke. "Senator Servius Hortius Suetonius, this is my nephew Octavius," he introduced. The senator looked closely at the young man, and gave a smile. "He will serve as your second in command, that is, if the senate agrees," he said, giving a laugh at the end. The senator's calm smile widened, as he said that he was sure that the senate would agree. Crassus smiled back. If they did not agree, which he was sure they would, considering the fact that about half of the senators were on his side, he could bribe them with money, and the permission would come without much difficulty. "Octavius, this is Senator Suetonius. He is very experienced in politics and in military business. He has put out a revolt in Hispania, and is a very good ally of mine." Octavius's eyes widened with new respect at the man who seemed to be in his early forties. "We were neighbors when we were boys," he said, letting out a low chuckle. Suetonius too gave a hearty laugh.

Suetonius too gave a hearty laugh. "Not one of my best experiences," Suetonius joked, shaking his head from side to side. Then he said, turning his warm eyes on him, "Pleased to meet you, Octavius."

Octavius blushed. "It's an honor having you as my legate," he said, and the man smiled.

"I wouldn't mind having you," he replied, and his eyes staring kindly at him. Octavius stared back, fascinated at the man had successfully put out a revolt in Hispania. He was also touched by the man's kind eyes that seemed to under-stand people— he had spoken the truth when he had said that he would be honored to have the man as his superior officer.

<hr>

Everyone had left but Arrius.

"You know what to do, Arrius," Crassus said.

"I do. I can make you a praetor. The war will not end soon. I can feel it," Arrius replied. "And you know how to repay me."

"How much?" Crassus asked.

Arrius shook his head and smiled gently. "No, my dear old friend. When you win the battle, you'll be popular. Might be elected to a consul. When you become consul, you will have complete power. I've grown old. You know what I want. A province."

Crassus nodded a little. That would be a piece of cake once he attained his consul seat. "Anything else?" he asked and Arrius nodded.

"Do you know Mummius?"

"Mummius? The ambitious fool? He is the worst legate I have ever seen."

Arrius gave a stern shake of his head. "That's the thing that you lack, Crassus. Information. Look at m! I have no relations in the senate yet nobody can dare ignore me because of my information. Be careful with what you say, Crassus. Mummius is my son."

Crassus lifted his eyebrows in surprise. He had not known the information before. Arrius smiled at the reaction. "You have never mentioned him before to me."

Arrius smiled again. "He is my adopted son. I adopted him when he was three."

Crassus could not imagine Arrius adopting a child out of mercy. The man kept some distance from philanthropy.

Arrius seemed to sense his thoughts. "He is the boy of my dead brother. He pleaded me to take his son in, and I could not refuse," Arrius said. Crassus hid a surprised gasp. So the man did have feelings after all.

"When you become praetor, you'll have many legions to command. One of them would be Mummius's legions. Then, I want you to pick his legion to fight in battle. Give him a chance to prove himself. And, whatever happens, do not punish him harshly."

Crassus thought about it. "No offence, Arrius. But that man is not so brilliant. He is ambitious but he is not bright. He is, in other words, clouded by his ambitions. I want smart legates. Also, if I do not punish him, then the commanding structure would deteriorate." he replied, cautiously watching Arrius. Arrius smiled bitterly for he knew what Crassus said was true.

"Nevertheless, Crassus. Nevertheless."

13

Octavius stared at the building before him in awe. This was the senate building, where all the influential men of Rome gathered to talk about how to rule the world. He had seen the building before, from far away, but today was the first time that he had actually set foot in it. Even though the senate was opened to all, Octavius had worried that he might not be allowed in. However, Crassus had reassured him that it was okay. Octavius, though he had nodded, had not completely trusted his uncle, and was relieved when no guards stopped him. He stepped gingerly onto the marble floor, respecting and taking in everything. His uncle had noticed his behavior and was standing next to him, clearly amused. Octavius tried not to make his feelings so obvious, but he couldn't help himself gasping when Crassus greeted a man who was addressed as 'Consul'. Octavius too greeted him, dazed by the fact that he was talking to the most powerful man in all of Rome.

"Octavius, maybe I should have left you outside with Titus," he said, frowning slightly. He had ordered Titus to stay outside, clearly displeasing the young man. Titus had told him that the senate building was open to all and that he had promised Marcus that he would stay by Octavius's side at all times, especially in times of battles. Political battles also count, he had said. Crassus had been amused at his bluntness. He hated men who stood up to him like that, but somehow this Titus was more amusing than annoying. He liked, and needed, men who had guts. Octavius, on the other hand, knew that Titus had only backed down because of the possible dangers lurking in the senate building. Although he was not persecuted anymore, there may still be senators who would still like to see him dead than alive. Titus had decided that keeping his life was more important than getting to listen to debates. If it had not been for that, he would have followed Crassus in no matter what Crassus told him to do.

Octavius apologized absently, heeding the senators who bustled about him. Crassus gave a loud sigh, and pushed Octavius down into a seat next to his. He poked his nephew gently to bring him back to his normal keen self. Octavius looked at him as if he had been snapped awake from some hypnosis, and Crassus laughed at that.

He put a finger to his lips, and gestured to the rostrum where the consuls were now standing. Octavius's gaze immediately snapped to them, eyes intent. Crassus smiled at his nephew's eagerness. The consuls began the traditional speech beginning the meeting— the verba fecit— and continued to talk about the current issues. The revolt in Capua was a hot topic.

"Reports say that they have grown their numbers up to three hundred, and are going to Mount Vesuvius. What have our legions been doing?" a senior senator asked, and the room filled with murmurs of agreement. "The governor should be punished!" he cried, and the room filled with men shouting agreements. Octavius felt sick as the senators descended on the governor like hungry vultures. Not that he minded the governor being punished— Octavius himself didn't like him— but he was Lucius's father. That counted for something.

The room quieted as another senator rose. It was Senator Arrius. Octavius could guess how much power he had by just seeing how the room quieted when he spoke. "Gentlemen, the governor is taken care of. We have given him the choice of restoring Capua in one year or to resign from his post. I was the first one to receive information, and I called all the important senators for a meeting when the news reached me about seven hours after the revolt. The senate needed to respond quickly, and so only a few selected senators were called. This issue has been agreed upon. I express my apologies to those who have not been called," he said, with an apologetic smile. Even though his face was smiling, his eyes were stony, as if challenging the men to object. Nobody dared to, and Octavius could see the guilty look on the consuls, and some others, including his uncle. The man sat down, and briefly rose again, smiling. "I believe that the most important issue here is how the revolt would be put down. Thank you," he announced, and resumed his seat, still smiling. Octavius felt a chill as he met Arrius's serpent like eyes.

Crassus raised his hand suddenly and, with a nod from the consuls, he rose. Octavius shuffled his feet in anticipation of his new post, his earlier worries about the governor forgotten. He leaned to prevent himself from missing a single word.

"Senators, it would be some time before we send out legions to wipe out the rebellion." He was interrupted by a voice that said that the slave rebellion was not anything serious to consider. The man was silenced by a consul's cold glare. Crassus nodded his thanks before continuing on. "Even though the legions on the borders are strong, our legions in the peninsula are weak. That is the truth, whether we like it or not," he said grimly. Many heads nodded. "Therefore, I believe that the rebellion might be more serious than we think, because it is a consecutive chain of events. We were fools not to have expected this— look at how the slaves and the plebeians live. They are impoverished. If Spartacus had revolted when everyone was content, he would have already been dead, killed by angry plebeian farmers. But there is news that even plebeians are joining the rebellion because Spartacus shouts for equality. And the ignorant peasants have craved for equality, equality in living status, especially after the Punic War—they are getting manipulated by the slave!

"It would be harder than expected to put down the uprising unless we call in legions from our borders. That is easier said than done." Crassus raised his hands to quiet the senators. "Thus, a better solution would be to create new legions to put down the rebellion—" He was interfered by many senators shouting, and the consuls had to bark silence at them to regain order. "Yes, new legions to help put down the revolt. Even the timing is right for it would soon be the season for the annual drafting. Also, even if the revolt ends before the legions are completely trained, they would be useful in maintaining order in Rome and in other cities that have forgotten the senate all together, the land being large as it is," he finished, and looked at the senators to see how his speech had gone. He could not tell from their blank looks.

"The slaves are not a threat," a voice said, and many gave murmurs of agreement. "Also, it would take a lot of senate money to create and maintain legions, Crassus." Crassus turned his head sharply to the voice. It was Cato, his most dangerous political enemy.

Crassus smiled. "Yes, and money is something that I am full of," he said with some bitterness. What use was the money if he had no legions?

"Are you offering to pay for them?"

"Yes, I am quite willing to equip, train and feed them, only if the senate will give the right to command to me."

"Is that all? And how many legions are you asking for?" Cato narrowed his eyes suspiciously.

"Three would be fine." Crassus said, and Octavius suddenly felt doubt at his uncle. What if his uncle couldn't secure his post as a tribune? He felt like a fool then, who had been feeling happy just over some words.

A consul interfered. "We first need to decide whether or not we need more legions, though all senators need to speak before we have a vote. The two of you can resume arguing before or after the vote," he said. After? What kind of advice was that? Octavius Octavius thought that he looked bored by the whole thing.

Each senator rose to speak, and, at first, Octavius listened with immense interest. His interest began to dwell as the fiftieth senator sat down. Soon, he was just pretending to listen, and he stifled a yawn as the hundred fortieth senator finished his speech. He could understand why the consul had looked so bored— he could not imagine his life being a continuous cycle of this. There was a short break after that, and Octavius used the time to question his uncle.

"Uncle, is that Arrius that powerful?" he asked quietly, and his uncle nodded.

"Very informative. He can probably blackmail almost all the senators here," he said, and Octavius nodded thoughtfully. He thought about yesterday's feast, in which the senator had attended. He was glad that the man was, or at least seemed, to be friends with his uncle. The man seemed a dangerous person to have as an enemy. Octavius put the senator out of his mind and guiltily thought of what Titus would be doing in the hot sun as the talking resumed.

"Now we shall have a vote. The first vote would be on whether or not we should grant Crassus his three legions," a consul announced, and he paused, giving the senators time to consider. "We shall go with a show of hands."

Octavius watched, his stomach churning. If they disagreed, it would be the end of his career even before it started.

"Those who agree raise your hands," the consul said in a flat, droning voice. Octavius closed his eyes, praying to Jupiter for the people's agreement. He dared to open his eyes a bit, and bit his lips to keep himself from shouting aloud. More than the majority of them had raised their hands, and the sullen looking Cato was looking on. Octavius studied him carefully, adding that man on to his list of people that he should be careful of in the future.

"Then the issue will now go on to appointing the officers," the consul announced dully, as if this bored him. Octavius hoped that his tone would not influence the votes.

Crassus rose. "The legates whom I had in mind were Senator Varinius, Senator Suetonius and finally Legate

Mummius— transferred to my new legion. Legate Mummius is in full agreement with this," he said, and was met with polite applause. He smiled. Varinius and Suetonius were respected in the senate, despite their comparatively younger age, and Mummius was under the direct influence of Arrius— something that never failed. He had chosen his officers well. The result was clear, and the consuls only called for a vote because it was the tradition to do so.

"For the tribunus laticlavius," he continued, "I will not name all of them. I do not care who they are, though they have to be talented. I trust that the senate will appoint me good tribunes. The only one that I plead for is Gnaeus Octavius Lupus, the son of Marcus Octavius Cornelius Lupus of Capua. He knows Spartacus well, and he is very capable, even though he is young. I believe that he will assist the legions of Rome well." There was a murmur of recognition at Marcus's name and a murmur of interest at Spartacus's. The consuls called for a vote, and the majority raised their hands to say that they agreed. Octavius closed his eyes in relief, letting out a breath that he hadn't realized that he was holding. He looked at Crassus, who was beaming. His gaze shifted to Arrius, whose face was inscrutable, and last, to Cato who looked more sullen than ever. Cato too was looking at him, probably guessing that he was the young tribune mentioned above. His eyes narrowed, but Octavius just smiled an earnest smile, to show that he was pleased by the results. There was no need to make enemies on his first day in the senate.

The consul quieted down the room, as he called for another vote. "The next vote," he said, glaring at those who were still talking, "shall be on which general would be appointed to destroy the rebellion while the three legions train. Does anyone have any ideas?" he said. Octavius thought that his words such as 'destroy' did not suit the man's monotonous tone.

"My legions can be situated near Capua for training, and we could still surround the Vesuvius," Crassus spoke.

"No," a single, strong voice called. One that Octavius recognized as Cato's. "The barracks for those legionaries need to be constructed, and it will be some time before they are able to take on the rebellion."

Crassus smiled before he rose to present himself. "Surely, Cato, you cannot object to them camping near the Vesuvius so that they could be of assistance to the general who is appointed to clear out the rebel forces, can you? Plus, I thought you were one of those who said that the revolt would be very easy to put down. If it is easy, my three new legions would also have no trouble with it. Furthermore, if you pardon my saying so, I am the one in control of the legions, so with the agreement of the senate, I am free to assist the appointed general," he said. His speech was met with a loud applause, and even some cheers. Crassus beamed inwardly as he noticed the men who were supporting him. They were his supporters. The consuls nodded their approval at the speech as they agreed to it. Cato's brooding face became even more so.

Cato rose, and raised a hand to quiet the senate. "Fine, Crassus," he spat venomously. Crassus did not fail to notice a spark in the man's eyes. "Gentlemen, I recommend General Claudius Glaber for this task. I'm sure he could put down the revolt. He does not own a legion, but I believe that he could wipe them out with only a militia and would not need any assistance in doing so." The man glanced at Crassus as he said the word assistance. This time, there was a loud clapping from the supporters of Sulla, or now, the supporters of Cato.

Crassus did not feel bitter at all when the senate voted for Glaber, even though Glaber was one of Cato's men. He had achieved his goal of commanding three legions, and he did not care about who the appointed general was. He knew that Cato had put in the word militia on purpose to show that there was no need for new legions. He chuckled to himself. Crassus knew that Cato would denounce him a general unfit to lead if the militia beat the gladiators. However, he knew that the militia was not better off than the slaves, and would be lacking far more when it came to fighting skills. There was no worry of the militia alone beating the slaves, and he knew that one of his legions would be helping out Glaber and his men pretty soon. He actually felt good, and was relieved that the Cato supporters, formerly the Sulla supporters, had not voted against his proposals. If they had, it could have been a difficult problem.

His time was not now. After Glaber's army was annihilated, he would step in and gain the praetorship.

Titus met them at the front of the senate building. Without even acknowledging the senator, he clasped Octavius on the shoulder.

"Congratulations, Octavius," he cried, and Octavius looked at him in surprise.

"How did you know?"

Titus laughed. He gave a shrug and evaded answers until Octavius pleaded him.

He gave a knowing, sly smile as he looked towards the senator. The senator was staring straight ahead, not heeding the man. "The door is left open for people to hear, Octavius."

Octavius shook his head. "Yes, but only technically. It is guarded by legionaries who won't let civilians near the door. Come on, Titus,"

Titus gave a reluctant nod, making a show of what had happened. "Well, all I had to do was to show a couple legionaries my sword skill, and the rest didn't really object after that." Octavius gazed at him, horrified. Titus understood his gaze and shook his head. "No, I didn't kill them. Just enough to make them wish they had died," he said, grinning. Octavius stared at him, aghast. "Nothing serious, really. The two called out some insults as I neared them. So I just made them pay for their insults. They didn't insult me after that. Actually, one of them couldn't," Titus put on a bigger grin this time and hopped onto his horse. "Race you," he said, and had turned the corner in a matter of seconds, leaving the young man and the senator to stare. Crassus shook his head at the man's behavior. The man was intelligent and old enough not to get into useless skirmishes like that. He turned to Octavius to say something about Titus when he was almost knocked over by a horse at a full gallop.

"Sorry, uncle, but he said that he would race me. No disrespects," the rider called over his shoulders, and was too gone in a blink of an eye. Crassus shook his head in disbelief at what had happened and walked slowly over to his horse. Usually he walked to the senate building, but today Octavius had insisted on riding. His light, victorious mood turned dark as he approached his horse slave, who also had a surprised expression on his face.

❧ *14* ❧

Octavius felt his veins pump as he planted a legion flag on the ground of Campus Martius, the place where the annual drafting would take place. The flag waved idly in the breeze, and Octavius just felt overwhelmed with emotion to see a wolf sewn onto the red flag with the word 'Legio III Victrix' beneath it. The wolf gazed down at him, reminding Octavius of his name, Lupus. The flag was his now.

Young men had gathered to watch the drafting. Officers, mostly centurions, would select the men to join the new legions, or the undermanned existing ones. Most men, however, were given a choice to enter a legion of their own choice before the officers called out to them.

Crassus frowned slightly at his young nephew's eagerness. He had been that way from the day when the senate had agreed to his demands. He wondered whether or not his nephew thought of what would happen if no man volunteered for their legions. Even if the officers drafted the men in, they would come with sullen faces, and it would be disastrous to have unenthusiastic soldiers on the field.

The crowd had assembled even more. Now, there were more than young men staring at them. Women and children had come to enjoy an annual spectacle. Crassus sweated nervously as he waited for the drafting to start. The young men were already scrutinizing the legion flags around them, and Crassus forced himself to stand taller. He hoped that both Octavius and Titus had the sense to do so also. Confidence was important for them.

Octavius cast a glance over the mass of milling crowd. He gazed at their number, and he estimated a number more than ten thousand. He knew that they would be from other places too, such as the provinces, hoping that life in the legions would provide a better life for them. He glanced quickly at the wolf flag to see if it was flying well as the horns sounded the start of the drafting. The crowd milled about, dropping back to give space for young men. They glanced at each other and shuffled among themselves, trying to stand in front of them legion that they wanted to go into. Although the officers had the right to draft any into the legion, they usually had the sense to pick men from the line in front of their legions.

Octavius watched as men separated into something that looked like a line in front of the legions. Some had a longer line while some were shorter than others. The officers too stayed silent as the men moved, watching anxiously. Once in a while a recognized officer would step out to show his face, enjoy his popularity and wave to the young men. The ranks would move again like a wave, men changing lines. He strained to see the line of the Third, his legion. It didn't seem like much.

He casually glanced at Suetonius, who seemed to be sweating. Any man would, if their line was comparatively shorter than others. Suetonius seemed to put on a smile, which Octavius thought as somewhat forced. Titus too looked a bit strained as he looked at the dwindling line. He knew it would be hard for three new legions without any name or feats to start out with a full number. He had expected this. Still, his heart ached to see the line so short. The five other tribunes too seemed to be feeling the same thing. Suddenly, one of them called out to the crowd the name of the legate, Suetonius, and the name of Senator Crassus. Some men picked their heads up in their direction as the name Crassus was called out, and a few made their way into their line. Titus wanted to hug the tribune who made the speech. Everybody knew of Crassus, the richest man in the whole of the Roman Republic, and they had the brains enough to conclude that they would get much more financial benefits than in other legions.

"What's the Third going to do?" a voice cried out from the lines.

"The Third shall go through a quick training interval and be stationed near Capua in case there might be trouble with the recent slave rebellion," the same tribune, Tribune Rufius cried out.

Men fidgeted. Some men walked away, joining the lines of other legions. Rufius sweated underneath his toga. He knew Crassus— his father was an equestrian merchant work-ing for him— and just hearing the man's temper from his father had always frightened him. To just think of one of those being unleashed at him was unpleasant enough for him to sweat furiously. Rufius did not dare to look at Crassus.

He let out a breath he had not noticed he was holding, as men from other lines shifted to the Third's. Those would be boisterous, overly courageous young man who loved to show off their skills. Men who had been in the Third's line from the start fidgeted uncomfortably, some clearly showing their dislike for upcoming battle. Still, moving out of the line would demote their reputation for courage— something they were not quite willing to risk.

More men sifted into the lines of the Third. At least, Rufius thought, they were getting a good share of enthusiastic men. The vast movements seemed to come to a stop gradually. Suetonius called for the man in the front to come and enlist, and the man gladly obeyed. He looked stout and eager to prove himself as he spoke his name and his family. A scribe furiously wrote the information down as the man spoke the oath that would bind him to his new legion.

It continued for a while, and Suetonius gestured for Octavius to continue as his voice tired. Octavius cleared his voice and clenched his sweaty palms together as he called for the next man. He came willingly enough, and Octavius sighed in relief. He continued for a while and let out another sigh as he saw the long line of men themselves waiting to enlist in the legion. It was going to be a long, tedious day.

• • ◄══►• •

Men camped in the barracks of Campus Martius, including the men of the Third. Octavius rubbed his tired eyes as he looked at them. He had spent all his afternoon enlisting them and had also helped Suetonius in dividing them up into centuries. They were nicely mixed with some veterans Crassus had managed to recruit.

Octavius was still staring at the men when Crassus appeared suddenly behind him. Octavius saluted smartly, well aware that he was playing the new role of a military tribune, and that Crassus was his commander.

"How was it?" Crassus asked.

"Tiring," Octavius replied earnestly, and Crassus laughed. Titus had risen from his seat beside the campfire to salute to Crassus. None of the cockiness shown before remained in his attitude.

"Centurion Titus," Crassus greeted him formally.

"Sir," Titus replied in a style Octavius thought as exemplary. It looked as if Titus was born to be in the legions.

"How do you feel on your first day as a centurion— or, on your first day as a centurion of the Third? I've heard that you have been a centurion before," Crassus asked, his voice affable.

"I have longed to be one again, and I am glad that the chance has finally come to me," he answered, this time turning his head slightly to meet Crassus's gaze. Crassus nodded as if he was satisfied before turning to Octavius again.

"Where's Lucius?" he asked.

Octavius hesitated, not sure of the fact himself. "I don't know. I think he needs time to decide. Still, I do not think that he will fail to show up," he said and quickly added 'sir,' trying to imitate Titus.

Crassus scowled slightly but then nodded as if content. "I hope he knows that I need to appoint all my centurions soon."

"He will know," Octavius responded with more conviction than he had.

Crassus mumbled something unintelligible before motioning Octavius to follow him. Octavius obliged, Titus following behind him. Crassus took them to a group of officers who were standing in a wide circle, each holding a finely made wine cup.

They hastily made way as they noticed Crassus. And Crassus acknowledged them with a nod. "This is my nephew, Octavius," he said, dragging Octavius into the circle.

Octavius bowed his head slightly and the rest of the officers nodded in return. "He is the Third's tribunus laticlavius," Crassus added, and the tranquil look that had been on the officers' faces vanished.

Some immediately saluted to Octavius while Octavius acknowledged with an awkward nod. Others stared at him, many with doubt.

"He's so young," one whispered to his companion, Tribune Rufius. Rufius shrugged as if it did not matter, but the whispering one scowled in obvious discontent. Octavius pretended not to see the scowl.

Suetonius had also seen the frown and decided to step in to break the ice. "Tribune Rufius," he said, pointing. Octavius nodded eagerly. "Tribune Serstus," he said, pointing to the one who was still frowning. The man turned his head away sharply. Suetonius pointed out each man, his rank and his name as Octavius struggled to memorize them.

"Tribune Serstus is a little jealous at the moment. Be gentle with him," Suetonius whispered only for Octavius's ears. "He has been stuck in that position for nearly eight years now, without any promotion. So naturally, he is jealous— he is a difficult person to have. Be gentle, all right?"

"Yes, sir."

Suetonius smiled slightly. Octavius thought he saw some sadness portrayed in the smile. Suetonius hesitated then spoke.

"My son, he... never mind," he said so softly that even

Octavius could barely make out the words. He shook his head briefly. When he met Octavius's eyes again, they were full of enthusiasm and kindness once again. "Go acquaint yourself with others," he said in a light tone.

❦ *15* ❦

Glaber looked at the men that had gathered. They were angry young men who had slaves, food, and other goods stolen away from them. Glaber smiled to himself as he smelled victory. His scouts had reported the slaves setting up a permanent looking camp on the top of the mountain, and he knew that if he managed to block the only way down from the mountain, he would have won the battle. Vesuvius was not fertile enough to feed a few hundred men for months. When the slaves clambered down, starved, he would end the battle then and there, swiftly. If he killed or captured enough slaves, he might be granted a triumph, or at least an ovation.

The men tried to form neat squares under their centurions' orders, but there was too much confusion amongst them to make them look like a real Roman army. Glaber gritted his teeth, vowing to himself that he would make proper legionaries out of them. Cato had trusted him. He would live up to it.

His initial hopes of forming a legion slowly dwindled away as he saw the men trying to form the squares. They still hadn't managed, even with the prodding of their optios and centurions. When they had finished making a loose rectangle, they were a crowded mass of confused young men. Glaber swore to himself as he saw the militia of nearly three thousand men. He would have to train them like the Spartans to make them a match for the gladiators, no matter how untrained the slaves were. Besides, he had to win the battle quickly, for he had been strictly advised by Cato to never let others help him, especially Crassus's legions. Yeah, right. Look at your men, said the rational part of his mind.

He ordered them to disengage, and the men tried to do so, pushing each other. One man in the front ranks tripped over another man's foot and landed on his nose. Glaber, his mood souring, grabbed the man up by his collar and pushed him into the ranks, causing more confusion. He glanced at the centurions, who too seemed frustrated. He knew that among the centurions were some retired legionaries, and they wore the look of disgust on their faces.

As soon as the men had somewhat disengaged to their

normal marching form, he ordered a march. If they could not form squares neatly and tightly enough, he would at least teach them how to march.

"We march to Vesuvius. We are not going to rest until we reach a ten mile perimeter of that mountain," he called sourly. He wanted them to be camped on the foot of the Vesuvius, but he knew that sending his untrained militia so close would mean literal suicide, at least for now. When he heard that he was to lead, he had been exhilarated, but all that feeling had long been vaporized. Cato had recommended him but had not even given him some useful, ambitious, young officers. Instead, he asked him to form a militia, not a legion, with a handful of old, unmotivated soldiers. Glaber did not have enough money to recruit some of the good veteran soldiers, nor ambitious ones.

He ignored the gasps in the ranks and the surprised looks even in the officers. "I call a forced march. Double speed. Quickly!" he barked, and the ranks dissolved into chaos once more as they tried to march in the best form.

<hr>

Octavius gazed down at the ranks of his legion. The men stood in shining iron squares, readying themselves for an attack. Crassus's other legion, the Fifth Aquila, commanded by Mummius spread out in a wide line, ready to charge. This was a mock attack between the legions, and the men used staffs instead of swords. They seemed relieved to be using only staves and shields, but Octavius knew better than to assume that the staff couldn't hurt or kill. He had experienced it with Spartacus as his teacher. Spartacus had helped improve his sword skills—only the legion sword masters could beat him now. He smiled bitterly at the irony. He would now be using the skills he had learned from Spartacus to crush down his rebellion.

Octavius looked at Lucius, standing in front of his own square. Lucius looked around and saw his friend staring down at him. He gave a smile and was rewarded by a cheery wave. Lucius thought about the day when a messenger had come to his house to inform him of the new post that he was offered. At first, he had been inclined to reject the offer. He could not bear to call Octavius 'sir'. Every time he imagined the scene, it hurt him like acid, and he had made up his choice to refuse when his sister had persuaded him to go. It would be a footstone in becoming a senator, she had said, and Lucius knew that it was true. Without any links back to Rome, like Octavius, it would be hard for him to become an

acknowledged senator, and he would have to do it by proving himself in battles. This was his chance, and he had to
take it in order to achieve his dream, whether he liked it or
not.

Octavius couldn't help exclaiming when he looked down
at the legionaries. Crassus had not fibbed when he had said
that he would salt the legion with the most loyal and the
best officers. The officers had really had made something
out of the men. They stood in perfect silence, staring ahead,
eyes focused on their mock enemies. Crassus was there too,
looking at the army spread out before him in glee. This
battle would be just a clash of staves, without any elaborate
tactics. Men who were hit would step out from the army on
their own conscience, and it would continue until the higher
officers could determine for sure whose legion was winning.
Mummius and Suetonius looked the most nervous of them
all. Each had bragged about how their legions were shaping
up, and they stood there, with cold sweat dropping from
their faces, as the time came to decide whose legion fought
better.

With a long note from the cornicerns, the Fifth went
into a wild charge, their staves pointed at the Third. The
legionaries of the Third spread their lines out to match their

enemy as the Fifth charged on them. Octavius leaned out in anticipation with the others near him. The first charge was met with a clang of shields, and the mock battle began.

At first, Octavius could not distinguish one legion from the other, as they fought wildly. However, as time passed, he could slowly begin to distinguish his legion as the centurions called for order. He smiled as he spotted Lucius among them. Lucius was fighting madly, and the men gave him space. Many flinched as he came toward them, preferring to match their skills against some other opponent than Lucius. Octavius was reminded again of the bitter irony as he calculated Lucius's sword patterns. It was Spartacus's favorite style.

Many men stepped out from the ranks, going over to the fountain where they drank and splashed cool water over themselves. Their numbers grew as the battle continued, and Octavius was relieved not to see Lucius or Titus among them. Most of them only seemed to have a light injury, but some of them were being laid out by their friends who tried to cool the injuries with water. He was satisfied to see the legion doctors rush out from their seats and take a look at the men, taking the serious ones with them.

"Look, Mummius! See our men winning?" Suetonius

cried out happily, enjoying Mummius's darkening expression.

"The battle isn't over yet. And it's got to do more with here," he said tapping his head.

"A hell lot of that you have," Crassus whispered silently so that no one could hear.

Octavius looked out to the battleground once more to judge who was winning. Crassus did so too, and was pleased that the two men Marcus had recommended were doing magnificently. They seemed to whirl around like twin tornadoes, beating up their opponents until they raised their hands and backed away to the perimeter of the battle to join their friends that had gone before them. Maybe he should ask them to serve as sword masters, though he thought it unlikely. Both enjoyed the power to command, and he believed that they would like to be a centurion more than a sword master. He spotted the tribunes also marveling at them.

"Maybe I should promote them," he commented lightly. Eyes turned to Crassus and he spotted his nephew's glittering, anticipating eyes. "And demote those who are not worthy of their positions," he said, throwing a casual glance at Mummius. Mummius did not notice. He was too engrossed in the mock battle scene before him. A few tribunes did, but Crassus's glance was so subtle that it was clear they did not know whether or not Crassus's glance was intentional or really casual. Only Suetonius caught the meaning.

He stepped back, standing next to Crassus. "Leave the kid alone. He has been fine until now," he said, lowering his voice so that only Crassus could hear.

"Yes, until now."

"Oh, Crassus. Cut him some slack."

"He's bound to cause trouble. I've seen him since he was young. Since he was a teen, he drank bottles of wine every day until he got knocked out by the alcohol. He is what you call a dissolute man. Never trust the man," Crassus said.

"Then why did you ask him to be your legate?"

Crassus grimaced. "Arrius."

Suetonius formed his mouth into a round 'O', nodding his head. "What is he to Arrius anyway?"

"His son," Crassus snapped bitterly.

Suetonius gave a start. "What?"

"His son."

"Gods help us," Suetonius muttered under his breath. "Under Arrius… he is then granted impunity?"

"How did you know?"

"That is the way Arrius does things. His sons, his relations—they are all immune to common law," Suetonius spat. Then after a moment, he asked, "Are you going to give him impunity?"

"Depends," was Crassus's ominous answer.

∾ 16 ∾

Octavius glanced behind to see men march in a perfect column behind him. He was still awed by the way how veteran centurions and officers train their man. They hammered a mass of unorganized young men, into a completely different group of men, a legion. All of them, officers included, had improved with the way of using their swords, and all the legionaries could now respond to complex sounds of the signal horns. Roman discipline, the veterans had called it. The cornicerns blew a note to sound a stop, and the column halted on the spot with a loud thump. Again, it made him proud to see them like that— they were his.

It was time to build a night camp, he realized, as the men began to form into neat groups. Some went to cut the timber, while others helped to make the food with the legion stewards. Suetonius kicked his horse towards the men to murmur words of encouragement, and Octavius followed suit. After spending more than three months at the barracks with the men, he knew about half of their names and called to them when he recognized the soldiers. They saluted smartly and continued with their work.

Lucius watched the scene bitterly. He watched how their eyes twinkled with pleasure when Octavius called out to them. Octavius was not so special enough for the men to be humbled. Not only that, Octavius had been given a horse while he had been forced to walk. And the reason had been just because Octavius held a higher post than his. Lucius wasn't even sure if Octavius deserved to get a tribune posting. Although Octavius understood tactics, he was the one who was better at fighting. What was the purpose of setting up good tactics when the army couldn't fight well enough?

He knew that some parts of his logic were flawed by his current mood, but he didn't want to think about it. He had marched all day, and he wanted to get a good rest before the food and the camp was prepared. Lucius swore as he saw that the tents had not yet been set up and snapped at his century to work faster. He sat on a stump, sourly realizing that it would have to do for now.

Octavius cast a watchful eye over the legionaries but could not spot his friends. He gave up, after some time, and walked over to where Suetonius. The other tribunes were standing.

The tribunes were all right, though Octavius had the feeling that they did not quite respect or follow him. He tried to understand their feelings. After all, they were more than ten years older than him, and nobody liked serving under men who were less experienced and younger. However, there were many times when he had to take in deep breaths to control his fury at them. When Octavius gave them an order, they would glance at each other, and weigh him before shuffling out to obey the order, clearly showing their unwillingness. Tribune Serstus made his feelings more blatant than others, always looking at him with mocking eyes.

The only tribune he liked was Rufius who seemed to have swallowed the fact that his higher officer was ten years younger than him. He kept his politeness, listened to his words, sometimes giving suggestions. The man, however, liked to keep to himself, and so Octavius could not form a tight bond with him as he had formed with Suetonius, Lucius, Titus and other legionaries.

The tribunes stopped their whispers as Octavius reached them. All five of them stared at him, as if he was an intruder. Rufius just lowered his gaze after a few seconds, and Serstus gave him a calm smile which only looked genuine from a distance. Octavius didn't bother to meet their icy gaze and headed to the legate who was standing a bit apart from them. The legate did not undermine him for his age and lack of experience, always encouraging him to give out the orders instead of doing it himself. Suetonius also listened to his opinion carefully, and when it was useful, he would incorporate the thought to the original plans at once.

"We made quite a distance sir," Octavius exclaimed enthusiastically, and Suetonius smiled.

"Well, we have to move fast if we want to help Glaber and his untrained militia, don't we?" the legate said, giving the younger man a wink. Octavius smiled, but his face clouded.

"What if he wins without our help?" he inquired. Even though he should hope for the rebellion to be put down soon, he didn't want Glaber to finish off the revolt. He wanted to participate, to do something great during the war. If Glaber won, he wouldn't be needed.

Suetonius seemed to sense his inner thoughts. "Don't worry Octavius. He won't. Many of the senators believe that the revolt is anything but serious, but that's not true. What does a pack of toothless men know about wars?" he said, smiling. "Trust me. I've conquered a revolt in Hispania before, and rebellions are hard to put down. Very hard! Slaves and farmers don't revolt unless they are in real desperation, and that desperation is the thing that fuels them on. They are fighting for their lives. They know that if they fail, they'll die — and so they know that they have to succeed, or die trying. There is no going back, and that makes them all the more harder to conquer. Do you understand me, Octavius?" he asked. He frowned as he tried to make his theory easier to the younger man.

"I do understand," Octavius said quietly, "Though I am still worried about Glaber winning without our help."

"Your thoughts are treacherous, Tribune," Suetonius said, staring at Octavius. In his eyes, Octavius saw a twinkle of humor and he too smiled. Suetonius broke into a laugh. "I've been a soldier as long as I can remember. Trust my instincts. Shall we have a bet on it?" he asked, and Octavius shook his head.

Octavius knew that Suetonius was a careful man and would not call a bet on something that was risky. "No, sir. I trust your instincts," he said, and Suetonius clasped him warmly on the shoulder. He was about to continue when the horn sounded for a meal.

"Call the tribunes. We'll talk later. Food comes first, always," the legate said humorously.

<hr>

Octavius sat in his tent, looking at nowhere in particular, and thinking about nothing in particular. He was awakened out of his reverie—like state by the sound of legionnaire sandals, and greeted his two friends as they came in. Octavius motioned them to have a seat.

"How was your day?" Octavius asked.

Lucius unfastened his centurion's helmet, showing hair matted by sweat. Octavius thought that Lucius looked more formidable with a helmet. It gave him a sense of some great warrior, untouchable. Octavius had been shocked at first. He could not see the playful boy he had always known before. Instead, with the helmet, he looked like a full grown adult. Even without the helmet, Octavius thought that he looked different; he seemed to have lost any trace of boy-hood in the past months.

Lucius tousled his hair a bit, and sighed. "How does this hair look like to you? You think it was a comfortable march?

I had to march every step of the way," he said with mock anger, and Octavius laughed. What Octavius did not realize was the fact that Lucius had spoken with some meaning in his words. Titus, however, caught it and frowned.

"We cannot spare horses for every centurion, though it's a pity," he remarked casually, not looking at Lucius. Lucius frowned. The man was devoted to Octavius, something that he could not understand. He did not know when or where it had happened. It had happened too gradually for him to notice. Their first few months together was not pleasant— he knew that much. But then, after that, they seemed to be getting along pretty well, until they referred to themselves as brothers. He knew that Titus was legally the brother of Octavius. Yet, he had felt a pang of jealousy when he had heard that. Octavius had never referred to him as a brother before. And then, after the two had received their posts, they had somehow gotten even closer. Titus was now some loyal follower of Octavius. He guessed that it was partly due to the fact that Titus was a natural soldier who was very constant in his loyalties, but he felt sour nevertheless.

Though he too loved Octavius, he couldn't quite see how men devoted their loyalty to him. He had heard rumors in the barracks and knew that Octavius was regarded as a young, humorous, and intelligent man. Lucius had tried hard to suppress a strange feeling that he had denied to call jealousy all the time it occurred in his mind, but he still felt bitter when he heard those rumors. To Titus, Lucius just gave a nod.

"And you, Titus?" Octavius asked.

"I've missed this," he said, grinning, and Octavius also smiled. "I know all of my men now. I know their histories too. My optio is pretty smart. He's a young man from Greece—Ajax—who came to Rome in search of a more energetic life. What he found was chaos, between the patricians and the plebeians, and between the patricians themselves. So he joined the legions in hope of a more orderly life, and now he's going out to the battlefront to fight a slave rebellion. Ha. I like him though. He's a nice kid, about the same age as you, Lucius." Lucius picked his head up, stared at Titus for a moment before smiling.

"I would like to meet him sometime. My optio is a sinister looking man who doesn't have a taste for words. But I hear that he's very good with a sword— I might want to challenge him sometime," Lucius said, smiling. He yawned a couple times and said, "I can't keep this on for much longer. I don't know about you, but I'm going to sleep.

Good night, gentlemen." With that, Lucius moved over to his bed and lay down with a big thump. Octavius and Titus looked at each other, amused, before following Lucius's example.

<hr>

Things weren't going as he had intended. Initially, Spartacus had wanted a small group of fellow gladiators to help him escape the gladiatorial school. It had been decided that they would escape to the Vesuvius until things had quieted down a bit, and escape north, to Gaul, possibly Thracia, his homeland. Small groups were forgotten easily, and they were also easy to equip and escape. Things began to turn for the worse when Crixus interfered. He glanced sourly at Crixus, who was helping the men to cut lumber. He should never have listened to the bloodthirsty man. The plan was to escape Capua quietly, but Crixus, exhilarated in finding the forces of Capua being weak, had suggested that they plunder Capua before going to the mountain. It was true that they needed supplies, so he listened to Crixus… but Spartacus now knew that pillaging Capua had meant their destruction. Rome would never allow one of her cities to be looted and the looters to escape unpunished. She might forget about a small group of troublesome gladiators who escaped, but he knew that she would take their plundering as a mutiny to Rome herself and would never give up until they all got their punishment. His thoughts pressed down on him, making his shoulders slump as he thought of their future. He glared again at Crixus, though he knew that he had been the one who made the final decision. He had been clouded by emotion that day. If he had been sane, he would have never listened… why did he listen? He asked to himself. The question tormented him continuously.

Now that he was level headed again, he could think back without emotion clouding his judgment. He was still grateful toward Octavius and Lucius for helping him save the lives of many other gladiators, though a slight resentment did remain. He knew that he had been wrong in trying to kill Octavius. If only he had kept his head… again, the 'if's. He promised to himself that he would not torment himself anymore on what happened in the past.

Spartacus gave a big sigh as he looked down the mountain. From his place, he had a vantage point, and he did not like what he saw. A legion was drawing close to them, ready to camp near Vesuvius, possibly blocking the only known way down the mountain. Soon they would all starve to death or become slaves again, at the best. He thought grimly of the worst consequences. There was a pretty good chance that the mountain would be decorated with crosses— his body on one of them.

His followers had grown to about two thousand. Everyday or so, Crixus led small raids into the cities near Vesuvius, freeing the slaves there. Hundreds followed Crixus back to their camp each night. Even though he warned the men not to harm the innocent civilians, they did so anyway, and there did not seem to be any ways of stopping the plundering. Sometimes, freemen who had grown sick of poverty would also ask to be recruited. Even though the numbers were growing, this was, in some effect, bad news. He had to make sure that there were enough supplies for all of them. Most of all, there was no chance that they would escape Rome undetected now.

His gaze landed on the men, training their bodies without respite. They wanted their freedom, and Spartacus envied how naïve. they were. They just trusted their officers, believing that the officers would grant them freedom. Believing that all Roman legions were easy to defeat like the untrained century at Capua. He knew that he had to live up to their hopes, though he doubted whether it would come true. There had even been some nights when he had thought of escaping on his own, but the revolt was something that he had planned, and he could not just give it up, leaving two thousand men who trusted him to die while he escaped.

"Sir!" a voice called, and Spartacus whipped toward the voice. "Sir, there's an army approaching. It's actually a militia, about a thousand more soldiers than us." It was David, Jacob's brother. David, after mourning in silence for a few hours next to his brother's body, had forgiven Spartacus. It was not his fault, David had said. He told Spartacus that he bore no grudges against him, just the Romans, and Spartacus was grateful for that.

"At what pace? It's nearly dark now. They should be stopping."

"It's really fast—"

"A forced march?" Spartacus asked, and instantly regretted it. These men had never trained in the legions, and they didn't know the words. Despite his hate for Rome, he had to admit that Rome's policies were very efficient. He would teach his men the words and the Roman battle formation.

David looked uncertain for a moment, but he continued, "Something like that sir. They show no sign of stopping." Spartacus nodded, thinking. If the general left it too late, he would lose men during the construction. His mind wandered to a possibility of a night attack, and discarded it. If he failed, the risks were too high. He would lose all his army, and they would be captured as the general's trophy before long.

"Call the council, David. Oh, you should send men out to a ten mile perimeter from now on. There maybe reinforcements arriving. Real legions. If not, then Rome does not think that we are a threat, and we will show them that we are."

David watched the man retreat to the command building, made out of lumber, and followed in, calling in the other officers behind him.

Spartacus seated himself at the head of the conference table, very crude considering the supplies they had. Crixus took a seat on his right, while Oenomaus took a seat on his left. Oenomaus was a careful man, well learned, and he contributed a lot of his knowledge to their 'campaign'. David took his seat next to Crixus, and Spartacus noted with some jealousy at David's features. He looked more like a nobility of Rome than a slave, and he wished that he could share the same comforting look that made the man look like a natural commander.

Spartacus cast a glance over the table to see if everyone was present and, on checking that they were, started the meeting. "Gentlemen, there is an army of three thousand approaching us, a militia by the way. There may be a Roman legion backing the militia up, but we cannot sight the legion yet."

"Where have they camped?" Crixus asked, and Spartacus told him that they were still marching.

"Well then, we can launch a night attack on these tired men, and we'll wipe out the three thousand in no time." There was a rowdy cheer of approval.

Spartacus closed his eyes, remembering the last time that he had listened to the man's advice. "No, it's too risky," he said, and Oenomaus nodded. Crixus started muttering a curse, and even went so far as to challenge Spartacus's bravery. Spartacus gritted his teeth at that and shouted at the man to be silent. "There will be Roman legions following. We are no match for Roman legions, whether we like it or not. That's the stark truth. We also have to form some other plan. Our original intention was escaping silently, but now, that is not possible."

"Spartacus, we are gladiators, those who have fought for all their lives. We are not scared of a bunch of untrained men," Crixus objected. "Let us take them on."

"You have never seen the trained ones, Crixus. I have served in one of them, and we will lose if we battle with a trained legion. A militia may be a different story, but still, the stakes are too high for me to command a night attack. For now, I want to discuss what to do in the future," Spartacus said.

Oenomaus raised his hand calmly. Spartacus nodded his approval, and Oenomaus cleared his throat quietly to command attention. Once he was sure that he had succeeded, he started to speak. "Comrades, I believe that we should continue our way up north. There is no choice now. Rome is on our trail, and now we have to battle every inch of our way north. But once we cross the Alps, there will be nothing that can stop us. We can return to our homes. We can form a country. We can do anything. Rome cannot find us in the vast Gaul." Spartacus's thoughts immediately started calculating the odds. He knew that staying in Rome was impossible—would be hunted down sooner or later. If they could just cross the Alps, it would be certain that they would gain their freedom and see no more of Rome. There were some mild cheers of approval, but others stayed silent. Crixus was one of them.

"Oenomaus, don't you want to have a chance back at them? The Romans?" Crixus asked suddenly, and Oenomaus faltered. "You do. Everybody does. I find it very boring to just go up north while we can wreak havoc in Rome," he said, eyeing the people around him.

Spartacus banged a fist on the desk. "I promise you, Crixus, that the journey north will never be boring, if we succeed in it at all. Men will die, including the people here. More will, if we decide to stay in Rome. Our only hope is to cross the Alps before Rome calls back her veteran legions. Once they come, it's over."

"You think too highly of them."

"With good reason," Spartacus said, his voice rising. "The Roman legions have never failed in crushing down a rebellion. They always succeed. It has been centuries before Rome has lost a war. Battles maybe, but they always manage to win in the end. Do you really think that we can succeed? Do you view us as immune?"

Crixus opened his mouth to say something when David grabbed the man's arm. "Crixus, what you truly want is to raid the rich cities around here, right?" he interrupted.

Crixus nodded blatantly. "Yes. I am going to kill every Roman I can find, loot any jewelry I see."

Spartacus thought he heard David let out a small sigh. "But Crixus, we can not stay in Rome forever. We need to escape this peninsula if we truly want to be free. Don't you agree?"

"Yes but—"

David cut in. "We need provisions if we want to escape to Gaul, and we do not have enough supplies. Crixus, we can raid provisions from cities around here, and when there is an abundance of them—at least, when we decide that there will be no shortage—we will head up north."

Crixus pondered on the idea. He then decided that it was good enough for him, nodding.

Spartacus looked at David, annoyed that David was making the decisions. Still, he thought the young man had proposed an effective idea that would lessen the disputes between Crixus and him.

"That is a good idea, David. Oenomaus, do you agree?"

Oenomaus nodded his head a bit reluctantly. Spartacus smiled. "So then it is decided, gentlemen. Crixus, I name you as General Crixus, second in command along with General Oenomaus." He paused to let the idea sink into their heads. Both stood up and gave large bows, with grins on their faces. The men banged the table and clapped— a rather rowdy revelry making.

"General Crixus, you shall overlook our raiding plans. General Oeminaus will continuously check on our plans to head north. General David, you are in charge of training the men. The rest of you, you shall come to me tomorrow, and I shall assign you all a general to help out. The council is now dismissed," Spartacus announced grandly, and claps followed his words.

⟋ *17* ⟍

Lucia touched her hair tenderly and stifled a yawn. She had woken up early today because she had heard that the legions would pass through Capua in the morning. Three legions were said to be coming, and rumors said that one of them will be stationed in Capua while the other two would continue south towards Vesuvius. In one of the legions, Octavius would be riding at the front of column in his flashing armor. She thought that Octavius's features looked even better when wearing the armor.

They, although unproven, were said to be trained by some of the best officers. She had been waiting for their coming since the revolt—every time she looked at her house slaves, she could not help feeling nervous. Some had already escaped, preferably, to Spartacus. The legions would bring her a feeling of security and she believed that the town becoming a little too rowdy with a few more thousand men was a fair price to pay.

The way her father was behaving wasn't so comforting either. Ever since a pale serpent like man had visited their house, her father had turned like him...only in the means of skin color, sickly pale. His usual ability to think fast was gone, and he seldom came out of his room. He would say nothing to her mother or her, but she knew that something was wrong. His nerves have never quite been the same, and she blamed Spartacus for it. The last time she had met Spartacus, Spartacus had been surprised at her ability to handle swords and ride horses. She didn't lack far behind Lucius or Octavius. He had been very polite then, and she still could not believe the things that he had done. He had slaughtered the young men in the town without giving a thought. Some of them lay in grotesque positions, a trophy of the things that the slaves had done. They had burnt down the insulas, robbed people of their money, and even had killed the women and the children. She hoped that the legions would crush the rebellion soon. They would pay for what they had done sooner or later, and Octavius would be one of the people who would make them pay. Her cheeks grew red at the thought of his hazel hair ruffling gently in the wind.

She woke out of her reverie as the door knocked. Outside came the voice of Flamina, her tutor. She was a slave by the law, but nobody really treated the Greek like a slave. She told her to enter, and she did, with a flushed face.

"Are they coming?" she asked eagerly, and Flamina looked sorry.

"I know that you will be very disappointed, mistress, but it turns out that only one legion would pass through Capua. The rest will camp near Vesuvius."

"What's the name of the legion?" she asked, hoping for her slave to say the Third Victrix.

"I think the Fifth Aquila, mistress." Lucia slumped on her desk. She had been waiting feverously to see her brother, and most of all, Octavius. Jupiter was so mean. He had made her hope, and now the hope was crushed.

Flamina saw the change and felt that she had to say something. "You can visit your brother, since he is close to you now," she said, and Lucia lightened up visibly.

"Yes, maybe I shall after they are settled." She stifled a yawn and asked Flamina to tell her another story on the Punic War.

⫘

Octavius thanked the messenger boy with a coin and opened the letter hurriedly.

Octavius, I am going to Rome because I need to handle some political upheavals. I am sorry that I have not visited you often. Even if I go to Rome, I am sure that you will do very well— Suetonius gladly reports so when I ask. I am sorry about the new arrangements—Mummius insisted on his legions camping at Capua, so you will have to go to Vesuvius. Though you will miss your chance to see your family, you will be more close to combat. Think of it as a chance. Good luck, and be careful if a battle takes place. See you, Crassus. P.S. Just to tell you, Julius has become a quaestor. He will probably leave for Hispania as soon as the revolt there is conquered.

Octavius reread the curt note. He didn't care much about his uncle going to Rome—they hadn't seen much of each other in the past days anyway. It was also good to hear that Julius had succeeded in getting the post. However, he was disappointed about the new plans for he had planned with his family and Lucia.

He fingered a gold ring that he had bought from a legion smith a few weeks before. He had planned on giving the ring to Lucia, with a letter maybe. Lucia. Whenever he was with her, there was a strange sensation, one that he had never felt before, consisting of high blood pressure, thumping heart and... warmness. A sensation he denied to call love. Octavius was pretty sure that she would agree to his proposal, and his main worry had been whether or not Governor Maximus had already proposed her to another man. He gritted his teeth as he thought of the possibility, shaking his head slightly. That entire plan was now ruined, and he slumped deep into his saddle, furious with how the situation was shaping up.

"What's wrong?" Suetonius asked without turning back, and Octavius looked up from his horse, surprised.

"Nothing sir, except, we are not going to Capua. I had actually planned on it, sir, and this is very... unsatisfactory."

"Why? Do you have a girl you like in Capua?" Shit.

"No, sir," Octavius said hastily. Suetonius gave a smile, frustrating Octavius.

"It's for the better. I let Mummius have it, because the closer we are to the slaves, the more we can engage with Spartacus's troops. We will camp about fifteen miles away from the mountain, five miles away from Glaber's militia. Someone will need to rescue Glaber sooner or later, and I believe that we are the most suited for the job, yes?" This time, he turned around to give a wink, and Octavius managed to smile, though he still felt disappointed.

A long note tooted in the distance, signaling the separation of the legions. Mummius's Fifth changed their path into the direction of Capua, while the other two legions continued their way south to the Vesuvius. Octavius gave a wistful sigh at the direction of his home and spurred his horse to go a little bit faster.

"Octavius?" Suetonius asked.

"Sir?"

"If I let you have an illegal break now and then to Capua, will you feel happy?"

Octavius grinned. "Yes sir. With Lucius and Titus, though." Suetonius gave a mock sigh and nodded his approval. He couldn't help acquiescing to his tribune's charms. It probably had to do with the memories of his son. His son had been very similar to Octavius. When he saw Octavius, it was as if he was seeing a younger version of his son... before his death.

He realized with a jolt that his second in command was speaking to him. "I'm sorry," he said.

"Nothing of importance, sir," Octavius answered.

The two rode their horses in silence for a while, each lost

in their thoughts. It was Suetonius who broke the silence first. "What do you know of me?" Nothing, Octavius realized with a jolt.

"Sir?"

"What do you know about me?" Suetonius asked again, his face dead serious.

Octavius faltered. "Uh… that you and Uncle Crassus are childhood friends?" he answered, frowning to think more. Oddly enough, he could think of nothing else.

Suetonius nodded his head, smiling a grim smile. "I have never told you of my family, have I?" he asked, and Octavius shook his head. He remembered the time Suetonius had mumbled something unintelligible about his son, but that was practically it.

"You can trust me. If you want anything, ask me. I think you as my son," Suetonius said, and Octavius's face turned crimson. "Don't blush. When I think of you… I see my son in you, ambitious, cheerful, outgoing, Talented, Intelligent, charming. He was that kind of a boy."

"Was?" Octavius managed to say. Suetonius gave a mirthless smile.

"Was. He is dead now," Suetonius blurted without emotion.

Octavius could not find the right words, and while he struggled for it, Suetonius continued.

"I am not the ambitious type. I prefer to live a peaceful life than to get myself involved in the politics. But my son, he was not like that. He loved power, and he joined the legions when he was seventeen, just like you. And then a year later… it was so ridiculous. He just fell ill, without any evident cause. He only lasted two days after that. When we cremated him… his heart didn't burn."

Suetonius stopped and stared at the sky, his eyes far away. Octavius maintained the silence, his mouth wide open. It was a well known fact that hearts of a poisoned body do not burn. "Sometimes, I just wish that I could go to my son…" he whispered in a very soft voice, barely enough for Octavius to catch it. Then a look of firmness entered his face. "It happened a long time ago. I have no need to grieve over it now," Suetonius said, bravely flashing a smile. It did not reach his eyes, however.

<hr>

It had been a few days since the legions had set up their barracks near Capua. The farmers were having some trouble feeding the extra mouths, but they did not complain, knowing that they could not risk another rebellion. It would be the end of everything.

Some made sure that the slaves were not mistreated, treating them nicely. Others set a tighter rein on the slaves. The two, however, were in common when it came to watching their slaves. They never slackened their watch and carried a weapon with them always, and would regard a slave suspiciously every time they approached near. Those who were caught trying to escape were killed brutally, without mercy. The legion had worked hard to maintain order in Capua and had left the day before with Mummius in lead to restore order in Doria. Only a cohort was left, and the cohort had grown slack with all the wine that had been given to them.

Lucia sighed in disgust when one drunken legionary offered her a hand, telling her how beautiful she was between his hiccups. She doubted that the man would be punished, for it seemed that the higher officers were too drunk. Mummius, she knew, also loved drinking, but at least he kept a tight rein on his men.

She pushed on her horse, leaving the man behind. She was going to meet Lucius and Octavius, and her heart pounded furiously. It had been a few months since she had seen them, and she had missed them a lot, partly because she had been used to their company. There had been many times when the three talked together, gathered beside the fountain on the governor's lawn. That had been some years ago, but the two young men had always included her in their conversations even after they had ceased to play like that.

The horse trotted out of the gate house, with only a nod from the soldiers. She was relieved that at least the soldiers on watch didn't seem to be drunk. Though it was her first time traveling to Vesuvius alone, she knew the way, and she tried to ride with confidence though uneasiness nagged at her.

She was not sure how long she had ridden—maybe an hour—when she saw a forest approach. Old memories came back to her as she remembered the time when the three of them had raced their way through the small forest. She knew the way as well as anyone, but, with the dusk approaching, she was not sure if she should go in the forest alone. It was just a small forest, she thought, and if she used the shortcut, she'll be at the camp in less than thirty minutes.

She took tentative steps toward the forest, when she saw a sudden flare of torchlight in the distance. There was a rowdy cheer in the forest, and that was all it took for her to swerve her horse around. She wondered if she should just go back but decided against it. She might not be able to ride to the Vesuvius again for some months, and she did not want that. Her heart beat furiously against her chest, but she ignored it, pushing the horse to go faster around the forest. She looked back occasionally to see if anybody was following her and was relieved that nobody was. She also glanced to her left, where the darkening forest loomed beside her. She kept on her fast pace until she was sure that she had lost even the speediest of them.

After ten minutes of berserk riding, she let out ragged breaths as she saw that the forest had ended and saw the open plain stretch out once more. In the distance, she could just make out the legion flags waving in the fading light. She ran her horse at a full speed once again, cursing Flamina for making her go through all this. Flamina had refused to let her go to the legions before she finished her studies, forcing her to leave Capua in the afternoon, knowing well that it would be dusk when she arrived. She thought sourly to what would have happened if the men in the forest had kidnapped her. The tutor would be.heart—broken she knew, regretting her decision in not letting her young charge go out when it was still light. When she returned home,

Flamina would be in tears, promising her that she would carry out every single whim.

Flamina had also been reluctant to follow her, and Lucia let her stay in the mansion, knowing that Flamina would only hinder her. She was too frail to provide her with protection of any kind. And she was the only one Lucia fully trusted. The others... she would feel uneasy to ride along with them. All in all, she had decided that it would be the safest and the fastest if she went alone.

She let out a breath she hadn't realized she was holding as she came closer to the legion. A soldier halted her as she neared the camp. He stood prominently on the wall, his hand on his sword hilt.

"Address yourself," the man said briskly, staring at the young woman in front of him. The woman gave him a smile, almost making him apologize for his curt greeting.

"Lucia Maximus, daughter of Governor Gaius Maximus from Capua, sister of Centurion Quintus Lucius Maximus."

"Why have you come, miss?" the soldier asked, his tone softer now.

Lucia smiled. "I came to see Tribune Gnaeus Octavius Lupus and my brother. Can I pass?" she asked, and the legionary nodded hastily. She sounded important, and he did not want to do anything that might aggravate her. "Where can I find them?" she inquired again.

He waved at the other soldiers below to open the gates, and the legionaries saluted as she passed. "They live in the same tent, miss. Go straight, and you'll see a big command tent. Their tent is next to the big one. You'll know it," he called out. Lucia thanked him and rode on with complete confidence, earning awed stares from the soldiers around her.

She did recognize the tent when she neared the big command tent, just as the soldier had said. The tent flap was open, and she caught a glimpse of Octavius. She jumped off her horse, handed her rein to a legion slave and rushed to the tent opening. Three men were sitting around a table, and one soldier who looked like a scout was telling a story urgently. All the men's face was grim as they listened to the scout. Her prepared greeting died in her throat as she took in the situation. She decided that the best way was to let them notice her, so she just cleared her throat. Octavius glanced at her direction, his annoyed face changing into surprise, and then joy as he noticed her.

"I'm sorry, Tinius. Just a moment, please," he said, as he walked over to Lucia. His reason he shouldn't. His mind said that he should. He had been a follower of reason until now, but one exception could be tolerated…ignoring the baffled look of all the men in the tent, he hugged Lucia. Lucia hugged back, and for a moment they stood like that before Octavius let go, his face crimson.

Lucius especially seemed to be dazed, and Titus was having a good laugh over it.

"I just so knew that. You're going to get married earlier than me!" Titus said, and clamped his mouth shut as Octavius gave him a murderous look. Lucia went and hugged Lucius too, giving her brother a kiss. Lucius kissed her back, and hugged her tightly. It had been a few months.

"I'm sorry to interrupt this happy reunion, officers, but…" the soldier said, and he pursed his lips in irritation as he was ignored.

"Lucia! I was about to go see you and my parents tomorrow," Octavius said. "Are my parents all right? They do seem very happy in their letters, but, are they? And the governor? He would be much stressed. What about the tutors—" Lucia held up a finger to silence the overjoyed Octavius and responded with a single nod. Octavius opened his mouth to say more when the soldier tried again.

"This urgent business—"

"I'm so glad to hear that," Octavius said. A grin stretched wide on his face.

"Tribune! This is urgent," the legionnaire said, his voice clear, loud, and irritated. Octavius sighed, looking at Lucia. There were so many things that he wanted to ask, things he wanted tell her.

"I'm sorry Lucia, but this is urgent. Would you like to stay or go out and wait?" he asked.

"I'd like to stay," she said firmly.

"All right," Octavius said, offering her a spare chair. Focusing his attention on the scout now, he asked, "I'm sure there was no one when I scouted the forest myself about three hours ago. Are you sure?"

The scout nodded. "Yes sir. Torch lights in the distance. I think it's the slaves."

"Yes, I saw them myself. I wanted to go through the forest, but then I saw the lights. So I used the other way," Lucia intervened, earning an annoyed look from the scout who had been interrupted just again.

Octavius looked sharply at her. "You shouldn't have come if that was the case. There are countless possibilities to what they would have done to you if they had caught you. You should have stayed within the walls." She thought about snapping at Octavius about treating her like a child when he himself was not much older. Maybe it was something about his new rank that made him speak with more authority than before. Just as she was about to speak, Octavius resumed. "If the two of you had seen it, then there is no mistake. Ask the general if we should go affront them. If he asks, tell him that I am for it. They might be aware that Mummius and most of his legionaries had left to Doria while only a cohort remains in Capua—the reason why they are staging their attacks now. I will prepare a cohort just in case in the drill yard. I have a feeling he will agree with me too."

The scout saluted smartly and rushed out of the tent. When he disappeared, Lucius held out a plate filled with fruits, and Lucia took them, marveling at their quality. She had always imagined the legions as tough and lean, without much comfort, but it seemed that her guess was incorrect, at least with the higher officers. When she voiced her thoughts, Lucius shook his head violently, telling her that she had never marched all day in the sun. Octavius grinned at his friend before strapping on his gladius to his belt. "Yeah. You should try on the armor. It weighs more than me," he said, adjusting his helmet gently as he looked at the mirror. The mirror reflected him, taller and leaner, the boyish plumpness gone. He gazed back at the new figure that stood before him, slightly wavering in the mirror. How would Lucia think of his new form? He glanced at her, and then back at himself, Lucia, the ring.

He felt warm blood rush into his cheeks as he thought of the proposal he was about to make. He had never planned on giving her the ring directly, especially with the other men looking on. But looking at her in the fading red light of sunset made him think that somehow he would never have a chance again. Maybe it was just his mood, his current thoughts that he might go into a real battle. He took in a deep breath and, from his tunic, took out a gold ring that glowed even in the fading light.

Octavius tentatively took a step toward her. And he could once again catch the whiff of her aroma, Sweet, luring and passionate. He mustered the courage to meet her eyes, and in them saw the bravery of her brother along with her kindness. Her eyes glowed softly in the fading light, and Octavius blushed, looking away.

He closed his eyes tightly, took one more step in her direction until her stola was brushing slightly with his armor, and opened them again as he stammered out the words.

"I—I love you, Lucia," he said, his face becoming redder

than ever.

He glanced sheepishly at the two men who gazed at him with open mouths. He did not dare look at Lucia. He pushed the ring into her hands, and waited trembling for her reaction.

She looked up at Octavius, her face showing a glad surprise. Octavius clenched and unclenched his fists in his anxiety and anticipation. Without hesitation, she put the ring on her finger, and tenderly kissed Octavius on his cheek. Octavius let out a sigh of relief, blushing again as he saw Lucius staring at him. He felt that he must do something in response, but with the other men, he simply could not do anything.

"I—I must go." he stammered, not meeting anyone's eyes. He almost tripped on his way out, hurrying his steps.

Octavius breathed in the cool air and wrapped his cloak around him a bit tighter out of habit. The embarrassment of the whole situation had not worn off yet, and he was not cold. He was still burning with embarrassment. Winter was coming, and the logical part of him wondered what changes it would bring to their campaign. Vesuvius would be bare, and the slaves would need to raid other cities even more to gain basic supplies. A slave handed him his horse, and

Octavius slipped onto the saddle easily. He had trained countless hours just to get familiar with his war horse and now he could handle his horse as well as anyone.

He jogged his horse to the drill yard and was satisfied with what he found. Two cohorts were training already making his job simpler. He gazed at them, wondering about which cohort to choose when there was a clatter of hooves behind him. It was Suetonius, his cheeks pink from riding against the chilly wind.

"I've heard," the general said as soon as Octavius was in earshot. "I have the same suspicion as you, that they might be mounting a raid on Capua. The Fifth Aquila has left Capua to restore order in another town, and the Ninth is controlling the south of Vesuvius. We're the only ones left. If you want to take the heavy infantry, it'll take an hour or two to overtake them. By then, it'll be completely dark— are you willing to risk it?"

"Am I willing to risk it?" he asked, blinking his eyes in confusion.

"Well somebody has to tend to the barracks, no? Spartacus doesn't seem like a fool. He is acting smarter than his predecessors of the first and the second slave revolt— I have some worries that this might spark into a real time war.

Anyway, he might attack the base while we're out defending Capua," Suetonius answered.

Octavius almost hugged the older man in glee at being given his first solo mission, but refrained from it, saluting instead. Suetonius noticed the younger man's feelings and gave a short laugh. His son had been like that too.

Octavius stayed silent, thinking. He had heard from the veteran centurions in the legion that forced marches in the night can kill many. However, he knew as well as anyone that Capua could not suffer another raid, and a cohort might not be enough to hold them back, even if they were sober. He doubted it.

He gave a nod, and Suetonius clapped him on the shoulders. "The second and the fourth cohort— Lucius and Titus are both in the second cohort, right? Good. The rest, I'll leave up to you, general," he winked as he said the word general, and rode off without another word. Octavius knew that the legate was doing so many things for him, extending Octavius's powers. He had put in his complete trust on the younger man, and Octavius vowed not to disappoint him. Though he loved the situation he was in right now, he knew he was burdened with new responsibility, and guilt. He would have to send men into battle, for some of them, their deaths.

"Legionaries!" he turned and called out to the two cohorts, and they looked up from their training, confused. "How are you today? Have you trained much?" some legionaries yelled out a positive answer, but the most of them stayed silent, baffled by the sudden addressing. "Well, then, for those of you who have said yes, your time to show off your skills have come. Are you eager to prove yourselves?" This time, more of them cheered, beating their swords against their scutums, their shields. "Today is the day. Capua is under immediate threat, and there is no one anywhere to save Capua from falling under the slaves' hands but we." A loud cheer rose as even the slowest realized what was coming. "And who are we? We are the Third. Today is our first day of battle, and the outcome of this skirmish will determine whether we are worthy or not. I'm sure that you, of all people, would not disappoint me, or your fellow legionaries." The cheer swelled, and Titus, who had by then arrived with Lucius, was cheering too. They chanted his name, and he had a sudden whim that Lucia might hear this chant in the tent and be proud of him. Octavius's eyes grew warm, and his heart was full as he listened to the cheer. The legion was his.

The two cohorts trampled everything in their paths as they marched on the uneven road. Octavius's breath grew shorter as he realized that the time for an engagement was getting closer. Scouts had reported that the slaves were still on the far edge of the forest, probably waiting for utter darkness until they made their move. They were being a bit too cautious, and Octavius wondered why. Were they in fear of the Roman legions? He doubted it, because the slaves had been raiding towns near Capua without any hardship. The untrained legions in the peninsula had fallen like leaves in autumn. His legion was different. It was salted with the best officers that Crassus could recruit, and the legions belonged to Crassus, the richest man in Rome, compared to the untrained legions in Capua that belonged to no one in particular. They were road guards, places for young men who had a bad history or those who had been dropped out from the veteran legions. The officers there were mostly unmotivated, unlike the officers in the professional legions. They did not care about making their legion the best of the generation. He, along with the other officers, had. There would be a difference, a big one at that. He wondered why he was thinking all this, and reached the uncomfortable solution—to console himself.

"Sir! The slaves are on the move!" A scout came rushing towards him, gulping for air. His horse wasn't better off, and the animal kept rolling its eyes in exhaustion. Octavius couldn't imagine what the scout had done to make an animal look like that, but that was of no importance at the current moment.

"Are they out of the forest?" Octavius asked.

"They are going to be soon, sir. The force is bigger than we realized. At least about six hundred men, maybe up to eight hundred."

Octavius paused. He had initially thought of taking out one cohort to engage the slaves, but he thanked Suetonius for giving him two cohorts. One cohort would have been too small. The fact that they had sent out so much would mean that they were expecting much from this raid. He wondered if he should suggest attacking Spartacus's base when there weren't many soldiers left, but swore as he remembered that they did not have authority to attack the main force. Their orders were to defend the town, engage any raiding forces and assist Glaber if necessary. Glaber. If the slaves were still free to raid at will, then it meant that

Glaber hadn't yet blocked the road. What was the man doing? He thought he heard Glaber say to Suetonius that he would be sitting on the only route down the mountain, and would be completely able to manage everything on his own—so be gone. He cursed the man for his laziness or cowardice—he was not sure which.

"All right. Keep track of them," he told the scout and turned towards the two veteran centurions riding next to him. "We change our route. We go around the forest, go ahead of them, and intercept them. There's a large plain from the forest to Capua, good enough for us." The two centurions nodded their approval and called out orders to their cohorts, making Octavius's chest swell with pride. He was in complete command here.

They were now wheeling around the forest, traveling at a fast pace. They would need the speed though it might cause some accidents. Octavius turned to a scout who had recently come back, and told him to bring Titus to him. The scout saluted and rushed off, coming back with Titus running behind. Titus gave a salute to Octavius, who laughed at the formality.

"You don't have to do that, and you know it. You're doing it just to annoy me," he said, pulling his horse out of the column to talk with the man, but Titus's face was still.

"Yes, sir," Titus responded. Octavius looked closer at the figure standing before him and noticed a playful twinkle in Titus's eyes.

"Fine," he said, rolling his eyes. "Anyway, I called you because I want you and your century to stay here. If—no when— we set the slaves running, you capture as many as you can, blocking off their retreat."

Titus thought staying silent for a moment before opening his mouth. "Will a century be enough?"

Octavius nodded. "They're going to be running for their lives. They won't regroup and fight. We'll be close behind them, and you'll be in no trouble." Octavius paused. "Look. I'm going to survive this, and win it through. I chose you because I can trust you. But...this is our first battle, and it may be tough. I mean... we only trained for several months. Will it be enough?" he said to Titus, though Titus got the feeling that Octavius was talking to himself rather than to him.

"The Third is better than average legions trained for a year. I know it. And wasn't it you who said that the Third had the best officers and that they had gone through rapid improvement? It's true Octavius, for them, and for you too.

You've gotten better, not only in your sword skills, but in your ability to command and plan tactics. Trust me. I'm not saying this to reassure you," Titus said, and searched the younger man's face for reaction. Octavius's face had brightened up a little, but he still looked unsure.

"I wouldn't be worried if I've seen a battle before. This is my first time in a battle, and I'm being given the whole command of it. This is too overwhelming. I should have refused Suetonius's offer." He hadn't planned on saying so much.

"The veteran centurions are very experienced— even within the ranks of the veterans. Ask them for their opinions, and listen to them, though the final choice is yours to make," Titus said. He had never seen Octavius so nervous before, and hoped that his nervousness wouldn't obstruct the man from making a good decision. "That's enough of worrying, Octavius. We've got the numbers, the weapons, and the soldiers are eager. They are good, I tell you, and we've also got element of surprise on our side. It's going to be easy, and maybe we'll get back to camp in time for breakfast," he said, keeping any doubts out of his voice. Even though he had been a centurion before, it was his first time engaging a troop of several hundred, and he too was getting a bit unsure about himself. However, he could not voice his doubts to Octavius, who, he thought was clearly having enough to ponder upon. "Before you go, Octavius, I want to clear my orders. Capture or kill?"

Octavius took in a deep breath. He was about to respond when a scout came racing towards the tribune.

"Sir!" the man shouted and Octavius stared at him, his anxiety growing at the man's urgency. "Two Roman soldiers have died!"

"What?" Octavius asked, stupefied.

"They were found slain near the forest, presumably on their way to Capua."

"Are they… deserters?" Octavius asked, his face clouding.

The scout shook his head hurriedly. "No, sir. Along with them also was a body, a body of a Roman woman who was slain a short while ago. She was still breathing when I arrived. She died very nastily; about ten or more arrows in her body," the scout reported, grimacing at the picture. "She was riding a horse, but the chestnut horse is dead also. The two legionaries seemed to have been escorting her. I thought I should tell you, sir," he said.

Octavius frowned, not being able to make head or tail of the strange report.

"Report to me after the battle. Find out their names, rank, and cohort," Octavius ordered briskly. Then he was about to dismiss the scout when Titus paled, grabbing the scout by the arm.

"How old was she?" he asked, gulping for air.

"About fifteen, maybe seventeen. I'm not sure, sir. She was very young. She was wearing a red tunic and a stola. She had black hair and dark brown eyes with good features," the scout said, and shifted uncomfortably as the two officers paled.

"Lucia. She's in the tent, right?" Octavius asked briskly, hoping, knowing, that the answer would be in the affirmative.

"She," Titus took in a deep breath. "She said that she must be going back. I asked her to stay but she said that she would rather go than to stay in our tent all alone. So I told two of my men to escort her." Titus answered, his voice coming out in short rasps.

"And?" Octavius forced the word out with immense strength. His voice was quavering.

"She…left," Titus answered. Octavius stood dumbly for a few seconds before shaking his head.

"She is not stupid. She knew there would be danger if

she crossed the forest. She would not have done that," Octavius gasped out in a pained voice.

"Her body wasn't so near the forest," the scout added helpfully— or so he thought.

"Did she have a ring on her fourth finger?" Octavius asked, his voice so large and demanding that the scout himself also paled.

"I don't know sir. There was no fourth finger. It was cut off," he said.

Octavius stood without saying anything. His breath grew into rasps, but he tried to calm himself, knowing that there was no proof that it was Lucia. She would be fine, he thought to himself. He knew her. She was not the one to die so meekly. He asked whether or not she said anything with a trembling voice, but was answered in the negative.

"She couldn't even open her eyes. It's a miracle that she even survived that long. By her way of dress, she looked like a patrician, perhaps from a wealthy family. I searched her for anything that might help verify who she is but nothing was left. I think the slaves have already searched her and have taken anything of value."

Octavius gave a short nod. It was better that he did not know who the body was. He could still hope. "But sir, I have ordered some other men to take the body to you," the scout said, and as if on cue, two horsemen arrived carrying a body. Octavius dared a glance, and watched in horror as his worst nightmare became true. He had been hoping that it was some other person, but he knew the blood stained face of the body very well.

He had a single thought.

No.

Never. Not possible. Surely he was seeing things? His mind said. His reason said otherwise.

"Take her to Capua. Don't come closer," he barely breathed out the words, his eyes wide with excruciating pain. Titus grimaced, and caught Octavius as he shook violently.

Octavius's eyes were blank as they stared into the open space. "Lucia," he whispered, and bit his tongue as he tried to hold back the tears. His hands shook and he clutched them tightly to hide the trembling. His men were watching.

"I'm sorry. I should have done something to keep her in the barracks," Titus whispered as he moved into a hug. As they embraced, Octavius let out the tears he had been holding. They flowed freely from his eyes and Titus could hear pained groans now and then. The younger man looked so different from before, a proud general, now a crumpled man.

Octavius let go of Titus suddenly, wiping the tears roughly. "I can't... I need time. She wasn't even part of the war. She was just... a civilian. She wasn't even a soldier," he whispered.

"I know, Octavius. I'm sorry. But you don't have time. The slaves, the murderers are out there, ready to kill more. Will you let them?" Titus said, feeling sorry that he had to be so harsh on the heart broken man. His words were true however. They did not have time. If they delayed, then they would kill even more.

Octavius shuddered violently. The slaves...the dogs. His eyes grew stony and his hands were clenched into tight fists, teeth bared as he let out a low growl. He was going to avenge her. Nothing restrained him, no morality issues, from killing. He had changed.

"They will regret killing her. I swear to the gods." Octavius's voice, though it was hardly audible, sent shivers down Titus's back. He had never seen Octavius look so devastated before. He looked utterly devastated, and his eyes that were once full of brightness were now shining with malice. He suddenly feared about the rash actions that Octavius might order. He had heard about the crazy commands that had been ordered by angered commanders, commands that drove the whole army into ruins.

The young commander cleared his throat, his eyes clearing a little. "Capture as many as you can, Titus. Let no one escape. This is my order, and I trust that you will not disappoint me." With the curt order, Octavius mounted his war horse and jogged off to his original place in the column, not once looking behind.

<hr />

"There!" someone in the column called out, making everyone's heads turn. Octavius could not see anything at first, but he soon saw a dim flicker in the distance. The slaves.

He felt his veins pulse, just like the time he had been near—death in Spartacus's chamber. His breath grew short. He was feeling something that he had never imagined he would feel. The boy who had cowered from dead bodies, and death itself, was now feeling lust, lust to kill, lust to revenge.

I shouldn't have let you go. Can you hear me? They killed you. Wait, Lucia. Wait. I will revenge you soon. I will find out the ones who killed you, and they will wish that they were dead.

The cohorts had arrived at the open plain about thirty

minutes before and were waiting calmly. The cohorts seemed to be energetic despite the cold and the dark night march. A few scouts had suffered injuries in the dark, but the injuries were light and everyone else was in good condition.

"Pass out the extra torches quietly and light them on my mark, one torch per three men. The torches are to be lit when the cornicerns blow the signal. Throw the torches. And then, rush the slaves. Make sure that they make a lot of sound when attacking," he ordered quietly and icily.

"Call Lucius to me," he told a scout softly before clasping down his hand to signal the cornicerns. The cornicerns blew two shrill notes, and soon the plain was filled with the eerie light of the torches. The cornicerns sounded once more, a deep long note this time, and the cohorts started to jog over to the slaves in perfect formation. They made a racket, following his orders, and Octavius smiled grimly to himself. The slaves would now view them as a legion force instead of two cohorts.

"Are we to meet them face on?" the centurion asked.

"Yes and no. I've already ordered a century to block the forest. We'll flank them and put them in between."

The centurion raised his eyebrows. "Will a century be enough?"

"There's nothing we can do about it now except to decrease the slaves' numbers so that a century will become enough," he snapped at the innocent centurion. He instantly regretted it. He did not show it, however. Instead, he turned to the column that was dog trotting ahead.

Octavius let himself fall back in order not to impede the cohorts' pace. A horse was capable of bringing chaos during the joggings. The two centurions tried to dismount to get to their places, the front of their century, when Octavius stopped them. "I need your advice," he whispered hoarsely. They looked at each other and grunted approval.

Lucius came running from the lines, panting. "Why have you called?"

"I can't risk you," Octavius whispered softly so that the two centurions could not hear. Especially when your sister is already crossing the River Styx, going to the Underworld, he thought, though he kept the thoughts to himself. Lucius would go wild, hot tempered as he is, and Octavius knew that Lucius would blindly fight until he got himself killed.

Lucius opened his mouth to object. "I can take care of myself without you having to baby sit me. Is this what you called me for? I want to go out and fight, not cower here," he whispered hotly with all the bitterness and jealousy that had been accumulated for months.

Octavius grimaced. He pursed his lips, thought about letting his temper loose on Lucius and decided against it. "I need you, Lucius," Octavius said finally. In some ways, he was grateful for this battle, this battle that was helping him greatly to numb his sadness. He just could not believe the piece of information, and it seemed almost to be a nightmare he had, just a nightmare. He was not feeling her death, yet.

Lucius gazed at his friend. "You just can't understand, can you?" he asked, trying hard to keep his voice down. He wanted Octavius to get out of his fantasy. Octavius had relations that traced back to Rome. He did not have to do anything but to just behave well in front of Crassus, and Crassus would just give his nephew a good post. He, on the other hand, had to gain every inch by proving himself to others, and the only way he could do that now was to fight bravely. He could understand why his friend had asked him not to fight, but he just hated the way how Octavius thought that everyone was born prestigiously. He gave a salute, and ran off without looking back.

He considered calling the man back, but decided against it sourly. Even though he wanted Lucius to be safe, a part of him wanted Lucius to regret not following his decision. He cleared the latter part of his thinking as soon as the thought formed and concentrated on the slaves ahead, partly to drive Lucia out of his mind. Focus on somewhere else, he told himself, thankful that it was working. The legionaries' torches were illuminating the plain, and he could now see the slaves, though he could not make out the exact features.

The centurion near him cleared his throat. "If you want to encircle them, you should form a semi circle with the cohorts," he said, and Octavius looked at the other centurion for his opinion. The other centurion stiffly nodded his head, and Octavius ordered the cornicerns to do so without the slightest hesitation. The cohorts responded immediately, and Octavius felt the savage thrill surge once more in his veins. The slaves would be terrified of the Romans, and he would not disappoint them.

The slaves seemed confused to what the Roman cohorts were doing, and Octavius was satisfied to see a little disruption in their ranks. The centurions had noticed it too. "Flank them in a faster speed, sir. Use the distraction," the same centurion who had advised him earlier, Caecilius, called out, and Octavius nodded.

By then, the cohorts had succeeded in flanking the slaves. The slaves were grouped in the same formation as the

Romans, and they too widened their lines to match the cohorts' semi—circle. They had been trained, probably by Spartacus who knew how the legions worked. Octavius gave an urgent prayer to Jupiter, hoping that they were not as well trained as them.

The slaves, even though they matched the cohorts' movements, never advanced, and instead stood still on their places, just watching the lines.

"They're scared," Octavius whispered, and Caecilius nodded.

"Of our numbers. They still believe that our forces are at least over two thousand. If you want to keep that fear advantage, sir, you should send men in the third line up to the front and lengthen the front line to make it look like that," Caecilius said.

Octavius nodded once. He then signaled the cornicerns. To the scouts he ordered them to pass the word to throw the torches before throwing their spears. He had imagined this moment to be filled with exhilaration. However, it was not so. He only felt nothing, his mind was blank, maybe except for a savage desire to avenge her. Even that, though, was not so strong. His mind had entered the stage of non—feeling.

His voice was still icy as he spoke. "I've done everything

you want, centurion. And now, we charge." His dropped his arm, and the sound to charge rang over the plain.

⚬⏤⏤⏤⏤❖⏤⏤⏤⏤⚬

Crixus swore as he saw the army of Rome before him. They looked like a legion, maybe a little less, but he was sure that they outnumbered his army by at least a few hundred men. They all looked eager in the light, shouting in a tone that betrayed no worries. His army, on the other hand, was shifting nervously, and he blamed Spartacus for that. Spartacus and his legion nonsense. Everyday he would say something about how strong the legions were in front of the army, decreasing the morale everyday. No doubt the man had his own purpose, but the negative influence was becoming greater than the positive one.

The heavy infantry certainly seemed formidable, unlike the ones that he had seen around here. The formation itself was different from the third class legions in this area. Where ever he invaded, they always fell back without much resistance, either running away or being killed. He had enjoyed their fear, making their deaths as slow as possible. They would feel trapped, then a little hope would flare, and Crixus would allow it to grow until he crushed the hope into pieces by sending in his core, the gladiators. They fought like crazy, with enthusiasm that had lacked in the arenas. They slaughtered for the joy of it, and did not stop when it came to civilians, plundering their homes. The gladiators also enjoyed torturing the civilians, cutting their body parts off one by one. They did not care whether or not their victim was a man or a woman or a child. They flung children back into burning homes. And they laughed. They were having the biggest revenge in their lives.

Last time, in Doria, they had almost left the town in ruins. No doubt the Capua legion would go there to restore order, leaving Capua free to fall to a similar fate. It had been all working out great until this legion interfered. You can do it, he thought. Show them the power of the gladiators. You have the most enthusiastic men in world history. Come on. With that consolation, he shouted the order for a counter charge.

~ *18* ~

As the cohorts neared the slaves, they threw their torches at them, and used the slaves' panic to throw their spears, adding to the confusion. There were screams already in the slaves' rank, though nobody ran. A hailstorm of spears could be seen through the now dim light. The flag bearers were the only men not to throw away their torches, sothere was not enough light for Octavius to distinguish the men's features.

Once the initial surprise calmed down a bit, Octavius held up a hand, and the cornicerns blew three long savage notes varying in tone that rang in the plain. The Third responded with enthusiasm.

Centurions rushed forward drawing their gladius, with their century at their heels. They crashed into the slaves' line, causing the line to buckle. Octavius could feel panic intensifying in the slaves, and hope surged in him. They were going to win.

"Their forces were just a raiding force. They never expected this," Caecilius commented, his eyes glued to the battle.
Now and then, he shouted orders at his cohort, and Octavius
followed the man's lead, shouting encouragements.

His gaze wandered to the far end of the slave ranks, and
he gasped in horror as he saw what he had done. A fire was
raging there, and though the slaves were even more terrified
because of that, Octavius knew better than to simply rejoice.
He had not seen rain in at least two weeks, and he knew
that the best fuel for a fire was dry grass. The fire would
become even greater, and he knew that once the fire reached
the forest, it would all be over for both armies.

He called to a scout waiting nearby and told him to lead
the other scouts and put down the fire. The scout looked
doubtful, and Octavius understood him well enough. They
had only about forty scouts, and the fire would need more
than forty men to contain.

"Do anything you can. You have my permission to take
men from the second line to put down the fire if you feel
that you are going to be overwhelmed," he ordered and the
scout saluted before rushing off.

"Sir, if our first line breaks, the second line might be
needed," Caecilius said, looking worried.

"It doesn't look as if we're going to need the second line. The fire is more of a threat," Octavius said, rejecting the centurion's doubts for the first time. "See how the slave lines are buckling?" Caecilius gave a short grunt, and resigned. He had met many others who could command less. This young man seemed to have no difficulty in commanding the men; at least he was not showing it if he did. Having, or pretending to have confidence was important in battles, and it had an enormous impact on the morale. Right now, he couldn't hope for the morale to be better, and the young man's plan to intimidate the slaves with extra torches had worked. The slaves had not attacked first, which had given them enough time to encircle the army, eventually cutting off their path to Capua. Furthermore, although they were unaware of it, they were now trapped in between two forces. Throwing the torches had caused complete panic, and he had to admit that even he was surprised for the technique had been new even to him. Night attacks were rare, especially since it was disadvantageous to the Roman legions who loved to charge at their enemy, something that could only be performed well with enough light. The charge, though it had been a bit awkward due to the lack of light, had worked better than he had first expected of the young commander.

The first lines were now buckling, and Octavius noticed men running from the outer edges of the slaves' ranks. The second line was holding, but the Romans were pushing the lines, battling furiously. He pursed his lips as he saw that the fire had not grown any smaller. He cleared his throat, and turned to the other centurion, Centurion Germanicus, standing besides him.

"Help the scouts with two centuries," he ordered.

"One, sir. Even though we're winning, two might invite a flanking move," the man said grimly. Octavius hesitated, but decided to trust the man. He was a veteran, while this was his first time in a real combat. He nodded, and the man trotted off towards his cohort, yelling orders.

The slaves' second line was being pushed back, and Octavius felt a strange disappointment. He had expected things to be a bit more challenging. He had expected to be in the heart of the battle but he was standing in the back, just directing out orders. Octavius could now understand why Lucius had behaved so, at least a part of it.

"Caecilius, I am going out there to fight," he said, still devoid of emotion, and Caecilius stared at him.

"You want to kill someone. I've heard that you don't like killing," Caecilius commented dryly. Octavius drew a sharp breath.

"That has changed."

The young man's voice was so flat and dominating that Caecilius did not dare ask anymore. He seemed to have grown darker suddenly, and Caecilius decided not to push it.

"The morale will increase," Octavius said with a wild fire glinting in his eyes. He didn't want to stand back. He wanted to get involved. That day, he finally knew that he was capable of killing. And also capable of wanting to kill.

Caecilius opened his mouth to object that morale was high enough already, and that nobody knew the outcome of a battle before it ended. It seemed as if the young commander was being arrogant about their situation. But before he could say anything, the young man was already gone.

Octavius trotted his horse into the battle. The legionaries who noticed him cheered, and struggled to fight better under his eye. Fury that had filled him moments before dwindled as he saw the grotesque figures of dead men lying around him.

He was still looking at the battlefield when a sword flashed near him. Octavius immediately blocked it, counterattacking as he had been trained to do by the legion masters, and of course, Spartacus. He felt his gladius push into the man, and gazed stupefied as blood started to pour out from the man's neck. His eyes were glazed, and Octavius just stared into the lifeless eyes, suddenly feeling as if he had done something very wrong. The feeling of sympathy and disgust soon changed into enormous fury as he thought of Lucia. This man might have killed her.

Out of the corner of his eye, he saw another metal weapon strike at him, and he broke from his stupor and raised his gladius in response. He was prepared to meet the sword. The sword, however, stopped in midway, and the slave who had been holding the sword collapsed onto the ground.

"I saved your life once again. Do I have to baby sit you all the time? You would have been dead if it wasn't for me. This is a battle, Octavius. No time to daydream." Octavius turned his head towards the sound to find his oldest friend standing there. A heavily armed slave dashed at him, but he slew the man with ease before turning back to stare again at Octavius.

"I could have blocked it well enough on my own," he said, truthfully.

Lucius stared aghast, and he practically shouted at his friend. "No, you would have been too late. Is this how you thank me?" he said, and Octavius shrugged. "By the way, we've almost broken the second line, and many slaves are running. Shall we chase them?" Lucius asked.

Octavius nodded and whipped around to block himself from an axe. The man was a giant, and he almost leveled the mounted Octavius. He sparred with the man, blocking the man's blow. He felt panic as he faced the giant, as it dawned on him that one fatal movement could lead to his death. Keep calm, he told himself, and managed to surprise the man by crashing his horse into him. The horse neighed in panic, and Octavius knew he would have to end it soon. This was a little trick Titus had taught him before, if he could call it a little. Horses could not be forced to be driven into someone or a shield barrier in most cases, and they would immediately panic if they did. Octavius attacked the momentarily surprised man's flank, and closed his eyes as he heard the giant scream.

Remember Lucia. You don't have to feel sorry.

The second line too gave away, and the slaves started to run into the forest in sheer panic. A cheer rang up from the cohorts, as they started to hail Octavius. Octavius raised his sword in response, and the cheer grew louder. Caecilius came running on horseback to congratulate the younger man, and Octavius's cheeks blushed as he heard praise from a veteran.

"We Romans never do night attacks unless it is absolutely necessary, and so naturally, we are not good at it. But today," he paused before he continued. "The might of the Roman legions showed even in the night," the old man said, chuckling, and he pointed to the fire. The fire was dwindling, it being cut off from more fuel by the stone wall the legionaries had built.

The cheering grew louder. Lucius felt a pang of jealousy strike at him as he saw his friend on horseback, holding out the red—tipped sword as if he had been the one who had fought the slaves' army and won. Sure, the plans were his idea, but he had not actually fought, and he had. He had ravaged through the enemy, cutting down their core group, the gladiators. He had been the one who crashed into the enemy's lines first, and the one to hurtle their line back by killing everything that moved around him while Octavius was settled safely in the back of the lines, watching the battle. Later, when he Octavius did come into the battle, he had been dazed at first. Yet his friend was there, alive and gloating, holding out his sword like a god. Like an imperator.

"You did not disappoint me; in fact, you made me feel like the most important person in all of Rome. Not because my plan worked, but because I had you," Octavius said, his voice ringing over the field. Lucius noted sourly that his friend even had the loud, commanding voice of a general. Other soldiers, however, cheered in a louder voice, chanting Octavius's name. Lucius saw pure joy in them as their commander addressed that he valued them. It was a political orating thing, he was sure. Octavius would be glad because his plan worked and because he had routed the slaves, he had something to show for.

Lucius saw Octavius gesticulating briefly to the cornicerns who blew order to the field. They soon formed the original Roman columns, and Octavius gave the signal to march. "Before we head to breakfast, how about completely routing the slaves to Vesuvius? More to brag to the men who are not here," Octavius announced as lightly as he could, pressing down every thought about Lucia. He knew that he could not hold back those thoughts forever, and he also knew that soon, these thoughts would just explode in him.

Those who heard it gave hearty, encouraging laughs. Not at all funny, thought Lucius, though he did not let it show. The men yelled their approval, and Octavius called for a double pace, marching through the forest this time.

"It's too dangerous. Too dark," Lucius objected, and Octavius merely pointed to a bloody red sun that had popped out over the horizon. He nodded, barely keeping his frustration in check. Why did Octavius get things right all the time and he didn't?

Octavius called to a centurion nearby, and asked him to lead a century to burn the dead before the civilians could see it and be shocked over it. "No doubt they heard the fighting, but it is a completely different story between hearing of a battle and seeing corpses on the field. And call back the century and the scouts who were ordered to contain the fire. The fire would have been consumed by now, and if it hadn't it would be very small and it would save your time from lighting a funeral fire." The centurion saluted smartly and no trace of weariness or disappointment showing through him. He looked professional, and Octavius smiled as he was reminded once again about how much Crassus had bragged about his officers being one of the best. He then took time to reflect on his current mood. He was feeling no joy. A degree of satisfaction maybe, but definitely not joy. A little sadness and some leftover fury remained in his mind. His mind, he realized, was still numb, too numb for him to feel anything.

They trampled over the wild roots in the forest, though the column was a little disarranged by the irregular distribution of trees. Some men tripped and one had his arm broken, but they all continued the march in good humor, bragging about what they had done in the night.

Octavius heard a sudden shout among the soldiers, and turned back to see what was happening. He was just in time to see a broken spear shoot out and hit a tree next to a legionary. Just as he was about to sound an alarm, a legionary rushed out and threw himself into a brush. He heard a terrible scream, and shortly after he saw the same soldier running back to his line once again. He had the look of glee on his face, and Octavius looked away in disgust. Some men here were a little better than animals, enjoying savage actions. Some others were more than that, completely courteous to women and the children but those who would not think twice about killing an enemy. Only a day before, he knew what type he was. Today, however, he was not sure.

It was becoming more and more stressful for him to push out thoughts about Lucia and to keep a light—hearted tone for the legionaries. After all, they had earned it, and he did not want to cheat them of their good mood.

He looked out for signs of the retreating slaves and for Titus, but could not see them in the dim light. He hoped it would get brighter soon. He took a drink from his water skin.

A horseman ran up to him, and quickly matched Octavius's stride. "The century you ordered back has almost caught up. I spread the other scouts wide in the forest and they should be back by now."

Another scout rode up to him, his face flushed with thrill. "Sir! There is a century ahead, commanded by Centurion Titus."

Octavius sighed, but then, he had never told anybody but Caecilius, commander of the second cohort, about the 'missing' century, so there was nobody to blame but himself. "Yes, I know that. I ordered them to be there," he said a bit impatiently.

The scout flushed red, this time with some annoyance, but continued. "Yes, sir. I think they've routed the slaves completely. The centurion told me so. The slaves arrived there a little less than thirty minutes before, running with all their might. He said that he captured most of them, and killed the ones he could not capture. He told me that Spartacus would have to find out about the loss himself because he was sure that those who had dared to come across his century are either prisoners or have not survived."

Octavius stared at the scout, then he asked. "How many did he capture?"

"I'm not certain about that, sir," the scout said, searching his commander's face for his response.

Octavius gave a curt nod. What's wrong with him? the scout wondered. He should be celebrating! "Caecilius, take command of the cohorts until I get back. Lead them to the barracks, on regular pace." Caecilius nodded. "You lead me to Titus," Octavius ordered, and the scout saluted. The man set off, and Octavius followed the scout easily, staring straight ahead, looking into an empty void. Something's definitely wrong, thought the scout.

Octavius's horse neighed nervously as it neared a silver barrier made of shields. The century was in a square position with the prisoners in the middle. Typical of Titus, he thought to himself.

The scout dismounted off his horse, handing the reins to a legion slave nearby. Octavius did the same, and he walked stiffly towards the barrier. The soldiers opened up for Octavius to pass.

Titus looked around at the sudden commotion, and found Octavius standing there.

"You look...angry," Titus finished lamely.

"I'm not. I mean, the fury inside me is exhausted. Or maybe it is yet to come. I don't know why. I feel tired, and actually, I'm not feeling anything. I've become senseless, apathetic. Like a shell, where there's only the physical you. Your mind has one off somewhere..." Octavius said. Titus stayed still, not knowing what to say.

"You still did a good job," Titus said lamely, not knowing what else to say. "We've got hundred prisoners, about twenty dead in our hands. That means you've left quite a ruin behind you. At least a five hundred. I thought you didn't want to kill?" Titus asked, and Octavius smiled mirthlessly.

"That was before. These men here will wish they have died on the battlefield," Octavius said, pointing carelessly at the prisoners. They stared back at him in pure fear, some pleading. He did not budge. There was no sympathy left in him. In each of their faces, he could see the face of Lucia, Lucia hugging him, Lucia taking his ring.

He then shook his head. There were other things to do.

Ignoring the nagging thoughts of Lucia, he ordered the cornicerns next to him to sound the signal for a march. The century gladly obliged, their neat squares disintegrating.

Octavius took a moment to gaze at the slaves again, and on seeing that they were bound secure, nodded his approval. The slaves all seemed weary, and some had hopeless, even self-furious faces. "Don't let them commit suicide," he said to Titus, and Titus nodded grimly.

"What are you planning to do?" he asked.

"Interrogate them. Suetonius would be pleased about that."

"Meaning?"

Octavius answered with a grim smile.

<hr>

Octavius heard the soldiers from his barracks even before he entered it. They cheered as they saw the victorious century coming back, no doubt that the other centuries who had arrived before had already spread the information.

Suetonius came to greet him as soon as he entered the barracks. "I've heard. It was brilliant, though there are some parts you could have been more careful on," the older man said. "No worries. It was excellent still. I'll tell you after what you could have done better, though I want to hear it from your own mouth first." Octavius nodded, not wanting to worry about anything anymore. He had enough sorrows at hand.

Suetonius sensed the younger man's feelings. "You did a nice job. I am so proud of you. Go have your breakfast and a rest before you come to see me," he said.

"Thank you, sir," Octavius said, and was about to turn around when he veered back again to face the Legate. "Sir, I've brought some prisoners. I hope we can interrogate them later on."

The legate looked surprised. "Is that so? You'll still want to refresh yourself anyway. We'll find time for it later on."

Octavius nodded tiredly and asked Titus to secure the prisoners somewhere safe. He stepped into the tent, and smiled softly as he saw Lucius already snoring on his bed. Titus smiled at Lucius once before following suit.

Lying on his bed, he closed his eyes. Sleep avoided him. Although he was too tired to even open his eyes, he could not sleep. The gentle snores of his two friends sounded in the tent, luring him to sleep. And yet, he could not.

Relieved he was alone, relieved that the others were already in deep sleep, he let his emotions come forth. He replayed the image of Lucia over and over in his brain—her death especially. Tears flew like a river, wetting his pillow. He hiccupped noiselessly between his sobs, all the while thinking of her. The reality had finally hit him, and it pained him more than imaginable.

❦ 19 ❦

Fools, he thought. No doubt they were all captured now, or killed. When the second rank broke and the slaves started to desert, he had also run, and his face burned at the memory of it. Never had he, Crixus, run from a battle before. He had cut down every obstacle in his path, and almost rivaled Spartacus in swords. He was their second favorite, and he had always continued to smile at them, knowing that it was his way of survival. However, underneath the smile, he has always loathed the men who grew fat on entertainment and food. He had vowed for their fall, and instead, he had fallen.

He remembered seeing Lucius somewhere in the battle to his immense surprise. He had been shocked to see the young man. He had tried to reach Lucius, but had failed, and he gritted his teeth as he thought of the Romans.

Spartacus had been right. They were strong, but not that strong. Their force would soon be enough to beat the Romans.

He swerved his head sharply to a rustle, but let out a breath as he saw it was only a curious rabbit. He had been hiding in thick groves, waiting for the cohorts to pass. He had been there when a crazy slave had thrown his spear at a legionary, calling his own death. When he had called to others, saying that they should hide now, they did not listen to him and kept running. They should have followed his advice and kept themselves hidden until the cohorts had gone.

Next time, he would be more cautious, and wipe out the whole Roman army as they had done to him today. Five hundred dead on the battle field was the estimated number. His eyes grew warm and watery as the truth began to dawn on him. Still, there was a lot of time left for revenge, next time.

<hr>

Curious men were chased away by guards, and only the higher officers remained to see what was happening.

Octavius took a deep breath. Suetonius was interrogating these men, and it was proving to be difficult. Serstus had advised the legate to interrogate them separately, and the legate had followed the man's advice, recognizing his reputation for interrogation and torture. Even so, no one had yet told them any of the information they wanted.

"Make the threats more forceful, sir. It helps a lot," Serstus advised again, and Suetonius nodded thoughtfully.

"Who's the leader of this raid?" he asked the new man. The man growled but didn't say anything. "I'm asking you who he is. Answer, you live. You don't, you die. Under Jupiter I swear it," Suetonius gritted his teeth, and the other men looked at him in mild surprise.

"Ole Crixus. He's not here. He's dead. Maybe escaped. Dunno." The man said casually. Lucius would hate to know that Crixus was not here. Lucius was currently sleeping in the tent, telling others not to bother him for at least a day. His friend still did not know about the fate of Lucia, and he vowed that he would not tell his friend for a while. Lucius would go on a suicide mission if he knew, and Octavius did not want to lose somebody, again. He listened half heartedly to the conversation, ignoring the picture of Lucia in his mind. The image of Lucia did not leave his mind however, no matter how hard he tried, and his sadness and apathetic mind had morphed into something more dangerous during the past few hours—uncontrollable fury.

Suetonius sighed as he ordered the guards to bring him the next man. "Wait," Octavius called suddenly. "Do you know anything about the death of a patrician girl?" he inquired, shaking a little to control his fury.

The man thought for a moment, and nodded casually. "Yes, I know the pretty girl. Crixus said that we should get rid of every Roman around this area. So he fired the first arrow, I the second and so on. Then he went and cut the finger off the gal because there was something valuable on it, a ring, nicely made. I saw it a little," the man finished. Titus gazed in horror as Octavius interrupted into a spasm of fury. He shuddered, and his hand moved to his gladius. Titus shot him a warning glance, but Octavius did not seem to have seen it. Each time Suetonius had called in the slaves to question them, he had resisted the urge to kill them all in the cruelest way he could think of. He had tried hard. But now, he could not hold on anymore.

"Very well," Octavius spat out with some difficulty. "Name the others reponsible."

"Why do you care? I'm not a rat."

"You will tell me, or I will go find out myself, and you will surely regret that. I care," Octavius took in a deep breath. "I care because I knew her. Now tell me!" His voice had almost grown into a shout, and Suetonius put a hand on his shoulder to calm him. Octavius didn't care, however. He was also glad that Lucius was not there, because he would have sensed whom Octavius was talking about.

"What's wrong with you? You liked her? She was pretty though. Guess I can't blame you. I loved her at my first glance," the slave remarked, and Titus closed his eyes. He knew that Octavius had been driven to the furthest edge of his temper, and he knew that Octavius would erupt soon. And he did.

Octavius stood, knocking over his chair. He calmly walked around the table, shaking, and slapped the big man hard on the face. The man staggered, but kept his stand, and was about to yell a curse when Octavius punched the man again. Then he kicked the man over with his iron soled sandals, knowing full well the impact it would have against flesh, letting out ragged breaths in uncontrollable fury. The fallen man tried to rise, his eyes also reflecting fury as he readied himself to body slam the younger man. He was quickly subdued by the legionaries who hit him over until the man was forced to kneel.

The slave groaned, spitting out blood as he writhed to get out of his dishonorable positions. The legionaries, however, managed to hold the big man still with the help of Titus who whacked the man's head with his heavy shield.

Octavius continued to glare at the kneeling man, a vicious look coming over his face. "Sir, with all due respect, may I sentence these men?" he asked Suetonius, his voice barely above a whisper.

Suetonius hesitated. Normally, he would have been glad to grant Octavius the right to sentence the prisoners. However, in the mood that he was in today, he worried that Octavius might make rash decisions that might result in too much blood. "If you promise to be clear headed when you make the decisions, they are yours. You are the one who caught them," he said, choosing his words carefully.

Octavius nodded slowly. "One more question, slave," he spat out, consciously angering the man in front of him. "Where is Spartacus headed next?"

"That's no business for Romans. General Spartacus would want it to be a secret. He will achieve our freedom for us and tear you all apart," the man replied, and the tribunes gave a short laugh. Suetonius frowned, but he too seemed amused.

Serstus cleared his throat. "You really think he's fighting for your freedom? He's fighting for his own. At least, that was probably his original intent, but you guys ruined it by joining him. He's not there to abolish slavery. He's there so that he can live a better life," Serstus sneered.

"You be quiet, rascal. You have no right. You are not in charge here. This man, and this man, no?" he asked in broken Latin, pointing at Octavius and Suetonius.

Octavius gave a short, dry laugh. "You are right. I am in charge. Send him to the ergastulum," he said, and the slave showed fear for the first time. His eyes were glazed in terror as he looked into Octavius's, but Octavius met his eyes without any sympathy. He had been the one who had killed Lucia. He would never forgive the slave for his doings, he had already promised Lucia that. He knew he had changed during the past few hours. He had turned from a more or less peaceful boy to a revengeful man. A few hours ago, he would have let the man go or at least would have let the man have a clean death. Now, it was different. He had a clear motive for winning the war, unlike before where the motive was something far away, for Rome. It wasn't close enough to be actually felt, and some moral parts in him had opposed his position as a tribune in this revolt. All the slaves wanted were to have freedom, and he was oppressing it just to fulfill his ambition. It didn't seem right then. Now, he did not care.

He admitted it. He wanted revenge. He wanted to kill

the ones responsible.

The slave was still looking into his unsympathetic, cold eyes, eyes that reflected no emotion, eyes that were embedded into a pale face striving for revenge. No doubt he was scared of the threat of being sent to the ergastulum, a workhouse for slaves. Each day the slaves were subjected to hard labors that killed hundreds. Each night was left to the guards of the ergastulum to torture the slaves as they pleased. There was no law in that place, and even the blood-loving Romans cringed at the name of ergastulum. It was every slave's nightmare, and the big slave in front of him seemed shocked at the name. It was a place where slaves would be tortured until they dropped dead, where even suicide was not allowed.

"Sir, please. I will tell you the names. Tiro, Sistus, Juba, Tumba, Cingento, Belenus, Ciro, Ogmius, Crixus and me. Rudiobus tried to shoot her but failed. Spartacus's next destination is Thurii," he said, rushing out the names in haste.

Octavius gave a mirthless smile. "There's a time for everything. You are too late." Something in him tugged at his conscience that he was becoming a slave of the goddess of revenge, Nemesis.

He swerved to the guard. "You heard him. Pick out the men he called and send them all to the ergastulum."

"You said you will let me live!" the slave cried in horror.

Octavius faced the man with cold eyes. "I am letting you live. I am not killing you, am I? I won't even bother. You deserve less," With that, he whipped his cloak around him once more and saluted to Suetonius.

"Your admission sir," he requested. Suetonius hesitated. Octavius was not the Octavius he had once known.

"Octavius, let us go out to clear some things up," he said quietly, rising to his feet and heading for the door. Octavius stared after the legate, and with a grim face followed him.

Suetonius led him around the barrack, to the far side where they could not be overheard. He watched as Octavius silently followed him with no expression. In the cold breeze, Suetonius saw Octavius as not the once cheerful man he had been but a lonely man with strong resolution on his face.

"In the name of all gods, what's the matter? You won by a large margin. By gods, you should be celebrating. What's this all about the patrician girl?" he asked, and Octavius dropped his head.

"I'm sorry."

"No, you have nothing to feel sorry about. Just answer

my questions."

Octavius let out a long sigh. He did not want the memory to be refreshed. "Today, somebody I loved was killed. She wasn't a soldier. She had nothing to do with the war. All she had done was to take a ride through the forest. And they killed her, just like that," he said, his voice trembling. He fought to restrain his tears. There was no way he would let them flow in front of his commander. "She was Lucia Maximus, daughter of Gaius Maximus, governor of Capua; sister to Centurion Quintus Lucius Maximus; proposed to today by," he took in a deep breath. "Tribune Gnaeus Octavius Lupus."

He almost broke down, but didn't, gulping in air. They had been together almost from the beginning. Every time they had played together, the time she had given him a silver necklace that still hung around his neck, the time when he had given her a pin, then today, when he had given her a ring just for it to be stolen by the slaves. It all came back to him striking him as if it was a massive blow. He felt dizzy, and the world rotated around him.

Suetonius clutched Octavius's arm. "Octavius. I'm sorry. I had no knowledge. Then you will have to tell Lucius."

"No. I will not. I can't. He'll go crazy. I'll go crazy. Please don't tell him."

Suetonius hesitated. "Will you not regret it? Or the man being sentenced to the ergastulum?"

"No, sir."

"Then you have my permission."

❧ *20* ❧

Glaber watched as his army set up camp on the foot of the great mountain. He had received a message from Suetonius that the slaves were defeated with only two cohorts and that their raids were going to get more frequent from now on. It didn't matter now. He would starve them and block off their water supply. Soon, men would start falling, and maybe then, Spartacus might surrender, to him.

"Shall we set up a fort, sir? With high walls?" an officer questioned him, and he frowned.

"Believe in your fellow comrades, and your general, soldier. There is no need to set up high walls, or trenches for that matter. We'll build them later on."

The officer tried to salute, his usual discipline urging him to. However, something in his guts told him that this went against every rule in the battlefields, and he knew that he had to offer some advice of some kind.

"Sir, but we are at the foot of their base. If they charge us from the mountain, we'll need the defense mechanisms."

Glaber glared at the man, and the officer instantly regretted speaking out. "They are only slaves and we outnumber them by at least a thousand," he said in a soft voice, and it was all that was needed for the man to scurry back to his work. Glaber was only worried about Suetonius's legion claiming victory for themselves. He would need to watch out for them.

The officer groaned to himself as he turned his back to his general. The men were not as hard trained as the legions. They were a militia, no more. There were no tribunes, no cavalry like the regular legions. He remembered his father telling him about the slaughter of the first and the second slave revolt that took years for Rome to put down. It was not because the slaves were especially good. It was because the Senate had not taken the revolt seriously, and had given praetorship to some untalented generals. Some men never learn, he thought as he thought about the amassing numbers of the slave army and his general.

⋅⋅⋅✦⋅⋅⋅

"You what?"

Crixus hung his head, glowering. It had never been his fault only, but Spartacus seemed to think so, and he could not bear the look of Spartacus right now. He looked as if in a fatal shock over the loss of about seven hundred men, men they had tried so hard to recruit.

Spartacus resumed. "I don't care. I really don't, Crixus. I don't give a damn to which side wins on a raid." He sighed. "But what I really do care is that you lost seven hundred men. When we first started out, all we wanted was to raid Capua and escape to our homelands. Now, Rome cares about us. They have sent legions close to this area, and that means they know about us. Do you think they are going to let us live if we lose this war? No! They are going to kill every one of us. Get it? We cannot afford to lose," Spartacus took a deep breath to calm himself. "Our numbers have shrunk to less than a thousand five hundred now, and that's going to take a whole long time to recover, longer than it did before, because the slaves are hesitant to join us. They now know how vulnerable we are. A loss is big enough to stop anybody from joining. Don't you even know that?"

Crixus raised his head. "Nobody knew a Roman legion might interfere with us. I did my best to keep my movements a secret," he said stubbornly, glancing around at other members of the table. They looked at him with accusing eyes.

"Seven hundred men can never be a secret," Spartacus whispered in a dangerous voice. "So why don't you just apologize? Don't keep arguing with me. You were wrong. You lost," he continued, his voice becoming louder. His eyes were narrowed, and he had risen from his chair to pace around. His hand was on his sword hilt, and Crixus wondered if Spartacus would use it on him.

The table erupted into chaos, as every man shouted out his idea. Some were in the idea of revenge, and some were blaming him. "Be quiet, all of you!" Spartacus shouted before speaking. "The only good this did to us was to tell us how good the Roman legions are. And this one was only a fledgling legion. Think about the veterans. Now do you believe me?"

"Spartacus," a calm voice called and everyone focused their eyes on the man, Oenomaus. "I think that legion, or cohort was better than it should be."

"Are you telling that to console me? That means they've got the best officers, unlike ours, who are eager but not trained themselves. The only ones that were trained are the gladiators, and we were taught how to fight and die bravely, never fight and live bravely. Anyway, who's the commander of the force? And how large was it?" Spartacus took several deep breaths. Part of it was his fault too, and he knew the might of the legions. He could never blame some eager group of raiding slaves to losing to a legion.

"I thought it was a legion at first, but then at the end of the battle it seemed to be about two, maybe three cohorts. The cavalry wasn't there, though I saw some auxiliary and scouts. The commander, I don't know. I saw him at a quick glance, and he seemed to be very young. I don't recognize him though. It was a tribune, I think. There wasn't any legion flag. Only cohort ones." Spartacus sighed at the report. Two cohorts would mean about a thousand soldiers, and it was probably only sensible if his troops lost. Crixus looked angry and miserable at the same time, though he didn't care. The man was rash, and he only knew about plundering, never using tactics or anything good.

Spartacus stayed quiet, and the other men did not dare to break his thoughts. He had been elected leader, along with Crixus and Oenomaus following at his heels on the first day of the revolt, and at that moment, he had felt optimistic about everything. Now things were looking pretty pessimistic.

"We need to do something to recover our reputation. We

attack Glaber. Scouts say that he's moving to block our entrance. Food will run short in a few days, even if we rely on rain for water supply. I say that we attack as soon as morale recovers. Glaber leads a militia, and scouts say that he has given up trying to spice his team up after a few tries. They are a militia, nothing more. They are not better than us, led by an arrogant Roman who thinks that his militia is enough. What's more, they report that he's not even setting up high walls, though I'm not sure if it's true. Either way, I know we can beat him. After that, we need to move into a city. This is no place to rest a winter," he said glancing at his men to see how they thought of it. They nodded, though some seemed more reluctant than others. "Go cheer the men up. We attack tomorrow night."

The men looked at him, astonished. "How? The way down the Vesuvius is blocked, and we can't have any frontal assaults. It's too overwhelming. It'll be suicide," a man called out worriedly, and Spartacus just smiled at the man.

• ⬦⬥⬦ •

Vines rippled in the air. The vines seemed to move by themselves, as the scout rubbed his tired eyes. His job was to circle the Vesuvius, and he sat dejected on his saddle. He had lost the bet, and now he was stuck here, in a moonless night. Glaber had ordered him to look out for Roman scouts. He had been confused at first, and asked the general if it was the slaves that he was talking about, but he denied it, stressing the word Romans.

Why any Roman general would order a soldier to search for Roman scouts or spies was a mystery to him, and his confusing task made him more miserable than ever. He rubbed his eyes again. He had seen something unusual. The vines. Yes, he was now almost sure that the vines were moving by themselves. The long vines were stretching from the top of the sheer cliff wall, and they kept rustling ominously. It wasn't possible that someone was using the vine, for the height of the wall itself would alone be enough to discourage anyone who tried to climb down the vine. Had he drunken too much wine?

Suddenly, he felt scared, standing in the middle of the wilderness without anyone near him. He had the feeling that something, or someone was staring at him, and he could not get rid of the thought no matter how much he tried.

He veered his horse around, casting one nervous glance back at the vines. He gasped in horror as he saw a torch flare up suddenly, and gazed at it, in trance. Someone was at the base of the cliff, holding up his torch up, lighting the way for other men who were climbing down the vines. Men hung to the thick vines like insects, as they slowly descended. He stared for a moment more before galloping his horse off towards the camp. He needed to warn Glaber. Their camp would be ravaged in the matter of time, it being without walls or trenches. Even as a new recruit, he knew that much from common sense, and he stopped his horse as he thought about what would happen if he returned. Glaber would order the militia to prepare a defending position, not taking the threat seriously. He would order every man to fight face on, without any special tactics, and then when their tents were on fire and the militants were driven into panic, he would order every one of them to fight to death. He shook his head. No, he could never rely on such man.

The man did not hesitate as he changed the direction and galloped off to the Roman legion, commanded by Suetonius. They had won the slaves before, and they would do so again. He would rather throw away his life to ones who did have the chance of winning, not Glaber, who would lose. Glaber was hopeless.

∽ *21* ∽

"What in the hell is the matter?" Lucius said, trying to cheer his friend up. His friend sat on a chair, dejected ever since his victory. He let nobody visit him. When he asked why not, Octavius would tell him that it was none of his business.

In front of Octavius sat a nice glass of wine straight from the wine chambers of Capua. Lucius noticed that Octavius did not mind drinking wine anymore. Something had changed definitely, and he was determined to find out what.

"Hey, Lucia didn't send me any letter on how she fared," he said, trying to lighten up the subject. "Or if my cranky father allowed the proposal. It's not like her."

Octavius shrugged, taking another sip of the wine. It wasn't so bitter anymore. He didn't tell his friend that there indeed had been a funeral letter from the governor. The letter was burned. Two slaves had arrived for Lucius but

they were stopped at the wall by soldiers who were instructed not to let anyone looking for Lucius in. He did feel guilty
about it. After all, his friend did have the right to know.
However, he felt that what he was doing was the best for
Lucius himself. Lucius would become even rasher than
before, and Octavius doubted whether Lucius would be able
to return to normal. He knew that Lucius loved his sister
more than anyone.

"I'm sorry, Lucius. I really am."

"What? I wasn't complaining to you. Are you worried
that the proposal might have been rejected? I mean, seriously. I didn't know that you two loved each other so much. I
thought there was only friendship going on. Maybe if Lucia
met a nice young man on her way back to Capua—"

Octavius smacked the table with his palm. "Stop. Stop it,
okay? Just don't talk about her."

Lucius stared at his friend, aghast. "Why are you venting
your anger at me? I never did anything wrong."

Octavius sighed. "Okay. I'm sorry. I'm just feeling down
these days. All I want is to get another chance at those
slaves. Especially Crixus." All the men named by the inter-
rogated slave had been sent to the ergastulum on his order
except for Crixus. Somehow he believed that Crixus had

survived. The fox.

However, it wasn't to say that condemning people to the ergastulum had brought him a sense of joy. He did not feel any satisfaction. Rather, he felt...empty.

"So you can all condemn them to the ergastulum? That was cruel, Octavius. Not like you. And if I say it's cruel, it really is."

"Things change all the time, so just get used to it," Octavius snapped.

"You've also grown arrogant. One success doesn't grant you a path of successes," Lucius spat, beginning to feel bad.

"Shut up."

Lucius was about to say something more when a legionary stepped into their tent. Octavius gazed up at him, his eyes empty and bloodshot. The soldier gasped, shocked at the change that had come over his commander, especially one that had led the legion to a decisive victory.

"Legate Suetonius wants you for an emergency meeting, sir." Octavius sighed. Why weren't people just leaving him alone?

"What kind? Do I need my armor? It's dead night." The messenger nodded his head, and Octavius sighed once more. Again, nobody really left him to be comfortable. "All right. I'll be there in a few minutes," he said.

<hr>

Octavius jogged over to the command tent, and saw that everyone was in their place. He blushed as he realized that he was the last one in, and quickly took his seat next to Suetonius.

"As I was saying, gentlemen, this scout, who by the way belongs to Glaber, reports to me that the slaves are on the move, again. They are probably headed for Glaber's camp. I want five cohorts with me. We will end these slaves for sure. Two more will be stationed in the west and the east in case the slaves try to escape. I want somebody to protect the camp just in case." Serstus looked up eagerly, but Suetonius didn't look in his direction. Instead he looked at Octavius. "You are in charge of the camp while I'm gone. I also want cavalry to widen out so that they cover the distance to Capua."

"Yes, sir," Octavius answered simply.

"You can do this, can't you?" Suetonius whispered silently, and Octavius gave a nod. "Good man," he said, clapping Octavius gently.

Octavius smiled. "Octavius, go out now and get the

second, fifth and the tenth cohort into defense position. Serstus, you take the third out to the east. Secundus, you take the fourth to the west. I will take the rest of the legion to engage the slaves. I want them light. Speed is good."

Octavius bowed his head and rose to leave. He saw the brisk form of Suetonius commanding his officers and smiled gently as he thought of his own commanding form. He still had a lot to go if he wanted to sound as professional as him.

⚜

Octavius rubbed his eyes. He had gone days without sleep. The thought of Lucia and Crixus would not let him sleep. Titus had worried that his eyes were red and filled with resentment and anger.

The effects of the sleepless nights, times of crying secretly, and perhaps too much wine were showing. He tried to keep his eyes from closing but they drooped anyway. He was gently nodding his head when a man called to him.

"Sir! Legate Suetonius has sent us a scout," the man said, rushing towards him.

"And?" Octavius asked, trying to look awake. He had been on the defense rampart supervising sentries since Suetonius left in the dead of the night. He did not want to be caught napping when the slaves attacked them. The sun was starting to come up, allowing Octavius to gain a glimpse of the imposing figure of Vesuvius.

"The scout says that the battle was almost over when he reached Glaber. Our legion arrived a bit too late, though we were able to save a few of the militants. The slaves ran off when they saw the legion, and Legate Suetonius said that he will chase them as far as he can. He said he will be back later in the day," the sentry said, motioning to the scout who was looking up at them from below the rampart.

Octavius gave the man a nod. "Are you to report back?" he asked directly at the scout, and the scout yelled back a positive answer. Nodding again, he gestured to the sentries below to open the doors so that the scout could go out. The horseman saluted and raced his horse out, leaving clouds of dust behind him. Octavius watched as he got further away, and when he could not see the scout anymore, he turned toward the sentry who had brought him the news. "Next time, bring the scout straight to me," he said grimly. The sentry blushed and saluted before returning to his post.

He watched as the sentry went, and as soon as he was sure that the sentry would not be able to see him clearly anymore, he started to shiver. The wind was fierce these days, and he sorely felt a need for another cloak. His feet, barely protected by his sandals were freezing too. Octavius gritted his teeth as he fought to stay calm. His thoughts wandered to Lucia...

"Sir!" Somebody called again, this time from below the rampart. Octavius looked down, surprised, and saw Caecilius standing there. The man indicated for Octavius to come down. Octavius frowned but obliged, and gingerly walked down the steps.

"What's the matter?" he asked, still frowning.

"I have some hot bread for you, sir. Sentry hours are restricted with a reason. Over three hours in extreme weathers can prove to be fatal and according to my knowledge, you've been up there for nearly seven hours," Caecilius said with a sly grin on his face as he handed the bread over. Octavius couldn't help smiling as he clapped the shorter man on the arm.

"Somebody's got to supervise things."

"Have trust in your officers, sir."

"I do. I just didn't wanted to be caught napping. Now that they are gone, I might," he said with a tired smile. Caecilius smiled back. "Thanks for the bread, Caecilius. I have my complete trust in you, so will you mind going up the wall to supervise the sentries?” Octavius asked with a wider smile, and Caecilius gave a mock groan.

“I shouldn’t have asked,” he said, groaning good humouredly. Octavius smiled back and stalked off towards his tent where he lied down prostrate on his bed, not even bothering to take off his armor. It had been such a long night, cold and deprived of sleep. He munched on the bread, still lying down, and thought about what he would have done if the slaves made their way here. He would have killed them all. For Lucia.

Octavius gave a pained sigh. He had pledged himself not to think of her death anymore and to regain his former self— the self that was not bound by revenge. He called for sleep, and sleep eagerly came. He was drifting off when somebody called him.

“What?” he asked without opening his eyes.

“Sir, there is somebody from Capua wanting you.”

“Tell him to come back later. If he’s from the governor, tell him to get out and never return again,” Octavius responded sourly, trying to keep his words from being slurred.

“I did. I told him that our legion was attacking the slaves, and that this was definitely not the time to meet somebody. But he said that he was your father. I couldn’t stop him. He’s probably almost here— there he is!" the legionary cried, and Octavius groaned. For the first time in his life he was not so enthusiastic to meet his father.

Octavius dragged himself out of bed and strapped on his sandals groggily. He checked Lucius was sleeping comfortably and walked out of the tent to meet his father.

His father was looking around, as if to pinpoint which tent was his son's. Octavius called to him, and he whirled around to face him. His face showed surprise, and he laughed out loud as he saw his son.

"You've grown! You're taller than me now," he said, his face beaming. "You're not my little boy anymore, are you? Especially in that armor you're wearing. Your uncle must have spent a fortune on it."

Octavius had to smile at his father's enthusiasm. "It's been so long, father," he said, allowing himself to be embraced.

They embraced like that for a few more seconds before Marcus let go. When Octavius saw his father's face again, it was clouded.

"Octavius," he started. "Look here, son. I'll be frank. Lucia is gone." He took a deep breath. "She was killed by the slaves on the day of the failed raid. Octavius, I'm not going to get into the details. I don't like this news myself. I mean,

I knew her since she was born. I know you liked her too…
it's so… just sad."

Octavius gazed at his father. It felt as if every healing
wound was split open again. "I know, father."

Marcus looked at his son in surprise. Octavius continued. "I was the one who ordered her to be sent to the governor. I commanded the assault on the slaves a few days
earlier. I meant to tell you, but I didn't have the time. I
didn't like her. I loved her. I proposed to her then, and she
accepted. An hour later, she was of no more," he said, trying
to keep his tears back. A few curious men were gathering,
and he would not break in front of them. "I didn't tell
Lucius. Don't let him know. He'll go crazy. He loved her the
most. Just don't, please."

Marcus looked open mouthed at his son. "You'll regret it,
Octavius. He will get to know it anyway. It's just a matter of
time. He'll be angry at you for not telling him. Think. If I
died, won't you be angry if he didn't tell you that I was dead?"
he asked.

Octavius hung his head, knowing that his answer would
be a definite yes.

"Go tell him. Go tell him that you and he are to come to
her funeral tomorrow," Marcus said, looking at his son

intently. "Make the right choice even though it might be hard on you. It would be selfish."

Octavius stood still with a stubborn look coming over his face. Maybe he really was selfish, but he didn't care. He wanted Lucius to be all right and what's more, he was worried that he could not stand the stress of narrating what had happened to Lucia and break down.

"If that is the case, Octavius, the governor would like you to tell the people what happened exactly."

Octavius gazed at his father in horror and shook his head violently. "Father, that is the exact reason I'm not telling Lucia's death to Lucius. I won't be able to stand it. I had my revenge. All those who knew Lucia in the last moments of her life were punished. They are currently at the ergastulum. Well, perhaps except for one, though he'll also meet his death sooner or later."

Marcus looked at his son in shock. "You sent them there? That is no place for humans, and you know it."

"They aren't humans," countered Octavius.

Marcus stared at his son. The death of Lucia had hurt his son more than he had thought it had. He knew his son. He knew that Octavius would never send people to be tortured—at least the former Octavius. He knew his son as a boy who hated blood. Standing before him now stood a completely different Octavius.

"Do you feel good now?"

Octavius hesitated. "…No."

Marcus sighed. Octavius was becoming dangerously revengeful. It would not be good to pressurize him. "All right. It's hurt you deeply. I won't ask you to come, nor tell Lucius about her."

"I want to go. I want to see her for the last time. But I think it'll hurt me more," Octavius said, feeling his eyes get warm once more.

"You'll do well by coming. See her for the last time and organize your thoughts about her. It'll help more than staying here. It always helps to have a little bit of time to organize your thoughts," Marcus said, watching carefully for his son's reaction.

Octavius stood still, gazing at nowhere in particular. His father was right. It would help him organize his feelings. The past few days had not been like him, fed up with revenge. It was time to return.

In the end, he gave a slight nod to his father. His father warmly rubbed his shoulders. Octavius cleared his throat. "But I'm not making any speeches. And moreover, I might not be able to go. We had a battle yesterday, and Suetonius emphasized that nobody may leave camp until the slaves are out of this area. They aren't yet. He said so very strongly to every men and officer, and he didn't forget to add that any that went out of camp off—duty without permission would be punished as a deserter—and he won't, not even he, will give permission. There is just too much risk. The slaves might return."

Marcus gave a sigh and shrugged his shoulders. "Decide for yourself. In the end the choice is all yours, though it will wager your friendship with the governor. Tomorrow morning. Starting at the hour Quinta. Decide well. Think about Lucius too," he said. "And get some sleep. You look like a dead possum. Deader than Lucia," he muttered.

"I don't know. I might be selfish, but it is too much for me. I will tell Lucius when the turmoil in me gets less."

Marcus turned to leave. "Think well. Do not become the prey of Nemesis, the goddess of revenge," he said as he walked away.

There were only a few hours left to the funeral. Octavius was still lying on his bed, staring at the ceiling. He was still deciding. He couldn't make out what he really wanted. Even if he wanted to go, he was not sure if he could for the fear of becoming marked as a deserter.

Yesterday night he had greeted Suetonius and the tired cohorts— which tired him out in turn. He had organized everything from a whole new schedule for the tired cohorts to feeding and providing them a good sleep. After that he listened late into the night reports from Suetonius on how they had chased the slaves. The legate had been thrilled to tell it to the junior officer though he had not slept for the last twenty four hours. Glaber was already killed when they arrived, and they only managed to save a mere five hundred out of the three thousand. Some other five hundred, Suetonius speculated, had deserted. He had followed the slaves until his cohorts were too tired to chase any further and had planted spies and scouts to follow the trail of slaves. 'We would be able to get good information soon,' he had said.

❖

People wore dark tunics. They cried. They sang mourning tunes. The body was on top of the stakes ready for cremation. The body, rubbed by incense, still carried an aura of dignity. The governor stood in the front, next to the pile of stakes while two women wept bitterly. One was the mother, people could see, and the other was dressed like a slave— maybe a personal tutor.

"Marcus, no sign of them?" the governor whispered, and Marcus shook his head. He had been hoping to see his son. In fact, he had thought that his son would come for sure. It turned out that he was mistaken.

"They'll be busy. They are fighting the slaves," Marcus said softly. Maximus sighed, putting his head into his cupped hands. Marcus felt pity as he saw the once glamorous man standing dejected before him. The Capuan revolt, the warnings of the senate, the death of Lucia, it was getting all too much for him. Marcus thought that Maximus' head had grown whiter over the few months. The governor had lost all his charisma and looked like a fragile empty shell ready to break at the slightest disruption.

"You don't know the feeling," Maximus groaned, his voice barely above a whisper. Marcus just stood, not knowing how to reply. He perked his head up as the bells tolled, signaling the hour Quinta. The funeral would begin.

People whispered among themselves as a young man appeared suddenly. He had been standing on the edge of the crowd, but he was pushing to get in and people snarled at his attempt.

"Where are your manners?" one whispered to him just above a whisper. The young man ignored it and continued to push his way. A girl screamed as the man stepped on her foot. The young man muttered an apology and continued. He was now close enough to see the body.

People saw as the man lifted his hands in prayer and followed his gaze towards the body. The man stood still as if drinking the scene in. Then he muttered some words that could not be heard.

The man was not a priest, they were sure. He looked to be some mysterious itinerant traveler. He wore a hood over his face which made him look all the more mysterious. On his shoulders sat pads of fur to ease the bitter wind.

"Who are you? This is a place for those who knew her," somebody said in the crowd, careful to keep her voice down so that it did not interrupt the voice of the governor who was narrating.

"I knew her," the man answered simply. The tall figure stood still, staring intently at the body.

"Do I know you?" the woman continued. The man ignored her.

With a last mourning word, the governor lit the flames, and the wood burned with crackle. The flames soon reached the body and covered it entirely. The man's gaze did not leave the pyre until the flames had gone out from lack of fuel.

The solemn crowd gave a mourning sound. People watched as the tall man began to weep softly. They gathered to see the man, but he did not seem to care.

"Strangers cannot see this," one said. The young man seemed oblivious to the surroundings around him. When he finally arose again, he was watching the smoke go up from the pyre. The body was of no more.

I loved your former self, he heard a voice. *A voice he faintly recognized as Lucia's.*

Did you? he answered back, not even thinking about what he was doing.

Yes. Go back to it. Don't feel sorry for me.

I feel sorry for myself.

(Gentle laughter)

I've revenged you.

There was no need for that.

Yes, there was.

No, there wasn't. Just win the war. Achieve your dream.

What dream?

Of becoming a famous general and politician. Of becoming a consul. Don't be surprised. It was kind of obvious.

I love you.

You're funny. Remember, don't become a slave of revenge.

But I can't help thinking about you.

Think all you want, but don't become caught up in me. The past is the past. You've got a whole lot of left before you.

It's not as easy as it looks. I've tried to get back to my normal state but it is difficult. I keep seeing you; covered in blood…I'm sorry.

No need to be sorry. How's this? All your mourning stresses me out. If you want to make me happy, you should stop that. Get

*some sleep, as your father said. Stop crying. I hate it when
somebody pities me like that.*

They took your ring.

I know.

I'll get it back and put it with you. I swear to that.

Don't get heated up. Why aren't you telling my brother?

He won't be able to take it. I won't either.

He'll find out anyway and when he does he'll be furious.

Doesn't matter. How am I talking to you? Am I sane?

(Laughter the sound of pearls) Why haven't you made a speech?

I told you, I can't stand it.

My father, your father— they were disappointed.

Doesn't matter.

What matters to you?

You. My family. The war. My career. My friends.

*Then have good luck with those who have not left you yet. And
good luck with your career too. I'll be watching. Before I go,
promise me you will return to your normal state.*

It's hard. Very difficult. I've tried several times before.

No, you haven't. At least, not in earnest. Promise me, please.

All right. I promise. Wait.

Good bye. Remember, I loved your former self.

Wait!

People watched as the man's moony eyes regained its sharpness. He had a look of determination on his partly covered face. They stepped back, not daring to get in his way.

⸎

Octavius cursed as he neared the wall. Before, he had been able to sneak out after sending away the door sentries and the front wall sentries on some petty errand. By doing so, he had escaped without being noticed. The wall was manned now with trained soldiers who would not hesitate to arrest and send him to Suetonius. Even though they were loyal to him, they were also loyal to Suetonius and the legion laws.

He thought about faking the guard that he had been on a duty, but there was too big a risk. The guard would probably sense that something was up for all officers on duties informed the guards before leaving. There was no other sensible way. He drew his hood completely around him and approached the gates.

"Halt!" a voice sounded above, to no surprise. "Address yourself," the voice commanded.

"Open the door," he said.

"I will not repeat my question again." With that, he

waved at the legionaries around him who drew their bows.

For the first time Octavius regretted the fact that his legionaries were so well trained.

"I want to see Tribune Gnaeus Octavius Lupus. Where is he?"

"None of your business. But he's here. Address yourself now or I'll call for the archers."

Octavius closed his eyes and let out a big sigh. He might be able to make it. Nobody yet knew that he was absent.

"I want to see him and Centurion Titus Aemilius Lupus. It should only be a while. I have some urgent message for them from Capua, from Marcus Aurelius— a father to both of them. It is very personal."

"The Legate has banned all visitors. And don't order me," the sentry replied coldly. Octavius risked a look upwards and saw a centurion in full armor standing on top. Maybe things were more urgent than he had thought it was. It seemed as if Suetonius was preparing to receive a big assault. If Suetonius felt so, then the slaughter on Glaber's militia must have been ugly.

"It's very urgent. Only a minute will do. Please call them out. It's about the slaves," Octavius tried again.

"Then the Legate should hear about it. I'll call for him."

No, damn. Things were definitely not working out as he had hoped it would.

"No! As I said, there's some personal stuff too. Just call for Titus only. You'll regret it if you don't. If he ever finds out that you banned me from taking a message to him, he'll cut your head off," Octavius threatened with a smile. He risked another look and for the first time saw a confused and frightened expression on the man's face. Every one who had dueled with Titus would not want to mess with him.

The centurion hesitated. "The tribune, especially the tribune you requested for will prevent it. He's very righteous though he seems a bit shaken these days."

"Oh no, he won't."

"Don't aggravate me, messenger. There is a good chance that I might call for the arrows just yet."

Octavius laughed. "He won't prevent it, and I'm pretty sure about it," he replied. He shivered a bit. It was getting cold. "Just call for Titus, will you?"

The centurion seemed to consider it. After a long hesitation, he finally shrugged his shoulders.

"Your life. If the Legate catches you and Titus, I'm not responsible."

"Okay. Just call," Octavius answered. The centurion

spoke something to the man beside him, and the man went rushing off. Few moments later Titus came running out, frowning.

He came out towards Octavius, and his confused face changed into disbelief.

"What the..." then to the centurion, he said, "I know this man. He will be out in five minutes. Let him in."

The centurion obliged and opened the door widely for Octavius to enter. Octavius did so gladly.

"Get back in five minutes," the centurion said. Octavius looked at him with something of amusement.

They walked briskly to their tent where Octavius took off his dark tunic and replaced it with another tunic. Then he put his armor over it. He quickly hid the dark tunic and his cloak deep in his trunk. They were good clothes and it would be a shame to discard them. He'll start wearing them again after this commotion was forgotten.

He sat on his bed and looking at the bewildered face of Titus, he laughed out loud crazily. It had been quite a time since he had laughed that hard, and he felt great about it. Lucia said that she wanted him back to his normal state. He would give her that.

"You went?"

"Yes. And I feel pretty good now. Well, not good, but better. I might just make it, you know. Stop being angry at the slaves, at myself, at her... I was angry at everyone, at the gods too. Her death should not have been so meek," he said, after glancing around to make sure that Lucius was not in the tent. "I remember her. I love her. I think about her, but I won't live in revenge for her anymore— though it is proving to be more difficult than I had hoped it will be."

"How come you changed so suddenly?" Titus asked.

"You wouldn't believe me."

"Yes, I would," Titus replied. Octavius raised an eyebrow in his direction.

He lowered his voice before speaking. "She talked to me. Seriously, I'm not crazy, and it definitely was not a figment of my imagination. She said that she wants me back to my normal state, before I learned of her death. It's difficult. Very. But I love her enough to try."

Titus stayed still for a moment before speaking slowly. "That's good. I was afraid that you might not be able to recover," Titus said, chuckling gently. "Yeah, I worried. By the way, what are you going to do now? The centurion would be wondering."

Octavius smiled. "Follow me. It is past five minutes and

he'll be crazy."

Titus grunted but followed Octavius out of the tent. It was good to see him so cheerful and alive. He had had the eyes of a dead fox before, but today he had regained the sparkle that had always shown in his eyes before Lucia's death.

Octavius led Titus to a rampart where the centurion was waiting impatiently. The centurion spotted them, and he rushed over to them.

"Sir," he said addressing Octavius. "There was a young man who had been looking for you. Have you met him?"

Octavius nodded his head casually. Titus greeted his fellow centurion and said that the man had bid them farewell minutes ago.

"He went this way. Didn't you see him? Maybe he's wandering around in the camp," Titus said casually, and the centurion's face turned gray.

"I can't let him loose around camp. The legate... if he knows," the centurion said.

"It's all right. I'll take care of it. I'm off duty," Octavius answered coolly, and the centurion's face lit up.

"You will, sir?"

"Yes."

"Thank you so much, sir," he said, genuinely looking relieved. Octavius shrugged to show that it was not much of a deal.

"Centurion, I came here because I wanted to ask you to do something. I thought hard about it, and I believe that there is no one but you to do it."

The centurion puffed himself at the praise. "Anything, sir."

"Good man. Go to the Vesuvius and scout every inch of it on foot. I want to know whether or not there are some remaining slaves there. Do it silently, and when you find one, capture him and report back immediately. On foot. No horses, remember. Take your century," he ordered, and the centurion looked crestfallen. "It's a big job. Do it well."

"No horses?" the centurion asked, feeling the freezing wind. They would have to spend the rest of their day marching and scouting the forest. The centurion saluted half—heartedly and turned to call to a group of his men. Before he left, Octavius called to him.

"Be back before midnight. I'll be up and waiting," Octavius said. He flashed a grin at Titus. "Don't stare at me like that. It's not as if I'm just asking him to go through an ordeal without purpose. I've wanted a team out there anyway and I have just found an adequate man. He's steady, despite of being inflexible and a bit rough— mannered. I like him, my next favorite centurion after you, Lucius and Caecilius. Don't you think?"

❧ 23 ❧

Octavius glanced at the sky. It was pitch black now, and Octavius began to worry slightly about the century he had sent to Vesuvius. They should be back by now, he decided, and climbed the ramparts to have a better view.

He walked over to where a soldier was standing in front of a torch, holding a spear, and almost laughed as he saw that the legionary's eyes were closed. He guessed that even the Roman training could not reverse a man's biorhythm, at least, yet.

Octavius stared at the man, amused. The man was nodding his head slightly, and the torch flames flickered slightly at his movement. He watched the man for a time before he heard a noise outside the walls.

The sound was a thudding sound of an army marching, though the sound was too small for it to be a fully fledged army. Octavius leaned across the ramparts, holding the torch out. He let out a small smile as he saw that the century was returning looking tired but safe.

"Centurion Germanicus. Open the door," the centurion called out in a loud voice and the dozing sentry jumped at the sound. He shook his head briefly and his mouth dropped in horror as he saw Octavius standing right next to him.

"What are you staring at? Open the door," Octavius told him and the man bobbed his head up and down. His eyes were still panicked as he kept glancing at Octavius to see if his dozing had been noticed.

"Yes, sir," he replied as smartly as he could before calling down to the sentries beneath the ramparts to open the gates. The order was carried out smoothly. Octavius grinned a vampire smile at the man before climbing down, and his smile broadened when he saw the man's face go ashen.

He greeted the centurion warmly as the centurion professionally began to report the remains of the slave camp—which were pretty well organized, and that there was no living soul left in the mountain. He had also found the route they had used to attack Glaber and did not hide his fascination at it. Octavius nodded his head, thanking him for his thorough search. The night was windy, and Octavius felt that he should reward his centurion more than just a 'nice job'. He handed the man a bag of denarii, telling him to share with his men. It'll be enough, Octavius said and the man's face lit up brightly at that.

⁘

Meanwhile, Varinius was enjoying himself in his friend's private bathhouse. He felt so cool bathing in the room, so normal to see people wear tunics instead of armor. All the dust that he had accumulated during his time in the legions had washed away, and he felt very cheerful for once.

His friend had invited him to his villa, and Varinius, happy to oblige, had followed the man to his house where he had had a nice dinner and was now relaxing his muscles in the bath. The hot water made him think about Crassus's private bathhouse, which was slightly better furnished than this house. Still, both were exemplary.

Crassus. Crassus had never given him any orders not to take a bath— it is something every general could do once in a while, right? And, the slaves have annihilated Glaber so they would probably not attack for a while, having had their share of blood, right?

Right, he answered his questions, closing his eyes. For a second, he thought he heard a boisterous noise outside, but the noise diminished so quickly that he decided to ignore it. Another noise, Varinius opened his eyes, alert for any traces of danger. The room was empty except for two legionaries and a slave who stood near the door.

The legionaries were calm, as if they had not heard the noise. He had pride and belief in his legionaries. He dunked his head into the water to refresh his head also. It turned out that dunking his head was the biggest mistake he had made in his life, because a person cannot hear well in the water—he cannot hear the sounds of battles nor screams.

"Sir, there is no one left in the outskirts of Vesuvius," Octavius said as he entered the command tent, shivering slightly in the winter night.

He walked in casually only to see a stony faced Suetonius. He froze on the spot and glanced at a cavalry legionnaire who was standing beside Suetonius. The man looked very grim.

Was it another battle? His questioning eyes landed on the eyes of the legate who apparently had been aroused from his sleep.

The legate indicated to a chair beside him. "Sit. I was

about to call for you anyway."

Octavius obeyed, taking his seat nervously. "What is it?" he asked quietly and for a long time Suetonius did not answer. Instead, he gestured at the legionnaire who stepped outside and walked in with another man.

Octavius gasped slightly at the man. The man's face was covered with grime, and only his clothes— or what was left of it— showed his rank as a Roman legionary. He had a long, ugly gap that ran across his cheek and several deep cuts in his arms which were still bleeding. The man looked faint from the blood loss, and Octavius noticed that the man was limping slightly.

Octavius turned his head toward Suetonius, expecting an answer.

Suetonius began with a sigh. "Varinius battled Spartacus. Varinius is a skilled veteran. He would have trained the soldiers like Mars himself. However, Spartacus's army had proliferated— like rats, and Varinius was taken completely by surprise, and so the man here believes that the odds are, or were, against Varinius—"

Octavius interfered. "It's not over yet. The Romans have a chance."

"Didn't you hear me?" Suetonius said, a little more sharply

than he had intended. "Were against Varinius. You see the man in front of you, a heavy infantry legionary from the seventh cohort. The battle is probably over now, so we can't even help," Suetonius said bitterly. He chewed his lips for a while before resuming.

"I can't blame the legion though. Varinius was not in the camp. Oh yeah. He was bathing when it all happened— bathing while Spartacus is at loose— and was caught half naked by the slaves. He managed to escape, all right, by racing his horse straight to his camp. What do you think happened?" Suetonius asked with much spite. Before Octavius could give an answer, Suetonius continued.

"So the slaves ravaged the camp also. If the bastard was even a little above an idiot he would have gone somewhere else to distract Spartacus. Instead he led them straight, straight, into the camp. The army of course was unprepared," Suetonius said, puffing out air. Octavius had never seen his commander look so vexed before.

"What will the senate do?" Octavius asked.

"They'll butcher the moron, who probably is still alive. I'll bet everything on the crafty fox. He loves his life too much. That's all the senate will do. They don't even think Spartacus as a threat. I wonder if they still think so now. We don't even have a permission to attack. We can't attack a single slave until they first kill our man or a Roman under our protection. Do you see how absurd this is Octavius? Hand me a parchment paper, will you? I'm going to write to Crassus. This whole thing is crazy."

<hr>

Spartacus gazed out at the ranks of his men. They were arranged in a Roman formation as they marched towards Nuceria. He was proud of them all. They had fought better than he had hoped them to fight. They had been loyal more than he had expected. They had been magnificent.

The slaves ravaged through the Roman lines slaughtering every soldier they could find. It was a massacre. Legionaries who were wearing only simple tunics were cut down as they hurriedly tried to escape. The officers gave up trying to command the soldiers after only a few minutes. Soldiers deserted. It had been chaos.

Spartacus still had to admire the officers. Even though they were all dead by night, they had relentlessly attacked the slaves— the gladiators. Instead of turning their backs, they fought until the end, hugely decreasing the gladiator numbers. His core group had been torn apart until he had ordered the mass of his army to concentrate on killing the officers. The officers, he had to admit, were one of the best. When they finally fell, they did not fall alone. They made sure to take at least one more gladiator with them before they died. It was this spirit of Rome that made him fear the Roman legions. It was this, he pondered, which had been the basis of becoming a large country.

To his regret, Varinius had survived. The man had disappeared—it was the only thing that had not gone according to plan. His running away half naked had become a great joke between the slaves.

"Crixus?" he said.

"Yes?"

"We were just incredible. We beat them. The Roman legions," Spartacus said, laughing gently.

"Told you they were easy. Did I tell you that Lucius was in the legion that beat me?" Crixus asked, silently regretting that he had brought up his loss again. Spartacus did not seem to mind.

Spartacus looked at him in surprise. "He was? Then Octavius must be in the legions too. They're always together," he said. Then, after a few minutes of silence, he continued. "I sort of feel sorry for trying to kill Octavius.

He was a nice boy. I do believe his story of being held up by the governor. He would have kept his promise, Lucius, too. They are both a man of his word. I'm glad that Octavius survived."

Crixus nodded. "Maybe. But I don't like Lucius. I've never seen Octavius but I guess he'll also be the typical patrician brat. I just abhor them. Just a question, Spartacus. If you ever meet them in battle, will you kill them?"

Spartacus was silent for such a long time that Crixus thought that his question had not been heard. He was about to repeat his question when Spartacus answered.

"No."

"What?"

"No. I won't. They've been good friends—saving my other friends. They have saved me from committing suicide," Spartacus said.

"I guess I had been kind of rash after losing Jacob. They helped me more than they realize. It is not manly to kill them just because they had not shown up in one game. I owe them a lot. I won't kill them unless I really have to, and I hope that time never comes."

⋅⋅❖⋅⋅

Crassus held onto the letter from Suetonius with sweaty hands. One of his legions had been destroyed. He frowned as Cato rose to speak.

"I believe that this fault all lies in Crassus. He did not train and equip them enough," Cato began.

"It is not. This letter says that Varinius was bathing when it happened. Varinius is responsible. Are you going to argue that it is me who is responsible? That I should have been there to tell him 'Don't wash yourself?' Glaber was destroyed and so was Varinius, and I am not blaming you for Glaber's loss because I knew that man was going to lose from the start. The slaves—those dogs—are not to be taken lightly—" Crassus was interrupted by a large stomp.

"I was speaking of some important matters here," Cato began again.

"You were speaking shit."

"Stop! Senator Crassus, watch the language or I'll have you go out of this room," a consul said, restoring order. Both senators glared at each other before Cato spoke again.

"As I was saying before I was so rudely interrupted, this is the fault of Crassus. He is not such a great military commander. He has never fought any big war since he helped Sulla, and that was a long time ago. I believe that we should punish him along with Varinius," Cato said.

"Senators," Crassus said, after checking that Cato was finished. "A letter has arrived to me from Legate Suetonius. He says that he has helped Glaber's militia though they were too late to bring victory. However, they still had managed to save the lives of several hundreds. If Glaber had not been defeated, Spartacus would never have had a chance to defeat Varinius. Am I not correct?" he asked and was satisfied by the nods around the room, both enthusiastic and reluctant.

"Then who had insisted on Glaber and a militia in the first place? Cato. Who was it that said that the slaves were not much threat? Cato. If he had only listened to me, I would have stationed my legions at the foot of the Vesuvius and would have starved them up there or would have wiped them out. My legions are perfectly capable. Two cohorts led by Tribune Octavius Lupus slaughtered a large group of raiders. The legion commanded by Mummius succeeded in restoring order to Doria. Do you doubt their ability?" he asked once more and many shook their heads. "It was Cato who had banned me from the right to command an attack. If we should blame anyone here for being responsible, then it should be Cato. If he, no you, my senators, would permit me, then I am sure that I can manage to beat the slaves. The slaves are not to be regarded lightly. I have two legions that are young but capable. They will be able to beat the slaves. The slaves' number has reached about four thousand and is rapidly growing not to mention that they are currently ravaging through Roman cities with almost no resistance. Right now, they are heading north, perhaps in the direction of Nuceria." He took a deep breath.

"Nuceria?" one senator cried, interrupting.

"I have a mansion there!" another cried in a horrified voice.

"The Nucerians would be able enough to protect themselves. Surely, Crassus, you would have the sense —" Cato started.

"I was speaking of some important matters here," Crassus snapped, smiling. "My point is not Nuceria. It is that we should take this revolt seriously, and that my legions are perfectly suited for this job."

"So you'll be asking for more legions to command? You'll be asking for a replacement of your devastated legion, am I not correct?" Cato interrupted, his eyes mocking.

Crassus smiled, a genuine smile.

"No. I'll be asking for praetura— praetorship, the right to command any Roman legion."

24

"Absurd!" Cato yelled in shock.

"Senators, I ask you to vote for me. If you give me the praetorship, I will do my best to bring down the rebellion," Crassus said, his voice full of passion.

The senators stayed still. Crassus began to sweat as he realized that they were not saying anything. He broke out in cold sweat and was relieved when a distant cheering came from a corner. The cheering soon spread out through the senate walls.

"But Crassus—"

"This matter is urgent Cato. Rome needs to act fast. This is aside from politics. I hope you know that," Arrius spoke out in a flat tone. Cato looked at the man. He gave a sigh. There was nothing much he could do against Arrius. Something about the man made him uncomfortable. His eyes were always darting around, scheming.

The consul clapped his hands for attention. "We shall take a vote. Show up your hands. Those who are for it," he declared. Crassus smiled as he saw the majority of hands go up. "Those who are against," the consul called and a few men and a sullen looking Cato raised their hands. Crassus gave a smile of triumphant victory.

"As a consul," the one who had called for a vote said. "I shall give him the command of six Roman legions plus your current two." The other consul nodded his head, casting a fleeting glance at Arrius. It was not hard to guess who had been very influential over this matter.

Crassus stood. He held his head high proudly and met the gaze of the other senators. "Senators, thank you. I pledge that as a praetor, I shall defeat Spartacus. I shall make an example of him to ensure that there will be no revolts like this any more. I shall make it so that when slaves born a century later hear about this revolt, they will shiver and plead to the gods that nothing like this would ever happen again. The people of Rome shall cheer for the victory while her enemies shall cower at the name of Rome. For Rome!" he said passionately and a cheer filled the room again.

Crassus exited the building feeling tremendous of himself.

He had done it. He was a praetor, technically a prelude before a consul. He hoped that his legions were shaping up well. It had taken a fortune to equip, train, and scout the best officers. He hoped that even with the slaves' numbers still growing he would be able to stamp the rebellion as easily as he had promised the senators.

Spartacus spotted Nuceria's walls. They were totaling over four thousand now including those who were not capable of fighting. Children, women and old people joined the column. Those who could not fight on field pledged that they would take care of all the army's supplies. Though he had been skeptical at first, Spartacus gladly agreed when he heard that. He had actually been worrying about the supplies which were getting harder to find. There were just too many of the slaves, and rapidly growing.

The slaves lined up facing Nuceria's walls. Civilians looked worriedly back at them, and the soldiers who manned the walls also looked uncomfortable. Spartacus flashed a grin at the soldiers and turned to face his own column.

"Ladies and gentlemen," he addressed. "We are now at

Nuceria. Once this city falls into our hands, we would have a steady supply line. We would be able to win the legions that come at us and break for Gaul where our freedom, our families lie." A cheer rose.

"The time of victory is at hand. But remember one thing, my soldiers. We are called barbarians and slaves because we are less disciplined than their so called legions. I do agree, though, that we are less disciplined, and discipline often marks an army's success. Are you wiling to go on a stronger discipline?" he asked and many heads nodded.

"Good. My first plea is to listen to the orders handed out by the generals. They know how the battle is going, better than a single soldier. Please follow their orders without question and no personal actions. The next is, do not, never ever plunder," he said, and a gasp rose. Some murmurs of protest came out, and Spartacus sighed. His army still had a lot to go if it wanted to be a real army. Real armies did not plunder unless the general gave the word.

"Plundering is banned. We are not barbarians. This is my ultimate order. Kill the soldiers. Kill anyone who goes up against you, but save the lives of those who surrender. Never harm the children, women and the elderly. Those who do I shall punish them personally. Is this clear?" he said with a stern face. He had his doubts though. The slaves looked at him in both disappointment and confusion. He was not sure if they would obey his command on not plundering. He hoped they would, for their own sake.

The legionaries stared nervously down at them and flinched slightly when Spartacus's army cheered. The slave army ran towards Nuceria's gates, slamming it with a battering ram that they had made a few hours earlier. The gates creaked at each impact, threatening to give away. Legionaries poured arrows to the slaves killing every time not because of their good marksmanship, but because there were simply too many slaves. Some civilians threw down heavy rocks at the slaves smashing some underneath, surprising Spartacus. He had estimated their victory with only a few casualties, but the Nucerians were resisting more than he had first predicted. He knew, and they knew that they could not beat his army. There were just too much of his followers. Still, they were fighting, and Spartacus felt a little respect for them.

He watched on as slaves continuously banged the gate. The gate's edges were giving slowly. More slaves helped to crack the door. Finally, gate gave a large moan and opened with a big boom. As soon as the slaves understood that the gate had been opened, they rushed into the city with a war cry… and dispersed.

Spartacus frowned. They should have been waiting in three columns inside the wall. Instead, his men had scattered. He galloped his horse into the gates and saw with dismay that two houses were already on fire. Streets were filled with screams, and legionaries who came down from the ramparts were slain without mercy.

"Stop!" he yelled at a group of slaves who were stealing jewelry out of a house. A man who looked like the father followed them out of the house and was killed. His wife let out a scream and rushed over to the fallen body where she too was butchered by one of the slaves.

"Stop. Stop it, now!" he yelled, racing his horse over to them.

"General," one said, looking up from his booty. He flashed an apologetic smile and held up a gold ring. "Would you like to have one?" he asked.

Spartacus struck the man's face so hard that he fell down. "Didn't you hear me?" he asked in a whisper.

"General, please," the man groaned out.

"The rest of you. Didn't you hear me also? I said no plundering. Go tell your other comrades to stop this! Go!"

he screamed at them, and they scuttled away to obey him—
or so he hoped.

Spartacus gazed at the fallen man. "Go put the jewelry
back," he ordered.

The man looked at him and actually laughed. "But then
others will take it anyway. It's better that I just safe keep it—"
Suddenly, he was cut off. The last thing he knew in his life
was that he tasted blood. And that his commander had just
cut his throat.

<hr>

It had been quite a while before he had managed to stop
the plundering, but he had succeeded. Many civilians had
made it through.

He had taken all the money out of richer patricians and
was distributing the money to the plebeians.

"People of Nuceria, listen to me. I have not come here to
slaughter, nor to plunder. I came here, just so that I can
borrow this city for the winter. As long as you do not
mutiny against my army, you will all survive. Merchants
would be allowed to leave the city and trade," he said, and
looked at the silent mass. He continued, an even more
shocking proposal.

"The money that has been looted from the rich would be equally distributed amongst the poor." Slaves, Nucerians, both the rich and the poor stared at him in disbelief. It was something unprecedented. "And more, those who feel that this republic has some serious problems are free to join. Impoverished farmers, freedmen, slaves, we would welcome you with open arms. For the patricians…we might let them join too. After all, we shouldn't discriminate people based on their classes, right?" Spartacus said and looked around as peals of laughter rose, mostly from the slaves. However, he also noticed some Romans smiling at that comment. He nodded to himself as some people of the crowd stepped out to be recruited. He began to think that there might be some hope in this after all. The rotten republic was shaking from its roots. They might win the war.

72B.C.

"General Crassus! General Crassus!" the legions cried. All eight legions had assembled and had created a long aisle in the middle for Crassus. Crassus nodded to the men as he marched through the aisle briskly. They hailed him, saluting as he passed. His helmet, which had a conspicuous plume, rested a little crooked on his head. He also wore a crimson cape that marked him as the top commander. Crassus's stern face surveyed the men around him and stopped casually when he spotted Suetonius and Octavius standing together in front of the Third. They were standing up straight, giving a more military look to them.

"I heard that your legion did a good job on the slaves," he commented.

"Thank you, sir," Suetonius replied smartly.

Crassus smiled. "Tribune Octavius?" he addressed his nephew, in which his nephew saluted.

"I know the job you did on the pack of raiders. It's quiet a talk in Rome."

Octavius's face colored a little. "Yes, sir," he responded, and Crassus nodded encouragingly at him. He went on to speak to the commanders of other legions, encouraging them.

Finally, after what seemed like forever, Crassus made it to the end of the aisle. Once he did so, the legions moved into squares, their armors reflecting sunlight. Crassus smiled to himself as he rose up the stairs of the makeshift platform.

"My legions," he addressed. They cheered in response. "As a praetor, I vow to you that I, no, you will destroy the slave army. The slaves have beaten other Roman legions before— but not us. We are different. After a few weeks we shall leave to affront them and show them the might of our legions. Are you ready to follow me?" he asked in a loud, commanding voice, and a wave of yes hit him. He stared at his legions with a pleased smile. At last, he had his own, proved legions and more, he had six other legions at his command. His power was almost complete. All he needed to do now was to win the war... and it would be perfect.

He stepped down from the platform, and the legions hurried to make an aisle for him again. They saluted him once more as he passed, and Crassus returned their salutes.

"Hail General Crassus!" they cried. "Hail the legates!" they said again, each naming their own legates. Octavius closed his eyes as his legion cried, "Hail Legate Suetonius! General Suetonius!" They cheered boisterously, and he knew that this exact moment, the war had started— for real.

72B.C.~71B.C.

Part 3

The War

"No one defies Rome"- Crassus

∾ 25 ∾

Crixus gritted his teeth as he killed another civilian. They were raiding again, contrary to Spartacus's orders. He just could not understand Spartacus. It was their ultimate chance to take revenge on those who had done wrong to them before. He still remembered the malicious face of the Romans as they smiled with glee as they saw gladiators killing another. They clapped if you killed the nastiest way you could think of. They laughed at how the loser died.

He stabbed the dying man again in uncontrollable fury as he thought about the blood thirsty Romans. His head snapped up as he heard a cry for help. It was Oenomaus. A few surviving legionaries were attacking him, and he was flailing in the middle of the legionnaires in complete panic.

Spartacus valued Oenomaus's opinion over his. Spartacus always implied that his opinion was too rash. Oenomaus was becoming the real second in command these days, and he was just a sword to help Spartacus kill the 'unnecessary' men. He shook his head angrily. He had wanted to be in complete command, but he had to give it up to the more talented—that he admitted—Spartacus. There was no way he would give up being the deputy. That was pushing him too far. His gaze wandered around and saw that everyone was busy in raiding goods and slaughtering people. Nobody was watching him.

His eyes met Oenomaus's, and Oenomaus called for help again, his eyes suddenly bright with hope. The three legionaries were attacking him from all sides, and Crixus knew Oenomaus would not stand for long. He moved a step to help Oenomaus and stopped. If it were not for that man, he would be the sole deputy. He stared at the helpless Oenomaus. The man looked at him for help, his green eyes pleading. Crixus smiled at him and gave a gracious bow…to bid him farewell to the afterlife.

Oenomaus's eyes grew large, and his face twisted in betrayal as he collapsed on to the ground. His dead eyes still stared at him, but Crixus felt no remorse at what he had done.

Spartacus sat dejected on a big, flat stone, high up in a rock mound, his face in his arms. Crixus sat next to him, staring at the bloody sun that shone its last lights over the devastated city.

"Why won't you and the rest of the army just listen to me? Is plundering that fun? Is bragging that we are barbaric and uneducated that enjoyable? Look at the innocent who died today. They were butchered without a cause just because they were Romans."

"Sometimes that's a disadvantage," Crixus murmured.

"I don't care, Crixus. The command structure is being ruined. At least a fourth of the army doesn't listen to me. I really wish that they would just go off somewhere. Don't say this to anybody, Crixus. Anyway, I want my army to have a lot of men, but I think that those who do not follow orders are more useful gone," Spartacus said, groaning. He still had not gotten over the loss of Oenomaus. He had made a funeral pyre for him and had given the man a sincere funeral. Oenomaus had been a steady friend who he could always rely on.

Crixus remained still. There was nothing to say unless… he brightened. "Spartacus, I have a good idea. If a big Roman army engulfs us, we would all be dead in a single blow. But if we split up, then we have less chance of being dead in just one blow, right?" he asked enthusiastically and Spartacus nodded his head calmly. "What if I take the fourth that you don't want and lead them?"

Spartacus's head snapped towards him. "Split up? But what about me? Oenoamus is dead. If you go away—"

"You'll still do well without my advice," Crixus said coldly, and Spartacus shut up. He knew what Crixus was referring to. To be honest, Crixus did not offer such good advice. The man was too full of spite. However, letting Crixus go away alone would mean that he was sending Crixus to his death. He knew just what Crixus would do. He would sack towns until he met the Roman army... and would be crushed.

But he also needed to get rid of those who would not listen to his command. They did more harm than good, and Spartacus knew that once the command chain broke, the army would break up— to the joy of the Romans. He could not allow that.

"Crixus, are you sure that you will not regret this? Next week we'll head for Gaul, and I really do want you at my side. We have enough men to do that, eighty thousand now, grown so much in six months, compared to forty thousand

Romans. Anyways, you are now my oldest friend since we were together at Batiatus's gladiator school. And... I don't want you dead."

"I won't regret it. And I'll always remember you. We can split up tomorrow morning. I'll be alive," Crixus said, in higher spirits than he had been in for days. Spartacus looked at his friend. Crixus was serious about this.

The fourth of the army, were they really more useful gone? Were they? He had been thinking about this issue for weeks now, but still, losing a fourth of their force would be fatal.

Spartacus hugged Crixus. "Are you really sure?" he said, wishing for a no.

Crixus nodded firmly as he hugged back. "I am. You won't stop me, will you?" he asked.

Spartacus stayed still for a while. "No," he said at last, still unsure. The command structure and the numbers, which were more important? "If that's what you really want," he responded tentatively. "I'll see you?" he asked, making it a question.

Crixus nodded. "Unless one of us dies. Wish you luck, Spartacus," he said with a smile. He patted his friend on the back and rose to descend the rocks. He flashed a long grin towards Spartacus, and Spartacus looked at Crixus sadly. He had lost two valuable men in just a few days.

Crixus leaped with joy. He was now going to be in complete command over thousands of soldiers. They would listen to him, and he would lure them with riches from the most luxurious towns. More and more would flock over to him.

Nobody would now deny that he was the full commander of a few legion forces. Spartacus had seemed genuinely sad to see him go, but it didn't matter. All that mattered was that he was going to be in full command now. He thanked all gods he could think of and went into a well furnished patrician house that he had chosen for himself. He felt that today had been a wonderful day overall.

$$\sim 26 \sim$$

Crassus pointed to a red mark on the map and looked around to see if the officers agreed with him. The slave force had split up, to his delight, and now he could engage them one by one and destroy them completely. Spartacus's army was heading north while Crixus's was still in the southern part, raiding the rich towns there. Most likely he would have grown fat on Roman blood from those cities and would be easier to take down than Spartacus.

"Spartacus has seen Roman blood a few times as a commander but not Crixus. We take out Crixus, and then we fight Spartacus," he added, and the officers present all nodded their assent.

Crassus spotted Octavius sitting next to Suetonius and smiled at him before continuing. "I would love to show the arrogant slave our full force, but unfortunately, we can't. If all of us leave southwards, there will be no legion to stand between the slave and Rome, and we cannot let it happen," he said, and paused. He glanced at the legates who stared at him in anticipation. They wanted blood, and he would give it to them.

"Gellius," he called to a legate sitting beside him. The man was a known fighter and a senior commander. "Your legion and Suetonius's legion are to go defeat Crixus. You are in command," he said, searching the men for reactions. Gellius gave a slaute and looked about proudly. Suetonius assented with the opinion also, with a calm smile. He showed no signs of jealousy that a more ambitious man might have shown. Crassus patted himself on the back for placing Octavius in Suetonius's legion where Octavius could perform more than his original tribune posting. Suetonius's love for Octavius and his un—ambitious mind helped Octavius to act almost as a legate, something that would be useful in the future.

"The rest of us shall wait here and engage Spartacus if necessary," he concluded, again pointing to the red mark on the map. "Gellius, you start the march today. Be back quickly. I don't want to meet Spartacus with only six legions." Gellius nodded and Crassus looked at him with pleasure. "Dismissed," he called and the legates rose to leave.

As they left, Crassus signaled Octavius to stay. "I'm so proud of you," Crassus said, smiling. "You managed to defeat Crixus once, you shall do so again. Go do something memorable, all right?"

Octavius smiled. "Yes...General," he responded awkwardly. He had never called his uncle a general before. Crassus laughed heartily at that and clapped his nephew on the back. Octavius thought Crassus was inwardly very much pleased at his new title.

"Are you scared?" he asked.

"No," Octavius replied earnestly.

"Good," Crassus said. "Because Roman politics is bloodier."

Octavius strode out of the command tent pondering about the brewing war with Lucia's murderer, Crixus. He hated Crixus more than anybody, and he vowed that he would make Crixus pay for the death.

Titus would be thrilled at the news of engagement. He was a real soldier, and he had been complaining about the lack of activities lately. All the officers did was to talk among themselves, he said, which Octavius also agreed. He too was bored of their endless conferences.

He first found Titus occupied with a dice gambling game, partly hidden in a corner of a tent. He was cheering when Octavius spotted him. The soldiers all rose to their feet awkwardly when they saw him, occasionally casting worried glances at the dice littered on the ground. Crassus had ordered gambling to be banned.

Titus was one of the last to spot him, occupied with his victory. "Tribune," he addressed slyly. He had a mischievous grin on his face and showed Octavius a small bundle that made jingling noises when shook. Octavius rolled his. He nodded casually to the other legionaries, pretending not to notice the game, who saluted back uncomfortably.

"Get ready to march. We are going south," he told them briefly before heading away, indicating for Titus to follow, leading Titus away to their tent.

"We're marching?" Titus asked, brightening up.

"Yes. To defeat Crixus," he said, and Titus grinned.

"Finally," he said. Then his face grew serious as he faced Octavius. Octavius has seen the face only a few times before, and looked back at him worriedly. Something told him that Titus was about to tell him something very unpleasant. And unpleasant it was.

Titus took a deep breath. "There's a rumor."

"What?"

"The scout. Remember the scout who first reported the death of Lucia?" Titus said. The words hit him like a blow. He had managed to forget her death, but nobody was trying to make it easy for him. "He has spread a rumor that you like her—that you even cried a little when you heard about her death. He even knows the name—Lucia."

Octavius stopped walking. "The bastard," he cursed, his face suddenly redder than a tomato. "Counter—rumor it," he told Titus, but Titus shook his head.

"That's not my point. Many don't believe it and even if they do, they don't take any serious meaning to it. I mean, they understand you and your reputation is fine. But the problem is that Lucius has heard about it," he said slowly, carefully choosing his words.

Octavius dropped his jaw. "No. Gods, no," he uttered. He felt his mouth going dry. "What did you say to him?" he asked urgently.

"I didn't. I wasn't there. I know because other soldiers told me that he was yelling 'Lucia' like a crazy man. He was also looking for you."

"Go pack up. I don't have time for this now. We march," Octavius ordered, his face paling. He had been a fool. He should have known that he could not hide the fact forever. He needed time to think on how he should handle it. He also needed time for Lucius to calm down before they met.

Octavius walked inside his tent, tired after the long march. During the march, he had thought about what to and how to tell the story to Lucius. He had to admit, he had been selfish, but he had done it to prevent the breakdown of both Lucius and himself. Maybe he should have told it to Lucius, be frank with it all, and then should have left it up to him to recover the mental wound, like he himself had done. It might have been better, but it was too late to fix that.

He was about to take off his armor when a pale hand grabbed him from the behind. He veered around, unsheathing his gladius, ready to protect himself from the assailant. It was Lucius.

"Lucius?" he asked, carefully sheathing his sword again.

Lucius continued to glare at him, his eyes burning of a cold fire. "Is it true?" he rasped out.

Octavius dropped his head. "I'm sorry. I should have told you before. I thought that it would be the best for both you and me if I broke the news gently, when you could, when I could take it—"

"You hid it all from me? What about her funeral? Why weren't there any messages or letters about her? Don't tell me that you censored them, or I'm going to..." Lucius took in a deep breath before continuing. He trembled slightly before turning his cold eyes on Octavius. "You knew and didn't tell me? I've been your friend all your life and you don't tell me? Is that how you treat your friends?"

"I'm sorry, Lucius, I really am. My intentions were good."

Lucius did not stop, however. He was too enraged to do so. "You scum," he whispered. "All you are is a selfish little boy wrapped up in his own shell thinking that he is so great. You shouldn't have proposed to her. You would have made her life miserable."

Octavius glared back at his friend. "Stop this whole thing. You are crossing the line. I said I was sorry."

"You aren't fit for anything," Lucius continued, not heeding the warning. "Not fit to love her," he repeated, knowing that it antagonized Octavius. "Not fit for your post. What is so different between you and me so that you become a tribune and I a centurion? Am I so inferior? All you've got is your heritage and a minor victory. You think you can succeed with that minor victory?"

"It wasn't minor, Lucius, and you admitted that. Stop it. I thought you wanted to hear my apology and then talk about her?" Octavius said through gritted teeth. Although he felt apologetic for Lucius about hiding the part of information from him— he could imagine the surge of betrayal that Lucius might be feeling at the moment— but Lucius was really crossing the line. He was hurting his pride, too much.

"Both," Lucius muttered, and shoved his face near Octavius's. Octavius took advantage of his height and leered back. The situation was soon broken by the cheerful Titus who walked into the tent without heeding the situation.

"Hey guys," he said, and stopped in mid—sentence after seeing the tension between Octavius and Lucius.

"Hey, hey," Titus called, splitting the two apart by force. They did as Titus willed, and yet they continued to glare at each other. "Guys, I have a feeling that I know what this is about. Lucia?" he asked, but no one answered him.

Lucius took a step towards Octavius and Titus placed himself in between the two. "No crossing lines, Lucius. There's a time to stop for everything, and that is now.

"How...did she die?" Lucius suddenly asked.

"She was killed by a hail of arrows, fired by the slaves.

Crixus included. Ten in all," Octavius responded, wincing at the memory.

"When?"

"Before the fight," Octavius said, his eyes growing distant.

Lucius whipped his moony glaze towards Octavius. "Before the fight? That means that she was killed…"

"When riding beside the forest," Titus concluded for him.

"How? How's that possible? She was in our barracks," Lucius asked, thoroughly confused.

Titus shook his head. "She said that she must be going. So I let her go with two legionaries—"

"She said that she must be going, and you let her? When you plainly knew that a raiding group was in the forest, ready to mount a raid on Capua? Didn't you even think about the consequences it would bring?" Lucius asked, seething, his venom directed at Titus now.

"I never imagined—"

"You should have," Lucius said, his eyes half—mad by now. Octavius also saw Titus's eyes glint dangerously at Lucius's words. He tried to pull Titus back before the two could fight, but as soon as he was about to grab for Titus, Lucius lunged at Titus.

Titus pushed Lucius away, grunting at the effort. Lucius stumbled, but he came back with an even more vicious looking face, snatching his gladius out from the holster. Titus groped for his sword but cursed as he realized that he had unbelted his gladius. Octavius came to his aid, blocking the initial blow with his own gladius. He winced as his arm absorbed the weight of Lucius's blow.

"Stop," Octavius ordered forcefully, but before anyone could react, Lucius swung his sword again, his eyes filled with something of madness.

At that moment, Octavius felt something.

Excruciating pain.

He screamed in agony as Lucius's gladius bit into his left arm. A long gash formed, and for a while it was numb before throbbing in a way that he had never felt before. He clutched the wound, watching as blood seeped through his fingers, falling like raindrops on the floor.

Eyes filled with shock, shock at the notion that Lucius would ever hurt him in such a way, he stared back at his old friend, unbelieving. Lucius stared back, the rage gone out of his eyes, instead filled with realization, realization of at finally understanding what he had done. The two gaped at each other for a few seconds more, both being too stunned to say anything. Then, Lucius's lips grew into a firm, straight line as he sharply sheathed his gladius and stalked out of the tent. Two pairs of eyes followed his movement intently, nobody saying anything.

None of them moved until Octavius let out a low groan and unclenched his hand from the wound. The blood had coagulated, but it didn't stop from hurting.

"Are you going to let him go?" Titus asked quietly.

"What do you mean?" Octavius answered, his voice cracking.

"What are you going to do to Lucius?" he asked again, his face hard.

Octavius did not respond, instead staring at a long gash on his left arm. The wound throbbed like crazy, though it was far better off than before, when it had felt like a fire razing through his body.

"Are you not going to do anything?" Titus prodded.

"What do you want me to do?"

"To report the fight."

"And?"

"And let him get what he deserves," Titus said without any trace of sympathy. Lucius had betrayed his trust once, and he knew he would never completely trust the man again.

Octavius glanced down at the long gash again. Clumps of blood hung to it and now a sickly fluid was coming out. Octavius was silent for minutes before he spoke again. "What he deserves, Titus, and I want to be very clear about this," Octavius took a long breath before continuing. "What he deserves is a sincere apology."

Titus's opened his mouth to protest. "You can't be partial to him. He's hurt you once, he can do it again."

"No. I would have done the same thing if I had been in the same situation. He was rash, but I was the one who gave him the reason to behave so. There is no need for further argument on this point, Titus," Octavius said, his face grim and determined. "He would be regretting what he had done."

"If you are so partial, the command structure—"

"This has nothing to do with the command structure. This is strictly private. It's finished. Forget about this. Understand? Finished," Octavius interrupted.

The two were silent for a while again, Titus glaring at Octavius and Octavius pretending not to notice Titus's glare, gazing at the wound.

Finally, Titus sighed, slumping slightly. "Fine. You win.

But this doesn't mean that I have to be amiable toward him too."

"Understood," Octavius answered coolly.

"Then go get that wound treated at least."

"What should I say to the doctor?"

Titus rolled his eyes. "You can't lie to him. Even I can see that the wound could not have been made with anything other than a sword. Tell him that you had a slight disagreement and shut him up. He's a pretty trustable guy. He won't tell if you speak convincingly."

Octavius nodded, rising. "Right."

27

Arrius irritably rolled up the parchment paper and gave it to one of his slaves to deliver it to Crassus. Crassus was not keeping his side of the bargain. He had heard that two legions had been recently deployed under Gellius's command, and it did more than to just displease him. Why was it Gellius? Why not his son? He knew that his son was not 'fit enough', yet he had had expected more from Crassus. Arrius bit his lips, thinking of the parchment paper he had just written. He had written that if Crassus did not hurry up, his position as a praetor might be rebuked—a warning effective enough to make Crassus do almost anything.

If Crassus, would not suit his demands, then he could always change the commander to someone else. He hoped Crassus knew that, for his own sake.

Gellius looked at the amassed force of slaves. They outnumbered the legions by thousands, and Gellius silently wished to himself for more legions.

The Roman legions were advancing slowly and grimly, stretched out in a straight line. Suetonius was sitting on his horse next to him with his young tribunus militium laticlavius. The young man was surveying the field with a serious eye and Gellius noted him with pleasure. He might not be as naïve. as he looked.

His eyes landed on the youth's left arm where an ugly scar ran long across. It seemed recent, and he pondered on where he had gotten the scar. He was still wondering when the youth turned toward him.

"Sir?" he asked, and Gellius nodded. Gellius put up a hand, and five arrows flew toward the slaves. They hit their mark, causing a slight disturbance. The slaves were within striking distance. This time, he clamped the hand down, and five spears flew, falling a little short, marking the range border. Once the slaves advanced within the lines, it would spell death for them.

"The cavalry are to protect the left flank. There is more risk on the left side than on the right," Gellius ordered and a scout galloped off to tell the cavalry.

Gellius watched the slaves advance a little more, savagely grinning to himself as he saw more and more of them come within striking distance. Once he decided there were enough, he signaled the cornicerns, and they blew a single tone, letting the arrows fly. The ground grew dark as thousands of arrows covered the sun. Even before the arrows descended, another was being shot.

The sky was covered with shafts of arrows that proved deadly to the slaves who did not have proper shields. Arrows that were shot always hit somebody— there were too many slaves to miss.

Octavius watched in awe as slaves fell like leaves in fall. He glanced at the archers who were intent in shooting the arrows, careful to shoot the arrow high so as to not hit the legionnaires. The sky soon thinned and the field grew silent as no arrows hailed on the rebels anymore.

When they realized that no more arrows would harass them, the slaves let out a roar of triumph and made a wild charge towards the legions. Even though the arrows had thinned their number, the slaves still outnumbered them.

"They are fighting in a Gallic style," Suetonius commented and Gellius nodded.

"Victory is ours then. We have beaten thousands of

Gauls before." Gellius nodded at Suetonius's comment. It seemed that Crixus was not as talented as Spartacus, wasting his advantage of numbers on a wild charge. The slaves crossed without hesitation the boundary that had been marked by the first five spears, trying to storm the legions, making as much noise as they could.

The legionnaires looked on with a grim silence. "Spears," Gellius bellowed, after noticing that many slaves were inside the firing range, and the sky grew dark once again as legionary spears were hefted into the sky. There was not as many spears as there were arrows, but spears had a stronger impact—if lucky, they were enough to penetrate two men.

The slaves staggered, but they doggedly regrouped and continued their run towards the legions.

"Suetonius, take command of the middle. Octavius, you take the right wing," Gellius commanded briefly. He had faith in the legions, but the numbers were worrying him.

Octavius saluted and raced his horse to the right wing. His veins began to pulse as he felt the thrill of a battle once more. He was going to command. As he rode his horse towards the right, many legionaries saluted him. Octavius felt his chest swell as he saw them. He would not fail them.

At a horn signal, the first line rushed out to meet the

oncoming slaves. The legion's first line buckled slightly at the first charge, unable to beat the numbers. A quick calculation told him that one legionary would have to face at least two slaves.

"Hold your position, Third! Remember Glaber! Remember Varinius! Remember all Romans who died during their raids," he yelled. "Gaius, don't fall back. Caecilius, you are doing fine. Germanicus, hold the line! We beat them before, we can do it again," he bellowed again. His throat was sore, but he noted with pleasure how the men he called strove to fight more furiously. However, to his dismay, he noticed that the first line was retreating and suddenly, Octavius felt panic. What if they lost?"

In his anxiety, he bit his lower lip and grimaced as he tasted blood. He surveyed the slaves' first line and noticed instantly what the problem was. Those fighting at the right flank were the gladiators. They wore spiked helmets and fought with ease as they slaughtered Romans. Even from a distance Octavius could notice their muscular forms. Desperately, he looked at Gellius but Gellius was not paying attention to the right flank. He decided that it would be too late if he awaited orders from Gellius and began to command. Never had he felt so utterly alone.

"Rotate the lines! I want the triarii—the most experi-enced—up in the front line," he called and watched with satisfaction the orderly retreat. The first line fell back while the third line—the triarii—sifted through the second—the princeps—and first line—the hastate—to take their positions at the first.

Octavius gazed at them, his face intent. The triarii were the best soldiers, and he knew that if they began to fall back also, the morale would plummet. The triarii widened and shortened the lines without any orders. They were experts, and they knew what to do.

They held the gladiators at bay, but they did not seem to be making much progress. Octavius sweated as he noticed that the triarii could not move forward. He signaled to a messenger who came shortly enough.

"Go to the cavalry and send about fifty men over here. Tell them to flank the gladiators," Octavius said, his words rushing out in a hurry and the messenger galloped off. In the corner of his brain he knew that he was disobeying the rules. He had no command over the cavalry, but that was not important. They needed backup and he had requested for it.

As time passed, his anxiety grew. What if the cavalry

refused to come? He let out a huge sigh of relief when he heard some horsemen rushing to him. He noticed that they were all from the Third legion and grinned savagely. He had trained with them before, and he knew what chaos they were able to bring.

"Go flank the gladiators," Octavius ordered swiftly. "Get behind their backs and aggravate them as best as you can. I'll handle the front," he told the horsemen and returned to watching the triarii.

He was glad to see the cavalry obey quickly and watched in anticipation as the legionaries made way for them to pass. Once they succeeded in trapping the gladiators, Octavius knew that they could destroy them.

"Hastati and Princeps advance! Support the triarii," he yelled and optios drove the lines forward from the back. Octavius narrowed his eyes to see where the cavalry was and saw them making a large circle toward the group.

"Think of the Roman blood that they have spelt!" he roared, hoping to encourage the legionaries. "Their blood must not be wasted," he called. One quick glance at the cavalry showed him that they were now riding at full charge at the gladiators, having completed their wide circle.

He looked on as the front lines of the cavalry met with

the back line of the gladiators and whooped with joy when he saw the gladiators falter. No matter how well they fought, they were not trained as an army and they could not face two enormous forces at the same time. Besides, Octavius knew the effects horses could have on men who have never been close to them. Many of them were slaves, and they never had the chance to be close to a horse, never mind a war horse at full gallop. It would panic them.

The legionaries too realized this, and they also roared in triumph as they set to massacring the gladiators with renewed energy. Gladiators began to fall back from both sides, and soon they were milling about with each other, trying to escape. The cavalry widened out making a semi—circle.

"Third, semi—circle," Octavius cried and was pleased when they obeyed swiftly. Now the gladiators were trapped between two semi—circles without anywhere to escape. He knew that their dying was just a matter of time.

For the first time, he turned his gaze to the left part of the field. When the slaves learned that their gladiators were trapped and helpless, they began to fall back. Romans roared and rushed the line, buckling their first line on the first charge. After that, began a mass slaughter. Legionaries slashed at everything in their paths, still in their formations. Octavius tried to imagine what it would look like to the slaves. To them, it would seem as if a huge iron wall was advancing towards them. He grinned as the slaves turned their backs and began to scatter for their own lives. Octavius glanced at Gellius to see if he would command to stop the slaughter, but apparently, Gellius had no thoughts whatsoever.

Octavius saw the legions rout the slave army and followed the exhilarated legionaries slowly on his horse, watching from a distance. Gellius and Suetonius too were doing the same. Then, he realized that the two were riding towards him, conferring with each other. His stomach churned as he thought of his unauthorized command.

"Nice job, Octavius," Suetonius greeted him, and Octavius was relieved to see him in a jovial mood.

"Good idea with the cavalry," Gellius said, looking intently at Octavius. Octavius caught the meaning.

"I shouldn't have done that sir. But the legionaries couldn't get past the gladiators so I thought that trapping the gladiators with the cavalry would not only help with our breaking through, but also with the morale of our soldiers."

Gellius smiled. "No, you should have done it. Just next

time, report before you do so."

"Yes, sir," Octavius responded, blushing, and Gellius laughed, clapping him on the back.

"It was fine. A good idea," he said.

◆—◆◆◆—◆

"Sir?" a legionary addressed Octavius. Octavius turned towards the voice and saw the legionary standing with a prisoner. They were at the slaves' camp, and he stood in the middle of it, watching the legion loot what the slaves had looted from civilians. "We caught this man trying to escape," he said, jerking his thumb towards a bound slave prisoner.

Octavius's eyes widened as he saw the prisoner. "Go call for Lucius and tell him to come immediately. He'll regret it if he doesn't," he told the legionary. When the legionary had run off to obey, he faced the prisoner.

"So how did you feel? What were you thinking?" he asked icily.

"What?" Crixus demanded roughly.

"Did you enjoy it when you killed her?" he asked.

"Who? I've slain more than you'd ever slay."

"Did you enjoy killing a certain patrician girl in the Capuan forest?" he asked, gritting his teeth.

The prisoner gave a laugh. "Oh, her! She squealed like a pig when she died. Did you like her?" Crixus asked.

Octavius kicked Crixus with his iron soled sandals. "Shut up, moron."

The legionary returned with Lucius at his side. Lucius met Octavius's gaze and dropped his eyes, averting them. "Lucius," he called, as if nothing had happened between them.

Octavius motioned at Crixus whose face was covered with dried blood. "He's the one who launched the first arrow at…her. He's the one directly responsible. Not me. Not Titus. I thought you would like to finish him off, more than I would want to do. I mean…I owe you this. I'm sorry for not telling you."

Lucius stared at Octavius and then averted his gaze to Crixus.

"Remember the time when I told you that you would die before you were able to bring down the republic? That day is today," Lucius whispered, his voice ruthless, and drew his gladius.

Octavius noticed that Lucius was going for the slow kill. Lucius aimed at the right side of the chest. He slit the part open with his gladius, then did the same with the left.

In other situations, Octavius would have stopped Lucius,

but this time was different. He closed his eyes at the brutal way Lucius was killing the man, but he did not stop it. Lucius was now sobbing frantically, so much so that Octavius seriously considered stopping him. Finally, Lucius regained control on his own.

"Thank you," Lucius whispered to him, and he opened his eyes. "I'm sorry," Lucius whispered. "I couldn't control myself. And I'm sorry about the insults. I didn't mean it."

"I know," Octavius replied simply.

"I'm sorry about your… injury," Lucius said, pointing at the long wound.

Octavius smiled in response. "I'll make it through," he replied and hugged Lucius. He had been missing his friend's companionship more than he realized.

They embraced for a minute longer before Lucius let go. "Octavius," he spoke and halted as if in thought. He kept still for a while and sighed. "You won't blame me even if I told you this?"

Octavius shook his head and gave his word. Lucius seemed to be relieved. "I—I'm sorry. Your hiding her death was mostly it, but that wasn't all. I mean, I was jealous. You a tribune, me a centurion, it didn't go well with my pride. I guess I've already told you, in a very rude way." Lucius looked at his friend uncomfortably.

Octavius was silent for a while, rethinking the bit of information. "I had been suspecting it. It's only natural, Lucius. I would have felt the same way. You don't have to apologize," Octavius said. "Are you still—?"

Lucius shook his head. "A little, if I want to be honest. But I'll be able to get over that feeling soon enough. Maybe," Lucius said and gave a small smile. He remained like that for a few seconds more and then his face turned suddenly stony. "Throw the man to the dogs," he ordered, remembering Crixus and faced Octavius. Octavius saw a trickle of tear running down his friend's face.

"She was my only sister," Lucius said, partly to himself. "Don't mind me. I won't talk about her death anymore. I'll talk about the days when she was alive," he said, managing a brave smile. Octavius bit his lips to stop his face from being crumpled as he thought of her death.

"Wait!" he called to the legionary who was dragging out Crixus's body. He knelt down, rummaging for a certain valuable... he found the ring inside a pocket of Crixus's tunic. His vision was blurred by his tears but he strove to maintain a calm face as he secretly kissed the ring before putting it in his. He would return it to her, as he had promised.

He turned again to Lucius after he thought that he had had enough time to compose himself. They looked over the battlefield in silence, seeing the damaged bodies of the slaves littered on the ground. "We made quite a kill, didn't we?" Octavius asked, and Lucius nodded.

"You have certainly changed," Lucius said.

Octavius just smiled. Then, he spoke. "You know, you've got quite a lot of work left to do back at camp," Octavius said, his eyes sly.

"What?" Lucius demanded.

"Apologizing to Titus. He's probably having the best time of his life, on the top of his mood. Never a better time to apologize than now. I have a feeling that he will accept it," Octavius said, and Lucius nodded.

"I'm sorry about blaming him for her death. I mean, he would have never guessed. And he also gave her two legionaries in case. He did the best he could. Lucia…"

"Hungry?" Octavius asked, trying to distract him. "Race you," Octavius said, jumping on his horse and racing it down the slope toward the legions' camp. Lucius jumped on an ownerless horse as he tried to catch up with Octavius, smiling softly at his friend's effort.

❧ *28* ❧

Octavius gazed at the brightening sky, the red fiery ball of fire mixing with the pale blue. The redness of the sun made him think of the blood that has been and will be spilled during the war. He shuddered at the thought as he mused about his precarious life. He could be killed any day. Lucius, Titus, Suetonius, Caecilius, Crassus… all were mortals who could be gone with a single blow from an opponent. One mistake and he would lose them, forever.

He thought of his younger self, when he had been in Capua—though it was only a year ago, it seemed to be about ten years to him—when he had been a completely different man. He had been a boy, leading a peaceful life. He had a good house, capable parents, an adopted brother to rely on, a trustable friend, an influential uncle, and a girl he had loved. He had only heard of the legions, admired those who served in them, listened to their stories, especially

Julius's, with great vigor, as he dreamed of the day he would become a part of these stories. Now that he was, it was not as thrilling as he had imagined it would be.

There had been minor skirmishes until now, the defeat of Crixus being the biggest and the most successful one. Sometimes the legions lost the minor skirmishes, yet they were managing to win the bigger ones, making Spartacus flee at a speedier pace toward Gaul. Each battle came with casualties, and sometimes the casualties happened within the Third. For Octavius who now knew all the members of the Third by heart, every death was like a blow to him. Every battle, he lost people. People he loved. And it was exactly this that made the engagements less exciting than Octavius had imagined it would be.

To his surprise, he noticed that he had not seen his parents for more than a year and that it had been a year since Lucia had died. Lucia. There was hardly a day when he did not think of her. The ring was still there, in a pocket of his tunic, near his heart, waiting to be given once again.

His urge to revenge had soothed meanwhile, but Lucius was still fed up with the thought of revenge. No doubt Spartacus too would be, trying to revenge the death of Crixus. Until someone finally died, he thought, there would be no end to this cycle.

Titus shivered slightly and breathed in the sharp air, staring at the scarlet disk that had popped up over the horizon. He was a typical Roman soldier, and he knew it. He carried the ruthlessness of the Roman legionaries, and he also had a devout belief in Rome. Although he hated what Rome was becoming, run by its ghastly senators, he still loved the spirit of Rome and the country itself. It was one of his personalities, he decided, his willingness to give everything to something he believed in. Rome, the legions, this war, Octavius…

He had always wished a chance to prove himself, to return to the legions since he had fled from the army. He had his chance now, and he thanked Spartacus for it. Everything was working out his way. Crassus, afraid to let one of his centurions go, had never asked nor had investigated anything about his background. Now he was a centurion of a fully fledged legion, the Third, which was getting noticed for its efficiency in battle.

He loved his life.

On the other side of the plain, Spartacus too looked at the rising sun, with a look of determination on his face. He knew that with the rising sun would come the revenge, the power of Rome—the legions. They had been chasing him for a while, and he knew that he could not turn his back to the legions forever. He would have to confront them anyhow, and better sooner than later.

He looked around the peaceful encampment. Men were sitting around campfires, grimly preparing themselves for the battle. Others watched the men with also a grim silence.

Spartacus nodded to himself. He would win. He had the numbers, and they were fighting for their lives, unlike the Romans, who were fighting for victory, fighting so that they could oppress others. Though he was fighting mostly because he could not run forever, Crixus's death also had a part.

When he heard that Crixus was dead, a wave of regret had engulfed him. He should not have let Crixus detach himself from the main army. He had known that Crixus would plunder until the Roman legions came to crush him down. And then Crixus would meet them face on, and. . . fail.

The legions had killed his best friend, and they would pay for it.

⸻⬦⬥⬦⸻

Octavius watched the priest with interest as he cut the lamb's throat. Spartacus had finally turned to face the legions, and a battle was inevitable. He, on Crassus's orders, was there to deliver the priest's omen. The priest began mumbling words he did not know as blood spurted out from the lamb into a readied bowl. After what seemed like forever, the priest stood tall and faced Octavius.

"I have prayed to the Gods to let the legions win and for you to come back safely."

Octavius blushed. "Thank you, though there was no need to pray for me."

The priest shook his head. "No, there was a need," he said grimly.

"I need to deliver the omen," Octavius said, ignoring the priest's grim words.

The priest sighed. Then, after a long pause, he said, "The legions will win." The priest gazed at the sky, refusing to meet Octavius's eyes.

"Tell me the truth," Octavius said, his eyes filling with

sudden worry.

"I have. The legions will win, though with many casualties. Many casualties. I want to tell you something else, but I will not. Omens are always right, yet they can be misinterpreted by people—like me—so I prefer to keep my mouth shut unless I am sure that I have interpreted the Gods' wills perfectly."

Octavius gazed at the priest intently, and the priest gazed back, his deep eyes searching Octavius's. "Be careful. And whatever you do, do not lose courage."

Octavius bowed his head in assent and turned to leave. Crassus, unlike he who only slightly heeded the priests' words, tended to believe everything the priests seemed to say. He was a very superstitious man, and Octavius knew that if he told Crassus about the many casualties part, Crassus would behave grimly, until it really turned out to be so. Omens could be misinterpreted, as the priest had said. Octavius consoled himself as he decided to tell Crassus only about the victory part.

❖

Octavius cast a nervous glance at his uncle. Crassus sat grimly on his horse, surveying the almost hundred thousand slaves that were coming toward him. His pale horse glowed red in the rising sun.

"Octavius, they've got the numbers, and they've got a good general." He paused and corrected himself rather hurriedly. "At least, for a slave. Anyway, the battle is going to be ugly, and I want you to be careful," Crassus whispered to his nephew and his nephew nodded. He had heard from Gellius about his nephew's involvement with their victory while battling Crixus. He was proud of his young nephew, yet he could not stop worrying. Octavius was just too young.

When they had beaten Crixus, Spartacus was already near Picenum. After Picenum lay the Alps and Crassus knew that the slave army should be defeated before they reached the Alps, out of Roman territory. It would be impossible to find and battle the slaves in Gaul. He had promised the senate a victory, and he would need to give it to them. Forcing gladiators out of Roman borders wasn't exactly what the senate had in mind.

He had forced—marched his legion to close the gap between them and Spartacus. For days they had followed Spartacus—who always was visible, but out of range. Today, finally, Spartacus had turned to meet the legions. Crassus vowed to himself that he would show Spartacus his mistake of confronting the legions. Even though they were a bit tired from the long marches, they were the Roman legions, the elites, or so Crassus believed, and Crassus had confidence in that.

"Legate Mummius," Crassus addressed, and the man gave a salute. "Take Gellius's legion and yours, and maneuver around Spartacus. Your motive is to panic them. Stay out of range and do not, under any circumstances, engage them. Are my orders clear?" he asked, and Mummius nodded.

Crassus looked at the man in disgust. He would rather have Gellius in command, but he had recently received three threatening letters from Arrius that implied the instability of his job—the news of the victory was not coming frequently enough for the senate to be pleased, and they were considering about rebuking his position as a preator, Arrius had said, while mentioning Mummius. It was a clear warning, reminding him of his promises about Mummius being given some important jobs.

Mummius had not caused much trouble recently. His legion was also shaping up well, though Crassus thought it had to do more with the officers than the always—a— little—drunken—Mummius. The man, no matter how well behaved he was lately, was still a trouble maker and could not be trusted. Though he was an ambitious man, he did nothing to endorse his ambitions, and when he did do something, it was always foolish and rather had an opposite effect.

"Never fight them, remember that, or else," Crassus said.

"I read you loud and clear," Mummius said. He saluted smartly and rode off to follow his orders.

He noticed his nephew staring up at him with curious eyes and smiled at him. "We are trapping Spartacus," he explained, and his nephew nodded again. "How old are you again?" he asked.

"A little over eighteen," Octavius replied, wondering why his uncle was asking such a thing.

"Be careful," Crassus said again. He was not sure if he should keep his nephew in the front lines. There were just too many slaves, and Octavius was just too young to die. Why he could not get rid of the ominous feeling was a mystery.

Octavius nodded, smiling. He knew the power of the legions and was sure that they could win. Maybe he had grown a little over confident, but still he believed in the legions. Among them were the Third. The Third was his, and he knew they would win the battle for him. The priest's warnings about the many casualties tugged at him, but he decided to ignore it, praying silently to the gods to be more lenient with them and decrease the number of casualties as much as possible.

The slaves sounded a long note which Crassus gave a short laugh. "Pretty impressive for slaves," he commented to no one in particular. The slaves widened out, matching the Roman lines, approaching steadily. Octavius dropped his jaws as he noticed how many of them were there. They were like a group of milling ants.

From their high ground, Octavius could see the whole field. Mummius's legions were marching at a forced pace. They sounded as many meaningless horn signals as they could, making their approach conspicuous. The slave army had noticed them and was shuffling nervously among themselves.

Mummius looked at the slaves who were rushing at his legions. He knew his orders had been not to engage the slaves, but if he did and won, his name would be known even back in Rome. His fame would cover Crassus's fame, and there was a chance that he might even become a consul.

He knew he would always fight under Crassus this entire war. This was the first and last chance he would ever get to command on his own, and he knew he had to use it. Crassus would not be able to punish somebody who had routed Spartacus's slaves. In fact, he would be awarded.

He knew what he had to do.

Or rather, he thought he knew.

<hr>

"Is Legate Mummius supposed to do that?" Octavius whispered to his uncle, who looked back at him with questioning eyes. Octavius pointed at the behind ranks of the slaves, where the two legions and the slave army were fighting.

Crassus gasped. He cursed himself for giving the command to Mummius and told a messenger to quickly retrieve him. He should not have given Mummius command on such an important mission. He felt as if he had been manipulated by Arrius.

"They'll get destroyed," Crassus said. He watched in silence as his words proved to be right. The slaves halted their advance suddenly, to let their rear lines destroy the legions only with their larger numbers.

He knew the single way to save his legions was to make other legions charge, in hopes of distracting the slaves. He quickly calculated and groaned as his brain turned up the near impossible probability of the 'hope'. Still, he had to try. He could not just stand and watch his two legions get routed. He gritted his teeth, vowing to himself that if Mummius survived, he would show the whole legion what he thought of those who had dared not to follow his command.

"Frontal direct assault," he cried to the cornicerns, and the cornicerns sounded the note for a charge. The distance was too far for the legionaries to make much impact when they charged the slaves. They would get tired before they even met them. More would die than were supposed to, all because of Mummius. He drummed his fingers on his saddle, feeling the ache of his heart as he saw the two legions getting torn apart by the worthless slaves.

The legionaries gave a mad roar as they ran across the plain to charge the slaves. They were met by the first line— the gladiators, and soon the peaceful field had erupted into chaos of shouting and slaying.

Octavius focused his attention on the Third. Titus, as usual, seemed not to have many problems even with the gladiators. He kept encouraging his century and killing any enemy within his gladius range. He was enjoying himself, not at all burdened by doing both at the same time. He turned his eyes towards Lucius, who was fighting besides the aquilifer, the bearer of the legion eagle. The eagle was very symbolic, especially in the fact that it represented the legion. If the eagle was stolen, the legion was disgraced and most times, they were disbanded.

He smiled contently at himself, relieved that his friends were safe. From a distance, he even saw Caecilius rearing his century on. He felt a little relieved at the fact that Mummius's legions were being engulfed, a treacherous thought, yet he had a sudden hope that those two legions would be the 'many casualties' the priest had warned him of. His Third would be fine then, he thought guiltily.

The gladiators were holding. As long as they held, keeping the other Roman legions at bay, the latter ranks would be free to attack Mummius.

And they did.

The two legions were being overwhelmed, and Octavius had a certain murky feeling that it would lead to a complete rout of the two legions. He closed his eyes and let out a sigh. The legions could not be defeated. Not now.

From his high position, he could see practically every-thing. The legionaries were managing to slowly advance now, but their pace was too slow, too slow to support the panicking two legions.

"First cohort first line, rotate lines with the second." Octavius heard Legate Suetonius shout. The second line, the princeps who were more heavily armed, orderly changed the lines with the hastati, the lighter armed soldiers. They soon showed the worth of being more heavily armed. The Third was advancing now, at a faster pace than the other legions.

"Match the pace, Third," Suetonius cried, but it hardly had any effect. The Third, exhilarated by their victory continued to advance. The legions formed an arrow shape, with the Third at its head. Octavius was proud to see it. What he did not see, however, was that when an arrow crashes, the head of the arrow is the first to get damaged. And he also did not see that the head was slowly getting engulfed by slaves who put the Third as their main target.

He sensed that more slaves were crashing themselves into the Third, flaying to make the Third retreat. The Third was not able to advance anymore, but they were holding, and Octavius did not see a particular need to call a retreat, a retreat to match the other legions' pace. It would mean that their advance had been in vain.

His eyes traveled once more to Lucius to check if he was all right, but saw something else instead. His eyes opened in horror as he saw that he had been wrong to leave the Third there, at the tip, to absorb the crash with the slaves. He saw that the aquilifer, who normally stood in the back of the lines, had advanced too much, probably in following Lucius. Lucius however, was nowhere in sight. His eyes grew even wider still as he saw the aquilifer fall. The gladiator then took the legion eagle with a cry of triumph, and he dove into his own lines— probably to show Spartacus his valuable present.

Octavius did not think. If he had, then he would not have done it, knowing that it was suicide. But impulse took over and ignoring a surprised cry from Crassus, he sprinted down the hill, toward the front ranks, in chase of the gladiator. No eagle meant no legion. He could not let his Third be disbanded.

He did not even feel it as his horse fell, eyes wide in panic, pierced by a spear thrown by one of the slaves. All his attention was on the gladiator who had stolen the eagle. Octavius continued his chase on foot, not caring about disrupting the Roman lines, but was soon hindered by a compact agile gladiator. The man would not let Octavius go, but instead weaved in and out of the ranks, aggravating Octavius.

The man was not dangerous, but Octavius felt himself grow impatient. He could not stand here to duel with this man while the gladiator went deeper and deeper into his own ranks, the standard of the legion right alongside him.

He yelled in frustration and in anger, his eyes keeping an eye on the agile man and another for searching the gladiator who had stolen the eagle. A part of Octavius knew that he was committing suicide, doing a very foolish thing that he would regret as he plunged himself from the legion's first lines to the slaves' lines. Centurions called him back but he ignored them, his thoughts only on the eagle, keeping track of the agile man who would venture and retreat in a series of consecutive movements.

Octavius battled the slaves, fighting to get deeper into their ranks. It was suicide, he knew, but it was too late to worry about it now. He was still managing to keep the slaves off him with his superior sword skills— he thanked Spartacus again for that with some bitterness. Just then, somebody grabbed his helmet from behind and threw him onto the ground. Instinct told him to roll, and he did, barely avoiding the blow of an ax. Out of a corner of his eyes, he saw the agile gladiator approaching. Great, he thought, two to one.

Octavius groped around for something he could use, frantically. He crawled toward a dead legionary and tore the scutum, the shield, out of his hands, using it to defend himself from a second blow of the ax. The shield rang with impact, and Octavius felt as if his arm was being torn apart. Staggering, he rose and faced the man with the hatchet. He slammed the man with the shield, and the man backed off, momentarily surprised. He took the time to face the agile man, kicking him off balance. Octavius did not hesitate to drive his sword into the man. He yelled in triumph, but his yell was cut short. The last thing he felt was a dull strike at his back.

Crassus screamed in horror as he saw his nephew fall.

Lucius dashed towards the man with the ax as he registered what had happened, plunging into the slaves' lines also. The ax man who was holding a scutum, the weapon that had felled Octavius, dropped dead with a big thud. He looked towards where he had first spotted the body of Octavius but only saw a patch of red ground.

There was no body to be seen.

"Third, advance!" Crassus cried shrilly. The cornicerns blew their horn and the legion followed his command. They pushed themselves on— Suetonius encouraging them on from the back, the optios beating anybody who did not advance with their sticks.

He had seen his nephew fall. Octavius had been fighting. He did not know why his nephew suddenly lunged himself into the front lines, and more, into the slaves' lines. It had been foolish, but the harm was done. His nephew was gone.

Most of his nephew's precious Third had seen what had happened—Octavius a conspicuous figure among the slaves— and were screaming and fighting in a frenzy, struggling to revenge their fallen Tribune. They were advancing, Crassus saw, fueled by uncontained anger. He shook his head, trying to forget what had happened. He could not simply believe it, his young nephew's body, soon to be trampled by the sandals of the legionaries and the slaves. Even if they won the battle and he had time to survey the corpses, he knew he would not have much chance in finding his nephew. The body would be too trampled for him to recognize Octavius.

He cringed to himself as his thoughts wandered to what

his sister and her husband would say to him. He knew he had nothing to say for it had been he who had asked Octavius to serve as a tribune. Licinia would go crazy. Her eyes would be filled with hatred at losing her only child.

He was awakened from his thoughts by the yelling of a scout. He swerved to look at the man who was sprinting at him in full speed. "Sir! The Third is at risk!" he yelled through his heavy pants, and Crassus looked at the battlefield to find that the man was correct. In his state, he had forgotten to let the other legions advance with the Third, making them an even more conspicuous target.

"Order the other legions to keep pace with the Third," he ordered, and his orders were soon spread over the field by the messengers. Crassus cringed as he saw the diminished number of the Third. A few centuries of the Third had been trapped by the slaves and were fighting futilely. He groaned at what the battle was becoming.

He gazed back at the battlefield, his eyes gloomy. What he saw there added to his shock. It might have shocked him more than the death of Octavius. He saw the Third run.

A few centuries were isolated from the main body, and the slaves seemed intent on taking them prisoner rather than in killing them. The main body was struggling with the slaves who stuck to the Third like sharks preying on an unfortunate fish. They lunged at the Third, winning by sheer numbers. The Third were driven back without any high ranking officers—the tribunus laticlavius dead and the legate suddenly nowhere to be seen—to guide them. Then it happened.

The front line of the Third fell at the charges of the numerous slaves. And then, Crassus saw a legionary drop his sword and turn his back to his enemy at the sheer fear of death. Those others who were barely holding followed behind, fear and panic portrayed in their eyes. They pushed at each other to get to the latter lines, toward safety.

"Optios! Hold them back!" Crassus shouted in rage. Once a legion started to turn its back, there was a good chance of it spreading to other legions. The optios obeyed, using sticks to force the legionaries back into the lines. Some legionaries were killed in the process, and the act discouraged the legionaries even more, and the second line started to crumble.

Optios and centurions ran about behind the third line, pushing running soldiers back. The legionaries fell but they stood and ran again, not heeding the orders of the optios and centurions.

The centurions started killing any who turned their

backs, and after they decided that they were killing too many of their own men, they changed their method to shaking any man who was running. The shaken men seemed to recover as they sheepishly went back to their positions. By now, other legions had come to reinforce the Third, and those who were running turned again to go back to their first positions. Only the third line had not run, and Crassus felt keenly how experience was important.

He gritted his teeth at the legion's cowardly behavior. Once the battle was over he would punish them so severely that no legion would ever dare to run while he was in command. Never.

~ *29* ~

Octavius saw her, standing there, as pretty as ever. She beckoned toward him, calling his name. Lucia. He wanted to go to her, but his feet would not move. He frowned, as he tried again.

"See? He's not dead." Octavius heard someone say and jolted open his eyes. But he realized with a groan that he could not see clearly. He felt as if he was in the middle of a fog. A man was standing beside him, looking at him grimly.

The man did not wear a legionary uniform and had a Gaulish look to him. His hair was unkempt, and his hands were grimy. Octavius closed his eyes again, wanting to go back to his dream.

"I know because I saw Draba hitting him. I brought him to show Spartacus. We've got about three hundred prisoners, some centurions. Only one high ranking officer, though. This one," the man said.

"How d'you know?" a man next to him cried in wonder.

"Look at his helmet. The plume, idiot," the man responded. "Draba's murdered. Poor Draba. The murderer came after me. A centurion."

Octavius listened to the rough Latin through his closed eyes. It took a moment before his dazed brain took in what was happening. He sat up suddenly, only to fall back onto the ground with a groan.

"Stay still. You'll have to be in good conditions when I show Spartacus. He's not back yet, still fighting. He'll love to see you."

"Shut up," Octavius groaned. The slave laughed out and gave a slight kick to his chest. Octavius gave an involuntary yelp.

"See how vulnerable you are? You got hit with one of those legionary shields," the man said, jabbing his chest. The man next to him was laughing.

Octavius gave another groan, and they laughed even more. "Please be quiet. My head hurts from hearing your uneducated Latin," Octavius managed to say, his tongue still slurred. Their faces grew dark as they stared at him. One pulled out a dagger and knelt down beside him.

He lowered his head until it almost touched Octavius's

and laughed. "I can kill you here," he said. "Does your head still hurt?" he asked with a dangerous smile.

Octavius smiled back. They were going to kill him anyways. Even Spartacus had been willing to kill him about a year before, in Capua. Spartacus probably had not forgotten his hate for him. He was going to die, and while dying, he would die with honor, showing contempt for the slaves and for death.

"Yeah. It hurts a lot," he responded genuinely. The man let out an angry roar and held the dagger up threateningly.

"Leave him. Spartacus would want to have him alive," the man still standing said, grabbing the kneeling man's dagger holding arm. "Let's go. Leave him here, close the door and don't give him any food or water. Just chain him. He would cap—capi—"

"Capitulate?" Octavius advised helpfully, his tone mocking.

"Capitulate on his own," the man said, looking murderously at Octavius.

"Congratulations. It's four syllables long," Octavius said with his angelic smile.

The man looked at Octavius as if he wanted to say something, but didn't, instead pulling the kneeling man to his feet. "Let's just leave him here. Spartacus will come, and then we can see how arrogant he is then." The kneeling man grudgingly obeyed. Octavius was too weak to resist as the man bound him in iron chains. The two went out, shutting the door behind them.

They had not, however, disarmed him, and Octavius smiled at their lack of attention. He might have a chance sometime later though now, they had bound him too tightly for him to move his hands. With that, he drifted back into unconsciousness once more.

He was roughly awakened by a person moving him. He did not struggle as they put him in a corner of the ware-house. They brought in more legionaries to Octavius's dismay. To his horror, many of them were those who he recognized, soldiers of the Third.

A legionary who was looking furious—probably at himself as well as the situation—gasped when he saw him. Octavius gave a slight smile, his humiliation growing. He was a tribune of a legion, and he knew that it would be very symbolically discouraging to the legionaries to see him in such a helpless state. His face burned as he thought of it.

"Caecilius! Tribune Octavius is here!" the legionnaire

cried and a crouching, dejected looking man suddenly sat up straight, his eyes alert.

"Caecilius?" Octavius asked in disbelief, and the man veered his head towards him. Caecilius too was bound in ropes but what was more, disarmed. Octavius realized that he was the only one they had forgotten to disarm, probably because of the two fools. He thanked the gods for it—it was the sword that reminded him of his uncle and Julius, though the sword did nothing to improve his current situation now. His back hurt like fire when ever he tried to bend, making it almost impossible for him to escape on his own by fighting. Still he did not want to lose the gladius.

"Tribune?" Caecilius asked, his eyes filled with consternation.

"Yes, it's me. How's the battle?" Octavius asked, shaking his head to clear his vision.

Caecilius sighed. "I don't know. Even if we win, it will be with many casualties."

"Are Lucius and Titus all right?" Octavius asked urgently. If somebody as experienced as Caecilius was captured, then there was a good chance that they might also be captured, regardless of how well they fought.

Caecilius stared into the air for so long that Octavius

began to worry what the response would be. "They are okay. At least, when I last saw them. Lucius saw you fall. He's a bit crazy, which is a good thing because he fights like a lion now," he said, and turned his eyes to him.

Caecilius looked mournfully at Octavius. "But Octavius…"

"Yes?" he said, wondering what could be more mournful than the situation they were in now.

"Legate Octavius."

"What?" Octavius asked, surprised.

Caecilius's black eyes bore into Octavius's eyes as he said the final words.

"I saw Suetonius die, a general's death. Died trying to rescue me and our century from the slaves." Caecilius closed his eyes as he remembered the scene. "Our century was trapped. The Third had advanced too much…I don't know. It just happened. We were isolated, and well, Legate Suetonius tried to rescue us by ordering men over to where we were, but it didn't quite work out. I guess the others were too busy to come to our aid…So Suetonius came, alone. And he fought well…he just didn't…By Mars, Octavius, I can't continue. I'm sorry."

Octavius closed his eyes. He felt nothing. There had been too many deaths around him lately for him to feel anything.

Suetonius, his legate, his supporter, and his second father, was gone. What he had been worrying had finally happened. Someone he loved had died on the battlefield, never to rise again.

"You are the legate now. At least, during this battle," Caecilius said softly. Octavius nodded briefly. He did not voice his thoughts that his legate—ship might be short lived. Very short lived.

"He was a brave man. He would be honored," Caecilius said.

"He'll be happy. He's with his son," Octavius murmured silently.

∾ *30* ∾

Night had fallen. The house was too black for Octavius to see anything so he lay still, thinking nothing in particular. He tried not to think about Suetonius. Then the door creaked open, and a slave entered with a torch. Behind him followed two more, and Octavius groaned as he recognized the figure of Spartacus in the dim light.

He turned his face around, not wanting to be discovered, partly in shame. Out of the corner of his eyes, he saw Spartacus look around the legionaries.

"This is the last group?" Spartacus asked, and the slave with the torch nodded.

"All legionaries, optios and centurions," Spartacus remarked with an unsatisfied tone. The one with the torch shrugged.

"All right. Get them out," Spartacus ordered, and the two men obliged. The bound legionaries were dragged out roughly by slaves who threatened and cursed at them.

Octavius too got out of the warehouse. He was not dragged, rather, civilly guided by the one holding the torch. Under the mocking civility lay enmity and Octavius was well aware of it.

"Off with their necks! Kill them! Kill them!" Octavius saw the crowd chant as he stepped out of the warehouse. The crowd was made of slaves of every age, both men and women. They shouted vulgar comments of revenge as they threatened to slaughter the prisoners. In fact, two dashed out at a legionary and shouted, "Revenge for those who have died!" as they clawed the legionary's face. The Roman howled in agony but the two did not stop. They were cheered on by the others who were also fighting to get closer to the victims.

"Stop! I have a great surprise for you—something that you will enjoy very much. Anybody who lays a hand on these Romans shall suffer," Spartacus announced, and the slaves backed off, grumbling to themselves. The legionary had stopped howling, but he twitched in agony. His eyes were fierce and glowed with anguish as he turned to look at Octavius. Octavius knew that he would never be able to forget the man's looks. The man, even after all the things that had been done to him stared at Octavius with trust.

There was no blame in his eyes; there was only respect and trust. It was enough for Octavius to go mad.

Spartacus was ahead of him, addressing the crowd. "Crixus is way worthier than you Romans. You need to experience what we have felt. What the gladiators had been undergoing for centuries. It is time for you arrogant Romans to learn that," Spartacus said loudly. They cheered at him. "So, I have arranged a gladiatorial spectacle in honor of Crixus. That's what the Romans do when an aristocrat is killed, isn't it? What are we different from their so called aristocrats? Are we inferior to the fat pigs? No!" Spartacus held up a hand as the crowd cheered madly.

"David, go get their precious legion eagle. Let them fight under it. Gannicus, I want to you to clear out a round arena space. Castus, pick out the legionaries to fight. Start from the front of the line," Spartacus ordered. He had picked Gannicus and Castus as his second in command after the death of his original two—Oenomaus and Crixus. Meanwhile, Octavius let out an inward sigh of relief. At least they had not destroyed the eagle.

The crowd eagerly made a large circle, and Castus picked out two legionaries—two muscular Romans who were shaking slightly. He then forced the others to kneel down.

Octavius pushed the man away with his shoulder but was repaid by a forceful blow to his back. He gritted his teeth to stop himself from shouting aloud. A slight groan escaped from his mouth as the man pushed him down with the others. The humiliation was unbearable.

The slave called David brought out the eagle and placed it in the middle. While he did so, he mocked an aquilifer holding the standard, earning many laughs.

Spartacus raised his hands, and two swords were handed over to them. "Our lives have been decided by Romans. It is our turn to decide theirs," he announced and the slaves cheered. It marked the beginning of the battle.

The two soldiers faced each other, each not wanting to harm the other. Reared by the taunts and threats of the slaves, one tentatively put out a sword towards his opponent and marking the start of the duel. They sparred, wrestled, kicked until the whole crowd was mad with joy. Blood spelt everywhere, and they fought like animals. One legionary finally managed to kill the other by driving his sword into the man's stomach. He stood still for a moment, and started to wail out in disbelief. He suddenly looked at Spartacus with a mad glint to his eyes. He rushed at the former gladiator, and the ex-gladiator killed the man with a nice stroke of his own sword. The crowd went berserk as they cheered their leader.

"Choose the next pair," Spartacus commented, and Castus began to search for a good legionary. He held a torch in his hands and pointed towards Octavius.

"Spartacus! There is a high ranking officer here," Castus announced and Spartacus looked at where he was pointing.

"Oh, gods, Castus! I didn't know. Bring him out immediately. This is getting to be fun," Spartacus said, giggling like a child. I thought you hated gladiatorial spectacles, Octavius thought to himself, seething.

Octavius felt terror as Castus forced him to stand. With his stunned back, he was not sure if he could survive if a well trained legionary came at him. And his Third were well trained.

"Spartacus, I had noticed him before, but he seemed to have broken his back or something. And he's too young. Almost no muscle in there," Castus said worriedly. Hurt and weak gladiators did not make a good show.

"And you have nothing but muscles," Octavius retorted, earning cheers from his legionaries. Castus kicked the younger man in his shins. He was about to say something vulgar when Spartacus interrupted.

"Really? Doesn't matter. He's a high ranking officer, and they value their honor more than anything. Let's ruin it for him. Bring him out," Spartacus called from his sitting position, and Castus shrugged. He roughly untied Octavius's bonds as he pushed Octavius out to the arena. Octavius gave a small groan as the man touched his back. He heard Caecilius calling a shocked no, and he turned back to give Caecilius an okay sign. He would face it.

Defiantly. Bravely.

Unlike the slaves.

Like a Roman.

<hr>

Spartacus gave the signal to start. Octavius faced his opponent, a centurion. The man, he now realized, was the one who had hindered him on the day of Lucia's funeral, and the man who had offered valuable advice on his first battle. A loyal man. Germanicus, Octavius said the name softly.

"Go on, legionaries. Show your bravery!" someone from the crowd called. The centurion faced Octavius, and he leveled his sword. If the man attacked, Octavius knew there was no hope of survival. His back would not grant him that.

The man held his sword, as if deep in thought. Then he faced Spartacus. "You will regret this when you lose. Your body will be thrown to the dogs after it is hung on a cross. The same for everyone else," the centurion said slowly. He took a step towards Octavius. Octavius stood his ground.

"Go on, Centurion Germanicus. I will not fight my men, including you. I will not give these slaves the enjoyment of watching us duel," he said, loud enough for the slaves to hear, and the slaves booed.

The centurion shook his head. "I am different from these animals here. I do not kill others for the joy of it. Legate," he addressed and paused. Octavius felt his eyes moisten at the title, the title that he had wanted so much, but at what cost? Lucia was dead, Suetonius was dead, and there was a good possibility that Germanicus here, Caecilius and he too would die.

"Please kill me. Quickly. I too will not give them the joy of watching us fight. This is my final plea as your centurion," the man said, and Octavius felt tears forming in his eyes. His eyes felt hot, and his breast felt torn as he tried to stop the tears. His throat burned hotter than when he had first heard the death of Lucia. He could not.

"Go on, centurion. This is my last order," Octavius

called. He would teach the animals around him the Roman spirit. Spartacus had questioned the difference between them and the Romans. He would show them.

The centurion faced the Roman captives. "Are you not ashamed to kill your comrades? I say that we fight these slaves. Make a way for our Legate," he said and saluted in front of the legion eagle. The crowd booed while he was doing so.

"I have followed orders all my life, and this order will be the first and the last that I shall disobey. Ave Legatus!" he hailed, holding his arm in front of his chest like the customarily legionary salute. Then he pushed the sword into his own chest. Slaves gasped at his courage, and the centurion laughed at them.

"This is why we are better than you, damned slaves. My only regret is that I can't see you get crucified," he shouted with all the energy he had and fell knee first to the ground. The man was dead before Octavius could rush over to him.

Spartacus gaped at the man. Truly, there had been no gladiators, at least those whom he knew of, that had committed suicide in such a way. He felt a little respect surging up inside him at the man's courage.

"Who are you, Legate," Spartacus asked in a mocking

tone, "for somebody such to commit suicide rather than to kill you?"

Octavius faced Spartacus. The man was a monster, the monster that was killing his legion. For every man died, he felt as if every piece of him was being torn away. He knew them all by name. They had fought alongside him. To kill them in such a way was unjust.

"Some say that you are their liberator. I almost believed it. I almost believed that you were fighting for the freedom of the slaves. But I now know who you are, a monster. You escaped the arena so that you could force someone else your own fate," Octavius whispered, knowing that he might be pushing Spartacus's fragile temper too far. Spartacus let out a fake smile, trying to mask his anger. Octavius was pleased that his words had bit so deeply.

"I asked you who you were!" Spartacus shouted, not succeeding in hiding his anger.

Octavius took off his helmet. "You already know me, Spartacus."

Spartacus strained to see the legate, and he dropped his jaws in surprise. "Octavius!" He stayed motionless for a few long seconds before he spoke again. "Congratulations, a legate," Spartacus said without cynicism, surprising Octavius.

He had expected Spartacus to be less welcoming.

"Last time you saw me, you wanted to kill me," Octavius said, watching Spartacus's reaction.

"That was last time. I'm actually sorry about it," Spartacus responded without any irony. "Is your back okay?" he asked. "I have a slave who was a doctor before. Would you like to meet him?"

"No."

"He's very good. He even cured me of my nasty leg wound here."

"No."

"He won't cut your veins like most Roman doctors do," Spartacus said with amusement and other laughed. "Come on, Octavius. This is my sincere offer."

"I don't want to hear any words of kindness coming out of your mouth, slave," Octavius said, consciously angering Spartacus. Spartacus's eyes flashed dangerously before he sighed.

"Have it your way," Spartacus said, shrugging.

"You murdered my legion," Octavius said, gritting his teeth. Spartacus shrugged which made him more furious than ever. If he survived, he would win the war and slaughter the whole lot of them. The dying centurion left him an image that he would not forget. He would live up to the man's words.

"You will be exempted from all this," Spartacus said.

"Why?"

"Because I owe you much."

Octavius took a deep breath. "If you owe me, then I want you to let them go. I saved many of your friends' lives than I care to think of, and this is how you repay me?" he asked.

Spartacus shrugged and Octavius cursed.

"When you lose, Spartacus, when you lose, there will be no one to save you from your fate if you kill them all. As the dying centurion forewarned, I shall personally nail every one of you who is currently watching this so called spectacle on a cross." Octavius warned.

Spartacus shrugged again, aggravating Octavius. "Let's hope it does not come to that. Castus, choose a new pair. Actually, I want a death match between eight legionaries, at the same time. We need to finish this quickly," he ordered, and turned to the horrified Octavius. "I'll let you live. Instead, you will have to watch the spectacle. You can tell that fat uncle of yours when you get back," Spartacus said. Octavius pretended to think as he walked slowly towards

Spartacus. He then suddenly whipped out his gladius at him, lunging. Spartacus ducked swiftly and unsheathed his own sword.

Spartacus shook his head. "Not with you injured. You can barely stand. Put that away before I disarm you," Spartacus said. He seemed to be genuinely worried for Octavius's back. Snarling, Octavius sheathed his gladius.

"Take a seat, Octavius, and no rash actions. I'll let you live, remember, so no rash actions," Spartacus warned.

"You don't decide my fate. I do," Octavius said flatly, turning his back on Spartacus. He faced the arena where there were eight trembling legionaries awaiting the start signal of the death match. On the opposite side of where Octavius and Spartacus were, were the Roman captives, kneeling down. Octavius vowed he would make the slaves pay for their doings. He could not bear to see his gallant Third being humiliated.

"As you say, Octavius. Castus, start the match!" Spartacus called, and the slaves started pushing the legionaries together using their sticks.

"You'll regret this," Octavius murmured, and Spartacus shook his head, grinning.

"This is something I've wanted to see for several years.

Enjoy it," Spartacus responded. Spartacus moved a little to make space for Castus who came to join them.

"Shouldn't we kill?" the man asked, jerking his head towards Octavius. Spartacus shook his head, narrating him of their relations back at Capua. Castus nodded, but he did not seem to be happy about it and cast mocking glances at Octavius. Once, their eyes met, and Octavius saw the man's eyes were full of hate. They were also full of derision.

Octavius stared back at him. "Jeer at me all you want now, because the next chance you are going to get is when you are hanging on a cross."

The man stood, his face twisted in anger. Octavius beckoned him on but Spartacus forced Castus down before the two could fight.

Octavius turned his attention towards the Roman legionnaires. They were reluctant to fight each other after all they have gone through. They exchanged meek blows that might have seen genuine to others, but Octavius knew it was not. It was similar to a training session. The fight was not to kill.

He shot a look at the prisoners. Some watched the spectacle, many kept their heads bowed. He saw one looking straight at him, and recognized the man. Caecilius. The gray haired veteran seemed helpless and small, kneeling there, and Octavius felt ashamed at his powerlessness. He had to do something. And as he stared into the eyes of Caecilius, he knew what to do.

⁕

Crassus threw his helmet on the floor of his tent. They had won the battle. The slaves had turned their backs at the last moment, but there was no thrill of victory and the legionaries too did not feel it. Victory had come with too many casualties. Suetonius was dead. Gellius was dead. Mummius had crawled back to him like a defeated dog. Two had been wiped out. He now had only six. Most of all, his nephew was dead. And his precious Third had run.

Nowhere was there the glory of Rome he had bragged about. The slave army, even though they had turned their backs, had gone through a quite orderly retreat. They had been in a cheerful mood, glad at the fact that they could face the Roman legions and give them such a great impact. It hurt Crassus to think that a mere army made of talking tools had been able to give such an effect.

Other legates watched Crassus in silence, not knowing how to react. They were afraid of the moody man. His eyes burned cold, and the legates who had never cowered before any enemy now cowered when they faced his cold face. The praetor's face was unreadable as they waited. They knew Crassus would order a harsh punishment on the Third and on Legate Mummius.

"I want," Crassus finally opened his mouth, and all the legates turned to meet the man's eyes only to drop their gaze at the cold fire burning inside the praetor's eyes. The torch in the tent crackled ominously. "Legate Mummius to be punished in front of all the legions," he said. The legates nodded but cringed, knowing that Crassus was warning all of them while he was punishing Mummius.

"For the Third legion, which has even lost their eagle, I will have them decimated," he announced monotonously, and the legates gasped. It was a death penalty that killed one man out of every ten legionaries. It was decided by a picking of stones, and the man who was chosen would be beaten to death by his own comrades. Those who had been lucky enough to avoid the punishment were given barley instead of wheat and were forced to sleep outside the camp, vulnerable.

"That practice has not been used for over a century. It is considered a barbaric—" a legate started.

"Are you, Claudius, trying to say that I am barbaric?"

Crassus asked sharply, and the man shook his head vigorously. "Very well. Then you will shut up and keep your head bowed unless you want to be punished alongside Mummius."

Claudius did as he was told. "Go prepare," Crassus said in a low, cold tone. "Dismissed."

<hr />

"Ajax," Octavius yelled, recognizing Titus's optio in the midst of the eight men. Titus had praised the young man whenever he could, and Octavius knew that Titus did not praise people lightly. If Titus said he was good, he was good.

The man turned towards him, his eyes pleading and also curious. Octavius stood still, not doing anything that might alarm Spartacus further.

Octavius took a deep breath. "I am the legate of the Third. I order you to go fight your real enemies!" Octavius ordered briskly and sprinted over to the opposite side of the arena, ignoring the severe pain in his back. It hurt, but he could move his back. And as long as it moved, he would move it.

He pretended not to hear a startled cry from Spartacus. Spartacus would not have expected him to do something like this because he had granted Octavius his life. Octavius laughed inwardly. While slaves might accept that offer, Romans did not. They did not think about only their lives. They also thought of their comrades unlike the slaves who only cared about themselves, another difference there. Octavius noted to himself that he would tell Spartacus when they met again—hopefully somewhere else.

He slashed at a stunned prisoner guard, killing the man at once. Strangely, he felt indifferent about the deaths of the slaves, enjoying it, unlike before.

He cut Caecilius's bonds in a swift motion, who immediately retrieved a sword from the fallen guard and went on cutting other's bonds. Octavius looked back to see Spartacus engaged in a fight with three legionaries. Ajax was fighting Castus.

It took a moment before the slaves realized that their prisoners were escaping, longer than Octavius hoped. The chain reaction had already started. Freed Romans began, at once, to free others using the swords of those who fell under the swords of those already freed.

Octavius shot a thankful look to Caecilius who fought at Octavius's back, protecting it. The arena erupted into chaos as slaves rushed into the arena to confront the Romans. It took one quick look to see that the Romans were winning against the normal slaves. They had more trouble with the gladiators, but in their enraged state—after all the deaths and the humiliation—they were recharged with savage energy.

A sword blow was deflected by his chest armor, and Octavius thanked his uncle for it. The sword was proving very valuable also. It cut very easily through the slaves' rough armor, to Octavius's glee.

"Legate! To the horses," Caecilius shouted, pointing at a stable near by. Octavius nodded his head and changed the direction towards the stables. He knew that their mere three hundred would soon be engulfed despite of how well they fought— they had to escape before more came rushing in.

Three hundred legionaries followed his direction, clearing a way to the stables. A big slave blocked him with a blow aimed at his neck, which Octavius ducked, barely managing not to fall. His back was going to give out soon, and he knew it. His footsteps were getting unstable. He thrust his sword at the man but missed, and the man broke into a grin. Octavius swung his sword again and this time their swords met with a large clang. They locked swords, trying to push the swords closer to each other's opponent. Octavius panicked as the man's strength overpowered him. Their swords drew closer to him, until the swords were only a few centimeters away from his neck. The man drew close, smiling at his victory. Octavius pushed, trying to unlock their swords, but the man's strength was brutal. The swords were drawing closer. Octavius shoved his helmet protected head towards the man, banging the man. The man stumbled, shocked at the blow against hard iron. Octavius took the time to wound him fatally.

Breathing violently, he made his way as fast as he could toward the stables, cutting down slaves in his path. Caecilius too was doing the same. Octavius surveyed the field and knew he had to hurry. Out of the three hundred, only a third of them were alive by now, and they too were covered with blood and grime.

Octavius slashed at the final slave standing in his way and cut the ropes that restrained the horse. The horse whinnied nervously at the commotion. Octavius patted at the horse carelessly, intent on the situation outside the stables. He jumped on the animal, surprising the animal once more. It shook its head violently.

"Caecilius! Where are you going?" he asked urgently. He had expected Caecilius to ride on another horse.

"To cut an escape path for you, sir," the man responded.

"Jump on a horse, quickly!" Octavius ordered, but

Caecilius was already out of the stables. Octavius cursed and followed him on his new horse.

Outside, there were even a fewer number of Roman legionaries left. They battled furiously, but Octavius knew that they would all be dead soon. It was futile. As he looked at fallen legionaries, he felt tears form once again, three hundred, risking their lives just for him. A drop fell, staining his armor. Then he knew that he could not leave them to all die while he went alive back to the camp.

They were cutting a path for him towards the exit of the camp. He spotted Caecilius fighting along the other legionaries.

"I am not leaving, Caecilius. I changed my mind. I can not leave all of you to be slaughtered while I escape," Octavius said defiantly, and Caecilius shook his head.

"No. You must leave. If you do not, then you are making the lives of three hundred legionaries worthless. They died so that you could escape, not for any other reason. They are not stupid enough to think that all of them could escape alive. They knew it from the start, but they did it because they wanted you, the legate of the Third, to live."

"I'm not a coward, Caecilius—"

"We knew it, Legate. I knew that I could not get out of

this alive. It was either dying in a fight with a comrade or dying in a fight with the slaves. I—we— prefer the latter. Go, sir," a deep voiced legionary interrupted, and Caecilius nodded.

"Go, Octavius. Go. All we want of you is to live and win the war."

Octavius hesitated. He had promised to himself that he would not run no matter what happened on the day he was made Tribune.

"This is not cowardly. Make their lives worthy!" Caecilius cried impatiently. "We are only a force of three hundred. There are more than ten times of our number back at our camp. They need you. The rest of the Third needs you," Caecilius yelled at him through the chaos. His eyes were desperate. Time was running out.

Octavius looked back at him, still unsure. His words were right however. If he did not get back, the command would probably go to Tribune Serstus. Lucius would not be able to accept his death, especially so soon after he heard about his sister's. Titus would blame himself for what had happened. What was more, the Third would be disbanded for losing their eagle. He gave a brief nod but instead of riding towards exit he went toward the arena. Ignoring

Caecilius's protest, he hurried as fast as he could towards the arena, where the legion eagle was reflecting the moonlight softly. It kept its place solemnly in the midst of the chaos. Octavius retrieved it, thanking the gods at the task being easier than he had imagined. Fighting on a horse gave him a lot more advantage than he had expected. Most of the slaves had never been close to horses before, and they panicked when Octavius drew near them on his new horse.

Octavius veered his horse again to a small road that the legionaries had made for him. They were fighting vigorously as they staked their lives to keep the road open for him to ride through. The road was crumbling as more and more legionaries fell.

Speed was fatal. Octavius ran as fast as he could on his horse, using the road. An arrow clanged off his helmet, and he cringed at the close call. When he got back, he would thank his uncle and Julius—the one who had brought up the idea of the armor—repeatedly.

He saw Caecilius fighting as he neared the exit. "Caecilius! I need you. The Third needs you," Octavius shouted, gesturing at him to ride with him. Caecilius flashed him a weary smile as he shook his head.

"I've lived long enough, Legate," he shouted over the

frenzy.

"No. I need you!" Octavius shouted. He could not lose Caecilius. Caecilius had been his subtle helper ever since he had helped him during the first battle with Crixus. The veteran's advice was more valuable than those of the other tribunes.

"This is the first order that I will not follow," Caecilius said, quoting Germanicus and still smiling. He managed to kill his opponent with a strike to the neck. "These legionaries need a commander. The Third needs a bigger commander. That is why I stay to command them while you go to command the Third," Caecilius said. "Go sir, go."

He then turned to face the handful of legionaries left. "Ave Legatus!" he shouted.

The legionaries shouted back, still engaged with their opponent. "Ave Legatus Octavius!" they shouted. Once more that day, Octavius felt his eyes warm and his throat beginning to thicken. He could not swallow.

Caecilius turned to have a last look at him. His eyes were full of determination. There was no regret. "Win the war for me. Crucify them, and I'll watch them from the Underworld," he whispered as he hit the horse from behind. The horse gave a panicked whinny as it galloped off. Octavius turned to look at Caecilius as Caecilius gave him a cheery wave. He could not see Caecilius clearly. His eyes were too watery for that.

⁕

"He's escaping, Spartacus!" Castus cried in distraught.

"Let him go. Someone needs to tell the Romans what happened," Spartacus said in a definite style, ignoring Castus's sullen looks. The man was similar to Crixus in many ways.

"They're shooting arrows at him," Castus said.

"Order them to stop," Spartacus replied, and Castus grumpily carried out his orders. A life for a life, Spartacus thought. He had thanked Octavius today for all Octavius had done to him before.

"Stop the chase, let him go," Spartacus said as he gazed at the last figures of Octavius disappearing into the night.

❧ 31 ❧

Octavius let out ragged breaths. The images of Caecilius dying flashed across his mind vividly, as his imagination escaped out of control. His back burned even more, and his head was dizzy from the loss of blood. As he escaped the slaves' camp, he had been targeted by some archers. Many missed and even those that had managed to hit him were deflected by the thick Roman armor. However, one had found its way to his arm, splitting open the wound he had gotten from Lucius. Blood flew but Octavius was afraid to take it out in case it might cause a vein to rip. If a vein ripped in his current situation, Octavius knew it would be the end of him.

He crossed the battlefield at full speed. The ground was littered with bodies and Octavius shivered at the sight of it. The field itself, however, was so tranquil that he could not imagine that this had been the death place of so many in the day. He could see the lights of the Roman camp from a distance and hurried on, relieved that he had come in the right direction. For a few minutes, he had been worried that he had chosen the wrong direction.

The light was like a savior to him, guiding him across the eerie plain. Finally, he managed to reach the gates. A sentry asked him who he was, and Octavius found it hard to answer. His voice was hoarse from shouting.

"Legate, Legate of the Third, Legate Octavius," he whispered weakly. It hurt him every time to say that he was a legate. He had become a legate through Suetonius's death. Don't think about it, he told himself. So far he had succeeded numbing his emotions.

The sentry seemed doubtful until Octavius lifted his tired face to look at the man on the rampart. "Tribune? No— Legate!" the man called. Octavius faintly realized him as a soldier of the First legion. "You have the eagle! Everyone thinks you are dead. By the way, General Crassus is planning to punish the Third," the man said as he came down to open the gates.

"What?" Octavius asked, his dazed head suddenly clearing.

"General Crassus is planning to punish the Third."

Octavius smiled. "Nothing to panic about. I have the

eagle," Octavius said.

"But that won't change a thing because the legion ran," the man said, stretching the word 'ran'.

Octavius could not believe his ears. His Third had ran? It was impossible. "You have to be kidding—"

"No sir. The Third did not have anybody to command them. You were thought to be dead, and Legate Suetonius had fallen in battle. They had been the legion that had advanced the most and so naturally, they were targeted by the slaves. It was complete chaos, and personally, I can't blame them," the man whispered.

Octavius shook his head as he let out a small laugh. "I don't believe a word."

"I swear on Jupiter," the man retorted. Octavius's face clouded. The man really seemed to be telling the truth. As much as he did not believe it, he thanked the man and raced his horse toward an empty lot where Crassus would be if the man's words were true. His hopes of a nice treatment and a hot meal were forgotten as he saw with a sickening feeling Crassus mounting a makeshift platform to speak. His uncle's face was cold as he began to speak.

"I had once thought that Roman legionaries would never run, especially from an attack from the slaves. They are lesser beings than us, but you still manage to run. Legate Mummius," Crassus called. The tied kneeling man wearily lifted his head.

"What were you thinking? You wanted to be famous. I know. You were thinking that if you managed to beat the slaves and perhaps capture Spartacus, you would be even more famous and popular than me. You would have imagined yourself on a chariot, parading through the gates of Rome receiving flowers and cheers from the crowd. The image blocked your brain, Mummius. It is enough blocked as it is," Crassus said coldly as he stared at the defeated legate. There was no room in his army for losers. Crassus decided his fate without any regrets. Arrius would be furious at him, but Arrius was a second matter to him. Mummius's impunity did not stretch so far as to being forgiven after losing two whole legions.

"Have this man whipped to death," he ordered briskly. A legate gave a whip to Crassus who stared at it in disdain. "Do you know how long it takes for a man to whip another to death? I am not going through the procedure. Centurion Regulus!" Crassus called to his most trusted centurion. The man saluted as he stepped forward. Crassus gave him the whip, and the man took it, somewhat reluctantly. He called to a few legionaries who tied Mummius onto a pole also half heartedly. They slowly ripped the chest armor and the tunic away, exposing bare skin. The centurion looked at Crassus, his eyes questioning. Crassus gave a nod, and the centurion lifted his whip, grimacing. He knew from his long experience that the death would be a long and painful death. Mummius seemed to know it too and had closed his eyes, his face filled with despair.

The crack of the whip rang out in the open lot. No sound came from anywhere else. The night was still and the legionaries did not dare to talk as they watched the death of Mummius.

Octavius too had been entranced by it. He could not do anything else but to stare at a legate being flogged to death. It was a brutal way to kill someone. He shook his head to clear his thoughts. He had to announce himself. When his uncle knew that he was alive, his uncle might reduce the Third's punishment in his new, cheerful mood. In a way, his uncle was similar to Spartacus. Both their emotions swung from side to side in short time.

He gently rode his horse toward the platform. The clatter of hooves earned everyone's attention in the silence. Even the centurion glanced back to see who the intruder was.

When they saw him, their mouths dropped in surprise. Some legionaries of the Third had recognized him and were talking among themselves, grinning. Titus and Lucius hugged each other.

Crassus was one of the last to look toward him. He frowned at the sight of Octavius until Octavius lifted his face to meet his uncle's eyes. Crassus gave an involuntary yelp. He recognized the armor. He recognized the face.

"Stop," he ordered the centurion who immediately let down the whip with some relief. Octavius cringed to see the man's once clean white back covered in blood red lashes. "Octavius?"

Octavius bowed his head in assent as he descended from his horse, not in his usual graceful style but a clumsy one. His back was literally killing him. Crassus descended from the platform swiftly. "Octavius. I thought you were— never mind. I had worried. We won the battle against those worthless dogs, but your legion had run and two of our legions commanded by Mummius were destroyed. Not a good price. I have been punishing them."

"My legion? The Third? Run?" Octavius asked, his eyes wide in shock. The sentry had been telling the truth after all.

"Yes, Your legion, the Third, ran. I will not blame you for the Third ran after you had fallen. But I shall still decimate them," Crassus announced loudly and a gasp rose from the soldiers. The Third looked at each other, their faces in panic. They had been expecting some kind of brutal punishment, but the decimation had been behind their imaginations. The practice after all, had been considered so brutal that it had been dead for centuries.

Octavius shook his head in disbelief. "I thought that practice was dead," he uttered slowly.

"I just revived it," Crassus said coldly.

"General, you cannot punish the Third with decimation. They had lost their legate and their tribune. They had nobody to command them. And I've heard that they were only engulfed because they had advanced too much. We cannot blame them for advancing, General."

"Who told you that?" Crassus asked, his eyes glinting coldly.

Octavius hesitated. "I heard it from those who were captured with me," he lied.

Crassus looked taken aback, and the legionaries murmured among themselves in wonder. "Captured?" he asked.

Octavius nodded. "Yes sir. Captured. I was knocked out

senseless and when I woke up I was inside a warehouse in the slave camp. Soon prisoners of the Third were thrown in with me. Spartacus ordered the prisoners to fight against each other in a death match. The slaves made fun of us. Then I ordered them to fight with their real enemies, and they did. They fought. They fought even though they knew it was hopeless. They provided me a route to escape," Octavius said and paused. He was afraid that he might burst into sobs if he continued.

"And you left them behind?" Crassus asked in a colder voice.

Octavius stared at him. "I did not want to. I preferred to die along with them. Then they said that most of the Third would be back at camp. They told me the Third needed somebody to command them. They threw away their lives for me, especially Centurion Caecilius. He could have lived but he died so that I could escape. He died for my future and the future of the Third. I owe them. I cannot let the Third face this fate. This fate would not be the fate that the brave legionaries had imagined."

Mournful whispers rose from the Third. All had respected Caecilius. They dropped their heads in further shame. They knew Caecilius had not died so that they could run and in turn be decimated.

"I have a feeling that there is more to this story," Crassus said, and Octavius nodded. He handed his uncle the eagle.

"I have the eagle. Do not disband the Third. Don't decimate them. Please," he whispered, and Crassus stayed motionless. A small cheer rose from the Third as they saw their eagle returned. Many lifted their heads again to glance at him, their eyes filled with hope and respect. Octavius held the gaze, but every moment was painful to him. The three hundred soldiers of the Third who would probably be all dead by now had also looked at him in the same way.

"I do not have any plans to disband the Third, but the decimation will carry out as planned," Crassus announced then gave a sudden jerk. "Octavius! Your arm!" Crassus whispered, low enough for only Octavius to hear, and Octavius nodded sheepishly. The arrow was still there. It did not hurt as long as he moved his arm— the wound did not seem to be so bad. Then of course, there was the possibility that he was feeling numb because of a greater challenge before him— the Third.

"Please," Octavius begged.

Crassus shook his head and without a word, the general rose on to the platform again. "Carry on," he announced to the centurion Regulus. "Legate Octavius," Crassus addressed, pleased at the new title. "Go have your wound dressed."

"What about the Third? They—" Octavius started but was cut off.

"Go to the doctor, legate. This is my order," Crassus announced, his voice becoming cold again. "The punishment shall carry on as planned."

The Third legionaries looked at him in despair. Their eyes were pleading, hoping for a rescue. Octavius hesitated. His uncle valued discipline more than any other thing, and he knew that if he did not obey a direct order, he too might be punished. However, he knew he could not let the Third die. Not after three hundred of them had sacrificed their lives for him. They had done so, so that he could save the rest of the Third. He would not fail them.

"Please. Please understand their position. They did not have any commanders. It was only natural that they ran," Octavius cried, tears welling up in his eyes once more. If they were decimated he would lose a tenth of his beloved soldiers and more from the lack of protection. They would be given a lesser of everything. They would be treated inferior. They would not be able to sleep inside the camp — becoming an easy prey for Spartacus. Soon most of his legion would be gone. All those he knew. He could not allow that.

Crassus's face turned icy. "Go treat your wound legate. This is a direct order, without any exceptions. Do not disagree with me."

Octavius shook his head, his voice trembling. He saw the faces of his Third. "Please rethink it! Do not decimate them! You will regret it! It would lead to a complete wipe out of another legion! General," Octavius shouted, his voice getting hoarser every second.

Crassus's temper frayed. As much as the young man was his nephew, the man was still one of his subordinates. His nephew, who had to obey his command, was still stubbornly standing there, talking to him so boldly. He had refused two direct orders from him. No one else would have dared to do so.

"Take him out of the lot!" he shouted. Two legionaries on guard slowly moved forward toward Octavius, doubt showing in their faces. Their steps were sluggish and indisposed as they continued their way, glancing nervously at Crassus.

"Immediately!" Crassus shouted once more, and the legionaries moved at a brisker pace. They hesitated to grab

Octavius and jumped when Octavius let out a painful yell as they grabbed him in the shoulders.

They moved their hands towards Octavius's arms, careful not to bother his wound. They gave a gentle tug but Octavius refused. He would not run again. He had run from the slave camp, whatever excuse. He had left the others to die while he was the only one who lived. Not anymore. If they died, he would die with them.

Octavius made a step forward, and the legionaries tugged him back, this time with more force.

"Don't decimate them!" Octavius shouted, his desperate voice ringing over the field. The legionaries pulled him back, and the tired Octavius could not resist the force of two sturdy legionaries as he was slowly pulled back. He desperately looked around for the other legates, but they did not meet his eyes, pitying the young man but more afraid of Crassus.

"Please legate. We do not want to drag you out of here like a criminal," one said, and Octavius shook his head.

"I am the only one left alive from the three hundred. They died for me. For what? So that I can run? Again? No. They wanted me to save the Third. I cannot disappoint them," Octavius spoke, his voice trembling with passion.

The legionaries glanced at each other, unsure of what to do.

Crassus lost his temper. He yelled at the legionaries to make their move if they too did not want to die with the others. That threat seemed to make them livelier as they half dragged his nephew out. His nephew weakly resisted, his eyes staring at nowhere in particular now. His eyes were empty— a look Crassus had never seen in his nephew. His nephew's eyes had been bright. Even when they were not, they had never been empty. This time it was as if he was staring into a man who had lost the reason to live. It tugged at his conscience, but Crassus did not let his conscience overrule him. He watched coldly as Octavius disappeared into the distance, probably to the doctor.

The centurion was still whipping the legate. The legate's eyes were closed, and blood had started to dribble out of his mouth. His back was red and blue, covered with a sickly red liquid. It was nothing. Soon would start the decimation. One in ten would be punched and kicked to death by their comrades—something even more painful physically and psychologically. It would be a long death, and a bitter one.

❖

"Who did you fight with this time?" the doctor asked

casually in a light tone but shut up after Octavius gave him a warning look. The two legionaries who had helped, or dragged, him here mouthed the word decimation. The doctor understood immediately, nodding briskly.

He carefully pulled the arrow out, ignoring the moans from his patient. "It could have been dangerous. You are pretty lucky," the doctor said but gave an inward sigh when Octavius did not respond.

He dressed the wound with infinite care, gently coating the wound with juice from herbs. "You should have come earlier. It would have been easier to cure. The wound is going to hurt for a while so don't use the arm if you want a fast recovery. Thank the gods it's your left arm," he said, looking at the young man intently. The patient's eyes were blank, and it showed sorrow—so much that the doctor could not help sympathizing with him.

Octavius stood up as soon as the doctor was finished dressing the wound. He could still use his sword arm. He flinched slightly at the sudden movement of his back.

"Sit down. You hurt your back too?" the doctor asked keenly as he tried to force Octavius down. Octavius shook the man free. He needed to go to his men. He had lost too many loved ones, Lucia, Suetonius, Caecilius. He knew he could not bear to lose anymore. It would be too much for him. As soon as he had somehow gotten over Lucia's death, two deaths had come barging in, now his legionaries. He could never allow that.

Octavius jogged for the door, his eyes intent now. He ignored the doctor calling for him and continued.

"Legate! Do not do anything stupid! There is nothing you can do!" Octavius ignored it and tried to make his way out of the tent.

However, before he even managed to get out, he was grabbed by two legionaries who roughly dragged him back. The doctor looked at him with sympathizing eyes. The legionaries also seemed to be unhappy with their job of dragging the legate here and there.

"I know this is hard for you, legate," the doctor said.

"Leave me. I want to go. If they die, I'm going to die with them. I'm not running a second time," Octavius rasped out. The doctor shook his head. He could see a fire burning in the man's eyes. The doctor, for a second, thought that the young legate looked better when his eyes were blank. The state the legate was in now was dangerous. He was half crazy, and able to commit headlong acts. The doctor sighed, as he decided what to do.

"I am doing this for you, legate." With that, the man forced his mouth open and poured something in. The last thing Octavius saw was the doctor looking worriedly at him.

⁂

Mummius was dead. Arrius would go crazy when he heard the news, but at his current mood, he did not care. Mummius had cost him almost ten thousand men and he would not forgive that.

He gazed at the soldiers of the Third. The gloomy looking centurions had forced the men down on their knees and were waiting silently. At least they did not wail out like his nephew. He had actually been embarrassed at how his nephew had refused to obey his command. If it had been someone else, the man would not have gotten away with it.

"The stones," he ordered and the centurions slowly walked toward their century to let the men pick the stones. The kneeling men picked their stones from a bag with trembling hands. Some almost smiled in relief when they saw that they were holding white stones. Then their faces turned grim as they saw their friends being condemned to die. Others cringed and stared blankly when they saw their stones were black. The centurions stood back, finished with their work.

Nobody spoke. Even those who had been lucky were silent as they mourned for their friends.

Four hundred men stood out from their ranks, staring blankly at the sky. Some were praying and some were weeping. Others were just casting their heads down, doing nothing. It was one thing to die in a battle. It was another to die by the order of their own commander.

Crassus gave a signal to start, and the comparatively lucky men started forming a circle around the men who were destined to die. They stood still like that, staring at each other, exchanging soft words of good bye.

"Tell my family I died while fighting," a legionary whispered to those who were circling him, and they nodded mournfully. One whispered an apology as he reached out tentatively to hit the man. The man stayed still, his eyes downcast now. Others followed suit, and the man remained still, never once looking up at his fellow comrades. The nine legionaries who were hitting the man wept as they did so, sniffling. Their sobs grew louder as their comrade fell knee first with blood trickling out of his mouth. The punches and kicks continued until the man had stopped breathing.

The nine others looked at their fallen comrade saying nothing. They stared at him, aware that they had killed the man. It was the same in other places—legionaries wept silently for the comrade that they themselves had killed.

"What an unmanly lot," Crassus growled to the other legates, hearing the soft sobs. The other legates just bowed their heads, afraid to even look into the man's eyes. Crassus had shown what a vicious commander he could be. They pitied the young man who was known to be only eighteen years old. He was too young to be a legate— he was too young to bear the responsibilities and the sorrows of decimation.

"Guards, clean the lot of dead men. Third, you shall now sleep outside the camp until I see you are fit to sleep within the walls again. Your rations shall be reduced to barely and wheat. You are not part of the regular Roman army anymore, though it could change. Now, get out," Crassus ordered impassively and stared with a cold eye as he saw his orders carried out.

❦ 32 ❦

Octavius opened his eyes groggily. It took a moment for him to remember what had happened to him and cursed the doctor aloud. He rose from the bed, ignoring a throbbing pain in his head. His back ached also.

"You've got good bones, legate. Nothing was broken. You just need some time to heal. Same with your arm, just need to dress it now and then," the doctor said, his voice light.

Octavius ignored him. As long as his spine was not broken, it was fine. He stood up and closed his eyes trying to lessen the pain in his head. It was probably the effects of being drugged yesterday.

"Oh gods," he whispered as the pain continued. It had moved from the side of his head to the back, and now they throbbed in unison. "What have you done?" he moaned miserably, and the doctor shook his head.

"Just a side effect. You'll get over it soon," he responded.

"What happened to the Third?" Octavius asked, his voice urgent and demanding.

The doctor took a deep breath. "Do you want the truth or do you want the good version?"

Octavius snapped his eyes open and reached for his gladius but grabbed empty air. He realized that the doctor had taken off his armor and had only left his tunic on. He cursed and looked around the room to see where his sword was. It was at the end of the room, his armor along with it.

"You're lucky I did not have my gladius with me doctor," Octavius said coldly. "What do you think I want?"

"The good version?" the doctor attempted, and Octavius shot toward the end of the room for his gladius. The doctor held up his hands, and tried to calm the younger man.

He could not think of a good way to tell him, so he hung his head and whispered that he was sorry, his voice low. Octavius stared at him, his eyes becoming blank again.

"Legate?" the doctor called worriedly.

Octavius did not respond for a long time. Then he shook his head as if he wanted to clear his thoughts. When he finally spoke, the content was of something the doctor had never even imagined.

"Help me put my armor on, doctor," Octavius commanded. "No word of this to anyone or else," Octavius added.

The doctor hesitated. He opened his mouth to object, but Octavius shook his head. "And no objections," Octavius ordered. He was already strapping on his chest plate. "Help me tie the back, will you?" he asked, and the doctor groaned.

"Why are you always dragging me into illegal stuff? Last time you also told me to keep my mouth shut, which is illegal by the way of not reporting things. Just tell me what you are going to do. Do you know how much trouble I had in keeping my mouth shut last time? And where do you think you are going with that wounded arm and back of yours?" the doctor protested indignantly, all the while helping Octavius strap his armor on.

The doctor stretched his arms after finishing his work. "You better pretend you are very sick, Legate, if you want to sleep within the camp," he advised.

"I have no desire to sleep here, away from my legion. They could be in danger from attacks. If they die, I will die along with them," Octavius responded. "Thanks anyway. Keep quiet," Octavius smiled and patted the man. The doctor rolled his eyes but stopped when he saw Octavius's face. His face mirrored his true feelings, grief and anger—something too much for such a young man. But what worried him the most was the sturdy determination that showed on his face.

"Don't worry too much. I'll be back," Octavius said with a slight smile on his face as he briskly walked out of the tent.

Octavius reached the gates of the camp at a hurried pace. The pain in his head had settled down to a mere nuisance, and he felt a lot fresher than he had the day before though he was still tired. He had been planning to call for his horse, but he realized that his horse was not there anymore. It gave him an odd sense of grief.

The sentries saluted him, casting a nervous look. They were not sure how he would react after the decimation.

"Tiberius, where is the Third camped?" Octavius asked briskly, as if everything was normal, and the man stammered.

"They are camping on the plain," he said and paused. "They... are not in such good conditions, Legate," the man said, and Octavius nodded. He had been expecting that.

"That's not what I mean...," the man said hesitantly. Octavius looked at him inquiringly but decided that it would be better not to waste time and go take a look for himself. It was when he stepped out of the high walled camp did he realize the true meaning of the sentry's words.

His Third were clustered on the side of the plain, watching the smoke going up from the field as Roman legionaries burned the dead.

They seemed to be at least a kilometer away, and Octavius groaned at the distance he would have to walk. Still, he hurried on. He needed to meet his men. He could not give up now.

When Octavius neared the Third, he almost regretted in coming. The once well polished Third now sat dejected on the plain, huddled in groups and muttering silently among themselves. Some had a fire going on, and soldiers sat around it, perhaps thinking of their lost comrades.

In one corner, Octavius spotted the centurions too clustered in a group. Their heads were down, and they seemed to be on the verge of crying. Only when he walked among the legionaries, did they realize that he was there with them. They lifted their heads in hope, sorrow and in embarrassment.

"Centurions," Octavius barked. The group looked up, surprise showing in their faces. "I want the legion in square formation," he ordered briskly ignoring their strange looks. The legion half heartedly listened to his command. And when he saw the empty spaces of the square, Octavius felt his heart rip. Centurions pushed others into the gap, filling the formation.

"You did not even know I was coming. What would you have done if Spartacus came?" Octavius asked, his tone flat. He watched as his legionaries bowed their heads, their humiliation and sorrows growing.

"He would attack soon. This is something I can guarantee on. He has good scouts. I want men ready for a raid. Set up barricades," Octavius ordered. The men lifted their heads again at the prospect of having something to do to forget their current situation.

"Do you want to camp here the rest of the war? I want all of you back into the barracks by tomorrow, and for you to do that, you must do something that the Crassus cannot deny." He took a long breath. "No matter what happened, I know you are the best legion of the generation. I will not have Rome's best legion treated such," Octavius said. He knew it was an overdose, but he was glad to see some spirit return. A few correct words were all it took.

"I know many of you have lost your fellow legionaries. I too have lost people who I love and respect, Suetonius and Caecilius among them. However, we cannot dwell on their deaths much longer. They will be watching, and we cannot disappoint those who have died for the Third," Octavius announced firmly, his tone growing somber as he remembered the two men. His speech also reminded him of Lucia.

"Serstus, I want you to set up a barricade," he ordered.

"But we don't have the tools," Serstus objected.

"I gave you an order. It is up to you to obey it," Octavius replied knowing that he needed to make the man understand that he was in complete command now. He could not tolerate the man's jealousy any longer. "Go get the tools from our real camp. Tell the sentry you need to visit the doctor and have the doctor bring you the tools. He will understand when you say you came under my orders."

Octavius did not hesitate to see if the man had understood. "Tribune Rufius, lead a cohort out to scout for Spartacus's movements. The camp is not far away, so be careful to not be spotted. Centurion Titus, I want you to be in charge of arranging the men in defense position. I will instruct you the details in person," Octavius said and took a deep breath. "Go do it," he said, and the legion cheered at the prospect of being able to act as a regular legion of the Roman army.

"But Legate," Serstus said. He barely said the word

'legate', and Octavius felt some inner amusement at that. "We have not eaten yet. The men are not rested enough."

"What do you propose to do then?" Octavius asked.

"I say we wait until food comes," Serstus said stubbornly. "This is a foolish idea," the man said, looking around for supporters.

Octavius shrugged. "You can. Anybody else who wants to wait?" he asked, and no one dared to raise their hand. "Very well. Centurion Lucius, you are in command of bringing the tools and setting up defense. Tribune Serstus, you can wait until the rations come," Octavius ordered, smiling mirthlessly.

The tribune opened his mouth to protest, but the young legate had already disappeared.

<hr>

Dannotalos giggled at the mere thought of it. Finally he would be able to lead his brothers in the battle against the Romans. He still remembered the day when he and his fellow tribe members had been sold as slaves by the Romans. They had acted as an invincible tribe of mercenaries in Gaul but their main fault was that they had grown overconfident. They had believed they could beat the Romans but lost by a large margin. In consequence, they had served as gladiators near Thurii. Now he could take revenge on a certain unfortunate, lonely, unsuspecting legion. Spartacus had granted him the honor.

"Thank you. You can rely on me," he said as he gave a slight bow to Spartacus. Spartacus gave a smile and waved him away. Dannotalos smiled back and moved toward the tent flap. He gave a wink to a fat merchant who was rumored to be from Thurii as he went out. Rumor had it that he was the key to preparing their escape to Sicily. The merchant was staring at a blue diamond with hungry eyes.

The fat merchant looked at the exiting Gaul suspiciously before returning his gaze to Spartacus. "Resume," he said, and Spartacus nodded.

"I am not sure if we can make it to Gaul with Crassus hot on our heels. He will do everything to stop us," Spartacus said frankly. He gesticulated at a golden cup sitting on the table, and the merchant helped himself to the wine. The man tasted it with his lips and purred at the delectable favor. Spartacus watched with some inner amusement. The merchant was getting the perception that they were rich. His plan was succeeding.

"And?"

"Well, I want to escape this cursed peninsula. There are two ways of getting out, one by crossing the Alps and one by the sea." Spartacus paused a little and tinkered with a gold ring on his finger. The merchant appeared relaxed, yet Spartacus saw that he could not take his eyes off the ring. "But crossing the Alps is easier said than done, so I'd like to go by the sea... Our army can do many things, but they cannot construct good fleets that will carry all of us out to Sicily. We need your help, Sempronius."

The man pretended to think about it. "So you want my help, Spartacus. But I am nothing but a merchant," he said.

"And a pirate if you don't mind," Spartacus added with some humor.

Sempronius shrugged, his overweight body trembling a little. "Some call me that, some don't. I am, Spartacus, a man of many trades," he said, winking slightly.

"You are outlawed, aren't you? Castus told me so," Spartacus said, frowning slightly. Sempronius gave a shrug again.

"No I am still a Roman though I don't give a damn about that. It was a good deal you put up. Two hundred talents for a shipment to Sicily," the man said. "Before we continue, Spartacus, I am actually wondering if you even have that much. It is quite a sum, you know," the man said, a little wistfully.

Spartacus laughed. He waved at all the goods that were in the room. "You do not believe me even now?" he asked as he led the man to a chest. He nodded generously to the questioning eyes of the merchant pirate who opened the chest eagerly. The man let out a squeal of delight as he saw the gold in the chest.

"Gold. Gods, gold," he said as he giggled. "Now that sapphire will cost about half a talent, the emerald, yes. It looks fine, could be forced at a quarter of one talent. The ruby! Gods! Lovely. Lovely. My everlasting wife, gold," the man said as he ran a chubby hand over the content. His face betrayed childish delight.

He admired the content a little more before speaking again. "I am very impressed, Spartacus. Looting?" he asked, and Spartacus nodded. "However, this is not the value of two hundred talents," he said, his face growing stern.

Spartacus nodded again. "Yes. I am aware. We have the money, yet we are afraid that you might not be very enthusiastic to take us to Sicily after you have received the whole sum."

Sempronius gave a hearty laugh. "You and I are partners

now. We should trust each other.”

“You were the first to suspect me,” Spartacus said casually, and the man laughed again.

“Very keen, very. All right. So you are saying that this is my first payment?” Sempronius asked, and Spartacus grunted.

“Yes. It should be a hundred talents, maybe more.”

“Nah, not more, less,” Sempronius said.

Spartacus shrugged. “I am paying you more than you are due for our ride to Sicily.”

“It shows how urgent your situation is. Anyway, fine, Spartacus. Give me another hundred talents of gold when you reach the bottom of this ‘cursed’ peninsula. My men will have prepared a fleet to take you all to Sicily in a hidden cove near Thurii,” Sempronius announced heartily as he drunk another cup of wine. “It’s marked here, on this map. I’ll give this copy to you. Anyway, when will that be?”

“Make it the Ides of November. We will be there.”

“One month? Is it enough?”

“Yes.”

“All right, Partner. I will trust you,” Sempronius said.

Spartacus nodded, and lifted his wine cup. “To Sicily, where we can start our own kingdom.”

"It was humiliating. Your uncle was relentless. The air smelled of blood," Titus said as he related the scene of the decimation to Octavius. "Now the legionaries know that their own commander is even scarier than Spartacus's gladiators," Titus said, finishing his rundown of the decimation.

Octavius nodded solemnly. "True," he said. "I am quite sure no one will run now, though the decimation must have decreased the morale."

Titus nodded and sighed as he looked at the legionaries of the Third whose spirits were returning at a rapid pace. "You did a good job," Titus commented, and Octavius smiled in reply.

"I have to fit my rank," Octavius said, his tone both light and somber. Titus gave a bark.

"No matter what your rank is, you are still a younger brother to me." Octavius rolled his eyes at Titus's words.

"Okay, older brother," Octavius started mockingly. "I want the defense line two lines deep, facing Spartacus. The length of the line is up to you. Be sure to leave out a few men for construction, scouting and for messengers. Leave the messaging to fast men. It is really a pity that our cavalry's horses are all at the barrack stables," Octavius said.

"Older brothers don't usually get commanded by younger ones," Titus said, frowning. Octavius gave a slight smile.

"Of course. Anyway, would you please hurry because I have a feeling they'll come soon. I did not order you this time. I asked you if you could hurry," Octavius said, putting on an innocent expression. This time it was Titus who rolled his eyes as he walked off to obey his orders.

❧ 33 ❧

Octavius felt adrenaline rush. His veins pumped rapidly and blood shot to his face, making him hot. It was as he had expected. A raiding force had come.

Then he relaxed a little as he saw that the force was only a little over thousand men. He regretted going through the trouble of building the defenses. Spartacus had underestimated his Third too much, even in their weakened state.

"Fight behind the defenses. Kill as many as you can with spears and rush out," he ordered briskly to the centurions. It felt odd to be in complete command. He had never been in charge of a complete battle since he had fought Crixus.

"Lucius, your spear," he called, and Lucius threw his spear, his spear falling a little short. Lucius's spear was known to be deadly in range, and only a few men in the legion could beat him. His spear marked the range of the Roman spears. The raiding group glanced nervously at each other. They knew what the spear meant, hesitating a little before passing the spear. Then they broke into a sudden rush, yelling and growling.

"Launch," Octavius said calmly. He had seen the effects of the spears before. Spears hailed through the sky making whishing noises. Even before one was down the legionaries were throwing another into the sky.

Thud... Thud... Octavius heard the dull sound of the spears hitting their target. The plain was filled with screams. When the spears finally ran out, Octavius surveyed the field to see about seven hundred men alive, three hundred dead under spears. It was a pretty good start.

Just as he was about to order a full rush, he stopped. A brilliant thought had just reached his mind. "Rufius, take the first and the fifth cohort and maneuver around them. Left flank. Purpose is to cause confusion. Do not attack unless necessary. Titus, your orders are the same with the second and the seventh cohort. Right flank," he said. He saw the confusion in the eyes of the legionaries. He smiled. They were about to get a good surprise, as much as the slaves.

The two men obeyed quickly, detaching from the main body. The slaves were no doubt confused and afraid after the slaughter by the spears. They seemed even more per-plexed when they saw the cohorts moving away. Octavius laughed savagely. They were too inexperienced with the Roman style.

"Flank them. Circle them. Trap them," he said. The cohorts easily succeeded in getting around the army and were closing in. Slaves murmured to each other and looked around at their enemy nervously. The enemy was at all sides now.

"First line, main body. Go make your kill," Octavius commanded, and the first line strode forward in the usual form, stepping out from their defenses. They shielded their companion on the left while stabbing with the right. Baffled slaves fell like a stack of dominos. Octavius could see their muscular bodies and gave a low whistle. They could prove to be formidable if they had a right leader. It might have been Spartacus. It definitely was not the man leading this raid.

Once he decided that the raiding force was on the verge of running, he gave the order. "Stop." Legionnaires turned to stare at him, also bemused. He ignored them and instead chose to speak to the slaves.

"Do you understand Latin?" he asked, and nobody

answered. He doubted they didn't. At least one would have understood. "I'll ask once more. Do you understand me?" he yelled, but silence was perfect.

Octavius sighed. There was only one way left to see if they understood him. "All right, Third. They are trapped. Kill them all," he ordered, and the legionaries held up their arms again.

"No!" A single voice called from the slave lines, and Octavius smiled. "What do you want, Roman?" it demanded hostiley.

"I want to negotiate," he said, earning bemused looks from his own soldiers. He was winning the battle. There was no need to negotiate. "Who is the leader?" he asked, and there was silence. "Quickly, before I order the legion to slaughter you again."

Octavius's threat was well received. A man stood up, the same one who had spoken, looking around defiantly. "Your want, Roman?" he asked in a deep voice.

"Put down your arms."

The leader shook his head. "For what? So that you could kill us easier?"

"I have no problem in killing you even when you are armed," Octavius whispered threateningly, waving to his legion. Hatred flashed across his face as he heard the comment, but the man bowed his head, thinking.

"Why?" he asked stubbornly.

"I will tell you after. I promise I will not kill you if you agree with me— and I promise to be quite reasonable. Take it or leave it," Octavius said.

"How good is the word of a Roman?" the man asked, his voice getting deeper. Octavius decided to ignore the question.

"What were you before you became a slave? You don't seem like a born slave."

"A mercenary, along with my brothers here," the voice responded grudgingly. Octavius laughed out loud in which all the men there jumped.

"Perfect, couldn't have been better. Are you still a mercenary? Or do you now serve Spartacus?" he asked. He opened his mouth to answer, but closed it again. Well thought, Octavius mused to himself. It was a loaded question.

"Depends," the man said diplomatically. Octavius smiled.

"I hope you still are a mercenary, for your own sake." The man perked up his head as Octavius said so. A slow smile crept into his face, and Octavius gave a slight smile back. The man was not so stupid.

"I am. Along with my brothers," the man responded, gazing hopefully at Octavius. Octavius nodded.

"Good. You will not be mercenaries from now on." Confused faces stared at him. "You will be Roman legionaries, unofficial members of the Third until I see you fit. Take it or leave it," Octavius said again.

Gasps rose from both the legionaries and the slaves. "No, Octavius. They are slaves," Lucius protested and was supported by many nods.

"Our legion is undermanned. We need to fill in the numbers soon. This does not mean that the former legionaries can be exchanged with them. We cannot, and must not, forget them. This just means that we are filling up our numbers," Octavius said and turned to the leader. "I do not have all day."

"The wages?" the man asked.

"I don't think you are in the position to ask me that now though I will answer you, 225 denarii per year for a regular legionary. Food, armor, and other basic goods are handed out to you. You will not receive that much until I see that you can serve as a regular." Octavius ignored the groans from the slaves. "A hundred denarii, remember, this is until you prove yourselves to me. After that, you will be treated the same with the others. If you agree with these conditions, put your arms down and sit. If you don't, you may stand up. I promise that our legion archers will take the man out in seconds."

The slaves grumbled and murmured but in the end they all sat down, leaving their arms on the floor. It wasn't of course, much of a choice. "Your arms will be replaced with legionary weapons. Lucius, take the weapons away from them." Lucius obliged, though his face told him that he was disagreeing with the whole thing.

"Remember, if you do not prove to be useful and loyal, you will be cut down without mercy. Understood? Now you may take the sacramentum, the oath that will bind you as a legionary. Titus, arrange a marching form for our legionaries. We will enter the gates of our barracks confidently. We deserve that much. We have proved ourselves once again. The Third is now reborn."

~ *34* ~

"Crassus has what?" Arrius yelled in fury at a messenger. The messenger did not dare to speak up.

"That man has dared to execute my son? Whipping to death? The man is out of his mind. He... I have warned him before, and I do not warn simply for the sake of hearing my own voice. I warn because I plan to carry out the threat if necessary. I will rebuke him of his position as a praetor," Arrius said, mainly to himself, and the messenger looked back at him, surprise evident on his face.

"Messenger," Arrius addressed. "You are to hurry to Pompey. I heard he has almost cleared out the rebel there. Give him this scroll," Arrius said, writing something briefly down in the parchment paper. The messenger bowed and exited with a flourish.

⋅•⟨❈⟩•⋅

Crassus gaped at his nephew. His nephew had just finished telling him all that the Third had gone through.

"I did not know of the attack."

"It ended quickly," Octavius replied curtly. He did not want to talk much with the man who had decimated his legion so violently yesterday.

Crassus nodded patiently. He was in a good mood today, Octavius noticed. "I agree with you. The Third is now free of their punishment. Take that order, Sextus," Crassus said to a legionary next to him, and the man obeyed. "You should not, however, have incorporated the ragged mercenary band. Once a mercenary, always a mercenary. There is a certain addiction with money," Crassus said, a little wistfully.

"I'm sure it can be cured," Octavius said a little stiffly. "We were short of about two cohorts— it was needed."

Crassus nodded, though reluctantly. "But Octavius, let me tell you. There is no advantage in incorporating mercenary bands. They can't seem to get rid of their habit. Think well on that. Anyway, we need to get ready for a march by tomorrow dawn. Spartacus is said to be heading south," Crassus informed him with a sigh. "He's leading us on a vicious march all across Italy terrifying civilians. I cannot guess why he has turned south."

"It could be that he will go northward again after he leads us south. Maybe he wants us to follow him so that he can put us behind them again. This time he will head straight for the Alps and not stop to fight us. All will be lost after that."

Crassus shook his head. "No. Even if he does, the northern legions would be enough to hinder him until we come to rescue. He knows that. He knows we will be hot on his trail. You, Octavius, have never seen the maximum pace of Roman legions. I am not even sure if there is a maximum. Don't worry about it. Go have a rest, Octavius. You look exhausted."

Octavius bowed his head slightly and retreated out of his uncle's commander tent. It was surprising how his positive feelings toward his uncle were gone, replaced by enmity that was masked by politeness. He had seen his uncle's true form, and it terrified him.

He walked slowly out of the command tent and walked into his. Relieved that both Titus and Lucius were elsewhere, he lay on his bed, letting himself finally think about Suetonius, Caecilius and the decimation. All the confidence he had brought up during the fight was exhausted. He closed his eyes and simply wept.

———❦———

Octavius exited his tent, a completely different person in the outside. He had erased all the traces of crying, and he was now back to his confident self, or as the legions viewed him.

Octavius thought it would be better to meet Dannotalos before he went to go find Lucius and Titus. The Gaul had a very interesting history and had a talent of telling it well. He had started the story on their way back, and it was a story that Octavius wanted to keep hearing. Dannotalos stood stiffly to attention when Octavius neared him. The man clearly knew how to behave.

Octavius smiled at the man casually as he sat down on a boulder. He gestured for the man to sit, and he obeyed though he glared at Octavius with guarded eyes.

"Continue," Octavius said, and the man stared.

"This was not part of the contract. I never promised to tell you my history." Octavius shrugged.

"If you have nothing more to tell me I will go away." Octavius rose but the man stopped him.

"I have a question. What post am I?"

"You aren't fully accepted yet," he started, and the man's face clouded. "Clearly you are their leader. Your Gauls have been dispersed throughout the legion. You can not hope to lead them all. What post do you think suits you?" he asked, clearly flustering the man.

The man thought for a long time before he opened his mouth. "I don't know. Roman posts, they all are—," the man stopped himself from saying a curse word to Octavius's amusement. "Not familiar," the man finally concluded.

Octavius smiled. "You know. You know the Tribunes, Centurions, Optios, Tesserariuses and more. What do you want then?"

The man smiled savagely. "A legate, but obviously you don't have any intentions of giving me that post. I don't think centurions would follow me even if I became a Tribune. I'd rather..." he blushed sheepishly. "Become a centurion."

Octavius laughed, frustrating Dannotalos. "Well thought. I have a shortage of centurions. I could use one. Someone who is capable, fights well, and has some brains." The man perked up his head and stared in anticipation at Octavius. "Do you have those traits?"

The man hesitated and nodded his head. "Yes. I led a

fearless mercenary tribe. All Gaul feared me and my brothers."

"Good. Then there is the final trait, the most important one, loyalty. I need someone who is loyal. Do you have that trait?" Octavius asked, smiling inwardly.

The man hesitated again, his face flushing. "That cannot be proven in words. You will not trust me even if I told you I was loyal."

Octavius nodded. Of course he would not. "You would have to prove yourself to the Roman legions. Then you can have a century of your own. Half Roman, half Gaul."

Dannotalos looked eager. "How do I prove myself? Spartacus is going south toward Sicily. He's not going to fight Romans—us—again."

Octavius looked at him in the face suddenly. "Sicily?"

The man's face colored. The time had finally come for him to decide his side once and for all. He could choose to be loyal to Spartacus and not tell the young legate. On the other hand, he could choose to tell his new commander. He and his brothers have been fighting for freedom. If he told and was accepted into the legion, then he and his brothers would attain their goal. Not only that, but he would have a regular pay and after twenty five years of service he would become a Roman citizen. The thought was very tempting. After all, freedom had been their ultimate goal.

He took a deep breath. "Sicily. He's made a deal with a pirate merchant to take him there. Don't ask me why. His name is Sempronius."

"That's it?"

"Yes," Dannotalos said truthfully.

"Sempronius? That will be hard to track. How does he look?"

"He's a fat man, oily black hair, green eyes. Don't go together, though I have no right to say so, rumored to be from Thurii. They say he also works in Sicily."

"Pirates aren't usually so fond of telling where they are from."

"Ah yes, but he's not an official pirate. He of course does some pirating and smuggling but officially, he's just a Roman merchant in Thurii. No doubt he smuggles money into the hands of Roman officers and avoid being caught."

Octavius nodded. The practice was common enough. "And how do you know this?"

Dannotalos smiled. "When I came to fight your—our—legion, he arrived at Spartacus's camp. I heard bits from here and there."

Octavius gave a smile at him that was growing larger. If Spartacus went toward the south thinking that a fleet would be waiting for him, he would be devastated when he found out there was no fleet. He would not be able to turn north again, meaning that he would have to stay in the toe of the peninsula. Once he was there, he was a lion in a cage. It would be easy to finish the rebellion off then.

"Do you know where to find him?"

"No, but I know how. The man is completely in love with jewelry."

~ 35 ~

Pompey wiped his bloody sword on a dead man as he gazed at the battlefield with the legions cheering him. He had succeeded in putting out the rebellion. He stood there, completely drenched in his own thoughts when a scout rode up to him in a tremendous hurry.

"What?" he asked, irritated.

"Sir, a message from Senator Arrius from Rome."

"Rome? Senator Arrius?" he asked. He had heard the notorious name before, yet he had never had a direct contact with him.

"Yes, sir," the scout responded as he handed Pompey a scroll. Pompey snatched it out of his hands to read.

> *My dear Pompey,*
> *I hear that you are doing a good job with the bastards in Hispania. I understand your full powers- I have watched you carefully since the reign of Sulla. Forgive me for introducing*

Pompey handed the scroll back to the scout, glaring at the man. He had been feeling perfect until now. Crassus was a long time friend of his, and Arrius was practically asking him to betray the man. He was pretty sure, from the rumors, that Arrius was manipulating him to help out his needs. Arrius was known to be a snake. A snake that used people until they were needed and discarded them without thought after. He could not submit his fate to such man.

Pompey snatched the scroll out of the scout's hands again as he turned the parchement paper over. He scribbled something briefly and threw it back to the scout.

"Senator Arrius, Rome," he said, and he turned back to his soldiers again to receive their salutes.

———— ·◆· ————

"Are you sure you can trust him?" Legate Claudius said. Octavius shrugged.

"I do. It was by an accident that he let the word out. He meant it for real. There is no reason to play false." Claudius shrugged at Octavius's response, not seeming to be persuaded.

Other legates too sat in grim silence. "We've got six legions. If the Third goes, then we will be left with five. It is not enough to take down Spartacus," Legate Bassus said, expressing his doubt.

"He will not waste time in turning to face the main body. He has made a contract to be in Thurii by the Ides of November, at least, according to the man. It will be hard for him to lead all the elderly, the sick, the children... He cannot spare enough time for a battle. He will continue south as long as he believes Sempronius is there waiting for him. When he finally realizes that he is not, it will be too late. After we get rid of Sempronius, we will join the main force again," Octavius announced. The others were silent, musing over the idea.

Crassus gave a fake cough to draw attention. "If we can only be sure of the information you are telling us…If it is true, then there is no flaw in your plan."

"It is true," Octavius said firmly. "I trust my men."

Crassus looked wearily at his nephew. He shook his head slightly. "Some just cannot be trusted. Anyway, I believe it is a good idea for you to find Sempronius. If Spartacus escapes to Sicily, the problem will get bigger. It will take a few months for all our legions to get to Sicily and set up encampments there. All the while Spartacus would be gathering a bigger slave force. I promised the senate a quick victory, and I need to give it to them.

"If this information is true… we cannot let Spartacus do as he plans. The risk is too high. I'm also pretty sure that Spartacus will not turn to confront us. He does not have time enough for that. He knows he is wasting precious time on enemy territory. Therefore, I allow your leave, Octavius," Crassus concluded. His eyes searched the other officers' expressions, and they all dropped their gazes in assent. Crassus smiled inwardly. They would never dare to oppose him, especially after the death of Mummius. Clearly, they all remembered it vividly.

"How are you going to find him?" Crassus asked, and his

nephew smiled.

"My new centurion told me that Sempronius is fascinated with jewelry. If you can lend me one, I might try putting it up on sale in Thurii," Octavius said, and Crassus frowned. "It must be very rare and expensive looking. If it is so, I am pretty sure he will appear by himself. Dannotalos—that is the name of the centurion—he has seen the man's face before so he will know."

"And if it fails?" Crassus asked doubtfully.

"It won't. But if it does, my Third can lead an effective search throughout Thurii. I have a feeling that many merchants, given the right levers, would know Sempronius. So would the Roman officers there," Octavius explained.

Crassus heaved a sigh. "The jewel. Will a large, clear diamond be all right? It is very, very expensive." Crassus saw his nephew nod and sighed again. "Octavius, will I be able to get it back?" he whispered.

Octavius was careful not to let contempt show on his face. Spartacus was leading a slave army that was ravaging the cities of Rome, and he had just proposed a move that might lead to the complete destruction of the slave army. He could not believe that his uncle, the richest man in Rome, was worrying about losing a diamond.

"Yes sir. You will. It is only a bait." Octavius kept a straight face as he saw Crassus's face relax. Crassus finally nodded.

"Good. Be careful and do not ever fight Spartacus's army. Understand?" Crassus ordered, hoping that his nephew would be more sensible than Mummius had been.

"Yes sir. I will give them a wide berth. I will try to go to Thurii in secret if I can, though a legion force would be easy to detect," Octavius said, and Crassus nodded pleasantly.

"Go quickly. I want to end this war quickly. And before you go, I will give you a letter with my mark on it."

"For what?" Octavius asked, perplexed.

"Those legions in Thurii will not listen to you, and that might cause a problem. It is a letter containing the limits of your power. I am giving you command of the southern legions until I reach there. Your word is my word," Crassus announced, pleased at the shock that showed in his nephew's face.

Octavius sat in silence and so did the other legates. Your word is my word. Octavius's head felt light in the thrill of it. He was to be in complete command of them until Crassus came. His vein pulsed. He could not believe it.

"I—" he stammered, and Crassus laughed.

"It's only temporary so don't become too happy about

it," Crassus said as he tried to meet his nephew's eyes. His nephew met his gaze directly for the first time since the decimation of the Third. He knew how his nephew had been feeling about him. He had been meaning to make it up, at least a little, to his nephew. His nephew bowed thanks and saluted smartly, but Crassus felt pain as he stared deep into his nephew's eyes. Before there had been love. Now he could not find the feeling anywhere in the young man's eyes.

<hr>

"Your word is my word," Titus called teasingly as they marched south. They were turning around Spartacus, giving the army a wide berth as he had promised Crassus. They were traveling at a forced pace, and the legionaries looked exhausted. Titus still teased him, making cat—calls, and repeating what Crassus had said.

"Would you do me a favor?" Octavius asked suddenly.

"Sure."

"Shut up."

Titus rolled his eyes, and was about to protest when Octavius spoke again. "I'm actually not even a legate. The Senate can send anybody to become the legate of the Third. They think me too young."

"Age is not an accurate factor when it comes to you, Octavius. You lead better than other legates," Titus said, and Octavius blushed. He looked around if the others had heard, but the tribunes were out of range and Lucius was tending to his own century. As much as he needed experienced advice, he needed someone who would be completely loyal to him if he wanted to succeed in this mission. Caecilius would have been the perfect person, but he was not here. The person he could rely on the most were his two friends, Lucius and Titus.

"They'll let you keep your post until the war is over, unless you do something seriously wrong. You'd better succeed in this mission. That will guarantee your post," Titus said and Octavius smiled.

"Oh it will. I've got the precious diamond," he said and patted his chest. He carried the diamond he had received from his uncle with him always. There were too many men who knew of the diamond, and as much as he trusted his men, this was a too big of a risk to be taken. There were some men who he could not rely on; especially among them were the tribunes. Many seemed to be accepting him now as their superior but for Serstus who tried to counter everything Octavius did.

Titus broke into Octavius's thoughts. "Octavius, can you trust Dannotalos?" he asked.

"Why?"

"Well, what your uncle said is true. Once a mercenary, always a mercenary."

Octavius reflected the point for a moment. Then he shrugged. "Mercenaries always try to be on the advantageous side. Right now, Dannotalos has more advantage here than he would elsewhere. There is no reason for him to betray us."

Titus shook his head doubtfully. "Maybe not now, but if the Romans start to lose..."

"Now is the most important, Titus. I have no reason to distrust that man right now," Octavius said.

Titus still looked doubtful. "You trust people too much," Titus said, a little worriedly.

"And you suspect too much," Octavius said, smiling.

❧ 36 ❧

Arrius laughed at the curt response from Pompey. 'No, I do not think it is necessary' was everything Pompey had written to him. Clearly, Pompey did not bother with manners. No introduction, no excuses, just a 'no' in a very fast cursive. He had, obviously, not even bothered to use another paper for a reply message. He had written in the back. Arrius chuckled at the man's impudence.

He took another parchment paper from his stocks and wrote another letter to Pompey. The letter was:

My dear Pompey,

I wish you would rethink on your decision. My letter did not ask you to betray Crassus. In fact, you would be helping him to put down the slave rebellion. I do not think he would be able to succeed without you. You are needed in Rome. Two rebellions crushed. It would guarantee you a successful career.

Pompey, please heed my sayings. If you come and succeed putting down the rebellion, you would become famous than ever.

Arrius knew that some parts of his story, for example, him doing this for Pompey were false. He was doing it so that Crassus would be overshadowed by the young general. He might be rebuked of his praetorship, or better, even if he won the war, Pompey would be the one who would be regarded as the general who actually finished off the revolt. He was pretty sure that Pompey would arrive before Crassus managed to win.

They had made a deal. Mummius was to be given impunity—at least, he was to be treated well. In return, Crassus had gotten the seat as a praetor, but now, Crassus had betrayed him. The man would pay, Arrius vowed. His fame would be gone, given to another general. There was no other suitable general than Pompey to do that.

⋅⋅◆⋅⋅

Arrius—

I know what you are thinking. Be frank with your words. I

know what you want. What do you have against Crassus?
Pompey

Ha, my dear Pompey,

So you are interested.

You read me too well. The man has murdered my son, and I intend to revenge him. If you come to Rome and defeat Spartacus's army, which by now is weakened out by Crassus, you will be commemorated as the greatest general since Scipio Africanus. Doesn't that appeal to you? All you have to do is to come to Rome, defeat the army, and send a letter to the senate that you have defeated the army. The rest, I will all take care of here. I have already appealed to the Senate about the possibility of a new general.

Arrius.

⸻ ⬦ ⸻

Octavius glanced up at the tall, formidable looking stone wall, flabbergasted. The sentries stationed on the walls of Thurii were being difficult. He looked back at his legionaries, all trying to look fresh and willing— yet tiredness showed on their faces. He would have men dropping to death if the sentries did not open the gates soon. The Third had walked at a faster speed than imagined for the last few days without much sleep or rations.

A man in a finely made toga, strewn with golden silk peeped over the wall to take a look at the tired legion.

"We do not offer refuge to legions outside Thurii," the man said in a mild tone.

"I do not want refuge," Octavius responded. "I am here on the orders of Praetor Marcus Licinius Crassus, senator and general of Rome. I demand that my legion be let in and given a good place to rest."

The man raised his eyebrows. His wrinkled yet plump face gave a certain distrusting look to him. He looked like any of the corrupt senators he had seen so much in Rome, and Octavius was not about to risk their plan. Corrupt senators were dangerous, and acted in benefit of themselves, not Rome. He had learned that much from his visits to Rome.

"And who are you, may I ask?" the man said in a mocking tone.

"I am Legatus Gnaeus Octavius Lupus, commander of the Third, also the commander of the southern legions, legitimated by the overall Praetor, Marcus Licinius Crassus."

The man looked at him doubtfully and let out a horse laugh. "You? A legate? The senate's gone mad. How old are you? Seventeen? Eighteen?"

Octavius glanced at Titus dryly. His age was his most formidable enemy when it came to strangers who did not know him.

Octavius ignored the man completely. "Open up. If you do not, you will regret it. My Third will tear down the walls of Thurii and have you punished for your insolence. This is my last warning. I hope you are wise enough to follow it for I do not want to declare war upon a Roman city unless it is unavoidable, like now." Octavius also held up the letter Crassus had given him, and he saw the man's attitude change immediately.

The man hesitated, weighing Octavius's words. If he indeed was from Crassus, which seemed likely after seeing the letter, he would get into enormous trouble after all this commotion. Everybody knew Crassus. They knew that he was a lamb in most cases, and also a wolf behind the mask of lamb. He could be cruel if he wanted to, crueler than imaginable.

For a governor his status, he knew that it would be wise for him to be seen as an obedient man if he wanted to rise up the ranks in the future. And opposing Crassus directly would put a complete end to his dreams of promotion.

"My city is quiet, Legate. It has not been long that this

city has returned to normal after that bastard slave raided this town. I have enough space in the barracks for your legion, but I will not have them roaming around the city drunk. Is that clear?" the man said with a reluctant voice, and Octavius glared at him.

"My legion does not do that."

The man seemed to let out a sigh and motioned for the gates to be opened. The legionaries obeyed, clearly relieved that the threat of a battle had not been carried out. The legionaries of the Third looked relieved also, their tensed faces relaxing.

Octavius paused before entering as he glanced up at the governor again. "Oh, one last thing, remember that the all armies of the south are under my command for now. Do not interfere with my plans, governor," he threatened, and the governor looked back sourly at him.

As soon as all the weary Third had marched into the town, earning frightened stares from the civilians, Octavius gave the order for Thurii to be contained.

"Titus, take care of the gates. Do not let anybody pass. I do not care if it is the consul himself," Octavius ordered, and the governor wailed.

"What? You are setting a blockade on my city? No. No.

That will never do. The merchants! They can't pass. You'll ruin this society! No trades. No incomes!" the man shouted furiously. Merchants who had been near looked up from their usual selling of goods and began to shout at him.

"I am a traveler. I need to get to Rome by next week, and I need to move fast."

"I am in charge of fresh vegetables. How do you expect me to get it?"

"My husband is currently out on the farms!"

Octavius turned toward them. "If I do not set up this blockade, soon this city will be ravaged by the slave army. Do you understand?" he said in a steely voice and then changed into a gentler tone. "Don't worry. The blockade will end in a day, two days at the most. I apologize for the inconveniences," Octavius said courteously, and they all shut up, though they glared at him venomously.

"Titus, take two centuries." Titus looked at him questioningly, and Octavius nodded. "I'll do it with Lucius and Dannotalos. I'll be safe," Octavius whispered, just for Titus's ears. He asked the whining governor to lead on to the barracks, and the Third marched behind him, taking in the scenery of the town.

"No. No. This is more expensive. From Greece," Rufius said. He held up a gem, a clean, enormous diamond. The diamond earned the eyes of many men from plebs to patricians and merchants.

A patrician stepped out to buy the jewel, and Rufius shook his head. "I call for twenty talents," Rufius said, and the man sputtered.

"That does not cost twenty talents, merchant," the man said, and Rufius shrugged.

"You'll never find another one like this. This was carried by King Alexander the Great himself. Used as a brooch of good omen and it did work. It passed onto many hands until it fell in my friend's. Poor man, he's dead now and having no family, he passed this on to me. It doesn't have to be you, sir. There are lots more," Rufius said, and as if to confirm his argument, many others called for the jewel.

Rufius gazed out at the throng of eager men, looking for a certain man with black hair and green eyes. He spotted a man of similar characteristics, looking at the commotion with an interested eye. The man was overweight, his stomach sagging. He also had a few bodyguards surrounding him, implying that he was an important figure in the town.

Rufius's heartbeats rose. It seemed as if he was the man Dannotalos had described to him. Rufius held the gem up, letting it catch the afternoon rays. The gem glowed more than ever, and Rufius himself was for a while indulged the gem.

"No one? Seems a shame," he said.

"Too expensive," one called out, and Rufius looked toward the voice. His heart thumped against his breast as he realized that the one who had spoken was the man with the green eyes.

Rufius pretended to think. "At what price will you buy it, then?"

The man shook his head. "Fifteen talents," he called.

Rufius shook his head vigorously. "I tell you, it is worth more than that. I had actually been planning to call this gem at thirty talents... Anyway, I can never give you this gem for fifteen talents," he said, and while doing so, he cast a sideways glance at Dannotalos, hidden amongst the crowd, who confirmed his suspicion.

"Sixteen."

"Seventeen," Rufius said. The man seemed to hesitate but sighed, nodding his head.

"The deal has been made," Rufius said jovially, imitating the merchants who worked with his father. He sighed to himself. What he had done today was more outgoing than the things that he had done before. All learned from his father, the great merchant. He thought back to the times he spent out on the markets, looking at his father and other merchants haggling with each other. The experience was proving to be very valuable.

The black haired man approached Rufius, and Rufius gave a courteous bow to him. His bodyguards followed him closely like shadows with an expressionless face. The man allowed his toga to slip a little, revealing a concealed blade. Rufius sweated. The man was no fool. Was he warning him?

Nonetheless the man was smiling at him, and Rufius wryly noticed that the man was wearing expensive looking rings on every finger. "Ah. Merchant, may I have your name?" the man asked, and Rufius sweated again.

"Spurius," Rufius responded, hiding his nervousness. He hated his nervous personality.

"Spurius, you must have your history wrong. I have no records that King Alexander wore brooches of luck," the man said slyly. His eyes bore through Rufius's eyes, and Rufius held them with difficulty.

Rufius gave a little laugh. "Yes he did, sir, or at least that is what my friend told me before he died in an unfortunate accident."

Sempronius eyed him suspiciously. "Your friend was probably lying, just to show it off to you. And if it really is indeed a gem of luck, how could he get into an unfortunate accident?" he said.

Rufius smiled, this time with more ease. "Nevertheless, it is still beautiful and the cost stays firm," he said, and the man laughed whole heartedly at that. He winked at Rufius, making Rufius all the more uncomfortable.

"Dear me," Rufius said suddenly. "I do not even know your name!" Rufius exclaimed casually, just to make sure in case Dannotalos was mistaken, and the man smiled gently.

"I have many enemies, Spurius. I cannot afford to give you my name, and I hate to lie. I will have seventeen talents handed over to you right now. My men have gone to fetch the sum. You see, Rufius, I have many men in Thurii. About a quarter of them are under my supervision." Rufius nodded, unnerved. Why was the man telling him all this? Did he suspect him and was warning him back? Rufius fidgeted uncomfortably and sighed inwardly. Then he decided to take the chance.

He reached inside his tunic. He pulled out a red cloth casually and wiped the diamond, smiling all the while.

At the exact moment, Octavius's hand clamped down, and two Roman centuries began to move toward the center square in stealthy formation.

⁂

They moved briskly. The two centuries, even after the march were still fresh due to adrenaline and moved at a great speed. People stared after the marching centuries. Some saluted them, some stared in fear. It was usual for the people to stare in fear when legionaries marched smartly with a purpose— because legionaries most of the time achieved them. And more often than not, their goals were achieved after a shed of blood.

The centuries arrived at the main square. Octavius spotted Rufius who was talking casually with an obese man with black hair. From the distance, it seemed genial and Octavius smiled to himself. He had chosen the right man.

It was sudden. Octavius saw the fat man raise a hand casually, and the three bodyguards around him dived for Rufius. People screamed. A sudden mass of men appeared between the merchant and the legionaries, baring their teeth and grinning at the prospect of a battle. Soon, the place filled with war cries and blood.

Rufius panicked. He thanked his usual training— it had just saved his life. When the three men had dived at him, he had jumped out of the way with uncommon agility, something that could only be found in trained soldiers. He had just failed a test by Sempronius.

Rufius feigned innocence. "Why, sir, are you doing this to me?" he asked toward the fat merchant, and the man just gave him a cold smile.

"You lied to me."

"Excuse me?"

"You said that you were a merchant, but you are not. How do I know? I am not stupid. I know that a legion entered the town and ordered it to be contained. Then you suddenly appear. I keep track of every merchant who enters this city. It is an unspoken rule that they report to me. The last straw was that you moved with uncommon agility. Don't tell me that you are just 'agile'. What do you think I would expect? I suspected you were from the legion, luring me with diamond bait. For a while, I had been fooled, you acted out your part very well. Then you take out your piece of cloth, and centuries begin to move. I have men everywhere, I warned you. I even showed you my concealed blade signifying the concealed men but you remained calm. Very good. I congratulate you on your acting before you die," the man said with a malicious grin. Rufius shook his head.

"You must be mistaken—" he started but was cut off by a roar of laughter. The man took out his blade and signaled his men.

"Take the legionary brat out," he commanded, and the three men advanced toward him with a similar malicious grin.

Octavius shook his head in disbelief. How could have the man— Sempronius, according to Dannotalos— have fore-seen the attack? He lamented himself on not taking much precautions, for he had relied on speed rather than stealth. It seemed that he had thought wrongly.

Sempronius's militants came at him, trying to attack his left arm where they smelled weakness. There was a big bruise along with a long scar, and it drew their attention. Octavius fought on relentlessly, smiling bitterly as he cut them down. His spine ached only a little now, and his left arm did not hinder him much.

Lucius called out orders to his century. "Advance! Never

let the man escape!" he yelled, and his legionaries gave a wild cry as a response. They were shocked from the sudden attack and were struggling to get back in formation.

Dannotalos saw Lucius commanding his century and also called orders to advance. He was proud and happy to see that his century obeyed— Roman and Gaul alike. Octavius was fighting grimly in the first line and Dannotalos hurried to join his legate. His legate would be surprised at his skills.

Octavius grinned at Dannotalos who fought at his left. It made it easier for him to keep an eye on Sempronius and battle on. He could see Dannotalos was skilled, maybe not in a Roman way, but still skilled. Romans tended to stab, but Dannotalos was slashing at his enemies with a long spatha sword. He was confusing the merchant's men with his different pattern of fighting.

Octavius fought on, not getting the least tired. His adrenaline was running high, and he felt as if he could go on forever. Despite the battles he had been in, he had never managed to really fight much. It was both a terrifying yet a thrilling experience. He was also astounded at the change that had overcome him. Before, he could not even stand the gladiators killing each other, and here he was now, efficiently killing those who opposed him. And he did not feel much remorse.

He sweated. There were just too many numbers though they were managing to get through. He looked up and saw Rufius fall.

Rufius rolled out of the way just in time. Three blades crashed down beside him— where his neck had been a second before. He rolled once more to avoid a fourth blade and stood up, unsheathing his gladius in a neat form. He dived for Sempronius, and the man dodged more agilely than expected. Rufius then decided to change his victim to a muscular bodyguard with a torn tunic and feigned a jump. The man was fooled and put out his gladius upward to block himself. Rufius used the time to dive for his legs, making him stagger. Rufius pushed him away, and the man fell down to the ground from their stand.

He blocked a blow, rising quickly to his feet and took a chance in glancing desperately at the centuries. They were advancing, though not as quickly as he wanted. He panted vigorously but doggedly continued to attack. He would never let Sempronius out of his eyes.

Octavius yelled in hope as Rufius came back up and threw a man off the stand. "Lucius, fan out! We're not leaving the man any escape routes," he called, and Lucius obeyed on the instant. Two centuries were blocking every route out of the markets. He hoped that the two centuries, disguised as common civilians might have escaped the man's eyes. They would not have in other cases, but with two centuries so prominently walking toward the center square, he might have just missed them. And it seemed likely too. The man was not hurrying to escape. He was backing off slowly, calling to other men. He briskly walked—not ran— toward the opposite side of where the centuries were attacking. Rufius was still flanked by two goons.

"Keep an eye on Sempronius!" Octavius shouted and lunged himself at the enemy. Others followed his lead and eventually they managed to break through the comparatively less trained men. Dannotalos left his century to his optio, a Roman, and sprinted at Sempronius, calling a few Gaul warriors behind him. Octavius had to admit, they were fast. They did not have anything but muscles, yet they ran with efficiency— something that was mostly seen in mercenaries. Lucius dashed towards the stage, where he swiftly climbed up the stairs and stabbed his sword into a bodyguard with a single blow. The other was taken by surprise and when seeing two legionaries facing him, especially a fresh one in a centurion's armor, jumped of the stage.

Lucius panted softly. "You okay?" he asked the faint Rufius. Rufius had always been a little pale, and now he looked even paler. He looked sick and tired, making Lucius worried. He patted his senior officer's back, their ranks forgotten. He handed Rufius his water skin, and Rufius took it gratefully. With that, Lucius jumped off the stage and gave a mad roar at the men who were blocking his path, cutting them down in swift blows.

Octavius felt confused for the first time. All around him was chaos. Some parts of the century were chasing Sempronius while others were still fighting. The centuries were not disorderly—they were orderly in their own way—yet things revolved around him too fast for him to command everything. He would have to just leave everything to his officers and the legionaries and trust them.

Dannotalos ran after Sempronius, thinking of his position. If he captured Sempronius, Octavius and others would trust him now. His conscience tugged at him a little, but he ignored it, saying that his loyalties were with the Third now. After all, there was nowhere else he could go if he was not accepted into the Third.

He made his decision. Dannotalos sprang at Sempronius,

tackling him from the behind. They both fell and rolled in the ground. Sempronius took advantage of his weight and pinned Dannotalos onto the floor. Then the man's eyes opened wide in shock.

"You!" he cried and Dannotalos nodded.

"Me!" he cried back.

"I didn't like you from the first time we met… You are the one who told on us, aren't you? The perpetrator! Even I have more loyalty in me than you."

Dannotalos kicked the man in the stomach, regaining the upper position. "I was a mercenary then."

"Are you still?" the man said with some hope.

"No, I've found a much more profitable business— playing legionaries," Dannotalos responded as he unsheathed his sword and aimed it at the man's neck. He was suddenly pressed flat by another man, one of Sempronius's bodyguards, and looked up as he saw the weight lift. A Roman legionary stood there with a bloodied gladius, a dead man at his feet.

The legionnaire saluted at him, and Dannotalos flashed a knowing grin at Sempronius. "See? This is more fun," he said and yelled at the top of his voice. "Sempronius is now captured!" he shouted.

He saw everyone halt for a moment, and Sempronius's

gangsters suddenly threw away their weapons and ran off toward the allies leading out of the center square. All they relied on was their powerful boss, and to hear their boss being captured, it was shocking and fearful to them. Some rushed toward Sempronius in hopes of freeing their leader but legionaries had begun to make a circle around Dannotalos and Sempronius, and held them off with ease. Soon, the men were all killed or running.

Sempronius tried to stop their flight, but Dannotalos threatened to kill him and gagged Sempronius with a piece of his tunic.

"Octavius! They're escaping!" Lucius called and immediately heard a response.

"Let them go!"

Lucius ordered the men not to attack Sempronius's soldiers, knowing fully well that they would be cut down anyways by the awaiting centuries. He did not care about them—all he cared was about Sempronius.

Octavius was already with Sempronius when Lucius arrived. Lucius saw his friend covered in grime and sweat, though he stood perfectly tall and maintained his noble like attitude.

"Sempronius," Octavius commented, and the man did

not answer. He seemed dumbfounded at his situation. He had almost made it out of the square— his escape would have been perfect if a centurion had not jumped at him from behind. The legate seemed to recognize it also.

"Thank you, Dannotalos. Our search would have been more difficult if not for you," Octavius said and nodded toward Dannotalos who seemed pleased at the comment. "Sempronius, have you ever made a deal with Spartacus?" Octavius asked, to the point and completely at ease.

Sempronius glanced at Dannotalos. The legate was just playing with him. He probably knew all the answers. He nodded slightly, and the legate smiled at him.

"Thank you for being so honest, Sempronius. It would have been difficult if you hadn't," the legate said, and Sempronius suddenly had a chill running through his spine. Something about the legate's smile, and his curious accent on the word 'difficult' was what made him nervous.

Sempronius glanced around to see if there were any possible means of escape, but he was surrounded by grim looking legionaries, and he knew that he could not escape by force. He needed to think of something else.

"Kindly tell me the details," Octavius asked, and Sempronius shrugged innocuously.

"It was nothing. We just traded gold," Sempronius lied and regretted it as he saw the exasperated look on Dannotalos's face. So the man knew more than he had actually heard—those damned rumors.

The legate's face suddenly grew dark, and his tone dropped a little. "Sempronius, I'd like it if you answered while I am still civil. You are a Roman, and I am doing my best to treat you like one."

Sempronius grinned outwardly, hiding his shudders. The man was still young— very young by the look of it, and he hoped the legate might be as naïve. also. He still needed to receive an additional hundred talents from the slaves. With that sum of money, combined with those that he had now, he could do everything he liked and still would not be able to use it all before he died.

"Can't we figure this all out in my chamber? Full of gold, something I would give you for free," he said, remembering all the other officers who had fallen for money.
Contempt crossed the young legate's face as he shook his head. "I have no need for any of it," he said.

Sempronius shook his head. "Yes, but you must have a general commander, a commander whom you follow. He might need some," Sempronius tried again.

"My commander is Praetor Marcus Licinius Crassus," the legate said, grinning.

"Oh," Sempronius said. It was all he could manage. The man had more money than he wanted to have. Money would not work.

"This is my last warning to you, merchant, smuggler, pirate. I am asking you for the deal you made with Spartacus. A fleet, isn't it?" Octavius asked and sighed when there was no answer.

"What do you value more? Your life or money?" Octavius asked, and the man stayed silent for a long time.

"Both," was the answer.

"You are a Roman, Sempronius. Would you like your country to be ripped in shreds by a mere slave rebellion?" Octavius asked, even though he knew that Spartacus's rebellion was not a 'mere'.

Sempronius bowed his head, a little ashamed. However, he did not do anything, and finally Octavius's patience ran out. He had been trying to deal as civilly as he could with the man, and it seemed that it would be impossible to make the man comply while talking to him in a civil way.

"I can hang you right here for all the illegal things you did. I can do anything to you and nobody would dare to object. Get out with it and I might spare your life. If you don't. . ." Octavius threatened, leaving the last part to Sempronius's vivid imaginations.

Sempronius resigned to the threat. The legate seemed pretty serious. After all, he needed to live to acquire the money and spend it. If he died now without ever spending the money, then his whole life would have been futile. He played his last card, however.

"Spartacus will kill me when he comes here. I can't do it," he said, fear reflecting in his eyes. Though he was not worried much about it, it might as well become true.

Octavius shook his head. "He will not reclaim Thurii." His voice was so definite that Sempronius gave up.

Sempronius took a big breath. His options had all run out. "I was to prepare a fleet to take him to Sicily."

"When?"

"By the Ides of November."

Lucius gave a low whistle. "That's fast for an army that size. They must be in quite a hurry," he said, and Octavius nodded.

"How many ships did you get together?" Octavius asked, and Sempronius thought about it.

"Twenty ships until now," he said, desperately wanting to

be elsewhere. He also had a sneaking suspicion that these legionaries might kill him after all after getting out the information.

"Where?"

"In a secret cove near Thurii. You won't kill me, will you?" Sempronius responded. "No, not if you comply nicely. Disband the ships," Octavius ordered, and Sempronius's eyes suddenly lit up.

"I'll go disband them. I give you my word that I will be back in two days," Sempronius said.

"What do you take me for? An idiot?" he snapped. "Dispatch a letter to your subordinates ordering for the fleet to be disbanded. I will give them two days to do so. For the time being, you will be detained. You should hope for the fleet to be disbanded for your own sake." Sempronius nodded meekly. "It was a pleasure meeting you," Octavius said as he left the area with Lucius, Rufius and Dannotalos, knowing that the legionaries would detain the man securely.

Before they left, Dannotalos stayed to talk with Sempronius who he felt a little sympathetic for. He had once been in a similar position, given a hard choice by Octavius, almost forced into the legions.

"Semp," he called. The man looked up with dejected

eyes. "Do what the legate says. One tip I learned as a mercenary— always be on the winning side. Right now, the
Romans are on the winning side," he said with a wink and
left the area, following Octavius.

❧ *37* ❧

Pompey looked over at his legions from the window of his building, his legions, so strong, so trustful. They were the glory of Rome, a legion that could crush the slaves in one step. Crassus was getting to be pathetic, and Arrius's warnings had hit home. What if the senate regard more highly of Crassus than of him? Then his conquest in Hispania would have been in vain. And that could not happen.

There was also that new quaestor, Caesar, who stared back at him with unnerving eyes, eyes filled with ambition. Whenever Pompey spoke with him, he had this uncomfortable feeling—and his gut instinct had always been correct. His time in Hispania was over. It was time for him to move on, to a new step, to Rome.

He looked at the piles of letters Arrius had sent him. The man must be desperate for revenge. If he managed to crush the slave rebellion— which would be a piece of cake— he would get an even higher honor, and then he might become consul, a consul at the age of a little over thirty. The thought mesmerized him.

He called to his scribe who came rushing up the stairs. "Write this. To Senator Arrius of Rome, I shall accept."

Spartacus gazed proudly at the trail of people following him. They trusted him. They followed him. They took him as their leader. He had once been an energetic man of Thracia. There his father had been a well respected man, and his mother too had been known as a wise woman— he too had grown as a respected boy. His wife had also been intelligent and beautiful. Everything had been perfect.

He had been playing war with his friends when they came. He remembered himself as nineteen, a little older than Octavius, he thought suddenly. They recognized his talents. The Romans saw his muscular body and his intelligence. He had been the commander of one of the two groups who were playing war.

They surrounded the area and came up to him, congratulating his efforts in the mock war. He had nodded briefly, wondering why the centurion had bothered. Then the man asked him to join the real legions. He refused. He knew that joining the legions might be useful for his future, yet he had learned from his father that they were the rightful owners of the land, not the Romans. Thracia had been a country, not a mere province. He could not turn his back on Thracia. Also, he had heard from many that the legions were a difficult place where he would be subjected to hard training. He liked his life here, in Thracia.

Then he had been courageous enough, or naïve. enough, to refuse. The centurion had asked again, persuading him this time. He refused yet again, telling the centurion that they had no obligation to serve in the military for they were Thracians, not Romans. He had not been wise enough to know that Romans, once they incorporated a piece of land to theirs, thought of it as a part of Rome, province or not, and considered those living there Romans without citizen-ships. It could be good in a way— there was less prejudice that way, but there were also downfalls.

The centurion's face had turned sour as he told him that he was conscripting him. He had been a fool to threaten the man with a gladius. The legionaries then had rushed at him, pulling him down until wind was knocked from his breath.

His friends tried to escape, but they too were caught by

the legionaries. Three of them cut off their thumbs thinking that if they could not use their hands they might be exempted. They too had not known that Romans did not care about that. The centurion, according to the customs, beheaded the three before incorporating the rest into the army. If only he had talked nicely to the centurion— the officer had seemed to have been level headed, he might have let him go if he had persuaded the man instead of threatening him.

After, he escaped from the legions, hating to fight for a country he did not like. A few days later, he was captured again by the legionaries and was sent to a gladiator school where he learned what agony was. Three years as a legionary, two as a slave, one as a commander of the slave force. He did not know what lay ahead of him.

What he knew for sure, though, was the fleet to Sicily. Sempronius would not betray him, two hundred talents just for preparing a fleet was irresistible. There were still two weeks left until the Ides of November.

❧ 38 ❧

"General, a messenger from Hispania," a scout called to Crassus, and Crassus looked up from his pile of papers.

"Let him in," Crassus said, irritation and curiosity showing. The messenger entered and handed him a scroll in a military way, which Crassus read urgently.

The messenger waited until he was sure Crassus must have finished. "The scroll must be burned," he said, and Crassus shook his head, his face pale.

"Is this... true?" Crassus asked, his voice wavering.

"Yes, sir. The scroll, it needs to be burned. Quaestor Gaius Julius Caesar does not want the content of the scroll to be known to others," the messenger replied smartly.

"But is it true? Arrius? Pompey coming—is it true?" Crassus asked, his voice desperate. The messenger nodded apathetically.

"This scroll is classified. Quaestor Caesar made it clear,"

he repeated.

"Yes. I will burn it," Crassus responded, dazed. Julius had just given the news of Pompey's sudden plan to get himself involved in the rebellion, due to Arrius's offer. If Arrius was behind all this, then Pompey would have no trouble in getting the permission of the senate. Crassus buried his head in his arms. The news was devastating. He would need to hurry before Pompey came and took all the glory away from him.

"The scroll," the messenger said stubbornly. Crassus obliged and watched with empty eyes as the messenger thrust the paper into the fire without a second glance. Soon there was nothing but ashes, no evidence that Julius had warned him of anything.

⸎

Vibius turned the letter over and over in his hands. A sudden order demanding him to disband the ships had come to him on a parchment paper. After all they had gone through! The handwriting was his master's, he was sure. He had been trained to recognize counterfeit handwritings as a slave in Greece.

It was strange that master did not appear, and so he knew

that his master was telling the truth when he said that he was under the 'protection' of the Roman army. Vibius rubbed his arms against a sudden cold and thought about the letter. Even though he was a slave, he had received better education than most plebeians. He knew what to do in these cases. The longer Sempronius was with the legions, the more their secrets they would get to know. Besides, he had been a slave too long to know how to refuse his master's orders. He could not refuse them.

"Master Albius?" he called, and a grumpy looking man appeared. Vibius bowed as he appeared and showed him the letter. Albius too knew that the letter was written by Sempronius himself. He was loyal to Sempronius. He could not risk the man's life. Without the man, he would be cut off from everything. No money. No contacts. The man was like a second parent to him, who had actually reared him since when he had been young as an adopted father.

He could tell Vibius shared the same thoughts. "Go disband them," he ordered, and Vibius bowed again.

❧ *39* ❧

Spartacus reached the silent port. It was the Ides of November, and the chill bit through his rough armor with some spite. The port was a secret port, almost a cove, rarely used. Only fishermen used them, and most of them were ignorant of what happened unless they were concerned. This time it did not concern them, and Spartacus was sure that he would be able to escape silently, burning all the ships, making Crassus have to wait impatiently on the peninsula until he could bring together enough galleys to transport his legions.

He admired the scenery of the cove, so silent except for some murmurs here and there in his own ranks. Silent. No. Too silent.

There was no one. No sailors. No ships. Not one in sight. Sempronius was not there either. His heart thumped with the suspicion that Sempronius had made off with all the money.

Sempronius paced his room. It was guarded by three emotionless legionaries. They kept their mouths shut unless he asked them something basic— for example, what day it was.

"The Ides of November," one answered monotonously, and Sempronius stopped pacing. He collapsed onto his bed with mixed feelings. He knew that he had chosen the right side— or, the winning side, according to Dannotalos. The war was bound to end soon, and he predicted that Spartacus would get the short end of it. He could not win. Not with six legions behind him. His only hope may have been Sicily. Sempronius was suddenly guilty at that.

He had destroyed their last hope. It had been a deal, and he had not kept it. Spartacus had trusted him and would now be waiting for him at the port. Conscience overwhelmed him. At least he had always kept his word when it came to a deal. Even when had he abandoned his consciences a long time ago, he had made a promise to himself— to always keep a deal. Now, it seemed keeping the promise was impossible.

On the other hand, he still remembered what the young commander had said. 'You are a Roman, Sempronius. Would you like your country to be ripped in shreds by a mere slave rebellion?'

That too touched his conscience, something he had never expected to feel. Rome was his country. He was a Roman though he had lived in ignorance of that fact for a long time. Rome was the place that made it possible for him to make money. He had many favorable experiences with Rome.

He was a Roman. He realized now that he loved Rome despite her corruptness—or maybe because of her corruptness. Anyway, he decided it was ridiculous for the great civilization to fall in the hands of a few ruthless slaves.

Sempronius then decided that he was almost glad he was locked up. He had no choice now but to watch Spartacus fall. There was nothing he could do. But if he had been free… he would have had to choose between Rome and Spartacus, Rome and money, his homeland and a freedom seeker's last chance. It would have been a difficult one, beyond his measures.

Spartacus collapsed onto his knees. Dawn was breaking

and still no sign of Sempronius, the traitor. He should have never trusted him, a Roman and a pirate— the most unreliable combination next to a Roman and a senator.

Wails broke out behind him. He could hear children crying. He looked at people sitting down dejectedly, weeping silently and comforting each other. He led a whole civilization behind him, one without the accursed slavery. And now the civilization had just come to an end.

"Spartacus," David said behind him. Spartacus did not answer, and the man also retained his silence. Spartacus looked at the rising sun, and the pinkish clouds in the sky made him think of blood, their blood. The rebellion was over. They could not turn north again. It would be too hard on most people. He would have to leave thousands dead behind.

"Let our deliveries be painless," Spartacus heard David whisper silently behind him, his eyes closed. When the man opened them, Spartacus saw pure fear.

"Wish for what can be wished," he said. "What you just said will be impossible if Romans capture us."

"I say we all kill ourselves," Castus, who had come up, said determinedly, and the men looked in horror at him.

"We are survivors, Castus. Remember that. Besides, it's a

sin—at least, in my religion," David said, and the pair lapsed into silence again.

It was Spartacus who first spoke. "We head south. There might be a little hope. And at least we would be able to take out more Romans… give more fear to them," he croaked, and David nodded his head.

"Where?"

"Rhegium."

❧ *40* ❧

Octavius knew he could not let the winter depression come over him. He shivered in his armor, adding an extra cloak around himself. Only a year and a half before, Lucia had been alive.

Suetonius, Caecilius, the honorable man who had died saving him, the kind general who knew of Octavius's ambitions and helped him out, Lucia, the person whom he had proposed to, the person whom he had asked to spend time together after the war, the person who had worried that he might die during the war, scoffing at his warnings to beware of the forest. Before it had been a joke, and Octavius shuddered at the irony that his words had become true. The forest had not been dull. It had been dangerous, a lurking trap.

He tormented himself for not letting Crixus have a much more painful death. Yet he knew that it would not have satisfied him no matter how much Crixus suffered. Lucia could not be brought back.

He recalled a story of a few Greek heroes who had gone down to Underworld to rescue their lovers. He wished that opportunity could present itself to him also— he wished he was on that kind of mission rather than fighting this stupid war.

Octavius shook his head. It was all because of the gloomy weather, wet and cold. He liked it dry and warm.

Crassus had chased Spartacus as far as the toe of Italy, keeping him holed in Rhegium. The war would probably rest until the weather improved. Crassus was thinking of brilliant tactics that would surprise Spartacus as soon as he dared to venture out of Rhegium. This recharging period was a little time to prepare for a deadly onslaught.

His parents had greeted him warmly, and he spent the days in Capua, during his short break, forgetting about being a legate and free of responsibility. He was their delicate child again. They had been informed of his news by the letters he had sent them, and they were pleased at the things that he had been able to achieve. They were still worried about his wounds, and the mental stress from seeing

· too much people die, but they were nonetheless happy to see him alive.

For a while it had been pleasant. He strolled in the garden, admiring the flowers that his mother and Aula had busily worked on.

Octavius received the congratulations of the folks of Capua and had been in a better mood than he had been for a while until he was greeted by the tired looking Maximus.

"Sir," he said, and the man nodded gently.

"Where's Lucius?" he asked with a trace of concern.

"He's still with the army. He said that he might get… unstable if he comes here," Octavius said, choosing words carefully. Maximus understood what he meant and sighed.

"Unstable. Yes. He would be. I had hoped that he might come. He's now my only child," he said with a trace of morose. No signs of his former greediness—greed for power and money showed. Octavius was surprised at the change he had undergone. The man was not what he had seen a year and a half before. But then, it had been a year so packed with events that he too had undergone many changes.

"And you? Are you…stable?"

Octavius shook his head honestly. "I loved her," he whispered, and Maximus did not reply.

"I honestly had no idea."

"I'm sorry, I should have asked your permission before giving her the ring," Octavius whispered.

"No, it's me who should be sorry. I should have done something about it before you went off to become a Tribune, a Legate now. What a feat, Octavius," he said, and it seemed as if he really meant it—a very drastic change in character.

Just then, Flamina came rushing out of the house, her face ruined with tears. "Lucia! Lucia! He's here!" she cried, and Octavius looked at her in alarm. He shifted his gaze at Maximus, and the man shrugged.

"You're not the only person who was affected by her death. She thinks it is her fault because she had not gone with her..."

Octavius looked at the governor, again feeling that he had changed much from the savage man he had once been.

"Flamina!" he cried, and she turned toward him.

"You! She died after she said she was visiting you! Where's Lucius? Did you kill him too?" with that, she jumped at him, aiming for his neck.

Octavius dodged and held her calmly, his brown eyes piercing hers. He hugged Flamina a little. "I'm sorry," he said, and he could feel her body relax.

Then as he let go, her face clouded with anger and confusion again, and she began her rant once more. Octavius watched her for a while and turned to Maximus. "I should get going," he said as he turned his footsteps. He walked, lonely, his vision blurred by tears. Lucia should have greeted him. She should not have died.

On his way, he stopped at her tomb, her tomb. Impossible. He almost expected her to come running at him, laughing at a joke she had made. The engraved letters were too much for him. It must be another Lucia. Thinking her as dead and seeing her tomb was a different thing altogether.

He wiped a few tears from his face, afraid to look around if anybody had seen him. He knelt in the front, and dug into the soft soil with his fingers. He dug deeply, yet not enough to unearth the box. He would break down for sure if it came to that. He reached inside his tunic and gently pulled out the ring, a ring that he had given to her a year and a half before. As he placed it down, he could smell her aroma, feel her warm touch, and hear her laughter like pearls— something he had felt on that day, when he had given the ring to her for the first time.

"I did it. I kept my promise," he said, looking at the ground. He thought he heard gentle laughter. He quickly filled the hole he had made and stood up softly caressing the top of the stone. He stopped when he realized he was resurfacing the wound that had taken him so much effort to cure. He could not— would not— go over the whole procedure again. He began to run, flee from his wounds. As soon as the war was over, he would follow Crassus to Rome and live there, only visiting Capua to see his parents and Lucia. Or maybe he would persuade his parents to move to Rome with him. He would forget about this village and bury himself in his new career— a general, a senator, or whatever. He could not stay in Capua.

"Hey. What are you thinking about?" Octavius looked up, surprised at the sudden appearance of Titus.

"Just my visit to Capua."

"Lucia?"

Octavius stayed silent.

"Not her again," Titus said as he gave a mock groan. "Actually, I just executed a slave who was captured by the sentries… and I am regretting it."

Octavius looked up again, interested. Titus was regretting killing someone? It was not like him. "Before he died, he asked me if the war was just. He said that if we only let them escape to Gaul, they would go in peace. And it sort of— very sort of— seemed right."

"After wreaking havoc in Rome?" Octavius countered. "They now want to escape in peace after massacring innocent people? Like Lucia?" he asked, his voice harsh.

Titus immediately regretted about the choice of time. Octavius definitely was not in a mood to debate about the moralities of this war.

"They are fighting for freedom. Something, he said, that all Romans have. They also want that right, just that. It was not their fault being born a slave."

"That's actually only a few. Many of them are war prisoners and criminals. Are you saying that we should give up now? Look, Titus. Now they are trying to compromise, but before, when they were powerful, they were ruining Rome, killing her innocent civilians. Oh I pity some of them for being born a slave, but what do you want me to do? Stop? After all this? We don't need to let them go. They are holed up in Rhegium without supplies. The war is literally over, understand? There is nothing to gain from letting them go. And how would the other countries see Rome if we just let them go? They would see it as a sign of weakness. Anyway, we can't stop, so just leave me alone, okay?" he said and turned his back to Titus irritably.

Titus fought a rage forming inside and stalked off. Octavius immediately regretted in speaking such to Titus but his worries were cut short by a messenger. He was to attend a meeting immediately.

Leave me alone! He wanted to scream. Instead, he irritably nodded his head and followed the man to the commanding tent where many officers were already there. He took his normal seat and saw immediately that Crassus was not in a good mood.

Crassus tried to restrain his anger at what his subordinate senators had told him through letters. "Pompey has received a grant from the senate to get himself involved in this war. Pompey. Then when we win, he will say that he ended a war— that it would have been impossible under my command. And the senate will fall for it," he said, raging. Cursed Arrius, the sneaky devil. I'll take care of you when I get back. You will regret it. You are not the only powerful men around here. With my legions, you would be dead before long.

"I wanted to wait until spring, but evidently, that is impossible. We are acting now. I want to keep them all in

Rhegium. Never let them a chance of escape. We are building a wall that runs from one side to the other side of the peninsula, containing them in the south."

The legates and the tribunes stared back at him, their faces shocked. The distance was over forty kilometers. Even with their numbers, they could not cover so much of a distance.

Octavius sighed under his breath, careful not to let anyone else hear it. His uncle was being rash again. He knew that his uncle had two different personalities that ran parallel to each other; one was love for his family and the wish to get recognized and popular, while the other was to vent his anger immediately, requiring rash actions, not contemplating hard on what effects it would bring, or whether it would be successful.

"A wall. I will give each legion their assigned place and three days to complete a rampart. It does not have to be strong though it would have to let our legionaries attack from above. In other words, it is more of a human wall than a stone one," Crassus said, actually feeling pleased about himself. Pompey would arrive in two months, one at the fastest, and by then, he would have starved them or beaten them or something.

The war will be over before Pompey comes greedily to take a share— something that he had not earned. "Octavius," he said, and his nephew looked up, his face calm. But Crassus knew enough of his nephew to know what he was really thinking, and it did not please him.

"You shall take the furthest south. Bassus, you are next to Octavius, see this map here? Yes, that is the place. Remember, three days." Crassus continued issuing orders in such fashion, disregarding all the officer's worried looks. Crassus rose after dismissing the men, hurrying out first. The other officers stayed rooted to their seats.

"Do you think that this is…productive?" Bassus asked, and some legates dared to shake their heads. They threw swift glances at the gate, alert for a pair of curious ears. Then, after reassuring themselves that Crassus had really gone, they turned their gazes toward Bassus, who shrugged. "A commander is supposed to promote council, yet this man is blocking our freedom of speech. Like a king," he said, spitting out the word 'king', the hated word in Rome.

"He's not really blocking our speech, but he covertly threatens us. The man is so subtle— it is hard to say what will happen when you oppose him greatly. For example, if I told him that the idea was an impossible idea—that the line would be too thin and the slave army would eventually break through— he will assign me some dreaded tasks and be biased when dealing with cases in my legion. He will seek to punish me in the most subtle way he could. I am daring this speech because I believe in the spirit of Rome. This cannot be tolerated."

Bassus's speech ended with a quiet round of applause. Bassus looked solemn, and the other officers were nodding. "What shall we do?" a voice broke out.

"Nothing we can do at the current moment. Remember the fate of Mummius, the poor man, though he did make some seriously wrong decisions," Claudius said, and other officers nodded again grimly. "All we can do is a mutiny," Claudius whispered, and the other officers stayed silent, rigidly gazing at Claudius.

"No. The safety of Rome comes first. If we break up, especially with Pompey coming to claim our prizes, we will be scattered. Besides, Spartacus will take advantage of it and escape—leading the war on a more frenzy goose chase," Bassus expressed his opinion and was supported by Octavius who clapped loudly.

"We cannot afford to break within ourselves. This is not because I am his nephew. I agree with you on your ideals. I am saying this because we might lose what we have fought to achieve after all this— just because we decided to go up against a non profitable general. Beating Spartacus is more important," Octavius spoke up. He felt a nudge of guilt as he thought of what he was speaking. He was actually saying that Crassus was not a suitable commander— his uncle who had made it possible for him to rise to his current status, and most of all, who trusted him completely. Bassus clapped support, and many others followed. A mutiny was foolish. It would risk everything.

"But the mutiny…" Claudius started, and Bassus stood up, enraged.

"Rome comes first. I will not have anymore of it. Three days is a short time," he said as he pushed back his chair and stalked off out of the tent.

Other officers gazed curiously at him, anticipating Claudius's reaction. Before Claudius could do anything, Octavius rose too and walked off without a word. He could hear others following suit and breathed a sigh in relief.

Bassus was walking away to his own legion when he suddenly turned to meet Octavius. The legate was young and yet he seemed to have some suitable senses in his brain.

"Legate Octavius?" he called, and the young man looked

up, his bluish brown eyes staring back questioningly. Bassus recognized with some envy his sharp features as he waited for Octavius to catch up. He sighed to think of his past when he too had been full of energy as Octavius. Octavius stood patiently with his dark brown hair ruffling slightly in the cold wind. Bassus ignored the feeling of jealousy and spoke. "Thank you for siding with me today. I mean, I call myself a patriot of Rome. Crassus can be tolerated at the moment—he is not so bad. Rome's situation is. Rome comes first, as I have said. A mutiny is the most idiotic thing we can do. I hope that we continue our good relations in the future," the man said and turned away with a slight smile.

"I hope so too," Octavius said as he turned his back on Bassus, slightly bemused.

• ⬦❈⬦ •

"Jupiter damn him!"

"The cursed idiot."

Curses flew back and forth as the legionaries of the Third slaved in the cold building Crassus's wall.

"It's gonna break! There is too less of us and too much of them, a wall across the whole peninsula. It's impossible. Can't he see it?" one called, and Octavius sighed. Yes, everyone knew except for Crassus.

"Vedius," he called, and the man turned abruptly, an apologetic smile forming on his face. "Take this piece instead. Looks sturdier," Octavius said as he picked up a piece of timber from the pile. Vedius's face relaxed as he realized that Octavius was not going to reprimand him for his curses and nodded his head gratefully.

"Thank you, Legate," he said, and Octavius threw him the wood which he caught in a swift movement.

"Vedius?" The man turned again. "One thing, I don't like this either," Octavius grumbled, and the man's smile widened.

"Of course. I always knew you were sensible," he said, grinning, and strutted off to complete the construction.

Octavius nodded with a crooked smile. He shivered in the cold, and comforted himself by telling him that it would be spring soon. After this cold draft, warm weather would finally come.

The construction was nearly finished, and they still had a whole day left ahead of them. He would concentrate on strengthening the walls, even though he knew that it would be futile. Spartacus would just choose another open space somewhere else and break through the thin line of defense.

The wall was pointless, and the only good thing about it

was that it completely blocked Spartacus from getting rations into Rhegium. Octavius hoped the shortage of food and water would kill Spartacus's army for them, less Roman lives thrown away. He did not care about the slaves. The winter, the visit to Capua, and the recent forced gladiatorial fight between the legionaries of the Third had strengthened his will to stamp out the rebellion for good, for Lucia, Caecilius, and Suetonius, and his three hundred.

He had ordered Sempronius to be freed after detaining him for two months—warning him to retire from his smuggling job. You have plenty of money already, Octavius had said, and the man smiled slyly. Something told him that Sempronius would not give up his life time practice so easily. That, however, was another matter which could be dealt after.

Octavius was not sure of the exact date though he knew that they were nearing the end of March. April would be a dreaded month for Spartacus.

⊷⬦⬦⊶

Legionaries were becoming optimistic. They had killed many without any casualties from the wall, firing arrows easily. There was no need for them to actually step out of the rampart to battle them. They could just leave it all to the artillery.

The slaves came at them continuously in groups, but they all either fled or died on the battlefield. Lucius watched the artillery pick off man by man, standing next to Octavius. He still felt the jealousy he had felt at first, though they were less intimate. Octavius would never know of the efforts he had put into containing his jealous feelings. At least Octavius was treating him like an equal, helping him in the process.

"Don't you have anything fishy about all this?"

"What?" Lucius asked.

"I mean, they are coming in small groups, continuously. They would have some point in doing this," Octavius said, thinking carefully.

"They might just want to escape," Lucius said casually.

"They know that they would stand a better chance in grouping together. Actually, you may be right. It's not important as long as we fend them off," Octavius said, though his voice was still doubtful. He had more things to worry about now, like how to spend his future after the war. He knew he should not jump to conclusions, but it seemed that the war was pretty much over.

They stood side by side, looking at the meadow. Slaves

rushed the walls and were killed. The groups were small yet it kept the legionaries occupied. They were not stupid— they knew that attacking like this would mean their deaths… unless it was a decoy.

A decoy, the thought struck him hard, and Octavius clasped Lucius's arm so tightly that Lucius gave a small yelp. Lucius turned, glowering, and was about to fly a sharp comment at Octavius when he stopped, seeing Octavius's expression.

"A decoy, they're decoying us. They are trying to find the weakest point and they'll break through there, leaving some of these suicide groups to consume the rest of the legions' time. In fact, they might be breaking through a wall right now," Octavius said urgently, and Lucius gave a half smile.

"They're not smart enough, Octavius," he said.

"It does not take a genius to think of a decoy. And Spartacus is far from dumb," Octavius said crossly. "Just because they are slaves doesn't mean they are stupid too."

"They are not called talking tools for nothing," Lucius said, though he seemed unsure. He became even more irresolute under Octavius's scrutinizing gaze.

"I need to warn Crassus and the other legates immediately."

"There is no need to."

Octavius and Lucius stared at each other, locked in a private battle that had prevailed since childhood. Both were glaring sourly at each other when they were shaken by an agonizing cry.

The Third looked terrified at a tattered legionary, covered in grime and blood. Octavius gasped as he saw that the man did not have an arm. He quickly descended from the wall and demanded the man his story, eliminating all the formal greetings. The man was barely alive, and he could not afford to waste time.

"An attack?" Octavius asked with a dry throat. The man, who had not even bothered to get off his horse, nodded morosely, life seeping away every second.

"Which legion?" he asked, worried that the time would be too short.

"Fourth, Bassus," the man said in an inhuman voice that roused the gasps of all men. Octavius leaned toward him to see that his vocal cords showed. He grimaced and turned the other way, pretending not to have seen. The man was bleeding too much, and Octavius knew that it was too late to save him. Still, he threw an inquiring glance at the legion doctor who solemnly shook his head.

How the man had survived up until now was a mystery in itself. "How many?" Octavius asked, feeling guilty as he pressed the dying man with questions.

This time the man held up five fingers instead of speaking. "Fifty thousand?" Yes, the man nodded.

"So the rest is all out decoying the other legions," Octavius said, mainly to himself, and the man nodded slightly at that. Then he gestured for Octavius to come closer, in which Octavius did so.

"Many have died, starved, or died out of exhaustion. All weak, but too many," the man said, and Octavius tried to keep from cringing at his voice. That was some hopeful news for them, at least. They did not have to deal with a hundred thousand, and he thanked the gods for it.

"And Crassus? Does he know?" Octavius asked urgently but it was too late. The man collapsed, sliding off his horse. He hit the ground with a thud, his vocal cords ripping even further. Octavius hurriedly knelt beside the man, whispering a thank you. The man did not respond but his eyes were relaxed as they became glazed forever.

"Okay. War's not pretty much over," he said, to nobody in particular. He ordered an optio to bury the man well as he turned to address his legions. Their eyes were all focused on him, burning with intent at the thought of revenge. "You all heard him," Octavius said, trying to keep his voice normal. "We are going to help the Fourth, several hours of marching. Before we do that though, we are eliminating all possibilities of risk here. Sestus, you'll enjoy this. Lead three cohorts out and attack any slave you see around this area. Be back in at least two hours. Lucius, take charge of sending messengers to other legions who might not have received the message. Titus, help me organize the march. Rufius, organize the rations. Go," he said and turned abruptly away. He shivered, consoling himself that it was only the last winter winds, not the image of the dying legionary.

❧ *41* ❧

Serstus had done a horrifying, yet a good job. Of the slaves around the area, none were left alive. Octavius took a peep at the battlefield, and immediately averted his gaze to elsewhere.

The march took a painfully long time. Even without the prod of optios the legionaries marched on at a forced pace, each imagining the horrible battlefield. Octavius could see from their pace that they were eager to battle the slaves, to revenge the messenger— or maybe they had gotten used to forced marching, he thought warily. His legion was always in a hurry. He could not remember the last day they had marched on a normal pace.

He glanced back at the solemn legionaries marching in perfect columns and pride washed over him. No one will believe that their legion was created only about two years ago. Crassus had guaranteed him that the officers were the best, and it was true. Now he believed that the men too were the best— each had a unique merit that he was proud of. They also were great in teamwork.

Maybe he was seeing his legion from a biased point of view— and he knew he might be right on that. Yet, he knew, or at least thought he knew, that even if he was looking at his legion from a third perspective, he would still consider his legion a magnificent one, a legion that all legates would be envious of.

It was as if he had formed a personal bond with many of them— and Octavius did not know if he could risk a legionary dying in battle. His reverie was broken by a scout.

"The battlefield is a mess, sir. The battle is over now, and the Fourth—it seems that they have suffered many casualties. Only five cohorts are left of its original legion. The slave army is going north eastward, with Praetor Crassus hard in pursuit. Other legions are following or preparing to follow. I met the General's messenger whose order was for you to pursue Spartacus for a final—he said to remember the 'final' — battle. Hopefully before," the scout paused and lowered his voice. "General Pompey comes."

Pompey. His uncle would do anything to defeat Spartacus without the man's help, Pompey, the man who Julius felt jealous of— no matter how much Julius denied it, Pompey, the youngest general to have a triumph. A shiver ran down his back when he realized Crassus feared Pompey more than Spartacus.

"I get your point. We change our course then. Lead on. I'd rather avoid the battlefield," Octavius said and the scout nodded, setting the direction.

<hr>

Spartacus stared at his troops in silence. Many had died in Rhegium by starvation. The children and the elderly went first, then went the women and men who were at their fighting ages. Epidemic took people without considering the person's age, gender, or status. The epidemic rushed on, killing those who were unfortunate enough to stand in its way. He had thanked the gods for the cold— the best treatment in containing an epidemic. Nonetheless, the epidemic had taken many. Others died from exhaustion, and some began to doubt whether their freedom was worth all this. They began to argue that it was not actually 'freedom' that they were having. After all, they have spent all their 'free' lives fighting for their lives, something that they had not actually planned on. All of them had suffered the feeling of losing someone who they loved. When they first started out, they had all thought that they would be in Gaul or Sicily by now, allowed to do what they wanted. They were hugely disappointed, and Spartacus could not blame them.

He grimaced at the shrunk numbers. Exhaustion picked up several, starvation more, and an epidemic even more. Betrayals within his ranks. He was sick of it all. Those that were left, despite the numbers, were the strongest. They were no doubt healthy and sturdy enough to make it all through alive, and they were also his staunch supporters. They believed in death rather than slavery, and they gave their complete loyalty to him. It was more than he could hope for.

Spartacus gave a resigned sigh. Sempronius had really been their last hope. Pompey had crossed over to the Italian peninsula and was nearing Rome. He would be on them in a few weeks at the most. In other words, Pompey should arrive by the end of May. He and Crassus together would be next to impossible to beat.

He continued his pace north, on foot. The horses had long been used as food. His stout followers marched behind him without a word and for the first time in his life, Spartacus realized how a cornered mouse might feel as it stared into the gleaming eyes of a hungry, open mouthed cat.

❦

Octavius scowled at the seventh scout that had been sent to him, asking him to hurry up. He was hurrying up; all he was doing was not exhausting the Third to death while marching. He knew Crassus must be in a great hurry to engage the slaves before Pompey came. The thought of Pompey coming did not really please him either, but at least he was being sensible enough to keep the pace at a level where legionaries would not die from exhaustion. If they finished the war before Pompey came, all would be better. If they could not, then too bad. Disputes within Rome comes after Spartacus. It was as simple as that.

Anyone could see Spartacus was meeting his end. Still, they should not underestimate him... what Crassus and Pompey were doing were rivaling against themselves, thinking that their real enemy was taken care of. Or maybe the 'real enemy' was Pompey to Crassus.

Octavius had a slight thought of Julius. He wondered how Julius would react to the rivalry between two men. Would he scorn it? Or would he take part? Octavius believed the latter to be more likely.

"Double the pace, he says," the scout told him with his most serious expression on.

"Double? Do you want all of us killed from heart attacks even before we reach Spartacus?" Octavius asked, not masking his irritability.

"That is Praetor Crassus's orders," the man said stubbornly in an even tone.

Octavius let out an exasperated sigh. "Can't you see that I am going in the best speed now? There is a certain limit to how long and fast people can march—I don't care if they are Roman legionaries or not— they still have limits, so don't give me the same crap that all your predecessors gave me. What do you think? Do I seem to be going in a slow pace?" he snarled out of fury.

"No but it is not enough. Spartacus is heading north in a faster pace."

"Then he wants to kill himself by exhaustion rather than to be killed in battle. Actually, I think that is a quite plausible idea," Octavius said, putting an innocent expression on. "Tell the Praetor that I will hurry there as soon as I can. I'll be able to reach him in a few days."

The scout's expression soured as he saluted reluctantly. "I

shall say all the things that you have told me. Insolence included," he growled.

Octavius could not help himself. "Tell him about my new theory too. Isn't it interesting?" he asked with a perfect angelic face. The scout grumbled something under his breath and headed off, the sound of the horse breaking rhythmically through the forest.

He turned to Lucius who was staring at him open mouthed. "Oh gods, you wouldn't want to upset him if you were there when he decimated— oops," Lucius said, immediately covering his mouth. Octavius didn't seem to notice however.

"I told him that I would reach Crassus's main body before long. Isn't that enough? I mean, I am going in a fast pace, am I not?" Octavius asked, a little too sharply.

"It might not be enough for him," Lucius said, shrugging.

"You don't know his temper," Titus broke in. Rufius kept his mouth shut but his eyes seemed to approve what Titus was saying.

Octavius rolled his eyes. He was having more fun than he had in the past few months— partly due to the warming weather and mostly due to teasing Crassus's scouts. The war ending also helped.

"I know his temper— precisely why I did not tell the scout

to mind his own business," Octavius said, grinning widely. Lucius smiled in return, his humor contagious.

"I would love to see Crassus's face when he hears that," Lucius said, imaging his own pouting Crassus. The fat man, all dressed up, his lower lip thrust out… it was too funny. He started laughing, and the people who were around him broke into laughter, each also thinking of Crassus's reaction.

"That's enough," Octavius called out responsibly, though he too could not help grinning. He tried to hide his smile, and soon the grin was replaced by a crooked smile. "Just a few more days, and we'll meet up. After that, we just fight once—the final battle, hopefully—and we go home, or where ever you want to go," Octavius said. He felt a tinge of sadness as he realized that he could not return to Capua—he had made a promise to himself the last time he was there. He knew he could not bear the sadness the town bore.

He tried to distract himself from thinking about her, forcing himself to join his officers' still gay conversation.

This was the end. Pompey had not reached them yet, though he was dangerously close. Spartacus was just ahead of them, a few kilometers away, preparing for a war that he knew he would lose. He still had the advantage of the numbers, but numbers mattered little when it came to trained legions that were hungry for the end of the war, hungry for revenge.

Crassus strapped on his helmet, adjusting it slightly in the mirror. He would have to make a clean cut. Destroy them all.

"Octavius," he said, and the young man answered, quietly gazing at the older man. "What do you want to do to the slaves?"

Octavius was still for a few seconds. "I don't know what I want to do to the slaves after we win."

"You what? You have fought all these years, and you don't

know? You don't want to see them tortured?"

"No, sir. I mean, if I think of Lucia, Suetonius and Caecilius, all those who have died in this war, the final three hundred who had sacrificed their lives so that I could survive, I want to kill them all. I especially remember Centurion Germanicus's last words, about wanting the slaves to be crucified. So did Caecilius. Both said that their regret was that they could not see the slaves getting crucified. 'This is why we are better than you, damned slaves. My only regret is that I can't see you get crucified,'" Octavius said, perfectly quoting the centurion. It was one of the many phrases Octavius remembered so clearly.

"I have also told them that I would crucify every one who had watched the gladiatorial games of the Third personally. I did it from temper, though. I don't know if I can really do it."

Crassus smiled. "A promise is a promise. A great general is somebody who keeps their word, your Julius too. He had promised the pirates while he was still a captive that he would crucify them, and he really did, though he told me that he killed them first before crucifying them because the scene was so grotesque. Scipio also kept his promise to his enemies, carrying out the threat, earning respects from his legionaries. Don't you want to be like them?"

"Yes sir. But I believe there are more ways to become a great general than carrying out grotesque promises," Octavius responded, testing his uncle's temper.

Crassus flashed him a look of annoyance.

"Look, Octavius. Your three hundred would be watching you," Crassus said, and was himself surprised by the agony in Octavius's eyes, his eyes flickered back and forth, suddenly uncertain about his words. Sorrow was there too. Octavius did not speak for a while.

"I intend to crucify them," Crassus declared, and Octavius's head shot up in alarm.

"Crucify?"

"According to the traditions, I will crucify those who has dared to rebel against Rome."

Octavius was silent. He thought about the soothsayer and his loved ones, his want for revenge and his conscience. He groaned. I won't be able to stand it! Two years ago, I couldn't even see a corpse. Now this is pushing me too far...

"Crucify," Octavius repeated.

"Yes. Don't worry about it, for my decision is made. I had just asked you, in case you had a better idea, which obviously you do not."

That decision made, he smiled and let himself concentrate on the future. He had no plans or whatsoever. He would just meet them head on and let a hidden legion finish the slaves off when they ran. Preferably, capture them.

He strutted out of his tent, Octavius at his heels, his pace brisk and confident. The legionaries too were confident—they were joking around certainly did not seem to worry about the war ahead.

"Spartacus is mine," he heard one centurion say.

"Never," the other centurion said, and they glared at each other for a few seconds before they burst into laughter. They clapped each other's back, wishing good luck.

"Remember, he's mine."

"Not so fast," the other called as they parted at the cornicerns' signal. Crassus was relieved that his legions were not worrying about the result of the war, though he knew that too much confidence could be worse than none. He would have to make a speech reminding them of this battle's importance. That should make them a little tenser.

Crassus smiled with pride at himself as he saw the six gleaming perfectly—squared legions stretched out below him. He only wished that there would have been two more legions— the legions that the bastard Mummius had managed to kill.

He thought he caught Octavius, who had resumed his position swiftly, staring at him and gave a slight wave toward the direction before he commenced his speech.

"Legionnaires of Rome! Thank you all. You have dedicated your life in fighting for your mother city, the city of Rome that now has expanded all around the Mediterranean Sea.

"Legionnaires of Rome! You have fought bravely for me and Rome for more than a year. Some of you have served for a longer time. I thank you again for it. I also want to request one more thing— this battle. We have gone through many hardships and battles, but none of them were as important as the battle that we are about to fight now. This battle will mark the end of Spartacus's insolent revolt against Rome. Rome shall not be beaten by mere slaves… and we have succeeded in cornering them. All we need to do is to give them a final strike— and it will be over. Over. All the glories wait for you in Rome once this war ends. Today will be the final day of the war— may the historians write it down." He let the legionaries shout and clap.

"I know you will win, soldiers of Rome," he said in a voice that rang out and the legionaries cheered again, making as many noises they could possibly make. Crassus smiled and waved at the legionaries before he stepped down and headed to where the legionaries were. A very short march, and then they would prepare themselves into their three lines— the hastati, princeps, and the triarii.

⚬⟐⟐⚬

"Why the gods does it always have to be us?" Lucius whined and Titus shook his head at him. "What? We miss all the fun, and now we are to wait in this dumb forest until Spartacus comes running, capture them all, and then baby sit them."

Octavius frowned at him but did not interfere and neither did Titus. He was mostly thinking about the 'dumb forest' around Capua that had turned out to be lethal. Now Lucius was saying the chilling words again.

"Be careful," he muttered.

"Of what?" Lucius asked.

"Of the forest," Octavius said and instantly regretted it. What a stupid thing to say. Lucius burst out laughing, and Octavius could swear that Titus was hiding a smile. "Seriously, that's what Lucia said before she... you know," Octavius said, his mood plummeting once again.

Titus saw it coming and tried to distract him. "What's

our position?" he asked and succeeded. Octavius brightened up a little, thinking of the end of the war.

"We stay in the front of the forest. All we need to worry about is being seen by the slaves when they approach the main body. After they come running in our direction, it doesn't matter whether we get noticed or not. We fan out as long as we can and catch as many as we can. Rufius knows it. He's in command."

"Rufius?"

"Yes. Until I get back."

"Get back?" Titus asked, his voice confused.

"I am certainly not sitting back. I am going over there, not to fight— just to have a look at how the battle's turning out. And perhaps distract a few slaves," Octavius said with a crooked smile.

"Right. So you are not going to miss all the fun, huh?" Lucius asked, his bitter jealousy returning.

"Yes," Octavius said, hiding a smirk. "Unless you want to come," he said, and Lucius lifted his eyebrows.

"What will my century think of me then?" Lucius grumbled.

"They'll come with you," Octavius said, putting on an innocent expression.

"What?" Lucius asked in astonishment.

"Just trust me, Lucius," Octavius said smugly, and Lucius glared at him, knowing that Octavius was up to something.

"And me?" Titus asked, knowing the answer.

"You stay here to baby sit the legionaries," Octavius said, and Titus's face crumpled in disappointment until he saw the gleam in Octavius's eyes. He rolled his eyes once more, a habit gotten from Lucius. Octavius flashed him a wide grin as he drummed his fingers on his horse. Octavius was clearly in a good mood today, Titus thought. Maybe because this war would mean an end to all grieving, or maybe it was just his teenage adrenaline. No one knew.

Titus suddenly stiffened. The two turned to look at him and held their breath as he put a finger to his mouth. They listened for a few seconds. Lucius's face was still confused but Octavius nodded in understanding. "They're coming," Titus whispered, the cheerful expression gone now.

Octavius nodded grimly. "Call the legionaries back. They must not get noticed. It shouldn't be difficult. The slaves won't even look in this direction, seeing the bigger army right in front of them," Octavius ordered, the atmosphere tense.

Lucius and Titus slithered off silently and swiftly to their centuries while Octavius waited quietly. He had not been allowed to send out scouts in case the slave army suspected their position. If the slave army found out, it would not have made any difference to the result of the battle, but Crassus wanted them captured. If they knew that a legion was waiting in ambush, they were not going to run toward the forest like they probably would do— a forest was an ideal place to hide. They would instead flee into another direction, something that Crassus did not want.

The legionaries began to slowly retreat. They slithered backward in total silence and when they were sufficiently deep in the forest, they crouched down behind the bushes. There was no need to crouch for the slave army would not see them through the thick veil of trees, but it was good to be careful nonetheless.

Octavius dismounted from his horse, putting a gag on his horse to keep it mute. He had been the only one allowed to bring a horse. He knew it would not be helpful while they were in hiding, but it would be useful when he would be spying on the—hopefully—last battle.

The sound of the slaves marching was impossible to ignore. More than fifty thousand men dedicated to win or die bravely marched on with grave expressions. The noise grew until they seemed to be passing right by them. Octavius clasped and unclasped his hands together, cold sweat running down his spine. His stomach fluttered a little as he heard the monotonous sound.

The amplified sound gradually descended as the slaves moved on, and Octavius let out a breath. The legionaries, who were clustered together, too seemed to relax a little. Their tense bodies slackened and a few sighs erupted from the legionaries. Yet none of them dared to talk.

Spartacus's keen eyes surveyed the Romans. He then shook his head and called to Castus. The man came quickly.

"See how a Roman legion is missing?" he asked, and Castus nodded only to please his commander. He had not noticed that there were only five legion flags.

"Crassus probably hid a legion away to capture us, but it seems as if he had not thought of the flags. It doesn't matter anyways. Even if we saw six legion flags, we would have known soon enough that a legion was missing," Spartacus said, and Castus nodded obediently by his side.

Spartacus turned to face his fifty thousand followers. They stood in perfect silence, solemnly looking at him.

"Gentlemen," he addressed. "I would like to thank you for trusting me, no matter what the outcome of this battle will be. You have sacrificed many things to gain your freedom, and I know that this is not your actual image of freedom. I too did not know that this war would take such a long time. My biggest mistake was when we were in the north, and I turned to face the Roman legions. I should not have. Even if I could not get my revenge and was tired from running, I should have kept our course onto the north. Who knows? Maybe we might have been in Gaul by now." The silence was perfect.

"But this is the reality. The reality is that Sempronius had betrayed us, and now we are left to face Crassus's bloodthirsty six legions. And Pompey is coming at us from behind. I know I should not say this, but if we do lose, I want to tell all of you that I am proud of having fought with you. And one more precaution: the Romans are missing a legion. If the missing legion turns up during the war, it is okay to flee wherever you want in case we lose. If not, then do not go into the forest," Spartacus said. No one's face was confident. Everybody looked depressed and grim as they nodded. They saluted Spartacus and called in one voice.

"This is better than being a slave!" they cried, as if they

had planned it. Then they let up a bloodthirsty war cry and rushed at the Roman legions, trying to engulf them with their sheer numbers.

The Romans responded eagerly. They shouted once and jogged in silent efficiency toward the oncoming slaves. Their faces were full of anticipation at the slaughter to come.

❦ 43 ❦

"I think Spartacus noticed us missing," Lucius whispered urgently.

"Of course," Octavius responded apathetically.

Lucius stared at Octavius confused, and then warily waited for Octavius to explain. He could think of no reason for Octavius to say so, unless he was bluffing his anxiousness.

Octavius however, did not explain, keeping still. When he finally opened his mouth, it was not what Lucius wanted to hear. "Spartacus is not a fool. He would have noticed a legion missing anyways."

"So?"

"There's no point in bluffing with him with the legion flags. He would have noticed."

"Then why are we here?" Lucius asked, confused. Octavius kept his mouth shut, making Lucius purse his lips in frustration. Titus put a hand on Lucius's shoulder, trying to calm him down.

Octavius strayed to the edge of the forest and detached his breastplate, revealing the tunic inside. Ignoring the strange looks from others, he took off his helmet and stepped out of the thick veil of trees, revealing himself.

"Octavius!" Titus hissed and sprinted after him. Lucius followed. Octavius veered around and shot them a look, gesturing for them to do the same. Titus stopped in his sprint, confused. However, he did as he was told, and stepped out of the forest with Octavius. Lucius frowned at Octavius's bossiness— there really wasn't the need to take off the armor that needed so much help in putting on, was there? Curiosity however took over his irritation, and he too followed Octavius out of the forest.

Octavius was gazing at the war scene. It was too far away to make out who was who, but they could distinguish one army from another. They could see the slaves fighting in Roman formation, but still being pushed back. However, even if the Romans were advancing, it was not enough to break the slave lines and make them run, at least, not yet.

He crouched there, careful not to let anyone notice him. The sun was glinting off his sword scabbard, and he cursed at the fact. At least, he had taken off his breast plate, which would probably reflect sunlight back like a mirror— letting the slaves know where they were.

Octavius did not move an inch, his body tense. Titus and Lucius followed his lead, and they soon forgot about their uncomfortable position, engrossed in the battle. Titus looked at the right wing of the battle—the battle was especially tough there. He wished that he too had been allowed to fight, claim glory in the presumably last battle.

He had still been staring when Octavius tapped him lightly on the shoulders and slinked back into the forest. The two others followed him, still perplexed. When they reached their taken off helmets and breastplates, Octavius broke the silence.

"Crassus wants us to move now."

"Now? I thought we were to wait?" Lucius asked.

"Spartacus will not run in this direction afterwards if he does not see the 'missing' legion. He will suspect this. We need to show ourselves to him so that he would not suspect. I am taking the cavalry, Titus you follow with the second cohort, Lucius with the fifth. Then we hit the hind part of their army and cause a little confusion—in other words, we put on a little show. We will pretend that we are losing and run," Octavius explained.

Octavius then smiled smugly. "What do you think? That I would miss this last battle? The last glory by hiding here? I was the one who had actually told Crassus of Spartacus's capacity to notice a missing legion, so I contrived this plan... something that will get us involved."

Titus grinned, saluted and rushed off to the second cohort.

"Just before you go, Titus. The second cohort will not fight. They will line up in a very long line on the horizon, all five hundred men to line up straight, same with the fifth. They are to move three steps forward, three steps backward every time."

Titus's face fell.

"Don't worry. If you want to fight, you can come with the cavalry," Octavius said, grinning in response to Titus's childish delight.

"But I thought you were the only one allowed to bring horses here?" Lucius asked, frowning.

Octavius nodded. "Here," he said, smiling.

<hr>

The cavalry looked disarranged from a long distance.

The two cohorts had marched to the end of the forest, and were marching around the forest to hit Spartacus's back. The cavalry was waiting for them. A few scouts from another legion had already prepared the Third's cavalry force— three hundred men. Octavius thanked the scouts, watching with gleaming eyes as his Third got ready to fight.

The second and the fifth cohort were given a head start, as they laboriously marched toward the back of the slave army. The cavalry followed slowly. Soon, the second and the fifth stopped, careful to keep a good range away from the slave army. They then lined up as they were told, all thousand men spread into a thin line. Then the cavalry got ahead of the cohorts, and started to approach the slaves, making a huge racket. The cohorts followed suit. From a distance— where Spartacus would be— it would look like a full legion approaching. The legion flag and the recovered eagle stood tall in the sunlight.

Titus, at the order of Octavius, left the command of the cohort to another centurion, grinning widely. The centurion gazed at him in envy. Lucius too left another centurion in command as they joined the cavalry.

"Second and fifth cohort, I know that you will do well. You have proved yourselves in many other occasions, and I know that this occasion too will not prove to be difficult for you. I know you want to fight, claim glory of this last battle. I am sorry that I cannot give you the chance to charge the slaves for a final time. Yet when these slaves run, the task of capturing them is ours. Killing and capturing are different. Which do you think is harder? Killing? All you have to do is to stick a sword through someone and they die. It is a different matter with capturing. You must avoid places where you might kill the opponent. Injuring the opponent to a right amount, chaining him, and dragging him to a safe place— it is hundred times harder and advanced than just killing. That is why Crassus chose our legion to capture the slaves instead of others. He knows we are skilled, skilled enough to carry out our tasks.

"Before I leave, I would like to remind you once more that I want you to keep a long line and keep moving. Our motive here is to look like a legion. When the cavalry comes back in a fake run, you too are to run in a supposed frenzy. The slaves will not come after us, unless they have completely lost their minds. In that case, you are to capture those that come after us. But most likely, they will stay where they are, and we regroup after we are out of their eyesight. I have trust in you," Octavius said, gazing into as many legionary's eyes he could meet. They bowed their heads in understanding, and Octavius nodded once to himself before he turned his horse to the direction of Spartacus, to follow the cavalry which had gone ahead and were waiting orders. Titus and Lucius followed eagerly.

⬧⬦⬥⬦⬧

Castus grinned. He was having the best time in his life. The missing legion had been spotted at last, and not only that, they were being engulfed. At first they seemed willing to fight, especially the legate. But then, after the slaves began to pressurize them, the legate had panicked. The cavalry lost their horses, and they ran in terror, pushing past others. It was the second time he had seen the Romans run, and it was exhilarating.

As the instinct for survival took over others who were still keeping formation, they looked anxious. A few more fell from their horses, and it was all they needed. The Romans fled. Even the legate turned his back, pushing his horse on at a breakneck speed.

Castus was about to pursue them when he saw a legion waiting on the horizon. He thought it more likely for the legion to run also, especially with their legate so terrified.

He decided that there would be no purpose in chasing the legion. The legion was out of play for now. It would not be late to slaughter that legion later.

Most of the soldiers had seen the missing legion return, their march being so boisterous. Castus scoffed at them, knowing that if it had been he, he would not have done so. He would have approached silently. Now, they could head into the forest without danger if they lost.

Crassus smiled to himself as he saw the running cavalry. All working out as planned. He had to thank Octavius for coming up with the idea— he had been the one who had told him that Spartacus would never fall for the flag hoax. He was even more pleased when he saw some of the cavalry dragging their fallen or injured comrades out of the chaos while on the run.

Anyway, the plan was working better than he had hoped. The cavalry had clearly made the 'missing legion's' return clear and while doing so, they had also managed to cause slight confusion in the hind part. The main body of the legions was having an easier time advancing. The gladiator line was on the verge of breaking. Once the strongest first line broke, he knew that it would only be a matter of time before Spartacus ran. He hoped Spartacus would be alive until the end of the battle and not try any heroics like suicide.

A cheer went up from the left wing, and Crassus sharply turned his head to the direction in hope. The legionaries had broken through. The first line was nowhere to be seen, already trampled under the legionaries' sandals. The second line was retreating at a great speed, only able to use numbers as their shields. Once the gladiators fell, the slaves were nothing.

The second line had retreated too fast. It left a gap wide enough for the legionaries to infiltrate.

It had a domino effect, a very fast one. Soon the right wing, aided by the other legionaries who had already broken through was butchering the gladiators, and the most of the second line too had been slaughtered. The legionaries continued to advance regardless, provoking fear into the other lines. They crashed into the third; the sound of metal smashing against each other rang over the plain.

The third line could not take it anymore. Many of the third line were being killed every second— they knew they had no choice but to run if they wanted to save their lives.

The ideal looking place was the forest, where a canopy of trees and ferns covered them enough for them to stay in hiding. They rushed toward the forest, their only wish being for the trees to have been more densely populated.

Spartacus found himself running with the others. He had intended to die in this fight if he could not win. And yet, his legs were moving across the plain to the forest, defying the thoughts in his head. The missing legion was somewhere long off. Castus had beaten them, easily, maybe too easily.

He stopped for a second, but knew that it was too late to change direction. Besides, if he was the only one running toward the opposite of where all the survivors were going, he would be the obvious and easiest target for the archers. He would have no chance of survival. He continued to the forest, and instantly regretted his decision.

He could hear those ahead of him calling for help as a Roman legion appeared from a forest, making a half circle around the running slaves. Spartacus whipped around only to see the five legions also forming a half circle. The half circles met, and Spartacus knew that they were trapped.

He looked around wildly for a place to escape but found none. "Die fighting!" he called and jumped to attack a

Roman legionary. The legionaries were making it clear that they wanted the slaves alive, and Spartacus believed that it was better to die cleanly than become their prisoner. He could not even imagine the fate that Crassus would have planned for him.

He assailed the legionary, yet the legionary continued to defend, not attack. Three other legionaries came to help the soldier, and Spartacus gritted his teeth. He feinted, falling on the ground, and when a legionary came toward him, he stabbed the man. The Roman fell, his eyes open in shock.

Spartacus quickly rolled to his feet, kicking at another legionary who was trying to take him down. With a bear hug, Spartacus pushed legionnaire down to the ground and was about to target another unfortunate legionary when he felt a sharp pain in his right leg.

He gasped, unable to control the pain. Then he heard a dense metal clang, and a sharp pain followed in his head. He gasped for breath, screaming. His vision went black, and his last thoughts were the chilling words Octavius had said: I shall nail every one of you standing here personally on a cross.

❧ 44 ❧

Octavius saluted as he let the general in his early thirties pass. The man paused to nod at him, surprised at his youth and his status as a legate. Then he smiled a warm smile before turning back to ride to the lot where the prisoners were bound. Pompey.

Crassus had been feeling sour all day about Pompey— a few thousand had escaped, and Pompey had easily killed them all with his legions. Probably, he said, Pompey would try to take all the glory, and he might succeed easily in that because he had Arrius backing him up.

Pompey would argue that he was the one who had ended the war, and Arrius would stand by him, forcing the senate to agree with his serpent like eyes. Damn Arrius, Crassus had whispered to himself, but Octavius had managed to hear.

Octavius followed Pompey to the lot, where most of the

legionaries were present. They tried to look serious, but Octavius could see that they were still groggy from all the wine they had drunken the day before as a celebration.

"I only wish that I could have been there yesterday to help you out..." Octavius heard Pompey say.

"We did fine by ourselves," Crassus responded sourly, and Pompey just smiled.

"Arrius wants me to take all the glory by myself, but I won't do so. You know me well enough to know that I am not such a person. A little maybe, but not all," Pompey whispered and Crassus jolted in his seat, surprised by his frankness. Then he narrowed his eyes, wondering if Pompey was telling the truth. The man was an ambitious man, a man who had changed sides during the fraction between Marius and Sulla so that he could achieve his dreams. He was a dangerous man, one he could not trust.

Crassus just shrugged and pointed at the slaves. Their fate had been decided and proclaimed to the officers while the legionaries had been busy partying. Many officers believed that this war should be the last slave revolt in Roman history, and to ensure that, they agreed to the need of enforcing harsh punishment, crucifixion.

Pompey had agreed with the punishment when he came

marching in the morning— in fact, he had called it a marvelous idea. He had suggested that they do so while following the Via Appia to Rome. Crassus had assented it eagerly.

The soldiers arranged themselves, a little sluggishly than usual, into their legion squares, coldly watching in anticipation of what would happen to the shackled slaves. Crassus circled the lot where nearly six thousand were kneeling on the ground as prisoners, with Pompey following right behind.

After Crassus had deliberately circled the slaves slowly, increasing the suspense, he suddenly jumped off his horse.

He straightened himself and gazed coldly at the slaves gathered in the lot.

"My warriors," he called mockingly to the slaves. There was muffled laughter from the legionaries who were clearly in a great mood. "I personally do not understand why you have gone through all this pain… to achieve nothing."

"We have achieved something! We have frightened Rome!" a prisoner called out, and Crassus whipped toward the voice.

"All you have achieved is this," he said, sweeping his hand across the lot, pointing to the kneeling slaves. "You have not frightened Rome. Yes, you might have frightened some civilians, but the civilization itself stays firm. Rome is not a country that can be brought down with mere slaves. It is an idea, a vision that remains firm. Rome is in here," he said, pointing to his chest. Pompey clapped loudly in approval.

"Our spirits will live on," the same man said.

Crassus smiled a mirthless smile. "Your spirits shall be wiped clear of Earth, I swear on Jupiter. This will be the last slave rebellion Rome will ever endure, may Jupiter hear this. I will make it so that no slave later will even consider the thought of a rebellion. The rebellion is over. No one defies Rome," he announced, and the legionaries erupted into boisterous cheers.

"You!" he called to a man closest to him, and the man lifted his head, trembling a little. "We have decided to crucify all of you on the sides of Via Appia." Shocked murmurs rose from the slaves, and Crassus smiled savagely. Pompey chuckled at their fear. "You too— unless you give me the information I want. If you do so... your punishment may be lightened."

The man continued to shake. "Tell me who Spartacus is," Crassus ordered.

The man dropped his head, clearly thinking. Then he whispered, "Spartacus was killed in the battle."

Crassus narrowed his eyes. It was unlikely for a commander to die easily in a battle. "Is it the truth?"

The man hesitated once before answering. "Yes," he said, his voice shaking.

Crassus stood back and took a deep breath. "Octavius!" he called, and his voice rang over the plain.

"Yes sir," Octavius responded smartly. He was still looking at the slaves— so many of them captured— no one except for the guards had been able to see the slaves before now.

"Spartacus is alive. Point out to me who he is."

"Sir?"

"Most likely he is here, disguising himself as a common soldier. Point him out for me," Crassus said coldly.

Octavius obeyed, swiftly glancing over each face. He saw no Spartacus. In a way, he was glad, for the man had once been his friend and teacher, and it saved him from making the choice of turning him over to Crassus.

He was about to tell his uncle that Spartacus was not here when he jolted slightly in his seat. A pale face was staring back at him, a face he knew. The face was hopeless, as if he had given up all hope. Spartacus.

Octavius wanted to open his mouth, point out where Spartacus was. But something was preventing him from doing so, his conscience probably. There was a gladiator, a leader of the slave rebellion, his teacher, his friend, the one who had made it possible for him to escape that day. If Spartacus had wanted to kill him, he would not have succeeded in escaping regardless of the three hundred who had died for him. Instead, Spartacus had let him go. The man had given the order for the three hundred legionaries to fight each other to death, and he had hated Spartacus then. However, Octavius could only imagine the cruel things that Crassus would have planned for Spartacus— Spartacus had been a leader. A leader, no matter what group he led, deserved more. After all, he had fought bravely for something he believed in.

"Octavius?" Crassus prodded him.

He jumped a little, knowing that he must make his decision quickly. He looked down, and then shifted his gaze at Crassus, his brown eyes penetrating. They were steady as he spoke.

"Spartacus is dead."

Lucius was groggily standing in front of his square, and accepted without doubt what Octavius said. Octavius was clear—headed, unlike he who had eaten and drunk too much the night before.

Titus opened his mouth and clamped it shut again. He

knew Octavius. He knew Octavius must have spotted Spartacus. Octavius, however, had chosen to keep Spartacus a secret. If Octavius wished it to be so, he would not object to it. He would play dumb.

Crassus let out a sigh. "What a misfortune," he mumbled to himself. "All right. We can do nothing about that now. Legionaries! We shall arrive in Rome in ten days. While marching, you may crucify the prisoners beside the Via Appia. I do not care in what form you crucify them as long as the point of torture is there. They are not to die quickly. Those who kill the slaves beforehand shall be punished, six hundred prisoners a day while marching; hundred a day for each legion. Start marching," Crassus said and the legionaries roared in approval.

They chanted his name, their thoughts already on the crucifixion. The thought of revenge was appealing.

The legionaries rushed out of the lot, eager to pack up their things and eager for the march, eager for the crucifixion that was to follow.

Octavius waited until the lot had emptied except for the guards and moved swiftly toward Spartacus. In his eyes was disbelief as he glanced up at the young legate.

"What do you think you are doing?" Octavius asked, his

voice full of sorrow, shaking his head.

"What are you doing here?" Spartacus asked as if amazed, and Octavius ignored the remark.

"What good did you think would have come out of this?"

"Our freedom. You don't know how it feels," Spartacus replied. Octavius noticed the wound on his leg, a wound that was not being treated and therefore, getting ugly.

"Oh, Spartacus," he whispered silently. "I don't know what to do with you."

"Thank you for hiding me," Spartacus replied casually, and Octavius continued to shake his head.

"I just thought I should. What do you think about death?" he asked suddenly.

Spartacus paused for a long time before speaking. "Death has always been a companion to me. I fought with and against death all the time I was a legionary, a gladiator, a leader of the slave rebellion. It has been with me too long that I do not shirk away from it. In fact, in my current state, now, I welcome it— except for the fact that my death would be painful, very painful. That's all I fear. My life was not worth living, Octavius. If a god asks me if I want to live my life all over again, I would not. My life has been miserable since I left Thracia. I would rather bid farewell to this accursed world."

Octavius too stayed still for a long time before responding. Spartacus's words rang in him. "So if you are able to go to Thracia, you will want to live, right?" Octavius asked and Spartacus nodded, his eyes curious of Octavius's intention. "Don't get any ideas, Spartacus. Just asking," Octavius said. He rose from his crouched position, glanced at the amassed slaves before stalking away.

～ 45 ～

It was clear that Lucius and Titus had not seen Spartacus, or at least Octavius thought. They kept lamenting Jupiter about how Spartacus was not alive, and Octavius kept silent through their talks. It was night, with the first six hundred crucified. The slaves screamed and moaned in agony, begging the Romans for a mercy killing. The legionaries were not shaken by it.

Octavius stared at his dinner, leaving it to cool as he stepped out of his tent to the open. He cringed as he saw a cross being erected right in front of his tent, only a few meters away.

"Aren't you eating?" Titus asked, and Octavius shook his head, hating himself for his weakness. The others clearly did not seem to have any problems with the slaves' pleas. He had not been able to stand the sight of their pain and bleeding, nervously watching from the sidelines as his legionaries went on with their grotesque project. They followed the traditional custom of scourging the slaves before crucifying them, and Octavius turned his head away at the blood that freely flowed from too much whipping. The sound, however, of the flogging and the screaming could not be blocked off. Octavius began wondering if they were his beloved Third. His Third had not been so cruel.

He noticed that his legionaries were especially vicious, probably because they wanted to revenge the three hundred who had died as prisoners. Dannotalos was not as vicious as others, probably due to his conscience and his old friendship of fighting with them, watching from the sidelines like Octavius. He too, however, did not seem to have much problem with watching the whole scene.

Lucius seemed to think of all of them as Lucia's murderers. He enjoyed his time in crucifying his ration of slaves leading a group of savage, almost crazy legionaries around. They crucified the slaves in a very innovative and crueler way each time. Titus did not show any personal feelings, just getting on with his work— always the typical centurion— of crucifying them.

The next day was worse. More than once a slave had knelt at his feet, pleading to him, apologizing, crying. Every time they did that, his heart weakened, but there was nothing he could do, so he chose to ignore them. Every night his dreams became distorted by the occasional screams and the moans of the slaves.

The only crucifixion he watched closely was the crucifying of Castus. Castus wailed, kicking his feet in desperateness.

"You!" he called, and Octavius even managed a smile.

"I told you that the next chance you would get was while hanging on a cross. Be lucky that I am not personally doing it as I had promised," Octavius responded, and almost regretted it when he saw the man's expression crumple into pain and regret.

The legionaries made swift work out of Castus, binding his hands and feet on a cross. After a day, Crassus had banned the legionaries from using iron nails, saying that they shouldn't be wasted for crucifying the 'just' slaves. They are not even worthy of iron nails, Crassus had said to the legionaries who had groaned when they had first heard his proclamation to ban the use of nails.

Castus would die of either starvation, thirst or due to the stretching of his lungs. The last option was probably the most plausible one. Octavius grimaced at the thought, and turned his head so that Castus and his legionaries would not see him grimace. He hated to be seen so weak.

"I hold you responsible for the killings back then," Octavius said, and Castus's face wrinkled. Octavius turned away from the man, not wanting to see the scenes of torture and agony. Even Castus's crucifixion was not so enjoyable now.

He strolled along the Via Appia, not being able to sleep, seeing the horrible message the Roman legions were leaving for those planning a revolt. It would certainly discourage them. He wondered what Spartacus would be thinking. Spartacus's crucifixion was scheduled for sometime later, and when he had visited Spartacus last, the man had looked up at him, eyes hopeless.

His strolling was cut short by a surprise.

"Octavius." Someone called, and Octavius turned around, but saw no one.

A laugh sounded, a distorted one.

"Up here."

Octavius jerked his head up in surprise, to see Spartacus hanging on a cross. With the blood red sun as a background, the image seemed more monstrous than ever. Octavius gazed in horror.

"What? I thought you were to be executed some day later," Octavius said.

"Someone died, and I was chosen to fill his space. At least, a sensible centurion tied me up to the cross, so I wasn't tortured— much, compared to others. Just a few lashes," Spartacus said, grinning to hide his pain. Octavius saw his tattered body and grimaced, and also at the intended cheerfulness of his words. Still, he agreed with the idea of the centurion being sensible. There were many others whose bodies were in a worse—very worse—situation.

"I've been up here for about half an hour, but it doesn't seem so bad. Though it will get worse after an hour, I'm fine now. The lashes bother me, but I've been through worse. What I worry is what will happen to me a few hours later. I know how this thing works. I might enjoy my last minutes of…sanity with you, if you have the time," Spartacus said. His tone was of the tone when he was nothing more than a plain gladiator, before he had become a leader of a rebellion, before he had been caught up in revenge for the death of Jacob, Crixus… and the revenge for himself, anger at the Romans for ruining his life.

"I just wanted to have my freedom. I did not want to kill Romans," Spartacus said sadly. "I guess it does not matter now. I have fought for what I believed, and still believe in, and most people cannot even do that... You too have fought for what you believe in and what you care about, though sadly, our purpose was different."

Octavius halted his pace. He looked at Spartacus intently. Octavius realized, with some surprise, that they were not enemies. Not friends, maybe, but not quite enemies. Just two people having different goals.

He saw Spartacus two years ago...

Octavius wavered.

The sun had risen, like any other day, pouring its warmth on the treetops, signaling a new day. Octavius gazed at the sun, thinking about his new promising career as one of the generals successful in a war.

Legionaries moved about, talking excitedly amongst themselves, playfully laughing. The legionnaires were still in a very good mood, congratulating themselves on the result of a long war that had finally ended. They were preparing to leave camp, to continue their bloody return to Rome. Already there were talks of who would get to crucify whom. However, they only looked at what lay ahead of them—

none of them took time to look back at the crosses that they had put up on the day before—except for one, Octavius.

He turned his gaze toward the crosses, where the slaves were still yelling and begging for mercy killings. His eyes travelled further down the road, and finally rested on a cross.

An empty cross.

No one was bound on the cross, though it was only Octavius who noticed it. He smiled faintly to himself, as if the news did not at all shock him, as if he was pleased at the fact that he had found the cross empty.

The sun's rays were warm on his back, creating a sense of tranquility. It was a feeling that he had not felt before. He had felt joyful after the last battle, after they had won, but tranquility had been another matter. There had been something that had tugged at the corner of his mind, a tug that had intensified every time he saw Spartacus. The tugging was now gone, replaced by a peaceful mind, a sensation of completion, and a feeling of hope. He imagined the optimistic career ahead of him, and perhaps the hopeful life of another person…

He took a long look at the empty cross, at the rising sun, and then finally toward the direction of Rome, toward a new beginning.

초판 1쇄 2009년 6월 25일
초판 발행 2009년 6월 30일
지은이 이소영
펴낸이 천봉재
주소 서울 성동구 금호동1가 1574번지 1층
전화 02-2299-1290~1
팩시밀리 02-2299-1292
E-mail minato3@hanmail.net
book@ilsongbook.com
등록 998. 8. 13. 제6-1382호
ⓒ이소영, 2009

잘못된 책은 구입하신 서점에서 바꾸어 드립니다.
ISBN 978-89-5732-096-9 03810